THE SEVERED
BREAST

To my dear cousin Sarah and Juan Lorenzo
12/20/2016
Stafford

THE SEVERED BREAST

by

STAFFORD BETTY

A NOVEL

www.whitecrowbooks.com

Published and printed in the United States of America and the United Kingdom
by White Crow Books; an imprint of White Crow Productions Ltd.

For information, contact White Crow Books
at 3 Hova Villas, Hove, BN3 3DH United Kingdom,
or e-mail to info@whitecrowbooks.com.

Cover Painting: Copyright © Stephanie B Morris
Cover Designed by Butterflyeffect
Interior design by Velin@Perseus-Design.com

Paperback ISBN 978-1-910121-84-9
eBook   ISBN 978-1-910121-85-6

Fiction / Religion / Historical

www.whitecrowbooks.com

Contents

Also by the author:

Fiction:
The Rich Man
Sing Like the Whippoorwill
Sunlit Waters
Thomas
The Imprisoned Splendor

Non-fiction:
Vadiraja's Refutation of Sankara's Non-Dualism
The Afterlife Unveiled: What the Dead Are Telling Us About Their World
Heaven and Hell Unveiled: Updates from the World of Spirit

NOTE TO THE READER

Did St. Thomas the Apostle reach Tamilakam (South India) in the first century? Scholars dispute this. To begin with, there is no reason he shouldn't have: Scores of ships sailed across the Indian Ocean from Socotra, off Africa's northeast shore, to Tamilakam every year, and just as many back. A great number of gold Roman coins bearing the face of the Roman Emperor Tiberius (14-37 A.D.) have been dug up in South India, and we know that the Roman Empire was addicted to the Indian pepper. Furthermore, many early Christian legends and documents speak of Thomas' going to India. Indeed, what is alleged to be his crypt can be found this very day in Chennai's Cathedral San Thome. It would be all but settled if the ancient Tamil literature mentioned him, but it does not. In the final analysis, our best evidences are an ancient, persistent legend and a living church that traces its ancestry back to Thomas.

If Thomas did get to India—and I think it likely he did—his success seems to have been limited to small pockets of the population. Today, despite centuries of zealous evangelization, less than three percent of India is Christian. The reasons for this are arguable. Most of them applied during the first century, when Thomas would have been there, as much as they apply today.

The personality I have chosen to give Thomas is entirely fictitious. I might have borrowed heavily from the *Acts of Thomas*, a second- or third-century Gnostic Christian tract that purports to describe Thomas' mission to India; but the characterization of him is unappealing, and most of the action takes place in Parthia and northwest India (today's Afghanistan and Pakistan). Moreover, most scholars regard his characterization and the many miracles he performed as a Christian romance.

Thomas means "twin." Thomas' real name was Judas—Judas "the twin." Whose twin was he? The ancient traditions disagree. One says he was Jesus' twin. I have used this legend but adapted it to my own use.

Thomas, on the basis of the well-known story in John's Gospel, is universally regarded today as "Doubting Thomas." I have adopted this characterization and in the process made him resonate with the modern reader. Whether or not he really had a congenital doubter's disposition is anybody's guess, although Christians have always taken the legend seriously: There have been twenty-four Pope Johns (including an antipope), but not one Pope Thomas. So much for doubting!

I have made good use of the Kerala and Tamil traditions about St. Thomas, and the experts will enjoy picking them out as they appear. It should not be assumed, though, that anything I have Thomas say or do in this book is historical. And on many occasions I knowingly deviate from the traditions. Some of my Christian readers will be shocked because my Thomas is a complex, struggling, sometimes sinful man. If they will stay with me to the end, they will see him change—whether into a saint or not, the readers must decide for themselves.

With India we are on firmer ground. The Tamils have a voluminous ancient literature that blends poetry, much of it superb, with liberal doses of history. The Tamil classics tell us a great deal about South India in the first centuries of the Christian era. The Tamil capital of Puhar, for example, is described in detail. So are some of the exploits of the famous King Karikal. But the literature is most remarkable for its portrayal of the customs of the people and for its delight in nature. When working on the settings for the events of this novel, I had to depend very little on my unaided imagination. India really was the way it appears here. To some degree it still is in the countryside.

The bloody event described near the climax of the novel might seem preposterous to many a reader. But not to a Tamil. The tragic but ultimately triumphant story of Kannaki, as told in the most celebrated Tamil classic of them all, the *Cilappatikaram*, has Kannaki doing the same thing that Queen Adimanti does here.

The experts on early Tamil history dispute the dates of events and personalities. Often they disagree by centuries. When did King Karikal rule? As early as the first century, or as late as the fifth? We are told a great deal about him, but we don't know when he lived—or when anyone else lived. And the great Battle of Venni which I've described here in detail is certainly historical. But when it happened we simply cannot say. As a result, I have not worried overmuch about dating. Many of the people, places, and events in this novel are historically based, but my pulling them all together into one historical space and time is fanciful.

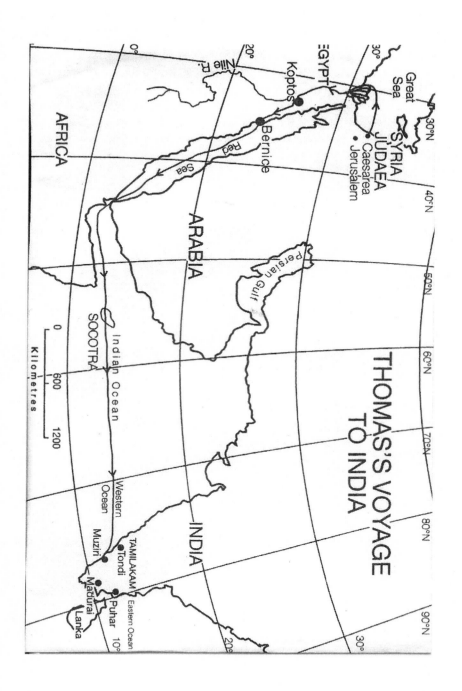

THOMAS'S VOYAGE TO INDIA

AFRICA

EGYPT

Great Sea

SYRIA

JUDAEA
• Caesarea
• Jerusalem

Koptos

Bernice

Red Sea

Nile R.

ARABIA

Persian Gulf

SOCOTRA

Indian Ocean

Western Ocean

INDIA

TAMILAKAM
• Tondi
Muziri

Madurai
Puhar

Lanka

Eastern Ocean

Kilometres
0   600   1200

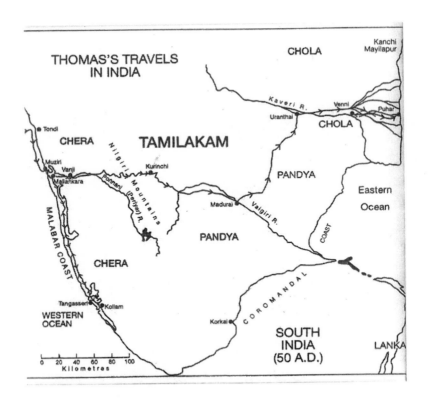

THE SEVERED BREAST
PART I: THE VOYAGE

1. The Lottery

Achilly drizzle fell as Thomas mounted the stone stairs leading to the upper room of John Mark's house in Jerusalem. He could hear singing, male and female, behind the door. He braced himself.

"Thomas!" and "the Doubter!" and "He's come!" and "Welcome back!" and similar sounds greeted him when the door opened. All faces were turned toward him, fifty or more; they moved in his direction across the large, mostly bare room.

They gathered around him and slapped his back or grasped his hand or kissed his cheek or patted his black bristly beard or, in the case of the women, smiled up at him from the perimeter of the crowd. Thomas' eyes misted over when he saw them all, especially when Bartholomew came up with arms outstretched. "May the Lord be praised! Look who's here!" Bartholomew, of superstitious mind but sweet, humble disposition. Bartholomew with his ruddy face and wide-set eyes and ample stomach. "Look who's here!" Bartholomew, Thomas' best friend.

"Welcome back. How was Parthia?" said Peter, gray and wrinkled but still of powerful build. "You've arrived just in time. Andrew, bring the Twin the bread."

"How's the family?" said someone.

"Well," said Thomas. "Both daughters now married off. Both have given themselves to the Lord, may He be praised."

1

"Master, I haven't seen you in five years. Do you remember me? Judith!"

A small, round-faced, middle-aged woman with big, trusting eyes parted the crowd of men and came up to Thomas. He had brought her to the faith shortly before his last journey. "Is it true you ate the ashes of the Torah, Master?"

"To save them from defilement, Sister, not because I was hungry."

A few laughed at this confession, but most gazed at him awestruck. For a second there was silence. Then—

"Thomas, we've missed you!"

"That we have."

"Did you hear about James son of Zebedee?"

"Did you know that they're talking about the Christ in Rome?"

"And they tell the story of your famous doubt."

"But not in derision, but in—"

"You're a hero, Thomas! The story is known and loved wherever we go. All over the world."

"You haven't aged a bit, Master!"

"Are you in good health?"

"Are you ready for the next round? Even as far as India? India!"

Thomas couldn't get a word in edgewise. He beamed at his friends, touched by their love. How good it was to be home! He hoped his next assignment wouldn't take him so far away.

Peter handed him a morsel of the Eucharistic bread. Thomas prayed briefly, put it in his mouth, and chewed it slowly while the crowd began to chant "Maranatha, Maranatha" ("Lord come, Lord come"). The room soon resonated with the sound he had heard through the door, but the faces that intoned the chant were now more solemn than joyous, more collected and interior, more intense, even anxious.

Thomas sipped wine from the cup, the cup of the Lord's blood, offered him by one of the women. He thought of the time Jesus broke bread and drank wine with them the night before his death. It had happened in this very room. Fourteen years ago. How fast the time passed, how far the Church had come. He caught a glimpse of Paul, Paul the indestructible, the one for whom he felt a secret camaraderie, Paul the persecutor, the one with a blacker past than his, Paul sitting in a corner weaving a cloak out of goat's hair as he sang. Even Paul was turning gray.

"Brothers and sisters, let us begin!" shouted Peter above the chant, his bald head shining over his long thin nose, unprepossessing pale eyes, and bushy beard. "You all know why we are here. Either in person or our stand-ins. As you can see, the palm leaves are arranged. Each has the name of a region inscribed on it, just as last time. Do you all agree to abide by your choices?"

"Aye!" said most of the voices.

"What's the order?" said someone.

"Come up as the spirit moves you, that's all," said Peter.

"Is India included?" said another.

"You know it is!" said Peter.

A hush fell over the room. If ever there was a sign that Peter and Paul were determined to see the faith spread to every corner of the gentile world, it was in this "You know it is!" For years the young church had been gathering news of India. Strange and awesome stories came by way of caravan travelers who had gone there to make a fortune in the spice and silk trade. Situated on the eastern edge of the earth, India professed a religion so disturbing and spoke so many languages that everyone feared going there. Everyone wanted to see it evangelized, but by someone else. It seemed beyond anyone's competency. Spain might be far away, but at least there were Romans there. But India was another world entirely. It was a stronghold of entrenched demonic forces, a hot, stifling, jungly continent, a mysterious hell on earth. It did not seem the sort of place that would take to the Lord's gospel or that one would ever come back from.

"Let us pray," said Peter quietly.

He closed his eyes and lifted his face and arms to heaven. It was chilly inside the house, for one of the window shutters was broken. The others could see his breath as he prayed:

"Father in heaven, Father of our Lord Jesus, guide our hands to the right lot. You alone know where each of us should go. Let this not be our choice, but Yours. And give us the courage and love to accept gladly whatever we choose. We recall the martyrdom of Stephen, who died by stoning. We recall the martyrdom of James son of Zebedee, whose head Herod Agrippa cut off just last month. They died right here in Jerusalem. Let us be prepared for even sterner tests than this in the farthest corners of the world, with none to uphold us but your son Jesus."

Peter opened his eyes and said, "Brethren, I love you all in Jesus' name. Come forth. And when you read what is on your leaf, call it out for all to hear. May God be with you!"

The first to approach was Philip, wearing his phylacteries on forehead and upper arm. He approached the thick cloak of goat's hair spread out across the floor with the tips of the twenty leaves protruding. He folded his hands, lifted his eyes to heaven, then knelt down. He pulled the left outermost palm out and held it out. "Egypt!" he called out.

Thomas felt a twinge of jealousy, for Alexandria was one of four places he wanted to go, the others being Cyprus, Galatia, and Cilicia. These places were close to home, close to his motherless daughters and friends; and they were places where Greek was spoken; they were cultivated places with a literate gentry, the sort of people he felt most comfortable with, the people he had had the most success with in the past. Who among the disciples could speak and write Greek half so well as he? And yet there was Alexandria the first place chosen—and by Philip! What if he, Thomas, should draw Spain, or Parthia, or—but he wouldn't let himself think of the worst that could be, the inconceivable, the unmentionable, that continent of Sodoms populated by sinister faces with gleaming eyes. Yet he knew India was inscribed on one of those twenty leaves. He knew someone would draw that leaf.

Thomas decided to wait until India was taken, then step up and draw. He hung back.

One by one Jesus' closest disciples and those who had risen in the young church to become leaders stepped up. Matthew, Bartholomew, James the son of Alphaeus, Andrew, Barnabas, Paul, Barsabbas, Nicanor, Parmenas, Ananias, Cornelius—one by one they came forward. Each had been chosen by Peter and James the brother of Jesus to lead a mission for the spread of the new faith all over the world. Each called out a name: Libya, Syria, Samaria, Thrace, Armenia, Cappadocia, Cyprus, Macedonia, Gaul, Ethiopia, Rome. Even Spain. Nicolaus, a widower from Antioch with eight children, yelled out the word as if it were Joppa or Jericho, a day's journey away, rather than a Roman colony so distant and dangerous that he could depend on never seeing his family again.

When Jude the Barrel-chested drew Persia, leaving only three leaves remaining, Thomas panicked and stepped forth. Galatia had not been claimed yet. Galatia, Crete, and India. What if he waited until last and the only leaf not taken were India? Who would he be able to blame but himself? He would be given India by default. India, that land of men "with teeth like milk and lips like soot," as a merchant once put it to him; of whole tribes with their feet turned backwards; of others with the heads of dogs who spoke by barking; of others with no necks and their eyes on their shoulders; of still others with ears so big they could curl up and sleep inside them. And it was said India was so huge that its population was a third of the world's total. No, not India!

He stepped forward. There remained one leaf far to the right, one toward the left, and one in the center. He imagined he was facing north. The one to the left seemed like Crete, the one far to the right India, and the one in the center Galatia. Just as if a map were laid out before him and Galatia were spelled out for all to see, he went for Galatia in the center. He put finger and thumb on the palm leaf and pulled it out with a jerk.

"What is it, Thomas?" asked Peter. "Tell us what it says."

"It's—" But he couldn't say more.

"It's India," whispered Matthew, who stood close by.

A murmur snaked through the crowd, and all eyes fixed on Thomas as he held the leaf in his hand and stared vacantly at the floor, his tall, muscular carpenter's frame slumped like a sapped reed.

"I'm not going," he said softly, moving swiftly toward the door as the crowd parted. "I'm not going!"

"You *are* going!" cried Peter. "Thomas, you *are* going! God has spoken!" Thomas began gathering his provisions from a corner of the room.

"You go, Peter. You or James. Let *me* stay in Jerusalem. You go. I just got back from Parthia. This isn't—I won't—the lots can't be trusted."

"You will honor the lots, Thomas. They are the will of God. We all agreed."

Thomas hung his head for an instant as if weighing what Peter said, then bolted out the door.

All that day Thomas walked like a man entranced, walked down, down through the barren hills east of Jerusalem toward the Jordan gorge. He looked down at the road at his feet, but he did not see it. He did not see the gnarled olive groves outside Jericho or hear the sounds of the city. He did not look up as he passed a traveler on the road. He was hungry but didn't stop to eat.

Night fell as he reached the gorge, but he did not bother to build a fire. He felt the hunger gnawing at his stomach and heard a leopard's growl coming up from the thick underbrush along the bank of the river. He lay down on barren earth a short distance away. A lone cricket chirped near his ear in the moonless dark. Did it, like him, prefer this lonely place in the desert to the intimate warmth of its own kind down in the gorge? He thought of Peter and James and the others, all vibrating to the same divine life. They were prepared to go anywhere. What was wrong with him? Why had he doubted fourteen years ago, and why did he doubt again now? Why did he doubt it was God's will he go to India? Or was it something else, something worse? Was it disobedience? Wasn't it just that simple? "No, Father, not thy will, but mine!" Wasn't it that? But he hadn't had much confidence in the lots the first time. And this time wasn't any better.Better that men decide, decide after fasting and prayer. Wasn't that how God led? Who could say for sure the lots weren't the work of the devil? Philip to Egypt, Thomas to India. The will of God? It couldn't be! He must resist this folly. He must stand up to Peter and go where he could best serve. He had been right to refuse.

But he didn't really believe this. Exhausted and hungry, his spirit flailing and twisting, he could stand no more. He let his muscles and bones slump against the ground and drew up his feet. "God, help me," he cried out in despair. "Jesus, come to me. I am your twin, Thomas."

He fell asleep in the mild air of the Jordan gorge wrapped in only his cloak.

2. The Poet of the West

———⟫●⟪———

At the time it had mattered little to Kumaran where he went, as long as he got as far as Rome, the city whose fame reached all the way to his home in Tamilakam. He wanted to see the world of the white-skinned yavanas, a world unknown to any of the Tamil poets. He had no itinerary and no host. His low-caste origin made it impossible for him to attract the notice of a king in the usual ways. He would have to do something, be something out of the ordinary. It had come to him in Muziris as he sculpted the head of a dragon at the prow of one of the yavana boats. No poet in Tamil country had ever sung of the faraway lands to the West. No poet had ever visited these lands. "Why not me?" he told himself. Had he learned to read and write only to keep accounts? Was it a mere accident that the teacher his father found for him was a poet, a hermit, a visionary who saw something special in his low-born pupil? Had he studied and learned to imitate the poets for nothing? "Why shouldn't I be the first? Why shouldn't I?" he kept prodding himself.

He let himself dream big dreams—dreams that no brown-faced son of a low-caste sculptor had any right to dream. He told himself, lowly pulaiyar though he was, that he would one day be the favorite of the mighty King Karikal. His writing skills might be no better than those of a hundred other poets who sought the King's favors. His pedigree would certainly be inferior. But his experience, and therefore his story-telling, would make him unique, indispensable: He would find himself living amid the splendors of Karikal's court, his permanent guest, in fabled Puhar. This had been Kumaran's wild, crazy ambition.

7

From Tamilakam he had worked his way across the Western Ocean, across the desert and up the Nile, along the Great Sea as far as Spain, and back east as far as Judaea. Over his shoulder hung a frayed rope which he wore with as much solicitude as any brahmin his sacred thread, for at the bottom of the loop that it made was a sizable leather pouch stuffed with the poetry he had written in the yavana lands he visited. He had carved totemic masks for the barbarians of Gaul, got drunk with a gang of Numidian slaves, worked on Ostia's docks, cleaned up human blood left behind in the great Roman amphitheater, experienced a snowstorm in Pergamum, lain next to a white Egyptian prostitute. He had spoken strange languages, eaten strange food, worn strange dress, slept with strange women, sworn by strange gods. About most of this he wrote, sometimes inventing words to describe things as yet unnamed in his own tongue. What does a Tamil call a giraffe, that freak of an animal brought to Rome for the games in honor of Caesar Augustus? Kumaran finally called it the "African camel." His pouch of poetry and notes carried more than a fortune. It carried his future, his destiny.

Now he found himself in Caesarea on the eastern shore of the Great Sea in the land of the Jews. Spring it was—Chitrai according to the Tamil solar calendar—in the thirty-first year of the reign of the Chola monarch Karikal, by Roman reckoning the seventh year of the Emperor Claudius. Five winters had come and gone since he left home. As the slaves below deck strained at their oars to the rhythm of their clanking chains and pulled the galley out of the crescent-shaped harbor through the stone breakwater, he stood alone on the stern and looked eastward beyond the Roman seaport named after an emperor. His gaze penetrated the flaming Judaean sunrise beyond the hills to the east. And he dreamed of the cattle, the elephants, the chariots, the chests of gold and silver that King Karikal would bestow on the humble son of a pulaiyar sculptor and poet.

3. "I've Seen the Lord!"

On the morning of the second day out, Thomas sat on coiled rope at the bow of a Roman galley. Seagulls screeched overhead in the cool sky streaked with wispy cirrus, but he didn't notice. His mind was on Jesus. He remembered how on a hillside Jesus taught the disciples how to pray, and he now said that prayer aloud: "Our Father in heaven, holy is your name. . . ."

He remembered the sendoff in the harbor the day before. A group of twenty, including Peter, had come down from Jerusalem to bless him. Others living in Caesarea, many of whom he did not know, swelled the crowd to more than fifty. He remembered the face of his daughter Tabitha, who had come all the way from Galilee; she held her hands over her mouth as a stream of tears flowed down her face; she was clutching her baby girl, his first grandchild. He remembered the face of Mary, who at sixty came down from Jerusalem to see him off. In her eyes he saw a tender, motherly love. Though she did not weep, he could not help weeping himself when he looked at her, for it was she who had taken him in and raised him alongside Jesus after his own mother died when he was twelve. He was known then only as Judas, Judas "the bastard" behind his back, for his natural mother had been a whore at the time of his birth. It was Mary who gave him the name Thomas, or "twin," for he resembled Jesus, even though Jesus was eight years older. Jesus had taken him on as an apprentice in the family carpenter shop and, together with Mary, had loved him.

Now they were all behind him. As the sun, squat and misshapen, peeped over the purple hills barely discernible in the east, something whispered in his heart he would never see them again, and he began to feel his courage fail.For the hundredth time he heard the voice inside him begin to complain, "Stay in Alexandria, that is where you can be useful." But he cut the voice off. It was Philip who was going to Alexandria; Philip was already there. He, Thomas, was going to India. He had known he would go from the moment he woke in the Jordan gorge three months before. If Jesus could die on a cross fit for criminals, then he, Thomas, could die in India as an honored martyr. That was the logic he couldn't resist when he woke. "You are clever with languages," they had all said. "India must be won over before the Lord returns," said the enthusiasts. "Parthia has prepared you for this greater challenge," said those who would reassure him. But none of those arguments meant much to him. He did not let himself dream he might be successful in India. He let himself think only that he might someday return from there.

He remembered how full of hope he and Bartholomew had been when they left for Parthia four years before. They had thought they would introduce the whole country to the new faith. They had the liveliest sense that Jesus was walking alongside them. Under the stars on warm nights or in drafty stables or shepherds' huts when the weather was wet or cold, they relived the events of his life, from the smallest to the greatest. During all the time in Parthia, Thomas had no doubts he was doing God's will.

He had not always been so fortunate. He remembered the time long ago, the first time he had doubted, the time of his famous Doubt which had given him his new name. He had come back to Jerusalem and found the disciples gathered in the house of John Mark's mother, the same house where they drew the lots. Only this time Jesus had been dead but a week, not fourteen years. Not just dead, but executed as a criminal, by crucifixion. With his own horrified eyes Thomas had seen the soldier pound spikes through Jesus' wrists and feet, with his own ears heard Jesus' anguished cry from the cross, "My God, my God, why have you forsaken me?" just before he died.

"Thomas, we thought you had fled for good," Peter had snarled at him as he unbolted the door.

Peter.Thomas had been present the day of Jesus' death when Peter, fearing for his life, denied three times in the high priest's courtyard he ever knew Jesus. Thomas, almost out of his mind with grief and confusion, cursed Peter and called him a coward in front of the other disciples. As a result, each thought the other despicable, and forgiveness was out of the question—or so it seemed.

But then the event happened that changed everything.

Mary Magdalene had come up to Thomas as Peter stood aside. With eyes wide and upturned, she said in a voice hushed with awe, "Thomas, we have seen the Lord."

The crowd behind her erupted in excited voices as soon as she spoke. "It's true!" they said. "We have seen him! We have seen the Lord!"

Thomas had walked the roads and footpaths around Jerusalem like a drifter after Jesus died. He did not know where he was going, and for three days he barely ate. Now he had come back—come back to grieve with his friends, to get their support, before going home to Nazareth. He expected to see faces like his own; it never occurred to him that it could be otherwise. What he saw instead he could not comprehend. No one shared his grief. Instead there was this nonsense about seeing him.

"Seen the Lord? What is this?—he's been dead for only a week, and you look like you're at a party. What are you talking about?"

"We have *seen* him, Thomas!"

"What do you mean, *seen him?*"

"He is risen!"

Thomas gaped at the excited faces before him. "Is he really alive?" He felt a faint hope stir in his heart.

A cacophony of voices thundered forth their good news. They had all gathered closely around him by now and were bursting to tell him their strange story.

"But he—*did* die, didn't he?"

"Yes, yes," the voices said, "but he is *risen!*"

"Risen?"

"Yes, risen!"

"What do you mean? Where? Where did you see him?"

"Here. Here in this room, in this very room!"

Thomas' eyes fanned over the room. There at the center was the long table where they shared their last meal with Jesus. It seemed so ordinary, so like it had always seemed, except that—and again the great lump rose in his throat. But why was everyone still here? Were they mad? Why didn't they all go home? "Who saw him?" he asked as he again allowed himself to hope.

"I did!" and "We did!" shouted many of the voices.

"But—but—this can't be. You're all—" Thomas looked at the mob and shook his head.

"But it happened! Thomas, it *happened*," said a woman's voice.

Thomas was sure not one of them except Mary Magdalene loved Jesus as much as he did—surely everyone must know of his devotion to the Master. *Is this one of Peter's jokes?* he wondered to himself. *Is he getting back at me? Or are they all—? Or by some miracle—? No! It can't be!*

So he said in a loud, almost furious voice, "Unless I see in his hands the prints of the nails, and put my finger in the holes made by the nails, and put my hand in the gash in his side, I will not believe it!"

For much of the day he sat in a daze, bewildered, resentful, unbelieving but wanting to believe, as the disciples gushed and rattled on with their giddy plans. He stayed with them overnight. They tolerated him, ignored him, wondered why he stayed. He stayed with them for part of the next day too, going from person to person, asking more questions, studying them, always studying them. It was impossible to deny that something extraordinary had really happened. They were all convinced Jesus, their crucified Master, had visited them in that very room even though they all had seen him crucified and dead. This was no joke. They were convinced he was the Messiah chosen by God to usher in a new age. They were even convinced they could carry their master's message to all Israel. What confidence they had! How their faces glowed! How weighty their words! They undertook the most commonplace duty as if it figured somehow in God's plan. And all he could do was look on, look on with wonder, increasingly astonished by what was going on around him. Every hour he told himself it was time for him to go. He should go back home to Nazareth and take up his place as a carpenter alongside James, his oldest brother. But James was here! He was one of them! As each hour passed, he told himself to wait one more. Just one more. He wanted to believe what everybody around him believed, but he couldn't. So the second day wore into the night. And Thomas found himself still in the upper room with the brethren.

He was almost the last to fall asleep. It must have been shortly before dawn that it happened.

"Thomas!"

A luminous figure stood in front of him.

"Thomas, peace be with you!"

Thomas jerked himself up and gasped, for it was Jesus.

"Thomas, look at my hands, and feel the wound where the soldier pierced my side with his spear; don't be faithless, but believing!"

Jesus was dressed in a white tunic that glowed with an unearthly pale yellow light. His unblinking eyes were compassionate and gentle but vaguely reproachful, almost sad; his beard and hair were clean and fresh.

"Master!" said Thomas in a voice that almost failed.

He fell upon Jesus, squeezing his body to his flesh. Then a demon rose up. Though holding Jesus in his arms, Thomas still doubted. Was this really Jesus, or a ghost? He felt his hand slide down Jesus' body. He felt for the wound. Even then he wasn't sure. Then he felt it, somehow felt it under the tunic, and his finger somehow slipped into Jesus' side and traveled the warm, wet length of the wound. Then, in an instant of incandescent certainty, the doubt shattered, the demon ran off howling into the night. Thomas was filled with an indescribable joy and power. It was as if God Himself had touched him and transformed him into an angel, into pure spirit, as if lightning had turned his blood into fire. He felt, he knew, that he was changed forever.

Then he heard, "You have believed because you have seen me; blessed are those who have not seen and yet believe."

Thomas fell on his knees and gazed up at Jesus, his eyes brimming with tears. "Master, Master!" he sobbed, "forgive me!" With those words Jesus vanished. In one instant he was there, in the next he was gone.

Thomas looked around him not knowing what to do. "What's going on?" muttered one of the sleepers. The voice then fell silent.

Thomas looked around in great excitement. The oil lamp glowed dimly on Bartholomew's shaggy face, and a cock crowed as the wind whistled through a chink in the window. . . . Darkness. . . . Stillness. . . .

"I'VE SEEN THE LORD!" he erupted. He went from body to body shaking each and shouting, "I'VE SEEN THE LORD!" Soon everyone was awake, slapping him, kissing him, embracing him, questioning him. Even the women, who had rushed up from the lower room. Even Simon Peter.

"He was just now here!" said Thomas. "He came to me. To me! I have no more doubts!"

"Tell us. Tells us what happened!" they said. "You're with us!" No one tried to go back to sleep. Instead they pressed him for details of the vision, and he told them all exactly what he had seen. And they were satisfied. "So you're with us?"

"Yes! Yes!"

The day broke, everyone bathed, prayed. The women brought up bread, yogurt, water. They breakfasted as he told them over and over what had happened. . . .

His thoughts returned to the present. A breeze had come up, and the sails overhead were beginning to billow out. The slaves churned up the bluish waters of the just awakening sea with their oars; soon they would be able to sleep. A black man with straight hair had climbed the mast and was letting out sail. He looked uncomfortable and awkward, even frightened, as he clung to the mast with one hand and slowly unfurled the sail with the other.

"That fellow's like me!" Thomas chuckled to himself. "Out of place!"

Yes, it was funny. It was ridiculous and outlandish. Here he was going to India to preach the gospel of his master and brother and twin. He didn't know the first word of the language he was supposed to preach in. He had no contacts there and no companion to help him. He had heard Indians didn't even grow the grape, so there would be no wine to celebrate the Eucharist with. He was like a man about to jump into a tub of wriggling snakes in the hope not only of escaping their bite but of taming them. Yes, it was ridiculous. As he contemplated the incongruity between the gigantic task and his own feeble ability, a quiet chuckle stole out of his throat.

He stopped himself abruptly. The salvation of souls was at stake and he was amused? A sacred mission was given him by God in heaven and he was making light of it? Yet he could not rid himself of a sense of bittersweet irony. That this grand and solemn mission should fall to *him*, that God should choose *him*—was it really possible?

He threw up his hands, looked up into the brightening sky, and called out: "I am your fool! Do with me what you will!" And like a man deranged he burst out laughing into the wind.

4. Teacher and Student

At sunset of the third day out, Kumaran sat cross-legged on the floor of the boat, leaned his back against the gunwale, and fished out a dirty scroll from his pouch. Then he mixed some ink, picked up his stylus, unfurled the scroll, and wrote in tiny letters crammed close together in Tamil: "Caesarea, a gaudy new city named after an emperor, in the land of the Hebrews. A pale blue windswept sky, the harbor with its fishy smells, the raucous shouts of its stevedores, the harried farewells of travelers, one of whom—"

Kumaran noticed sandals and white hairy legs standing in front of him. He looked up into strange eyes, the eyes of the man he was about to describe. This was a man of some importance, for a throng of well-wishers had seen him off. This was the man who slowly paced the deck with an anxious brow and seemed to be in perpetual conversation with himself. Kumaran wondered who he was, but years of experience dealing with the white man had taught him to be wary. But there was no contempt or insolence on the face of this white man.

Kumaran blew on the letters he had just written and rolled up the scroll.

"Pardon me," said the man.

Kumaran looked up suspiciously at the long face with the high forehead and sharp, prominent nose looking down.

"Do you speak Aramaic?" the stranger asked.

"Yes," said Kumaran, trying to size up the man so strangely amiable.

"My name is Judas, Judas Thomas. I am known as Thomas. I am from Galilee. I was curious. It's not everyday that one sees a sailor who—writes."

The man was gazing down at Kumaran with an embarrassed smile, and Kumaran could not help wondering if the man was trying to sell him something. Was he a dealer in parchment?

"I am not a sailor," said Kumaran sullenly.

"You are Numidian? Or Ethiopian?"

"I am a Tamil."

"Tamil? I haven't heard of the place."

"You would call me Indian."

Kumaran was surprised at the man's reaction. His ascetic face lit up as if someone had told him where treasure was hidden. His black beard fluttered though there was no wind, and his nostrils quivered.

"You are from India?" said the man. "India, did you say?"

Feeling he had something the man wanted and that he was in a position of advantage, though he hadn't the faintest idea why, Kumaran let his eyes scan the man with professional detachment. Spiritual eyes, the eyes of a yogi; incongruously broad shoulders over a wiry frame, a strong man, very, very tall; a kindly but anxious face; a man of the world—no, that wasn't quite it; too otherworldly; but competent. Yes, competent. A man of much experience; well traveled; perhaps an adventurer. No, that wasn't it. There was something strange about the man's eyes he did not understand.

"Yes. Your merchants consider me from South India," Kumaran said reluctantly.

"May I sit with you?"

Kumaran nodded. He could hardly believe what was happening.

"Would you tell me about your country?" said the man.

"Well, I . . . I will try," said Kumaran. "If you like."

"You speak our language well. Do you know Greek? Or Hebrew?"

"A little Latin, a little Greek. But I prefer Aramaic."

"As do I. And what is your name?"

Should he tell him? He was by now intensely suspicious. Nevertheless he said, "Kumaran."

"And you are really an Indian? No, you are an angel sent to me by God!"

"I do not understand," said Kumaran.

"I mean—never mind."

"And where are you going?" Kumaran ventured after a pause.

"To India."

"India? You are going to my country?"

"India, yes, to India. I am going to India. Actually Tamilakam."

Kumaran was amazed. Nothing about this strange man made any sense. But that would at least explain why there were so many people on the wharf. He was going so far. "So that is why you want to know about India," said Kumaran, trying to hide his interest.

"Yes, but I don't speak the Indian language."

"There are many Indian languages," said Kumaran, suppressing a smile.

"I would like to learn one," said the man.

"Which one?"

"Well, I don't know. What about yours?"

Was the man asking him to be his teacher? It almost seemed so, but Kumaran could not believe that.

"Would you teach me your language?" said the man.

It was so! Should he accept? "What did you say your name was?"

"Thomas. Call me Thomas."

Kumaran looked at Thomas sitting beside him stroking his beard, then looked out toward the horizon. The sun had set and a beautiful crimson glow dominated the sky on the other side of the boat. He thought to himself that of all the adventures he had had on his long voyage, this was the strangest. In Tamilakam he had grown up knowing he was low-born, and nothing in his karma had changed since he set foot on yavana soil. For five years no white man had considered him so much as an equal. But here, suddenly, was one willing to sit at his feet and learn his language. And a tall and handsome one, a man of some importance, at that.

"Could I become your student? We could pass the time as teacher and student," the man persisted in his gentle but anxious voice. "And I will teach you Greek or whatever you like."

Feigning nonchalance, but inwardly excited, Kumaran accepted Thomas as his student. "But each region has its own language," he warned. "There is no such thing as 'Indian,' nothing like your Greek or Aramaic, no common language."

Thomas looked troubled but recovered his good cheer momentarily. "Then I'll have to go to *your* country and speak *your* language," he said decisively as he stroked his beard.

Again Kumaran was amazed. Here was a man with a destination as indefinite as his had been five years ago when he left Muziri for the

West. Apparently this strange yavana had no itinerary and no host. He only knew he had to travel as far as the vast land he thought of as India. Where exactly—the country of the Tamils, or the Konkanas, or the Kalingas, or the Gangas, or the Aryas far to the north—made no difference to him. Kumaran was intensely curious, but it was not his nature to ask a yavana outright what his business was. He would find out in due time.

So the black-faced Tamil in his twenties and the white-faced Jew, the yavana, about forty, spent their days on the deck of the galley as teacher and student. Sometimes the patched sails would billow out and give them shade. At other times, especially early in the morning, they were glad to feel the sun's rays. Since Kumaran had no parchment or palm leaves to spare, and since he was a sculptor by birth, he carved the thirty letters of the Tamil alphabet—the twelve vowels or "souls," the eighteen consonants or "bodies"—on a broken oar. These Thomas memorized, first learning to recognize them, then to pronounce them, then to trace them with eyes closed. Kumaran next carved the 204 modifications arising from the combining of all but one of the bodies with each of the souls, and by the time the boat reached Alexandria Thomas had memorized all these. Kumaran also taught him how to converse—quite a different skill.

"Why do you have two syllables for every one of ours?!" Thomas cried out once in exasperation.

"We are twice as civilized!" Kumaran said. Then he burst out laughing in his usual high-pitched warble.

As they got to know each other better, Kumaran told Thomas he was a sculptor and a poet. What Thomas called himself in the midst of that seaman's world of open sky and swarthy faces Kumaran had never heard before—not in Greek, not in Aramaic, certainly not in his native Tamil. Thomas called himself a Christian. And when he carried his precious oar off the boat in Alexandria, carried it under his arm—"It's crucial to the success of my mission," he told the guffawing sailors who slapped him on the back—he won Kumaran's affection.

They got passage on a small freighter carrying processed papyrus wrapped in skins up the Nile to all the major inland towns. The twelve slaves who poled the boat were blacker than the ribbons of silt that hugged the river to right and left. Always the sun beat down on their gleaming bare backs as they struggled against the current, sometimes with the aid of the north wind which filled the single sail of the low snub-nosed boat, sometimes not. Sometimes Thomas volunteered to help with the poling, but mostly he sat at the bow, oar in hand, studying Tamil, struggling against a different kind of current. To what purpose Kumaran still did not know.

They made many stops along the way to unload cargo. Finally, after twenty-three days, they reached Koptos. There they procured food and water and rented space on a camel for their baggage, including Thomas' oar. The caravan set out across the desert for Bernice on the Red Sea.

5. Desert Silence

They traveled by day over the Egyptian desert under a terrible sun, for the caravan leader feared meeting brigands at night. When they camped at sunset at one of the halting places along the route, Thomas set out in search of a place to study, pray, and sleep, away from the party. Once he located it—sometimes on a promontory, sometimes in the middle of a flat sandy tract, once in a cave on the side of a cliff—he rejoined the group, checked his provisions, and in other ways readied himself for the night and for departure the next morning at sunrise. Then he retired, always carrying his oar and a scroll, usually the collected sayings of Jesus or a reading from the Prophets, to his private camp. He would study and read by the waning light of day, spend an hour or more in prayer, then settle down to sleep.

He knew Kumaran could not understand why any man would leave the security of the camp to go off by himself. But Kumaran did not ask about this, and Thomas felt the time for Kumaran to know had not yet come. Their roles would be reversed soon enough, but for now he needed a teacher, not a student. He would let Kumaran think whatever he wanted.

But at the end of the fifth day, as the setting sun reddened the barren, craggy ridges that hemmed in the wadi along which the road wound, Kumaran followed Thomas to his private camp a quarter mile distant on the other side of a jagged ridge.

"Thomas," Kumaran called out softly from atop the ridge.

Thomas, who had been praying, turned to look at the voice.

"It's me."

"What brings you here, Teacher?" he said, standing up.

Kumaran picked his way down over mossless, dead rock, and did not answer.

The still air was hotter than human flesh in spite of the deepening twilight, and Kumaran's voice seemed eerie in the absolute quietness of the windless heat.

"I wondered where you had gone off to," he said.

Thomas loosened the phylacteries tied round his arm and head while Kumaran stared. Thomas could see Kumaran wondering what they were. But, as always, Kumaran shied away from asking direct questions. So Thomas did not tell him.

"I'll go," Kumaran said. He nervously blew mucus out of his nose onto the rocks, which made a spanking sound. "I just wanted to see where you—what you were—"

"Don't go, Teacher," said Thomas, "Since you are here, let me teach you something for a change."

For an instant Thomas thought he would tell Kumaran everything, but just as he opened his mouth he decided better. He must not confuse his own needs for companionship and understanding with Kumaran's. The time was not quite right.

Kumaran stared and waited.

Thomas didn't know what to say. He looked around him at the landscape to see if there was anything close at hand to tell Kumaran about. Then it occurred to him what to do. "Be very still, Teacher, and listen."

Kumaran looked around him in every direction, then up at the sky, which was a fiery scarlet in the west.

"Listen. What do you hear?"

Kumaran listened, listened and waited, as he looked out at the silent sunset.

"What do you hear?"

Thomas could see Kumaran concentrating. "Nothing," he said as he gave his head a peculiar sideways wiggle.

"Try harder, Teacher. Tell me what you hear."

Kumaran listened, waited for a sound. But there was no sound. No sound at all. Absolutely no sound in the whole vast, still desert. "I hear nothing," he said with an apologetic half-smile.

"Nothing," said Thomas. "Nothing. No cricket, no cicada. No bird, no frog. No wind. Not a grain of sand moving. Not even a flutter of hair at the ear's opening. Silence. Listen to it, Teacher."

They stood perfectly still and listened to the hot, darkening silence. Then Thomas said, "Kumaran, what do you hear *in* the silence?"

Thomas heard the voice of God in the silence, and he wondered if Kumaran might hear something similar. But Kumaran did not understand the question.

"*In* the silence. What do you hear *in* the silence?" Thomas repeated.

"Ah, now I understand." Kumaran stood very still and concentrated, closing his eyes. "Only a slight buzzing, like a swarm of insects far off, inside my head."

Thomas scooped up a handful of sand, studied it, and said, "You are welcome to stay the night if you like. Shall we trust our baggage to God?"

That night, and each of the desert nights that followed, Thomas had Kumaran as a companion. Most of the time they had a visitor, a silent, bright moon with a personality mysterious and alluring. Every night it grew rounder and began its descent from a position higher in the sky. Several times Thomas thought he noticed Kumaran, lying on the warm sand, watching him as he prayed. Once Thomas wrapped a Torah scroll around his head instead of the phylactery. Another time he wept aloud. And he frequently fingered a cross-shaped ivory pectoral which hung around his neck on a thick, unbreakable thong. His friends thought of the cross as a gruesome symbol of public execution and thought of him as eccentric, but Thomas didn't care. He wore it as a reminder of what Jesus had gone through and what he was prepared to go through; it kept Jesus close to him. He knew he had eccentricities and hoped that Kumaran would accept them, as Bartholomew had learned to do. Already he had almost gotten used to one of Kumaran's: his habit of explosively clearing his nose one nostril at a time.

The caravan reached Bernice after thirteen days, and Thomas swam in the vivid blue water of the Red Sea. He was a good swimmer, and he enjoyed his healthy, muscular body. As he cut through that wonderfully refreshing water, he saw Kumaran studying him. And he wondered if Kumaran might be persuaded to join him as he journeyed across India. And if Kumaran did join him—for the first time Thomas began to dream. He and Kumaran, wouldn't they make the perfect team? Kumaran could translate, advise, and prepare the way. He looked over at Kumaran squatting on the beach. If the spirit really took hold, there was no telling what the limits of this man's abilities were. Did Kumaran love him? It seemed so. Thomas was no fool, and he well understood the power of love. He also understood the plight of the slave and the dark-skinned. Give them love, treat them with respect, and they will love back tenfold. Love was the secret of Jesus' gospel; love was the magic that empowered it and made it irresistible, especially among the oppressed. Wouldn't India find it irresistible too? Suddenly an extraordinary hope was born in his soul. All the fantastic expectations of the enthusiasts back in Jerusalem made sense. Love, just love—that was the recipe for success. The whole dark continent could be gained for Christ. The faith would climb quickly like a creeper, like ivy up a trellis. All he had to do was plant it in the rich, virginal soil. But first he had to win Kumaran.

Three days later they found work on a ship bound for Socotra, that desert island off the northeast coast of Africa, and set sail.

6. The Exorcism

Sometimes a hot wind out of the northwest favored them as they made their way down the Red Sea, but just as often the wind died down altogether. The heat was horribly oppressive. Everyone woke up stinking at dawn in a pool of sweat, and the sun that rose high in the sky and boiled the water below took on demonic properties in the minds of the sailors as it roasted their flesh. Kumaran wasn't surprised the first time Thomas dived off the becalmed ship into the salty water, but some of the sailors disapproved. After one of these swims, the boat's owner, Philetus, a vintner from Rome carrying wine to Socotra, glowered at teacher and student as they sat in the shadow of a sail practicing Tamil. "Get out of my way, you filthy Jew! You and your nigger boy teacher!"

Kumaran had grown accustomed to abuse, so it didn't particularly bother him. But he had never before seen Thomas abused. What would he do? Kumaran watched Thomas study Philetus, tipsy with wine. Then, without rising, Thomas said in a voice as gentle as a maiden's, "And you, Philetus, are a child of God, precious to Him."

Philetus' behavior had been peculiar from the beginning of the voyage. He was either drunk or abusive or both, and he had a distracted, roving look in his eyes. He doted on a pet monkey—a tiny spider monkey named Julian—that sat on his shoulder. But on the sixth day out he seized the monkey, hacked off its head, and ordered him to be boiled and mixed into the soup. By that night everyone whispered that Philetus was mad. But it was not until the next day—the summer solstice, as it happened—when Thomas delivered that mysterious, kindly rebuke, that everyone found out what was really wrong with him.

As soon as Thomas said "child of God," Philetus let out a bestial growl and, with fingers bent like claws, lunged at the "filthy Jew." Thomas, a powerful man, could not fight off the smaller Philetus by himself. Kumaran tried to pull him off, but Philetus hurled him aside as if he were a piece of straw. Finally six or seven sailors pried him loose.

Thomas, bleeding from bite marks on his face and neck, was transformed in front of everyone's eyes. The gentle, brooding, seemingly ineffectual eccentric suddenly took on the character of the *chakravartin*, the "wheel turner," the Universal Emperor told of in Indian legend.

"Bring a cot up from below!" he ordered. "Bring it, bring it now!"

At once two open-mouthed sailors disappeared down the hatchway.

"Hold him! Hold him tight! Pick him up! You two, grab his legs! You, get some rope!"

Everyone did as Thomas bid. Everyone felt that something remarkable—and dreadful—was about to happen. They forgot about the sun cooking their flesh.

The cot and the rope at hand, Thomas, bare-chested, directed the men to tie Philetus down. Then he removed his most precious possession, the ivory cross, and held it out at Philetus. "In the name of Jesus the Christ, come out of the man!" he roared.

Philetus' mouth suddenly became square in shape, and his face became contorted with an unbelievable, horrifying malevolence. He spoke not in his own voice, but in high-pitched parrot-like echoing tones that zinged down to the bowels of the horrified onlookers. "No! No! You are no match for us! There are two of us, and you are only one!" the voice, or rather voices, said.

"Come out, come out, in the name of God and his son Jesus the Christ!" said Thomas repeatedly, streams of sweat pouring off his face.

By now all the sailors had gathered. Unutterable obscenities began pouring out of Philetus' mouth. Interspersed with these were howls and growls. His mouth was ringed with foam, and his eyeteeth glistened like a dog's fangs beneath quivering lips. Then he began jerking with superhuman strength, so much so that the cot to which he was tied bumped up and down on the deck like a beached shark. Meanwhile Thomas alternated between periods of intense silent prayer and loud commands to the demons—as he called them—to come out.

Then with amazement the sailors and passengers watched as Philetus' body began to swell. The cincture he wore round his waist popped like a slingshot as his belly swelled to the shape of a wind-filled sail. His thighs, hips, chest, and neck swelled in the same monstrous way. "In the name of Jesus the Christ, leave him! Leave him!" Thomas roared, never once glancing away from the grotesque body, which seemed on the point of exploding.

Suddenly the body shook, and out of every pore oozed a stream of the most sickening substance imaginable. The sailors, used to every kind of fishy rotten smell, retreated as if one man. Thomas never budged, but asked Kumaran to bring him his bag of scrolls. He read out loud from them as the horrid effluvia streamed out of Philetus and rolled across the deck.

Finally Philetus resumed his natural size. Thomas then handed the scroll back to Kumaran and took up his cross-shaped amulet again. "Give up! You are defeated! Leave him! Leave him in the name of God, the Supreme Power!" he shouted.

Then a new horror transpired. Philetus grew quiet, his eyes closed, and his muscles became as taut and rigid as stone. Although of normal size, his body began to sink against the rope matting of the cot. Lower and lower it sagged until, with a crack, the wooden bedstead broke in two, and Philetus' rump lay against the hot deck. Thomas then ordered the men to pick Philetus up, but not even the strongest could budge him. He might as well have been made of iron or stone. Meanwhile Thomas prayed silently with eyes closed. His brows knit together, and sweat poured off his face. Sometimes he opened his eyes and muttered something, then he resumed his silent prayer.

Suddenly and without any warning Philetus was his normal weight again.Thomas again held out his amulet and commanded the demons to come out.Then he cried victoriously, "You are defeated! Christ has won! Get out! Get out!"

But Philetus, or rather the demons, began to twitch and then to struggle and convulse in a final paroxysm of resistance. They cursed and threatened Thomas and clawed their victim's body. Philetus' eyes rolled up until only the whites were visible, and foam again gathered at his mouth. Gradually his face and body took on serpentine features. His eyebrows became hooded, his eyes reptilian. From time to time they opened wide and blazed out at Thomas in a fury of hatred, then they sank back torpidly beneath their almost-closed, hooded eyelids. As the climax came, Philetus' whole body began to writhe like a mortally wounded snake, and the color of his face changed continually, as if invisible shadows stole across his face, went away, then reappeared.

Finally he was still. He opened his eyes and asked where he was. For the first time since the sailors had seen him, he looked and sounded like a normal man.

Thomas slumped down against some coiled ropes and lay exhausted. Craggy old salts came by and bowed or knelt down in front of him or just gazed in amazement. He still gripped the precious ivory cross in his right hand, its thong splayed out over his hairy chest.

More and more Thomas intrigued Kumaran, who studied his face with a sculptor's eye. He noted the anxious self-confidence creasing Thomas' forehead and the jaws moving slowly and almost imperceptibly, as if chewing a cud that would not quite break down and dissolve. He watched once as Thomas gazed into the night sky with eyes blazing and mouth pulled back in a strange smile. What kind of man was this Thomas? It seemed that a mysterious and powerful sense of purpose informed all he did. Yet at other times he seemed haunted by some secret fear. And why did he, a man of obvious stature, volunteer to help black slaves pole the boat on the Nile? And what was behind the gentle reproof he gave Philetus? And where did the power come from to cast out demons? Kumaran knew of such things back home, but one expected them of yogis. More and more Kumaran wanted to reverse their roles, to learn from his student, to discover the secret of his nature. Thomas made him think of Mother Kaveri, the river on which he was born and about which he had written many a verse. Every other river in the Chola Empire dried up in the hot season, but the Kaveri, from her highest reaches in the Nilgiris to the broad, flat delta a continent distant—Mother Kaveri always rolled on. She bent around mountains and parted before islets of granite, but she was always moving. Part of her was diverted to this or that ditch or canal or tank, part of her overflowed and irrigated the land, part of her was drunk up by the sun, but her main stream flowed tirelessly, infallibly to the great ocean. What was Thomas' great ocean? What kept him on course and drew him onward?

He waited for Thomas to tell him. Thomas spoke openly, often with deep feeling, of every other subject: of his wife, Huldah, who died giving birth to their one and only son; of that son, who breathed earth's sweet air for only a few weeks and was buried beside his mother; of his two married daughters, one of whom was with child at the time of his departure; of the carpenter's trade that was his profession; of the places he had traveled to; but especially of his "master"—"more than a man" he would say with a faraway look—who had been crucified in

Jerusalem by his own people for some mysterious reason that Kumaran could make no sense of.

Keeping in mind one of the maxims drilled into him by his uncle—"a prudent man will never tell his thoughts to another before he knows that other's faults"—Kumaran began to wonder if Thomas suspected him of hiding his faults. So he began speaking openly of himself. He told Thomas about the girl of sixteen, his betrothed, whom he had left behind and who now, at the advanced age of twenty-one, might still be waiting for him to return and marry her. He told him of his boyish—"pranks" he called them, although one of these had left a playmate blind in one eye and taught him early in life that one can survive by lying. He told him of the floods, famines, and wars by which his people marked time and that drove them sometimes to theft and murder. He spoke of the bloody feats of Karikal, the tiger-king whose patronage he desired beyond anything else that life offered. He described the horror of his father when he told him he would break with the ancient tradition of the family and leave the sculptor's trade to his two younger brothers: "You were supposed to learn how to write *accounts*, not poetry!" he had bellowed. He described how his father would substitute inferior woods and bilk his clients, and how he had come to despise his father, who was either drunk on toddy or all business, and who never had time for play like other boys' fathers. With a lump in his throat he described his mother, who died when he was eight, and whom he had adored; he described her for Thomas in detail, right down to the sandalwood hairpiece and rose-tinted pearl nosering she wore to her funeral pyre. He even spoke of his religion and of Murugan, the God with six faces who sees all and protects his devotees.

Thomas listened with interest to all of this and asked many questions besides. But he would not volunteer the piece of the puzzle that explained who he was and why he was on his way to India. And Kumaran, though often tempted, did not ask him the question that burned inside him. So the game of cat-and-mouse continued. Thomas was not one to make a person feel relaxed to begin with; there was a nobility, an augustness, a dignity, a formality about him that attracted people to him and made them feel privileged to be in his presence and be noticed by him; but this same quality served to keep them at a certain distance. He was an eagle among smaller fowl. This was not so by conscious design; it was not a matter of Thomas' putting on airs; indeed he was uncommonly warm and cheerful. But there was something impersonal about his warmth, as if he were holding back a part of himself.

At least that is how Kumaran saw it. Nevertheless Kumaran was proud of flying in the eagle's shadow. At times it almost thrilled him. In some obscure part of his heart he had even begun to love the eagle. Yet he could not bring himself to fly as high as the eagle; he dared not be too familiar. He was a black man among white yavanas in yavana country. Not even Thomas could make him forget that fact.

As they sailed out of the Red Sea into the Gulf of Aden, they picked up a good wind and trimmed sail. With the lines creaking and groaning again, the ship sped east toward the Indian Ocean, or what Kumaran thought of as the Western Ocean. Soon they were hard by Socotra, that impoverished desert island and transfer point where East meets West and only the date palm grows. The solstice had come and gone, but Thomas' heart, along with the secret that Kumaran was convinced it carried, was locked as tight as the inner door to a god's sanctuary.

7. The "Shipboard Letter"

Thomas and Kumaran found themselves on a great three-masted ship heading east toward the Land of the Tamils. Thomas had been hired as a carpenter and Kumaran as the "ship's translator." The Captain, a Roman named Hippalus, had discovered fifteen years earlier the direct passage to Tamilakam across the Indian Ocean. Even the wind, which blew from the southwest during the summer, was named "the Hippalus," as was the ship itself. The cargo included thirty-two milk-white horses from Arabia, a hundred casks of Roman wine, and fifteen trunks of gold coins with the image of Tiberius Caesar. Three smaller vessels followed the ship for protection from pirates and because Hippalus knew the way.

The wide open air stretched in all directions to the gray horizon. Thomas liked facing backward into the wind as it blustered out of the southwest and washed his body with its warm rain. He would lift his head high and relive his success on Socotra, where he had just baptized one-hundred forty in the span of a mere six weeks. India was dead ahead, only a month distant. Was Socotra an omen of what was to come?

He had not intended to write the brethren back in Jerusalem so early, but there was already much news. And the captain of the freighter on the Nile had given him a roll of papyrus twenty feet long because he had helped out with the poling.

Early one morning two weeks out of Socotra, he sat on a coil of salt-caked rope near the bow and took pen, ink black, and the roll of pale yellow papyrus out of a rough wooden box. As the moist breeze blew through his hair and beard, he closed his eyes and visualized the dock at Socotra. He saw the throng of converts to the new faith: sailors and merchants from Assyria and Greece, local people and their families, even three prostitutes painted with henna standing apart—they had all come to see him off, more than a hundred. The names of "Thomas" and "Christ" were on their lips as they stood or squatted on the jetty—such a variety of ages, hues, and dress. Many wept while others shouted that he must come back soon. One man—a Socotran holding a goat—yelled above all the rest, "Unless we see you *first* in the Kingdom!" And the whole lot of them took up the chant, *"In the Kingdom!"* As the ship's dinghy moved away from shore, the crowd quieted. Out into the harbor they went. The crowd continued to shout out their farewells and wave. Finally the wind had covered up their voices, and all Thomas heard was the creaking and plopping and swirling of the oars in and out of the water as they made for the ship.

Now, sitting on his rope as the clouds rolled in off starboard, he marveled at his success. The Socotrans had drunk up his gospel like men dying of thirst. He had never seen the work go so fast. Had something happened to him, had he been touched by the spirit, could miracles be expected? He knew better than to think this, yet this time he had the testimony of his own eyes. How was it to be explained? And he was catching on to Tamil—simple phrases only, but that was a beginning. "I am going to Tamilakam. . . . Please give me some rice. . . . Where is your home? . . . My name is Thomas"—the words rolled off his tongue with ease. "Why do you study Tamil?" the Indian sailors asked, their heads bobbing in that strange, ever-mobile way of theirs; for they had never before seen a yavana study their language.

His mind turned to Kumaran. That he should happen upon an Indian in a boat while still within shouting distance of Jerusalem, and that this Indian should be literate, even a poet, rather than a common sailor or close-fisted merchant—what unbelievable luck! Maybe not luck. Maybe not luck at all. But what would he do if Kumaran left him alone in the harbor at Muziri where no Greek or Aramaic was spoken? Muziri, that sinister sounding place that was the ship's destination. Thomas felt the old fears grind away at his innards.

But what if Kumaran converted and was willing to stay with him through his travels? But Kumaran was an ambitious man in his own right; he was bent on fame; his sights were set on the courts of a king, on the glory that this world offers. But with God's help—with God's help—no, he mustn't count on anything. Well did he know that God was not in the business of pulling strings for his servants, least of all him. Things had not always gone smoothly in Parthia; he counted himself lucky to be alive. And only six months ago Simon had been sawn in half in Damascus for his zeal.

But there was no denying that Kumaran seemed heaven-sent. Kumaran, or someone like him, was the key to any mass conversion of India, no doubt about that. Sitting on the rope and facing ahead with the breeze at his back, he visualized Kumaran, asleep on the deck near the stern. He imagined the wide-set eyes with the consistency of honey, mobile, almost dancing; the nose aquiline and narrow, the delicate lips turned up at the corners, and the smooth narrow chin that gave his face the shape of an inverted equilateral triangle; the short frame carried lightly, almost with stealth, and the bright rags that he wore; his habit of pacing the deck like a caged cat, as if he were under some compulsion to get from stern to bow and back again; the way he looked around him as if there were enemies about; his quick speech, even in a language not his own, and his high-pitched, twittering laugh; the hands that waved as if they were throwing dice when he talked heatedly about something or when he was drunk. All this gave the impression of someone not at ease with things as they were. Then there was the habit of whittling, the nervous, ever-moving hands; they reflected, Thomas thought, the perpetual movement of his restless soul. Yet Kumaran was a man of undoubted talents. Not only was he a good, if impatient teacher, he seemed to get along well with his countrymen. The Indian sailors who boarded at Socotra and who might have been expected to have little in common with a poet laughed from their bellies at his jokes. They seemed to delight in his company whether he was tickling them with ribald sailors' puns or inspiring them with tales of the gods. If only all this charm, or whatever it was, could be put to good use!

Thomas mixed a few drops of water into the ink but still did not know how to begin the letter. His mind drifted off to the days following Jesus' death, back to the time when he said he did not believe. Now he was known from Sicily to Parthia as "Doubting Thomas." Every convert to the infant faith soon heard the story. At first it had troubled him greatly; he had hoped to make all the brethren forget his famous lapse. He worked with the ardor of ten men, but it was no use; "Doubting Thomas" he remained. But now it bothered him less. For the brethren now used "Doubting" not out of a desire to censure or warn, but with the deepest respect. He was not merely the Doubter; he was the one, above all, who had conquered his doubt.

"The First Letter to the Brethren in Jerusalem, from Thomas, the Lord's Twin, Apostle to India"—should he begin that way? He visualized the brethren gathering in Jerusalem with hundreds of the faithful to hear it read by Peter or James. He imagined it being referred to by all the Christian churches as the "Shipboard Letter."

"Silly!" he chided himself, chuckling anxiously as he came to his senses. He thought of his old friend Bartholomew, who could be depended on to strip him of his pretensions. He picked up the pen and, as the rigging groaned and the ship rocked, began to write:

To the Christians, the followers of Jesus the Nazarene, the Christ, in Jerusalem.

From Judas Thomas, apostle to India, on the Indian Ocean.

Grace to you and peace from God the Father and our Lord Jesus Christ.

By the grace of God my mission to India on the Earth's edge has already borne fruit. Socotra, a parched island off the African coast where only the date palm grows, was ripe for the Lord's harvest, and with the help of a rich convert named Philetus, who earlier cursed me, I baptized 140 souls during a brief stopover.

An Indian who believes in a six-faced god and that I was an Indian in my "former life" is teaching me the language, which is known as Tamil. He has a keen, crafty intelligence, and his manner, though strangely excitable and fidgety, is marked by a kind of grace that endears him to his fellow countrymen. I have great hopes for this man, whose name is Kumaran. With God's grace he will be my first Indian convert and will become my assistant. Without his help I dread to think of what could happen.

For the conversion of India might be more difficult than any of us imagined. From what I have learned, Indians love their gods; they will not be easy to displace. And they are everywhere; every asterism has its residing deity, and every deity is associated with fantastic stories which these innocent people accept at face value. It will not be enough, I fear, merely to preach the gospel; I will have to dig out their superstitions one by one. Let me give you an example of one, for this is like nothing I ever encountered in Parthia: After a feast, Lord Ganesha (an elephant-headed god) ties a snake around his stomach. Amused by this, the sun and moon make fun of him. Ganesha becomes angry and orders the snake to swallow the sun and moon. Darkness covers the world. Thousands of the "lesser gods" pray and get them released. An agreement is reached that the sun and moon are to be swallowed only on certain days. This is the way that Indians explain the eclipse. And there are many other stories just as strange.

But I am hopeful that God will have mercy on this land. The day of the Lord's coming is close at hand, and the time remaining is urgent. Imagine what the Father's power could accomplish through his humble servant: the whole dark continent wrested from Satan's grasp. Pray for me, brothers and sisters in Christ, pray that I may not fail Him! For the truth is that I feel completely unprepared for this mighty task. Some of you know how I doubt my abilities. Even after Socotra not much has changed. Pray for me.

Yet I am encouraged to believe that the power of God is flowing through me as never before, and I tell the following story to embolden all who trust in Christ. The same Philetus whom I mentioned above, a rich Roman shipowner and merchant, cursed me in front of everyone. At first I returned love for hatred, as Jesus taught us on the Mount, but I could see that this approach had no chance of working by itself, for the man was possessed. So I challenged the demons to come out. At the time we were becalmed in the middle of the Red Sea, which was like a lake of fire. But as soon as the demons fled, favorable winds came up, and we reached Socotra nine days later. Philetus in the meantime converted to the faith and helped me in every way while on Socotra, for he has influential friends there. Perhaps you will meet him before this letter reaches you, for he plans to seek you out on his return voyage. Give him a holy kiss of greeting from me.

May God use me to do his holy will. May He be glorified in his lowly servant and in all of you, my brethren. Blessed be God on High, and blessed be his son Jesus.

While writing the letter, Thomas felt as if he were in the company of his friends. But as he looked up from the papyrus, looked out at the broad sea and the dark clouds dropping purple rain here and there on the choppy water, he felt afraid. By nature he was shy, introspective, and cautious. It never ceased to surprise him when someone told him that he was a "great man" or a powerful orator or inspired with the spirit, as many of his converts claimed. He did not exactly disbelieve them, but neither did he quite believe. For there was something artificial about his efforts; they did not seem to flow naturally out of him. Sometimes he wondered if he was miserly with love. Did he love like the other apostles? With all his might he tried to, but he suspected that what others accomplished with sweet feeling he had to accomplish with raw willpower.

He thought again of his daughters and his friends back in Judaea and would have given anything to be anyplace but exactly where he was.

8. A Deal is Struck

They sat under a clear, breezy, moonless sky at the ship's bow. There was no warning, nothing to tell Kumaran what was coming his way. He leaned back against the low railing, where a lamp hung, and tried to see into the eyes of his yavana friend, in whose presence he had begun to glow with a confident, proud satisfaction. He heard the snorts of horses below—horses destined to pull, four abreast, the Chera king's war chariots—and the clopping of their hooves when the boat rocked. The wind was stiff but warm out of the southwest as it strained against the bulging ghostly sails and listed the ship to port. The sails vibrated in rapid snaps under the steady push of the wind, while the flags on top of each mast whipped. The prow swished and ground as it cut through the black and silver waves. Occasionally flecks of spray peppered them, but there was no place on the ship, unless one climbed the rigging, as a few of the sailors did, so isolated as the prow. Kumaran thought of it as "his place"—the place where he could remember and think and compose once the sailors had retired.

They had drunk good wine that night in the captain's quarters, and Kumaran was in especially good spirits. He looked into Thomas' shadowy face and imagined the bemused, slightly ironic smile that complemented the candor and raw power of his personality. Or was Thomas wearing a different face, perhaps the intense, kindly expression that he had seen on other occasions and that made him think of the Buddha?

"You are like the Buddha, the compassionate one," Kumaran said playfully, helped by the wine to bury the last vestiges of awe he felt in Thomas' presence.

"Buddha? Who is this Buddha?" said Thomas.

Kumaran thought back to the last day on Socotra. He had come in from an outlying date plantation where he had found work, for the embarkation date had arrived; he hadn't seen Thomas in three weeks. There in the harbor stood Thomas exhorting a throng to "come to Christ." At first he had been merely astonished. Then it occurred to him that Thomas was going to India for the sole purpose of preaching this message, that his life's work was to preach, just as the Buddha's had been, and not to make money.

"Tell me about this Buddha. Is he another one of your gods?" said Thomas.

Kumaran, feeling playful and bold, giggled at Thomas' conceit. "So you think you're good enough to compare to a god, eh?"

Thomas didn't answer.

"I tell you you are like the Buddha, and you turn around and ask if he is a god. You are bold tonight, my friend!"

Kumaran had never dared be so bold himself. Had he insulted Thomas? He imagined he saw Thomas smile under the starlight. Suddenly the question he had been wanting to ask tumbled out of him before he could stop it: "Who is this Christ, and why are you going to my country?"

"I wondered if you would ever ask," said Thomas.

"What are you trying to sell?"

Kumaran heard Thomas laugh quietly in the warm darkness, then said: "The people on the wharf told me about some man who died for somebody's sin. Is he the Christ?"

"Yes."

"And didn't I hear the same name when you were throwing the demon out of Philetus?"

"You did."

"Tell me about him, then! I wonder that you didn't a long time ago if he means so much to you."

"Kumaran! Kumaran!" Thomas placed his outstretched arms on Kumaran's shoulders. "I wonder too, but I knew this moment would come. Kumaran, listen to me carefully. Trust me. I have known a man in whom God lived. He is Israel's Messiah and the world's salvation. He was raised from the dead. Now he dwells in heaven with the Father, sits at the Father's right hand, but he is coming back to earth soon. He is coming to bring all of us, Jews and gentiles, Israelites and Parthians and Africans and Romans and Indians—yes, Indians too—to the Father. There, in heaven with the Father, we will dwell without end."

"So you are going to India to tell the Indians about this—what did you call him?"

"Messiah. Christ. His name was Jesus."

"Your brother!"

"My 'twin.'"

Kumaran laughed aloud. What tickled him so? If Thomas wasn't a god in his own right, then at least his twin brother was! What an utterly strange man was this Thomas!

"And now we are brothers," Thomas continued.

"Brothers?" Kumaran was no longer tickled. He thrilled at the intimate sound of the word "brothers."

"Kumaran, I want you to give your life to the Father. I want you to help me with my work. We will work like brothers."

"Help you? Am I not already helping you?"

"I will need you to translate, to continue teaching me, to travel where I travel. I can promise you eternal life."

Kumaran stared straight ahead into the night and let those strange words "travel where I travel" go straight to his heart. "Eternal life" meant little to him, but "travel where I travel"—those were momentous words. He felt that some extraordinary fate was descending on him. He had no such feeling when he embarked for the West five and a half years ago, for that was a fate that, by comparison, seemed fashioned by himself. But this was different. It seemed as if he were in the presence of a fate that the Gods had chosen for him. It had nothing to do with any choice that he might have made. It at once thrilled and threatened him. It was the exact interstice between two conflicting sets of karmas. It felt like the close of one history and the beginning of another.

"Kumaran, will you trust me? Will you put on a white robe and let me baptize you? God help anyone who has not been reborn. Kumaran, will you receive it? . . . You and I, together, we are called to bring news of the Messiah, the Savior, the Christ, to India. I need you, Kumaran. I need you to give me, to give the Messiah, your life."

Hardly believing his ears, Kumaran looked up at the stars blazing in the firmament. It comforted him to know that they were listening and heard this strange, preposterous request. They were witnesses.

"Kumaran, he preached love and forgiveness. He promised eternal life."

Kumaran sat as still and mute as stone, still scarcely believing his ears.

Thomas lowered his voice. "Kumaran, do you love me? Do you love me as a brother?"

Love him as a brother? He thought of his brothers back home. He loved Thomas *more* than a brother. But what was Thomas angling for? Was it a trick?

"Yes," he finally said, almost out of a daze.

"It's not *me* that you love, Brother Kumaran. I, Judas Thomas, am nothing special; I am a common sinner, a stupid blunderer; there is nothing lovable about that. It's the spirit you love. The spirit can dwell in you too, Brother. It can dwell in every Indian. The time is short, Kumaran. We, you and I, must be about the Father's business. Together, Kumaran. It can't be put off. Will you help me?"

"But what are you saying?" Kumaran's head was reeling. "What can I do? What is this baptism? How long will you need me?"

"I don't speak the language well enough, you know that. I need someone to translate. The work—it's such a great work. We will carry the gospel of Christ Jesus, the Redeemer, the Messiah of God—"

"*Which* God?" cried Kumaran.

"What? Kumaran, there is only one God."

"One? Only one? What's his name?"

"Does it matter? His proper name we're not allowed to speak, so holy is he, but my Master called him 'Father.'"

"Father? I've not heard of him. And the Mother?"

"Mother? What do you mean?"

"The *Mother*, Thomas. The Goddess. You never speak of her."

"Kumaran, there's only the Father!"

"No Mother?" Kumaran was amazed. "Thomas, there are many Gods. There are Murugan and his mother, the War Goddess Kotravai. There is the Sea Goddess Manimekalai and Mayon, the Black God. And there are the northern gods Vishnu and Shiva. How can you say—?"

At that instant the prow plowed downward, and a chilly spray dampened their tunics.

"They are all false gods," said Thomas. "I want to baptize you into the truth. You are claimed, you belong to him—if only you acknowledge him. Kumaran, you've already acknowledged him. You acknowledged him when you said you loved me. For it was *him* that you loved, him *in me*."

"What? Who?"

"The Christ! And the Father."

"Then there are two Gods?"

"No, brother! Only one! Kumaran, the Christ is God's Messiah, his anointed messenger."

For a moment Kumaran was silent. He half understood what Thomas was saying. He remembered now that he had heard somewhere long ago of the Jews with their odd belief in only one God. But why did he insist on only one God for *others?* In Tamilakam, Kumaran's neighbor respected his Murugan, and Kumaran respected his neighbor's Shiva. Both Gods were real, both true. Perhaps Thomas' Father was real too. Why shouldn't he be? Thomas got his power from somewhere. That must have been where he got it from. Yes, yes, of course.

"I acknowledge him," Kumaran said firmly.

"You acknowledge the Father?" Thomas sounded as if he wanted to be sure.

"Thomas, you're a yavana, but I swear to you—never mind. Yes, I acknowledge this Father of yours."

"Kumaran!"

Kumaran felt Thomas' hands on both his arms.

"Kumaran!" Thomas pounded him with his muscular carpenter's hands.

Kumaran imagined he could see a crescent of white teeth blazing out of the dark.

Thomas cupped his hands over Kumaran's beard and kissed him hard on the mouth, then stood up, exclaiming, "Oh, Kumaran, Kumaran! How I love you, Brother! How I love you! What great things we will do together! Oh, you can't know what great things! You've been chosen, touched by the Father himself! You will become one of the Lord's apostles—you, Brother, chosen, God knows why it should be you from among all Indians! You and I together, we'll cast our nets over the whole land of India, and the fish that we'll catch—oh, Kumaran, you'll see! The fish, all the fish! And all those gods, that god you used to worship, that Murugan. That stone image!"

"Thomas," Kumaran broke in, horrified, "Thomas, what are you saying?"

"What do you mean?" Thomas was still overcome with joy.

"No, Thomas, no, I can't give up Murugan. Is that what you expect? You don't understand what you're asking. Murugan is *my* God."

"What?"

"Murugan is *my* God!"

"But you just said—you acknowledged—-surely you—" Thomas' voice trailed off in the breeze.

"I did. And I will."

"Then—"

"Thomas, I've seen with my own eyes that your god has power; I saw the change in Philetus. And I've seen how real your god is to you. I accept his reality, I acknowledge his power, I'll greet him in my daily prayer because you are my yavana brother. I'll call down blessings upon you from him. But don't ask me to give up Murugan. That's unthinkable! You don't understand what you're saying. Do you know what he does to his enemies? He has six faces and twelve arms. He sees everything, and nothing is beyond his power. He strikes his enemies down like thunderbolts. Once he cursed the great God Brahma to be born on earth, and it was so. A glorious light shines from his head. If I want to, I can see it, with my eyes closed, in my mind. Any of his devotees can. I see him now in my mind, see his purple dress, ear pendant, silver girdle, anklets, wreaths of the *vetchi* flower around his head, one of his arms twirling a spear. He has a peacock for a mount, and he leads a goat on a rope. All about him musicians play stringed instruments, flutes, drums. Sometimes he dances on the hills with beautiful maidens wearing girdles—girdles of the finest gold, inlaid with gems. Undyed garments. Flower designs."

Kumaran's speech, partly Tamil and partly Aramaic, bubbled and squirmed out of his mouth. He took a deep breath and went on: "He lives in forests, in rivers, in lakes, wherever he pleases. He appears where many roads meet and under trees where his worshippers gather. Thomas, you'd do well to honor him along with your Father. He'll protect you while you're in my country. I'm certain he understands Tamils better than your Father does. He would be of much greater help!"

For a long time they sat without a word as the ship mounted and dipped, mounted and dipped. Kumaran wondered if the Gods in the starry constellations on high were enjoying their airy celestial sports and disputing the destinies of embodied beings. He brought his attention back to Thomas' dark face.

"Kumaran, will you stay with me? That's all I ask." The voice sounded weary and spent. Defeated.

Kumaran had never felt so bold before. "You ask a lot, Brother," he said. "I tell you, you ask a lot. I've told you I have to go to Puhar, to Karikal's court."

"And I have to—!" Thomas paused, seemed to swallow his anger, and continued in an apologetic, subdued voice: "I was going to say I had to go about my Father's business."

Kumaran had the upper hand. He felt sorry for Thomas. "Can you go about your Father's business in Puhar?" he said.

Thomas pounced on the question. "Anywhere! As long as it's India!"

There was something about Thomas' eagerness that made Kumaran want to laugh. Such a lion of a man, but look how he begged!

"But Puhar, you say, is on the other side of the continent," Thomas said. "Isn't there something we can do on this side first, in Malabar?"

"I will take a wife in Malabar," said Kumaran with a giggle.

"And after you've taken a wife, will you travel with me in Malabar while I go about my Father's business?"

Kumaran hesitated.

"What have you been preparing me for—on the Great Sea, on the Nile, in the desert, on the Red sea, and now on this ocean stretching to the edge of the world? What have you been preparing me for? Kumaran"—his voice quavered—"you said you loved me."

Kumaran wanted to see just how desperate Thomas was. Would he grovel for his Christ? Kumaran knew he would go with Thomas, but Thomas' weakness made him hesitate. He felt like Thomas was trying to bully him into agreeing, and Kumaran despised being pushed around. But he could not deny that he loved being with Thomas, and he meant to travel through Tamilakam anyway, for he wanted to see the five regions described by all the poets with his own eyes. But this! Kumaran wanted to see just how far Thomas would stoop, to gain even more power over him. If Thomas could play the bully, then he could bully back with interest! But then he felt again the pull of his karma. He felt its strangeness. Was it a destiny he had created for himself in former lives, or one that the Gods had decreed for reasons known only to them? Whatever it was, it was unlike that of any Tamil who had ever lived. What bizarre deed could have ripened into such a life as his? Perhaps it was all apparent to the Gods, but to Kumaran it was an unyielding cipher, a metaphysical zero. But that made it all the more exciting. It was like a game of dice with stakes one could not see. Of course he would go with Thomas. At least for a while. For as long as it suited his purpose.

"All right, I'll go," he said rather airily.

"Good." Thomas paused, then lightly touched Kumaran's arms on both sides in a tentative embrace. "Good," he said again. "God be with you." Then he got up and walked away into the darkness.

For a long time after Thomas went below deck, Kumaran kept watch with the captain and the helmsman. Abaft were the three smaller ships convoying with them to Muziri.The sailors said that Hippalus could navigate by smell and had never missed Muziri by more than fifty miles. Kumaran wondered what Hippalus was doing now. Was he studying the stars, setting the course for the night? Kumaran knew how to locate only one star, the polestar. He found it gleaming faithfully at an unaccustomed latitude low on the horizon, lower than he had seen it since leaving home. How long would he stay with Thomas? What had he gotten himself into? Would he desert Thomas at the first chance? It was an extraordinary idea: traveling all over Tamil country with a yavana. What would there be in it for him? He had grown to love Thomas in yavana country, but would it be so easy to love him in India? What if Thomas became a burden, an embarrassment? Many Indians despised yavanas. But Thomas had such a powerful and good effect on people, and he cut such a fine, tall figure.

While these thoughts tugged back and forth inside Kumaran, he drifted off to sleep. He dreamed of feasting on curried rice, of getting drunk on toddy made from the palmyra or coconut palm, of bare-breasted maidens wearing wreaths of fresh flowers in their hair, and of seven-storey mansions lining the great avenues of Puhar.

9. Black-Faced Jesus

On the fortieth day Thomas crept out through the hatchway, out into the fresh air of dawn. The decks were wet from the squall that had passed over the ship around midnight and sent the men below. The ship dipped and rolled and creaked as it rode the choppy waves on a brisk wind. In the east the first golden rays rose out of the sea beside a billowing column of clouds.

This was the day that the first of the sea birds was to be released to look for land, and it occurred to Thomas that land might already be in sight. He climbed the main mast to the crow's nest.

Perched high up like a bird himself, he searched the horizon ahead for a sign. Failing to see any, he looked around him. Everywhere there was sky, sky even below. Looking down he saw the sailors going about their chores, and sometimes he heard their cries above the pulsating swish of the ocean. When the ship reached its maximum pitch, he was suspended over the gray and white waters. As he watched the sun rise and the sailors emerge from below, he prayed, "Maranatha, Maranatha" ("Come, Lord"), until the very wind seemed to join in the prayer. He was a bird riding on a high wind, the high wind of God, to the ends of the earth.

That night he slept next to Kumaran on the deck under the stars. In a dream he saw an infinite, shoreless ocean of light that seemed to throb with consciousness, power, bliss, and love. Everywhere he looked, in every direction, he saw shining waves, one after another, rolling toward him. He was at the center of his little private island,

and the infinite Ocean of Love was encircling him, approaching him. The waves were high and overpowering, but they did not rage, did not threaten. They swallowed him up, but he was unafraid. For a moment he seemed to lose consciousness, but then—he found himself in the middle of an inviting green meadow under a cloudless blue sky. He could see all round and above him, everything at once, with a panoramic eye. He saw the burning bush that appeared to Moses and declared, "I am the God of your father, the God of Abraham, the God of Isaac, and the God of Jacob." He saw a withered old man, an ascetic, riding on a bull, and with each of the man's breaths, out and in, worlds were created and destroyed; and every time the man blinked his eye in the middle of his forehead, an eon passed. He saw Jesus, not as he was known in Galilee, but mounted on a great serpent; Jesus rode the serpent as another man might ride a horse, reins and all; and his face was black. He saw an old woman, and in her hand was a blood-stained arrow which she had pulled from her body. He saw a beautiful woman give birth to a boy. At first she suckled the child with the greatest tenderness, but then her expression changed and she became fierce and terrible, and she began to eat the child, grinding his flesh and bones between her teeth. Then he saw the child seated serenely on his smiling mother's lap. All these figures, all these and many more, were at ease with each other. People of all colors and dress walked around him in a wide circle, and no one seemed a stranger to anyone. Inside the circle children and animals frolicked. Lions and tigers licked the ears of lambs and kids, and little boys rode on the backs of bears. All in this land lived in harmony.

When he woke up, he recalled the dream in vivid detail. He felt excitement—as if the dream carried some tremendous significance, as if it were a kind of revelation. Yet, upon analysis, he was far from sure what the dream meant, or even whether it came from God. A black-faced Jesus riding on a serpent, a mother eating her child—what could they mean? He did not know, he did not know. But he could not deny that the dream as a whole promised peace and a kind of reconciliation. Reconciliation between what? He did not know.

He scanned the horizon ahead. Nothing. Only a huge black cumulus outlined by light as bright as lightning. "Maranatha," he said. Again and again, "Maranatha. Maranatha."

PART II. MALABAR

10. Sacred Land

Home, the *punya-bhumi*, the "sacred land." Kumaran's heart leaped at the sound of "Land!" on the afternoon of the forty-second day out of Socotra. There it was, unmistakably, dead ahead, a faint dirty streak dividing sky from sea. "To be born in this land is to be superior to the Gods." For the first time he understood the meaning of this proverb.

Soon hawkers rowed out in long dugout boats laden with every kind of fresh food, drink, and medicine. Plantains, coconuts, mangoes, jackfruits, the *badam* nuts that he relished as a boy—Kumaran ate them greedily. Sour curds, sugar cane, delicious syrupy rice cakes. Home!

"She's all yours if you can win her!" said Kumaran to Thomas as they filled their stomachs and stared toward the shore at a thick line of coconut and palmyra palms standing tall on a golden-white beach dotted with fishing boats. The buildings of a city could be seen through the trees, and beyond it a line of dark green hills and still more distant mountains. As seagulls screeched overhead in the pale blue sky, Kumaran giggled uncontrollably.

The hawkers told them the city was Tondi, famous for its high beaches, its beautiful flower gardens, and its delicious rice. Tondi. Kumaran had heard it described in many a poem. "To Captain Hippalus!" the sailors shouted. "Hooray! Hooray!" Coconut juice and toddy flowed abundantly. Meanwhile Hippalus, his gray-blue eyes dancing and his lips drawn back in a tight-lipped smile, turned the ship in a southerly direction, and the wind hit them broadside and made them list far to port. Muziri was only forty-five miles to the south.

The sun had set by the time they reached the mouth of the Shulliyar River, from where they could see Muziri's great harbor lit up. Muziri—or Kodungallur, as it was still known. Kumaran remembered it was here he had first thought of traveling to the West. They took in sail, dropped anchor, and spent the last night aboard ship.

The next morning, under a scudding gray sky threatening rain, they docked. At last they disembarked, and Kumaran stepped off the ship with his baggage of palm manuscripts and white-skinned, black-bearded Jew as tall as a tribesman's bow. With his heart beating fast and his eyes misting over, he fingered the swollen pouch of poetry hanging around his neck. The brahmin might have his sacred thread worn over his shoulder, but Kumaran, the lowly pulaiyar, had his sacred thread too. That frayed thread had carried its growing booty to the western edge of the world and back. Kumaran felt with glee that he had taken something he had no right to, stolen it from unsuspecting yavanas spread out over the world from Spain to Assyria. He felt superior to his ignorant countrymen, even brahmins. In five years he had compassed the world to the west, and no one in all Tamilakam, in all India, had ever known what he now knew. No one before him had ever been willing to make that sacrifice, to undergo that unique, unheard of *tapas*. He alone knew the magical password by which a pulaiyar could steal into the hearts and palaces of kings.

Kumaran and Thomas made their way through the maze of cages, crates, baskets, bales, and bundled heaps of every kind of cargo strewn over the wharves. Behind the wharves they made out high warehouses, some of them newly built, and behind them the thicket of palms and underbrush that shut out the sights and noises and smells of the harbor from the city itself. All around them was a din of men and carts. Kumaran heard the familiar lowing of hump-backed bullocks, the squeaks and groans of pulleys and hoists built by black Tamil hands, the shouts of stevedores and vendors in his beloved Tamil, and it thrilled him. He looked up at Thomas and said, "Isn't it wonderful!" But Thomas looked anxious and answered with only a quick glance.

They jostled their way along the street fronting the warehouses past ship after ship, each with its flags waving in the wind. They found the ferry jetty just as a heavy rain broke out, waited for the rain to abate, then boarded a boat to Maliankara, Kumaran's home.

Gradually the gray-blue of the bay gave way to the gray-green of the backwaters, and the two boatmen exchanged their oars for poles. Down the wide channel the ferry boat pushed on, enclosed now on both sides by forests of coconut and areca palms. As it came up on Maliankara, recognizable only by the whitewashed walls of the wealthier houses along the shore and the cluster of people gathering, Kumaran heard shouts from the shore. "Kumaran is back! Kumaran! Kumaran!" How did they find out? How did they know? For the moment he was brahmin, landowner, general, and king, all at once.

Kumaran and the towering white man stood side by side as the boat anchored. Among the crowd that was still gathering, Kumaran recognized—he blinked hard to make sure—his mother—his dear mother who had been dead twenty years: there she stood, smiling, in her favorite blue sari! Even the rose-tinted pearl nose ring was in place. His scalp tingled and he could barely breathe. He tried to point her out to Thomas, but the ghost had vanished by the time he looked back. "Oh Mother, Mother!" he called. He got off the boat shaking, no one but Thomas knowing the reason.

Kumaran introduced his yavana companion to the family as if Thomas were a great holy man from the Ganges. He tried to explain to them why he was here, but they simply did not understand. A yavana come to convert all India to his religion? It made no sense, it was laughable. They did all they could to make Thomas feel welcome, even when he got in their way and made a fool of himself in small ways.

Kumaran was too preoccupied to take much notice of Thomas during those first days. He wept with joy as he walked alone through the perpetual twilight of Malabar's coconut groves and cavernous rain forests. He had come home.

11. "Kumaran, You Didn't Tell Me about India!"

Nothing had prepared Thomas for this. Everywhere he went people stopped doing what they were doing and turned and stared. If he stayed in one place for a while, soon there would be thirty gathered in a semicircle studying him. They did not lower their heads or avert their glances when he looked back; they showed no more embarrassment than they would have if he had been made of stone. When he walked, people followed him, especially the children, who swarmed after him and tugged at his tunic. He felt like a freak in one of Caesar's spectacles. Some people tried to get him to talk, not because they were interested in what he had to say, but just to see if he *could* talk—like a parrot. And when he did, they would clap their hands gleefully and giggle. He reminded himself that he was already tall for an Israelite and that he towered over the average Tamil male by almost a full head. And his skin was so curiously white—Kumaran had once described it as pink. Even at the harbor people had stared, but they had at least seen white men before. Not so in Maliankara, and Thomas dreaded going outside.

And then there was the stifling showery heat, the devouring deep shade which shut out the sun and the stars, the maze-like lagoons and canals which restricted walking, the lack of a single hill to escape to for prayer, the warnings about paths to avoid at night because of venomous snakes. And the black skin all around him—even the seagulls were black. It all seemed bewildering and hostile.

But he reminded himself that these were small things and that he would get used to them. What was important was his work. "What a harvest of souls!" he exclaimed to himself over and over, as if to prod himself on. But he was more afraid than ever. If only he had Bartholomew with him—he would take one Bartholomew over ten Kumarans. Kumaran knew all about his own country, but what did he know of an Israelite? Kumaran told him the names and habits of all his relatives, but what did that matter? Better if he had explained how Indians ate, or bathed, or defecated. So many peculiar rules. So many different ways to give offense. Everyone seemed so finicky about everything. And all their baffling customs: Scribes wrote by pressing dung into the etchings they made with their stylus. Soldiers wore flowers in their hair. Shopkeepers counted starting with their little finger and moving backwards. And their language contained words for things he had never heard of and lacked other words for things he took for granted. To Thomas it all seemed very strange and threatening. He wanted to board the next ship and go home. But when he looked into the eyes of the children, those big, trusting dark eyes, he saw a beauty the equal of a child of Israel. And he knew that there were immortal souls underneath that black husk, souls that hungered to hear his Master's gospel but were hindered by Satan. He remembered the psalm that described Satan as lurking in the villages and killing the innocent. He promised God that he would drive Satan out.

But Satan was busy working on Thomas. Many years ago he, along with many of the brethren, had made a solemn vow that he would never again lie with a woman. He swore to forego every work of passion, both in thought and deed; he would have taken this oath of celibacy, of this he was sure, even if Huldah were alive. In any case, he had taken it in the presence of Peter and the others. Yet in the ferry over to Kumaran's village, then in the village itself—"Woe is me, for I sojourn in Meshech, I dwell among the tents of Kedar!"—he had found himself sneaking glances at the giggling young women sitting across. Nothing that Kumaran had said prepared him for this. How could he not see their shapely close-set thighs, the leafy loin cloths over their broad hips, their narrow waists with beaded belts, their bare navels, their firm breasts peeping through wreaths of white jasmine and smeared with sweet-smelling sandal paste and brightly colored beauty spots, their smooth shoulders, their modest deer-like eyes, their carefully combed tresses falling down their backs? How could he not see them? Even when he looked away, he still saw them. And they all seemed to say to him,

"I have spread my couch with coverings, with colored linens of Egypt. I have sprinkled my bed with myrrh, aloes, and cinnamon."

On the morning of the fifth day, after he had ceased to be a curiosity to the villagers and could come and go without too much fuss, he sat beside the lagoon in front of Kumaran's house and looked out across the water to the other shore, trying to pray. A young woman came to wash her clothes—she stopped only ten paces to his left, smiled shyly at him once, then went on about her business. She easily could have washed her clothes elsewhere, he thought, but she continued to wash where she was. He tried to put her out of his mind but instead imagined she had come there to tempt him. A melancholy loneliness spread over him. He felt cut off from the consolations of his faith, and for a moment it did not matter that the Father was his eternal companion, or that Jesus sometimes visited him in his dreams, or that Kumaran was in the house just behind him. Everything felt unfriendly and threatening. Everything except the woman washing. He fought his desire, gave in, fought it with new determination, gave in again. He could have walked away, but he felt riveted to the spot. He could have looked the other way, but he was entranced by the firm youthful breast that dangled so plainly and vibrated to the woman's movements as she bent over. "What will she do?" he asked himself. "What is she bent on?" But curiosity was not the real reason for his staying. He stayed because he enjoyed looking at the forbidden sight. He even let himself hope she might turn and smile shyly at him again, invite him with a quiet nod of the head to touch those dark breasts, lift the loin cloth, see and touch and smell the one thing that would be familiar, that he would understand. Suddenly he follows her, he remembered the proverb, "as an ox goes to the slaughter, as a bird hastens to the snare" She walked away with a quick glance over her shoulder, but he did not follow. Only in his heart did he follow.

"Kumaran, you didn't tell me about India, you didn't tell me!" he cried out to himself in his room late that night. As the breath lay stagnant in his lungs, like the still, thick humidity before a thunderstorm, he fell on his knees and asked God to forgive him.

12. Temple-Building

It vexed Kumaran that the week of feasting and storytelling in his honor should come to an end so abruptly. How quickly he was becoming just another member of the family! Already his father was beginning to make noises about work. Work! Did the man not understand yet that his son was a great adventurer and poet and storyteller and not just a common pulaiyar sculptor? There was talk of making money, of pulling his own weight. Were they too stupid to realize they could measure their success in elephants and gold if King Attan should like his storytelling as much as they did? Idiots!

"There is plenty of work in Vanji on the Great Temple. We've never had it so good," said his father in that stiff, commanding way of his. Kumaran sulked and hated his father, just as of old. "He's putting off my destiny," he complained bitterly to himself. Yet deep down he was relieved, for the thought of meeting King Attan, the mighty ruler of all Chera country, made him quiver. On the ship it had seemed exhilarating, but now that it was a real possibility, a ferry boat's ride away, it seemed more frightening than anything else. He knew that Attan was a lavish patron of poets, but would the royal hospitality extend to pulaiyars? And if it did not, where would that leave him? His whole life would seem pointless and futile. He had broken caste restrictions, he had tasted freedom. To sculpt because he chose to was one thing; to sculpt because he had to was quite another. He realized as never before how important it was for him to dream his big dream. And he was not yet ready to test his dream against reality. His date with the

King could wait a few months, couldn't it? Besides, he needed time to organize and polish his poetry, didn't he? So it seemed advisable to work for a while on the great temple in Vanji, the new Chera capital that King Attan was building inland in a curve of the Ponnani River. He would never admit to his father that he had decided to obey because he lost his nerve; indeed he could not quite admit this to himself; it was, after all, easier blaming his sorry fate on another. And by the time he told Thomas of his plans, one might have supposed he was eager to sculpt again.

"It's an honor to work on a temple," he said. "It tests the sculptor's skills to the utmost. Only the best is permitted. And all the materials are supplied by the King. The very best of woods. Maybe once in a lifetime an opportunity like this comes along for a sculptor. Besides, we earn the grace of the Gods."

"But you are not a sculptor. You're a poet," said Thomas. "And Muziri is just up the bay. And that's where the King lives. And—"

"We'll see if I'm not a sculptor!" Kumaran snapped. "I'm going north to Vanji! Come if you want!"

Kumaran hadn't the slightest sympathy with Thomas' scruples over working on a "pagan" temple. He had promised to travel with Thomas, but not on Thomas' terms.

"If you won't help me, I won't help you," Kumaran said. "You can help me on the platform, and I will help you with the language as I work. There is no other way."

Kumaran was paid by the job, and he contracted to carve a large image—taller than Thomas including the pedestal—of a minor northern goddess named Kali whose popularity was gaining in Tamil country. Thomas had finally agreed to help Kumaran. He even agreed to help erect and strengthen the scaffolding that surrounded the temple, built entirely of wood, on its four sides. This immense jungle of vertical, horizontal, and diagonal bamboo stalks, mounted on trunks of the areca palm as thick as an elephant's leg and held together at ten-thousand joints by tangles of coir rope, was almost as imposing a structure as the temple of fine woods that it encased. Thomas was glum when the superintendent told him about this "side duty"—all assistants had to do it—but at this point he had no choice. He could submit to this unholy task, or he could go it alone, and he was not ready to go it alone. He told Kumaran that he hoped God would forgive him.

Kumaran still scorned Thomas' scruples. "Look at it this way, Brother. You're working for a wage, that's all. You're paying your teacher."

After an agreement had been struck, the master-carver took them up a long flight of winding stairs in the dark interior of the temple, which was structurally complete, to the sunlit opening in the western wall that led out to the slab of wood which Kumaran was to transform into the goddess. It was Thomas' primary job to make Kumaran's work area both safe and comfortable, and this he set about doing as Kumaran directed him to place a support here or a platform there. Meanwhile Kumaran consulted the authorities, mostly priests, on the goddess' many characteristics, and listed the qualities that they wanted included. He looked at other images of the goddess and studied sketches of others housed in temples far to the north. He kept foremost in his mind the proportions of the human figure: the distance from the tip of the chin to the beginning of the hair is a tenth of the figure's height; the span of the arms outstretched is equal to the height; the distance from the tip of the chin to the bottom of the nostrils is a third of the face's length; and so forth. He sharpened and beveled his tools—gouges and spades and chisels of different sizes and sweeps—with special slips of stone. It took almost a week to draw up the plan and ready the tools and worksite. During that time Thomas climbed the stairs a hundred times, often with a burden of timber or rope. Sometimes he complained of the food, never of the work. Whatever misgivings he still had he overcame.

High above the tallest surrounding trees and propped against the railings Thomas had built, Kumaran, with the mountains at his back, went to work. First he carved the demon whose head served as Kali's pedestal. Then, keeping in mind her peculiar protrusions—the trident in her bangled hands, the great Mount Meru resting on her shoulders, the angry serpent Vasuki engirdling her waist, the moon in her hair, her long tongue dangling out of her mouth, and similar details—he roughed out the perimeter of Kali's figure. Meanwhile Thomas roosted like a pigeon in the opening next to him. Much of the time he practiced writing prayers and sermons in Tamil, trying to manipulate palm leaf and stylus in the Tamil manner. But when asked to adjust a prop, add a platform, hand over a new tool, or even help Kumaran as he answered the call of nature, he would put down his work and help.

One day Thomas told Kumaran a story from his scripture about some proud men who tried to build a tower that reached to heaven: God, he said, made the workers speak different languages so that they could not understand each other, and the tower was abandoned.

Kumaran peered over at him. Thomas' golden face with its black beard was half-visible in the opening as he looked out over the treetops toward the jungle-shrouded mountains. "So that's what you think will happen," Kumaran said.

"Not even the temple in Jerusalem is as grand as this," Thomas said darkly.

"Nowhere in the world, not even in Rome, not in Alexandria is there wealth the equal of ours," said Kumaran.

"The Greeks are better sculptors."

Kumaran did not take offense, for he himself had been in awe of Greek sculpture. But still he said, "How would you know, Brother?"

He looked over at Thomas and saw that Thomas was smiling.

It was good having Thomas as a companion, very good. Sometimes he would look at Thomas' shiny-eyed, ironic smile and feel—was it friendship? Loyalty? Love? He didn't quite know what it was, but it made his heart glad to have such a friend.

In time, as Kumaran made progress on his Kali, Thomas even began to admire the work. "That's good!" he said as Kumaran shaped the unwinking eye in the center of Kali's forehead. But at other times he assured Kumaran with that doomful but powerfully magnetic look of his that God detested all images of him, not to mention images of "false gods." At first Kumaran took offense, but now he just shrugged it off.

It was while they worked together on Kali that Kumaran grew almost to understand Thomas. He was not much in awe of him anymore; he was not even particularly curious to learn more about Thomas' religion, as he had once been. But since he had nothing better to do as he carved on his Kali the long day through, he was glad to have Thomas talk about anything. And of course there was nothing Thomas would rather talk about than his religion.

Kumaran couldn't help but admire certain features of it. It lacked romance, color, and imagination—Thomas' favorite sacred stories were dull compared to India's. But the homely stories about forgiveness and love—what Thomas called "the gospel"—intrigued him. He found them peculiar and somehow wrong-headed, but he could not help being impressed. They forced him to think in a new way, and even though he ultimately rejected them, they at least helped him understand why Thomas blessed Philetus on the Red Sea after Philetus insulted him, and why Thomas had the annoying habit of giving things away, especially the money he had saved from his ship's wages.

"Aiyer, please, please, I haven't eaten today!" a beggar cried out.

Kumaran, waiting with Thomas in the temple courtyard for the signal to go up and begin the day's work, felt disgust for the miserable fellow, who was a leper in the most advanced stages of the disease.

Without hesitation Thomas, who was just about to eat a banana, held it up to the man's mouth, which was ulcerous and threatened to join the nostrils in one horrid gaping orifice. The man looked at the towering, pale apparition with incredulity, then took a bite and massaged it into a sticky, glistening, sickening blob in his open mouth.

"What is your name?" said Thomas, smiling down. Kumaran had never seen the fellow before.

Thomas and the beggar made small talk as Thomas peeled the banana back bite by bite and fed the man like a baby, while fellow workers and chance passersby gathered round, whispering and nudging each other.

When the man finished, Thomas took the leper's stubby, clawed hands in his own and kissed his forehead. Kumaran thought he saw tears in Thomas' eyes and half understood where they came from, but on balance he was appalled and outraged by the deed. Mortified, he slunk away from Thomas' side as the crowd began to murmur and break up.

Thomas drew eyes to him wherever he went. He was the tallest man that most Tamils had ever seen, and his pale glowing face radiated a peculiar power and beauty that drew eyes to it. But it was this particular work of feeding the leper that made him more than a curiosity. Many people had noticed this horribly polluting act, including at least one brahmin priest, for it took place on the temple steps facing the new cobblestone square on the east side. Overnight Thomas had only enemies and friends; no one remained neutral. In general, the higher the caste, the more likely it was that an enemy had been made; the lower the caste, the more likely a friend. And what of Kumaran? He began to resent the attention his helper received, even more resented the attention Thomas gave back. Kumaran could not have admitted this to himself at the time; he would have denied with uneasy conviction that he felt a twinge of jealousy even for the leper whom Thomas kissed.

Thomas regularly gave food to beggars, always feeding them himself if they needed help or dining with them if they did not; always risking their laughter and derision by conversing with them in his wobbly Tamil; always smiling at them and in other ways going out of his way to show the pleasure he took in their company. It seemed to Kumaran that Thomas took as much pleasure in their company as in his—a preposterous, humiliating thing for him to admit. The despicable creatures were taking Thomas from him, and he, Kumaran, was spending more time after hours by himself. He resented this. He did not understand what Thomas saw in them. Thomas even knew all their names, even joked with them about their vices or afflictions.

One of the most grotesque of them was a man named Kunju who walked on his hands. His legs were no bigger than twigs and dragged along behind him like two enfeebled tails. He had a powerful neck and shoulders and a ferocious face with thick brows that met in a wad at the center of his forehead.

"You look like Kali," Thomas told him one afternoon. "You keep your third eye hidden behind brow, eh?" Then he put his thumb on Kunju's forehead and made as if he were feeling for the eye. "No eye!" he then said. "You are not Kali. You only Kunju!" Then Kunju and Thomas exploded in laughter. And so did those who watched this strange play, whether more out of delight or embarrassment it was difficult to tell.

Thomas was always touching people, smiling at them, listening with apparent compassion to their litany of problems, sharing what he had with them. He pretended to like them—and they were fooled—at least that is how Kumaran saw it. Or did Thomas really like being with them? But how could that be? Not even Kumaran's poet's imagination could understand how. So he concluded that Thomas did not really care for them. They were but pawns. They were the means by which Thomas practiced the language and gave his yavana God what he thought the God wanted. He, Kumaran, was Thomas' only true friend.

The "pawns" shared a joke with their new friend and sponsor. It was always the same one, and Thomas encouraged it as much the hundredth time he heard it as the first. "Don't trip as you walk, Master, for you'll die from the fall!" they would say in reference to his great height. And Thomas would joke back in his broken Tamil, "Ah, then I cut head off!" to the great amusement of everyone. This joke was almost like a challenge and password, and all who joined in signified that they were Thomas' friends. In fact they were more like his devotees.

One day he told all the beggars to gather with their families next to the temple pond a little before sunset. Until then he had said nothing about his religion to anyone except Kumaran. But he had been working quietly for weeks, with Kumaran's help, on his "first sermon." He told Kumaran he intended to deliver it himself in Tamil, and he wrote version after version of it on palm leaves—the usual eight lines to a leaf, four on one side, four on the other, and each leaf smeared with cow dung so that the lettering could be seen. He cut a hole through each leaf at the center, just as Kumaran showed him, and strung them together.

He carried this booklet with him wherever he went, as he once had carried his precious oar, and was always glancing at it.

By the day of the meeting Thomas had memorized his sermon along with several prayers that Kumaran helped him translate. Thomas said he was ready, and Kumaran worked uneasily on his Kali throughout the afternoon as the sun descended. The effect that Thomas would have on his audience Kumaran could not imagine, but he had a feeling that, whatever happened, things would never be the same between them again. As for the fate of the religion Thomas came to India to preach, he never even gave it a thought. Either things would get better between him and Thomas, or they would get worse. What else mattered?

13. The Lord's Twin

Thomas had recited his sermon out loud in front of Kumaran a dozen times, and he knew every syllable of it. He was as ready as he would ever be.

As the afternoon of the climactic day wore on, the prayer to Jesus grew more and more urgent. "Maranatha," "Lord, come," he repeated again and again. *I must not fail*, he exhorted himself. For the fate of India turned on his success. He told himself that there was every reason to expect success, but in his heart of hearts he felt, for no particular reason other than his natural state of mind, that failure was just over the horizon, that it lurked in the shadows behind his back.

With two hours still to go before sunset and Kumaran working away at his Kali, Thomas began to daydream. Had he hypnotized himself by constantly repeating the prayer? Was he bored by the twentieth recitation of his sermon? Was he fleeing the sense of doom that settled on him like a cold sea fog? He found himself in the grip of ancient memories.

He remembered that he was born in the thirty-first year of the Emperor Caesar Augustus. He could see the groves of olive trees and the busy threshing floors in his hometown of Nazareth, and he remembered the peculiar lilt of his mother's voice as she called out his name, "Judas," which meant "May the Lord be praised." Judas, his real name, the name he now never heard—did she choose the name, or did a rabbi choose it? Why had he never asked? Or did his father, the man he never knew, the man no one could ever tell him about because his identity was not known—did his father perhaps name him?

He remembered how it was when he was five, how it always hurt him when the older boys taunted him with that name "Judas ben Rabbim" ("Judas, son of many"), and how he had not understood why they called him that until much later when he found out what a whore was. He remembered how his mother defended and reassured him—how she said he cut a "fine little figure" and how she compared his arched back to the "upright of a lyre" and how he did not believe her, and how at night, when her perfumed arms were not busy with someone else, he sometimes crawled into them and wept himself into a bitter sleep.

He remembered that at a very young age he learned to doubt everything his mother said. She did not lie outright but merely changed her mind from one hour to the next. Often she simply could not muster the energy, when the time came, to carry through what she had thought such a good idea earlier. The things she promised him—a trip to Sepphoris, a climb up the mount behind the village, the building of a small Sukkoth hut on the roof of the house, even the weekly lighting of the Sabbath candle—had a way of not happening. She gave the impression of one who was overwhelmed by life, and she made him feel guilty when he reminded her of a promise unkept. He did not stop loving his mother, but he learned to distrust her. He remembered how he used to scream his disappointment at her, and once, on a whim, how she pacified him with a small gift: a black puppy with white markings on its tail and feet. For some reason she named it Mitzvah. He carried Mitzvah all over the village, fed him stray bones and scraps of food that the crows missed, and slept with him at night. An older boy once told him it was fitting that a *mamzer* (bastard) should love a filthy dog, but he did not understand for a long time what the word meant. He knew only that animals were more trustworthy than people.

He thought back to the school he attended when he was seven and how he had to sit on the floor of hard earth in the shadows at the back of the room and how it was there that he first met Jesus. James, the teacher, would sometimes bring Jesus, his half-brother, along with him. He remembered how Jesus noticed he always finished writing the alphabet on his wax tablet ahead of the other boys, and how one day Jesus asked him to write the alphabet backwards as the boys began their daily exercise.

He picked up his stylus and stuck it into the wax at the bottom left-hand corner of the tablet.

"Too easy," Jesus said. "Start at the top, Judas. Start at the top, but go in reverse. *Taw* to *aleph*."

He remembered Jesus' long face with the deep-set gentle eyes and the thin wisps of beard—how those eyes encouraged him, wanted him to succeed, even to be first. Something buried deep inside him had sprung to life for the first time, and the letters seemed to etch themselves into the wax. Even going backwards he finished ahead of the other boys.

He remembered how from that day forward his named had changed: "Judas, son of many" gave way to "Backwards Judas." He hadn't understood at the time, but later he realized that the nickname was both a compliment and a slight. It complimented him for being good with words and slighted him for being lowborn. It would not do to praise a *mamzer* without in the same breath reminding him what he was. But he had not minded at the time. All he cared about was that Jesus looked at him with love. And when he went to sleep, he imagined Jesus smiling down at him, smiling down—

Kumaran asked for a drink of water, and Thomas jerked back to the present, back to the pagan temple on whose scaffolding hundreds of sculptors were spread out like spiders on a single vast web.

He poured Kumaran some water in a wooden cup, reached out toward him and gave him the cup, but barely noticed the brightly colored Kali, the last details of which Kumaran was painting and polishing. Like a man just awakened eager to resume the dream that fascinated him, he tried to recapture the spell of Jesus' face. Settling back into his niche, he closed his eyes and concentrated, and for a moment he saw the face with the same vivid clarity of his daydream. Again he felt Jesus' presence, and Jesus was buoying him and dispelling his loneliness and reminding him how good with words he was and one day even bringing him home. "How much like you he looks!" Mary, Jesus' mother, had said to Jesus. "He's your little twin!" And thus he became Judas Thomas, Judas the Twin. "Judas the Twin." How could he fail? Was he not Jesus' twin? Was he not the Lord's twin?

"The Lord's twin." The phrase tugged at a long chain of associations, and Kumaran and Kali and India and the sermon that was to be India's salvation rattled against each other inside his head.

The present moment burst upon him in its full reality; the meaning and climax of his entire life loomed. A terrifying thrill skewered his tall pale frame from top to bottom.

14. First Sermon, First Lie

Hundreds of people—not only the beggars, but architects, engineers, sculptors, carpenters, carters, messengers, vendors of every kind, fishermen, women and children, prostitutes, even brahmin priests who looked on from a discreet distance—gathered next to the sizable pond to hear the "proclamation" of the "yavana prince," as some of the beggars called him. When Thomas arrived, this curious multitude was seated on the open grassy area between the temple and the pond. They had their backs to the sun, so Thomas accommodated them by facing the sun, which hovered just over the tree line in the West. A golden light haloed him; he might have been the very Sun-God himself. Kumaran squatted off to the side and brushed away a mosquito that wouldn't leave him alone. He wondered if Murugan and his mother Kotravai, the War God and Goddess to whom the temple was chiefly dedicated, were looking on.

Then, minutes after the sun disappeared behind the trees, a sound boomed from Thomas' mouth in Tamil: "Citizens of the great Chera Kingdom, subjects of Attan, children of the one God on High! Greetings!"

A virgin concubine on her first visit to the king's bed could not have been more nervous than Kumaran. To him Thomas did not represent an apostle of some exotic new religion; what did he care about that anyway? Thomas was simply his student, and this was his first great test. He had no idea how Thomas would do. Yet there he was, speaking the Tamil text that he had quietly rehearsed twenty times on the tower—or rather not speaking it, but hurtling it forth like missiles!

"Many of you know me as Thomas the yavana, and in truth I am a Jew from Judaea in the Roman Empire far to the west; but I do not come to you as a yavana. You know me as a carpenter, but it is not to practice this trade that I have come to your country. You know me as Kumaran's helper" (he pointed to Kumaran), "but it is not to assist a sculptor that I have come to Vanji. You know me as the patron and friend of beggars, but it is not to feed and joke with you that I stand before you now. Why do I stand here? To bring you news that will violently shake the earth from edge to edge and corner to corner! Friends, brothers and sisters: God on High, God infinite in holiness and might, Lord of all creatures and all nations, your Father and mine, has sent his messenger, his anointed Messiah, a man who walked among us and whose name was Jesus, a Jew from my country, to invite all men to the Father's banquet. And Jesus has sent me here to invite you. Make ready! Prepare yourself! For the time of this great banquet is near. It is upon us even now! Before the rains come, you fertilize your fields. When the damp monsoon wind begins to blow, you sow the rice. When the rains fall in abundance, you dig canals and flood the fields. When the paddy stands green and high and waves in the wind, you bend over double under burning sun for hours on end and gather the roots in clusters. And now that the rains have stopped and the grain is ripe and yellow? And now? . . . You prepare for the harvest! That is what we must all do now—prepare for the harvest!"

Kumaran's heart beat with a fierce pride at the performance of his student. But there was more than pride in that heartbeat; there was love. Even though Thomas' words did not touch him, Thomas himself did. How could one not respond to him—so tall, so golden, so magnetic? What in the world could make a man do what he did? What stupendous vision drove him on? Kumaran still did not understand.

"*We* are the harvest! *God* is the harvester! *Now* is the time of the harvest! Prepare yourselves! Or be passed over and left in the field to wither and to burn! That is what the Master, Jesus, has sent me to tell you.

"How do you prepare yourselves for God's harvest, for his banquet, for his Kingdom? By *changing* yourselves! What kind of world is this? Look at it, brothers and sisters: Servants leave a master who has been reduced to poverty; ministers desert a king facing defeat; women take advantage of men who have become old; landlords cheat their tenants who are ignorant and weak; husbands betray their vows when their wives lose their youth and their beauty; businessmen undertake nothing without hope of profit. Self-interest is the motive of everyone in this world. Self-interest is the supreme law of this world.

"I say to you, Renounce this law! Repent! Change yourselves! Your Father in heaven demands this of you. The price for disobedience is the fire of hell. Woe to him who is not ready for the harvest!

"But how do you renounce? By fasting unto death? By going about naked? By walking on glowing embers? By standing on one leg? By wallowing in mud and dust like an elephant? I have seen all these things here. But they are perversions, detours, obstacles. How do you renounce? By making your neighbor's interest the equal of your own; by offering your persecutor your left cheek after he has slapped your right; by feeding the hungry, nursing the sick, clothing the naked, sheltering the homeless. That is how, brothers and sisters. That is the only way. I have discovered a saying among you: 'A virtuous man ought to be like the sandalwood tree, which perfumes the ax that destroys it.' What is renunciation? Does a yavana have to tell you? It is summed up in that very saying of yours!

"Hear me now. This is the final truth. True renunciation is impossible without God. Only God can consecrate the good deed that you do. Men of means, do you give to the beggar? Then *love* the beggar as you give; it is your love that he needs more than your gift. Beggars, do you take from the giver? Then *bless* him as he gives; it is your prayer that he needs more than the merit he thinks he is making. Love is the final truth! God, your Father, loves you, each of you, as you love your own sons and daughters. Each of you is precious to Him. What are you called to do? Return his love, that is all! Before you break open the jackfruit, you rub your hands with oil, or else the gummy juice of the fruit will stick to them. In the same way anoint yourself with the love of God, then attend to the business of the world and it will not stick to you. Or be like the mother tortoise. She moves about in the water of a lake, but her mind is on the bank where she laid her eggs. In the same way, do your duties in the world, but let your heart dwell on God. Love Him with all your heart, all your soul, all your mind. Ask Him for your needs as a child asks his father—full of trust, full of confidence, full of love!

"How light is our yoke, brothers and sisters! What joy there is in this life of love! Your Father is infinite Love. And all his love is directed at you. How light is our yoke, brothers and sisters!"

Listening to Thomas, Kumaran was agog with admiration. Here was a yavana, in Tamil country for four months, preaching in Tamil with spellbinding effect! Kumaran was also proud of himself: How good his metaphors sounded coming out of Thomas' mouth! From that moment Kumaran knew that his poetry was worthy and good—worthy of any king. A third feeling was an unconscious wish to surrender to Thomas and follow him anywhere, even to Thomas' heaven or hell. For a few moments Thomas held Kumaran in the palm of his hand. Thomas was simply stupendous. He could have made his Jesus into an avatar, and who knows what might have followed?

Then Thomas began to speak words that Kumaran had not heard him rehearse. "So renounce the law of this world. Wash away your sins in the water as I pray over you. Receive the holy baptism that the Father offers you now. Prepare yourself for the heavenly banquet, for the glory of God in your midst. Come up to me now, yes, come, stand up and come forward, walk into the pond, and I will baptize you. . . . God will wash your sins away in the water. . . ."

As Thomas majestically waved his hands at the stunned crowd, he stepped toward the pond. "Come, the time of the harvest approaches, don't hang back! . . . Come! . . . Come! . . . Come! . . ."

But the crowd, now almost lost in the shadows, did not come. Mumbling and whispering, tittering, looking behind them, the people began to rise. The infirm somehow managed to stand up and looked as if they might hobble away. The able-bodied stood, gathered in circles, gesticulated as they looked fearfully at Thomas and the pond. Mothers tugged at their children, who eyed Thomas soulfully as they sucked their thumbs.

"Thomas!" Kumaran said running up toward him. "Brother, they're afraid of the pond. They're *afraid!*"

"What!?"

"They're afraid of the pond. It's consecrated to Manimekalai, the Sea Goddess. It's filled with snakes. They wouldn't dare!"

"WHAT!?"

"I didn't know—it wasn't in your sermon—you didn't tell me—"

For an instant Thomas was struck dumb. Then he said, "What should we do? What should we *do?*"

Meanwhile the voices of the people buzzed louder than ever in confusion.

"To the river," said Kumaran. "Yes, tell them to go to the river!"

"You tell them, Brother!"

The crowd waited, waited for Kumaran to solve the problem. They all wanted the show to go on. They all wanted to join in the harvest. They wanted this thing that the yavana prince called "baptism." They wanted to feast at the banquet of the "New God," as they called him. They wanted to be like the mother tortoise. They wanted to change themselves. Yes, they even wanted to change themselves!

"Go to the river!" Kumaran shouted, pointing.

Then Thomas repeated in a booming voice, "GO TO THE RIVER!"

The people waved their fists and their torches in the air—for the twilight was deepening—and took up the cry, "To the river!" Droning their excitement into the still evening air, they moved off like a single giant bee hungry for nectar.

Then a brahmin priest with white paint on his face who had been looking on from a distance came up to Thomas and said proudly, "Yavana, who gives you the authority to speak for God?"

Thomas was not ready to talk to the brahmin in Tamil, but he understood him. He turned to Kumaran and said in Aramaic, "Tell him that Jesus, the one anointed by the Father, has given me this authority."

Kumaran told the priest.

Then the brahmin said, "And what of Vishnu, the Unborn? Is your Father greater than Vishnu?"

Again Thomas looked at Kumaran. "Tell him that Vishnu is a false God, that I've come to reveal to India the true God, that all who hear my word and believe it will go to eternal life, that those who don't will perish."

Kumaran flinched at the words Thomas spoke, then turned to the brahmin and muttered as rapidly and indistinctly as he could so that Thomas would not be able to follow, "The yavana says that Vishnu and the Father of all men are one, and that those who believe this will go to eternal life, and those who do not will perish."

The brahmin frowned but was satisfied, and Thomas made his way to the river to begin the baptism. Hundreds came forward, well on into the night. They included seventeen from one family, members of the despised butcher caste. Many were his friends, the beggars and their relatives. Five cripples, four blind men, a rich widow with a goiter, a toddy merchant with a scrotum swollen to the size of a melon and unable to walk—all became "Christians." Several lepers, one of whom was the man Thomas fed the banana to, joined their ranks. Many more were ordinary workers, not a few of them Thomas' fellow assistants. One by one he dunked them in the cool water flowing down from the mountains, pronouncing the same formula over each. To each he gave a new name to go with the real name: "I baptize you, Mary Kavunti," he would say, "in the name of the Lord Jesus."

Kumaran wondered what they saw as they looked up into Thomas' face by torchlight. What did they see as they stared into those intense, shining dark eyes? Did they see Murugan, the Tall God, the God of the Hills, the Child of Six Mothers, the Beautiful One? Kumaran was sure that Thomas was seen by a few of his converts as a God in his own right—more of a God, perhaps, than the God he preached.

"Converts"—that is what Thomas called this bunch of human flotsam. Kumaran wondered if Thomas thought they gave up their own Gods, their own traditions, their own caste ways for his. Thomas was just such a fool—he had made that mistake before.What did he think they converted from? What did they reject? Yet he rejoiced at what he called the "new faith" that God gave them. Who knows? Perhaps these wretches had nothing to lose. Perhaps they really did convert. Kumaran could not believe it though. At least no sculptor had succumbed to Thomas' spell, and this for some reason made him proud.

Kumaran did not tell Thomas that he lied to the brahmin. In fact he did not know why he lied. What indeed was his motive? Did he simply delight in foiling a brahmin, as any low-caste pulaiyar might? Did he want to protect Thomas from the brahmin's power? Did he remember that yavanas made good eunuchs in the court of the Chera King, especially after their tongues had been cut out? Or did he simply say what he believed to be true? Kumaran might have asked himself why he so cleverly lied, but he did not. Even if he had asked, it is likely he would not have been able to sort the answer out. Kumaran's powers of observation went outward, and there they largely spent themselves. His earliest training had taught him to look outward at things—at the woods and stones and clays that he shaped into contours for the delight of the eye—rather than inward at himself. He could chart the high terrain on his map of life, but its subtler grades were as mysterious to him as the folds on a hippo's back.

15. Big Dreams

Since about the time of his marriage and the birth of his first daughter, Thomas had suffered from insomnia. Often he could find no reason for it. It seemed to follow its own laws and rhythms; there seemed not to be any clear connection between it and the circumstances of his life. But as he grew older, as Jesus' example shamed him into a more steady devotion to God and his prayers grew deeper and more sincere, he learned to sniff out the different layers of quiet worry that huddled together in the hidden recesses of his mind. And he began to see that his sleeplessness did not follow some arbitrary law, but was anchored to these depths. If something, however minor, remained undone or unresolved, he could not sleep. Even the slightest suspicion that all was not quite right might gnaw away at him for hours, especially after his sleep was interrupted. Sometimes he would lie turning on his bed until sunrise, while his brothers around him, down to the last man, lay around him as limp and heavy as cadavers. In time he learned to work his worries out before retiring, and sleep came more easily. Strangely, on the hard, rolling deck of Hippalus' ship, sleep had covered him like a thick cloud; but on arriving in India the old problem returned, and not even the most careful soul-searching could scare away the old ghost.

But on this night the old ghost came for a different reason. As Thomas stepped out of the workman's hut to escape Kumaran's snoring, he saw a sliver of a moon dangling in the clear starlit sky. He noticed that a breeze had sprung up; it was rustling through the palms, and it came not from the sea but from the mountains. Going back into the hut, he lay down next to Kumaran, who now slept quietly. Again he tried to fall asleep, to quiet his mind, to make it stop picturing the bodies that had come to him in the dark, one after another, hour after hour, to get baptized.

"Father, let me sleep," he prayed, "oh, let me sleep!" But his mind danced away from that prayer like heat lightning skipping off clouds. It had is own agenda, it seemed to be a separate thing and to laugh at him.

Finally he gave up the battle and slung aside his cover. He crept out into the cool dewy night one more time and started walking toward the pond. He was exhausted but happy, as happy as he had been in a long time. "The Sea Goddess Manimekalai!" he thought. He threw his hands out at the night, looked straight up at the stars, and laughed aloud. They twinkled down at him, and he almost felt they understood his joke. It was as if the whole universe understood.

When he reached the pond, he still felt restless and excited. He would have to walk some more. But it was a high place he wanted. A high place, like the Mount of Olives where Jesus and his disciples would get away to pray, or the hills surrounding Nazareth where as a boy he often roamed to get away from the bigger boys who teased him. "The temple," he thought. He would climb it, get to its top. He knew the way by heart, knew exactly where to climb out onto the scaffolding. He did not need a torch, he would be safe. He would give some excuse to the guards, who knew him anyway, and climb the tower.

The climb was more awkward than he had thought, and once near the top he slipped on some shavings and nearly fell; had the god he fell against not had a weapon protruding from its hand, he would have fallen to his death. With a pounding heart he finally reached the summit where the great god Murugan stood proudly between his mother Kotravai and his wife Valli. Holding on tightly to Murugan, who was twice his height, he surveyed the moonlit world from his precarious perch. And he let himself think that a cross would be mounted in place of these gods someday; and all the garish gods that cluttered the sides of the monstrous building would be dislodged and thrown down on the polished brick of the square below, and their smashed remains gathered for firewood by grateful pulaiyar Christians who would sell them to brahmin Christians. Then his mind and heart turned to prayer, and the words gathered and poured out of him like bubbles gurgling out of a Jordan spring.

"Father, I belong utterly to You. It does not matter what You do to your servant. You have given me everything that I have, You have blessed me with a life that is full and filled with joy. You have turned me into your instrument, and my heart is glad. You overlook my faults, You do not count my sins. You look away as I build this temple. Instead of punishing me You bestow on me every bounty. You thrill me with the mysteries of your grace. How my brain reels with thoughts of You! I belong to You wherever I am. I will do your will, moment by moment. You will be pleased to rest in my heart, You will find it a congenial place, a place of comfort and congeniality. Help me, Lord! And I will delight in your ways forever."

Effusions like these poured out of him until a pink dawn lit up the eastern sky, and finally the sun squatted on top of the highest, most distant mountains. Thomas noted that it sat in solitude; not a ray reached out from it; only the thin clouds immediately surrounding it partook of its indefinite red-orange shape. It was the homeliest of sunrises. It made him think of the way God sits, unappreciated by men, acknowledged but unloved. Still leaning against Murugan, he felt tears gather in his eyes. He was determined not to neglect God ever again. He was done with doubting. Had not the Lord worked a miracle for his benefit the night before? Hundreds had been baptized, the great movement begun. And he, Thomas, would never forget.

He was so high that he could almost see over the hills blocking his view of the ocean, twenty miles to the west. He imagined the golden beach with its row of black, high-prowed fishing boats lined up side by side and stretching out in both directions as far as the eye could see. Closer in he saw dark green groves of banana, coconut, and mango, and light green fields of rice paddy, sugar cane, cotton, pulses, pepper, cardamom, and ginger. He saw the gleaming Ponnani River winding down from the eastern hills, from which the morning breeze carried a faint scent of some mysterious jungle flower. Directly below, far, far below in the courtyard and on the roads and paths surrounding the temple, men moved. They went about their chores like so many ants; they bathed, they ate, they answered the call of nature. Thomas thought he recognized Kunju waddling up on his hands to his begging post. He remembered that Kunju was a Christian now, and he was pleased.

He looked down at the hundreds of lotus-seated gods spread over the four sides of the huge pyramid. Everywhere on that mountain of wood something was carved, everywhere a different god. How bare and simple was Jehovah by comparison. Someday all those gods would topple like sticks resting against each other. Like ivy on a trellis the new religion would cover India, all India. It was just a matter of time. All would be accomplished, with God's mercy, within his very lifetime.

Then he thought of Kumaran. Still Kumaran fended off baptism, and this bothered him. Thomas gave God the credit for his successes and took the blame himself for his failures. So far he had failed with Kumaran. He must pray harder, set a better example. Then Kumaran would be drawn to it irresistibly. "Bring—him—to—You—Lord!" he prayed. Each word throbbed in his brain like a drumbeat. He repeated the prayer, pounding its content into his soul until his very heart beat with the prayer. And a great peace, an ecstasy filled him like incense. As he climbed down to eat and go to work, he knew without a doubt that Kumaran was as good as the Lord's already.

16. "A Dirty Bitch of a Trick"

———————

Kumaran sat on a coir mat in a toddy bar among other members of the sculptor caste. On the walls hung bright paintings of a dozen gods, all favorites of the patrons or owners. Kumaran was with his own kind, both human and supernatural. None reminded him of Thomas' "new dharma." He could speak his mind without risk of a challenge.

Kumaran and Thomas had argued about religion earlier that day, and Kumaran knew he had had the worst of it. Didn't he always have the worst of it when they disagreed? All he could think of now was how sure of himself Thomas had seemed. Thomas made him feel guilty, made him feel small and low. He did not know exactly why, but he knew what to do about it. The day's work was done, supper eaten. Now it was time to relax, drink toddy with friends who didn't care if he was damned or saved, who knew nothing of the ambitions he secretly clung to, who couldn't care less if he was literate and a poet. These were the people who regarded him as nothing special, as merely "Kumaran the sculptor," who didn't care if he got drunk or complained or lied or fought or cursed—just so long as he entertained them and made them forget the drudgery of their lives.

At the moment Kumaran was holding forth on Thomas. "He's a trickster! It's always 'Brother Kumaran.' That's what he calls me, you know. He always makes people feel like he loves them, then he springs his religion on them!"

Not even toddy slowed Kumaran's rapid speech; he wielded it as a juggler wields his balls: it was an impressive show, but one never quite knew where to look.

"I'm telling you, it's a trick," he went on. "It's a sham. He doesn't love anybody. He uses love to bring people around to his religion. It's all a trick. You saw what happened at the baptism that night. You saw his face all lit up. You heard him preach. Do you think he meant it? But he *believes* he meant it. It's a trick, a dirty bitch of a trick! And he believes his own trick! Piss on him!"

Kumaran looked down into his cup and jiggled the toddy. "Sometimes I feel like killing him," he said. Then he looked up at his companions and nodded his head significantly, as if he were trying to convince them of some great truth. "I really do, you know. Someday I might throw him off the platform." Then he laughed with throaty violence, though his eyes never changed their stricken expression.

"Why don't you replace him?" said one of the circle.

"He's a good worker. I have to admit it, he's a good worker. I've never had better." Kumaran paused to blow mucus out of his nostrils onto the hard clay floor off to the side behind the circle of men.

"That freak has you by the twat!" bellowed a scarfaced man seated across from Kumaran.

"Get rid of him," said the first man.

"Get rid of him, Kumaran!" someone else urged.

"There are plenty of helpers available, you know that," said the scarface. "What do you owe him? Why do you put up with him? All he does is make you feel like a worm. He hates you. He hates all of us. He's a whore-screwing yavana. It's just as you say."

Suddenly Kumaran held up his hands with great ceremony. He looked as if he had just remembered something fundamental that changed everything. In place of the twisted lines of hatred on his face was a look of wounded solemnity. With a grave air that belied his red-eyed drunkenness, he said quietly and slowly, "What do I owe him? I'll tell you what I owe him. In all my travels in the West I never met a white man who was kind to me until I met him. Do you know what it feels like to go for five years without a kind word? FIVE YEARS!"

Kumaran looked slowly around the circle at each of the men, who cowered and stared back speechlessly. "DO YOU KNOW WHAT IT FEELS LIKE?" he screamed as toddy flew out of his cup. "Let me tell you something," he continued, his voice choking with suppressed passion. "That man—that man you all saw preach that day—have you ever seen anything like that? That man is my BROTHER!" Kumaran slammed down his cup on the mat, toddy splashing all over.

"Brother?" one of the men said in amazement.

But Kumaran had begun to sob hysterically. A cacophony of dirty words was all that anyone could make out.

17. Little Chakki

Thomas and the little girl Chakki sat on top of the hill above Chakki's thatched hut, where she lived with her widowed mother and older brother. It was the rainy season, but a break in the clouds revealed one of the most beautiful sunsets Thomas had ever seen—orange, gold, pink, deep crimson, even a small patch of green. They looked down over the city cradled in a curve of the river. "There goes the ferry boat," Thomas said.

"Will you take me on the ferry someday, Uncle?" Chakki said, looking back up at Thomas, who bounced her up and down on his foot as he held her hands.

Thomas loved the poor, bright-eyed pulaiyar children who capered under the deep shade of their tiny hillside world. He especially loved three-year-old Chakki, whose mother converted on that first night. His own granddaughter was about her age. Was she, like Chakki, playing horse on someone's leg at that very moment? Did Galilee have that much in common with India?

"Chakki, who made that sunset?" he said.

He stopped bouncing her so she could think it over. "The sea goddess, Uncle?" she said as she looked up at Thomas with a dimpled grin.

Thomas looked down at the little black girl with fine white teeth and impish eyes. How long had it been since anyone brought him so much happiness? She made him feel faintly intoxicated, the way one feels after a particularly long and deep sleep as he lies in bed remembering his happy dream.

He chided her gently, "No, Chakki, God made the sunset, not the sea goddess. Chakki, now Chakki, who made your mother?"

"Murugan," she said at once, looking up at him with hopeful, mirthful round eyes.

Thomas chuckled and stroked one of her loose curls. "No, Chakki, God made your mother too. Now Chakki, who do you think made you?"

Chakki said nothing.

"Who, Chakki? Who do you think?"

But Chakki only smiled quietly to herself.

"God made you, Chakki. Yes, Chakki, God made *you.*" Thomas stroked her tiny arms and repeated the question, "Who made you, Chakki?"

"God," said the little girl softly, as if she were uttering something strictly forbidden until that moment.

"Good, Chakki. Now, who made *God*?"

Chakki stared up at him and said nothing.

"Think, Chakki, who made God?"

Again Chakki said nothing, but then, as if visited by a sudden revelation, she blurted out across the hillside, with every sign of seriousness, "You did!"

Tears came into Thomas' eyes as he quietly shook with mirth. Oh, if only he had Bartholomew next to him to share this moment with!

"No, Chakki," he said finally. "Nobody made God. God always was."

Every night Chakki wanted to "play God" with Thomas. She learned to answer "God" to every question except the last. "N-o-o-o-body," she would say to the last, her tuneful speech suspended like a hammock. "N-o-o-o-body," Thomas would repeat in his elementary Tamil, which was getting better by the day. And for a little while he would forget that the new faith was not spreading like ivy on a trellis. He would forget that signs of the old heathen religion were reappearing in the homes of his converts. He would forget that the sunrise eucharist—the breaking and sharing of bread, which signified Jesus' presence among them—attracted fewer of the faithful than it once had. He would forget that he was putting in too many hours building a grotesque temple and too few ministering to his precious flock. He would forget how much he was growing to resent Kumaran, who kept promising to quit and move on down the coast "any day now" but ended by contracting for "just one more sculpture." He would forget all his troubles and, with Chakki on his foot playing horse, be happy.

18. In the Ocean

By the time the rains stopped and the cool season set in, Kumaran felt he understood Thomas' religion. Much of it he could not help but admire: It regarded all men as equal and, like Buddhism, rejected caste as a measure of worth. It taught that the poor and the despised are as dear to God as any brahmin or king. It held that God overlooks a man's sin as soon as he repents it and that He even cancels their karmic debt. It offered salvation not at the end of many rebirths, but at the end of this very life. It offered the selfless, loving, forgiving Jesus as a guide and model for a life well lived. And it promised a joy not only in the next life but in this one. Kumaran found none of this very plausible, but it attracted him nevertheless, especially joy here and now. It was impossible not to feel this joy radiate out of Thomas from time to time, even through all the cares that lay heavily against his heart. It was this joy—an enthusiasm, a sacred, spiritual lilt in the voice and expression—that in Kumaran's view attracted Thomas' first converts. Was it this, the very thing he sometimes described to others as a "trick," was it this that attached *him* to Thomas too?

But Kumaran also saw another side to the religion. As he traveled with Thomas after work or on holiday to the villages around Vanji; as he listened to his sermons, translating when necessary, and helped him explain the meaning of the prayers to his devotees after they memorized them; but especially as he confided what he believed to his closest followers—Kumaran called them the "inner circle"—around whom he spoke with less caution, Kumaran discovered something that he hated. Thomas thought anyone who did not convert to his faith was damned to hell—not damned for a while so as to expiate bad karma, but damned forever. Kumaran had long heard Thomas speak of hell, but only now did he grasp that there was no end to it, as there was in every other religion he had heard of. Even worse, a virtuous man might end by going there, even a saint. "One truth" is the way Thomas described his religion. "One truth and one scripture." And those who did not bow to it, however virtuous they might be, were damned to this hideous place forever. For the brahmins' holy Veda, that beginningless scripture breathed out by God at the beginning of each age, Kumaran was sure Thomas had nothing but scorn. For the Tamil scripture written by the immortal yogi Agastya, one verse each year for three thousand years, he had the same scorn. Thomas, of course, never showed scorn outwardly—he kept a studied quiet at the mention of these scriptures—but Kumaran was certain that is what he felt. Kumaran learned to scorn parts of Thomas' faith as much as Thomas scorned all of his.

The months passed. The dry season scorched the groves and fields along the Malabar Coast with its flaming desert heat, then the summer rains came. Thomas and Kumaran had been in Tamil country for almost a year when Kumaran finally decided to quit work on the Great Temple. All together he had carved seven figures, one major—the Kali—and six minor.

By the end of the hot season Thomas' Tamil had improved to the point where he was almost independent of Kumaran. Kumaran was glad of this, for it gave him an excuse to leave Thomas if he should want to. But so far, though he often flirted with the idea, he hadn't wanted to. For reasons not quite apparent to him, he let Thomas take the lead and accompanied him to the fishing villages below Tondi and then farther south. He told himself this would be a good time to write more poetry. As is the custom in Tamil country, he described what he saw in meticulous detail and with the aid of elaborate metaphor. For example, he once noticed a "sapphire-hued" kingfisher fly off with a "red-jeweled pendant" that a girl laid aside while she swam in a pond. He noted how the bird perched on a priest's sacrificial stake nearby and how the jewel gleamed in the sunlight, and he compared it to a "lamp burning on the mast top of a yavana boat as tall as Mount Meru." He had not forgotten his life's ambition, oh no, not at all. Every new adventure was a preparation for the courts of Attan and Karikal. And Thomas' travels suited him well. So did his companionship, in spite of their frequent disagreements.

Eight months after they left Vanji for good, roaming from town to town among the simple, magic-minded fishermen, staying about a month in each place, a strange event halted them. They had gotten as far south as the coastal village of Tangasseri, near Kollam; Thomas preached tirelessly in Tangasseri, baptized one-hundred fifty, ministered to the sick, cast out demons, and appointed a local leader, or "deacon." After a month there, they traveled farther south toward Kumari, then reversed direction and traveled north back up the coast and found themselves back in Tangasseri. But there was no sign of the Christian life. Thomas was angry at his deacon when the man told him the Sea-Goddess was taking revenge on the village.

"She's given us so few fish," the man pleaded.

"Gather the villagers on the beach," Thomas said dourly, the veins in his forehead popping out.

The fishermen and their families gathered on the beach after they sold the afternoon's scant catch to the fishmongers.

"The Sea-Goddess is an abomination to the one true God!" Thomas thundered. He went on to say that anyone who worshipped her would go to hell, which he described as fire and brimstone. He exhorted them to bring all their petitions to "the Father, the universal God, the God who alone is real!"

"But we tried that," they said. "We tried for two weeks. But the sea only turned red, and our nets are empty."

"The Sea-Goddess is only having her period!" shouted a woman trying to defend Thomas. "It happens every year. It will pass. It always does."

Along the coast many believed in Manimekalai's period. Kumaran was half inclined to believe it himself, for why else would the water take on a reddish hue? But others were just as sure the poor fishing was due to the Sea-Goddess' anger at them for their infidelity to her. The red hue represented her wrath at Thomas' rival god, they said. Arguments broke out; many said that Thomas would have to go.

That afternoon Thomas made inquiries, and by sunset he made a daring proposal to the village chief. He would show the villagers that his God was more powerful than the Sea-Goddess. He asked to be dropped off in the middle of the ocean as an offering to Manimekalai. If he disappeared, that would mean they could go on worshipping her. But if he came back unharmed, that would mean that his God was stronger.

All the villagers were frightened of the ocean, even the fishermen. No one even swam in the sea. It was home to poisonous sea snakes, sharks and dragons farther out, and of course Manimekalai. When

Thomas made his proposal, the village council looked at him as if he were insane and laughed aloud. Those who opposed him eagerly accepted the proposal. Thomas was making their job easy; he was removing himself—forever.

"And you will renounce the Sea-Goddess if I come back alive? You and all the village?" Thomas said.

They all nodded.

"And you will serve and love the New God, and Him alone, and ask Him to restore the sea to its natural color and give you many fish?"

Again they all nodded.

That night the word traveled fast, well beyond the boundaries of the village. By dawn the next morning people from other villages started to gather on the beach. All that day the "yavana sage," as many called Thomas, stayed inside the village chief's house, while a steady stream of people passed by the door to get a glimpse of him.

That afternoon Thomas' supporters brought him rice, fish, bananas, coconuts, and curds. They touched his feet with their heads and warned him of the sea monsters and poisonous sea serpents and whirlpools that sucked a man to the bottom of the ocean. Every man in the village feared the Sea-Goddess, even those most prepared to devote themselves to Thomas' "New God." No one gave Thomas much of a chance—only one man wagered he would come back, at twenty-to-one odds—and many of the wrinkled old salts who knew from long experience that the Sea-Goddess was powerful and jealous relished the certain fate of the "foreign blasphemer." But others came to offer their help. "When you hear a hissing, that's a monster," said one old man. "If you hear a great rush like a waterfall, swim the other way," said another, "that's the sound of the Sea-Goddess swallowing." One old woman, a madwoman or a shaman—it was hard to tell—put her hands over Thomas' head and prayed. Then she said in a voice from another world, "Child, give homage to Manimekalai, the Sea-Goddess, and she won't eat you!"

The boat was scheduled to cast off a half hour before sunset, and Thomas was to drop into the sea with the sun.

"You're not afraid?" Kumaran asked him as he came out of the house.

"If I get into trouble, I'll pray to Manimekalai. Like the old woman told me," Thomas joked without the faintest hint of a smile.

"I'm afraid. I'll build a fire on the beach and keep it burning all night," Kumaran said.

"No need, the sky is clear, the stars will be up. I'll swim east, that's all. Get your sleep, Brother."

"I'll stay up, Brother."

"And will you pray?"

"I will pray."

"To whom?"

"To Murugan. And to your Father." Kumaran knew Thomas wanted to hear this.

Thomas finished a banana and gulped down a cup of water. Then he embraced Kumaran, and for once Kumaran thought he felt Thomas' love go out not to the future convert that he, Kumaran, represented, but to him himself. And he savored that moment.

Minutes later the boat cut through the languid gray-green surf as two-thousand people looked on, murmuring quietly to themselves—people from as far away as Chavara. The four oarsmen rowed in unison, two on the left, two on the right. Kumaran heard them hiss to establish their rhythm as they dug their oars into the water. Thomas crouched in the middle, his right hand clasping the ivory cross he wore around his neck. It wasn't long before the boat was a speck on the horizon.

That night hundreds of people slept on the beach. Several of the men fed logs to the fire while a few of the women sang to keep up the vigil.Finally all was still except for an occasional star shaking loose from the firmament, the wind stirring faintly in the high palm leaves, the white waves lapping the shore and rhythmically drowning out the endless roar of crickets and frogs, nearby sleepers snoring, and the softly crackling fire.

In the early morning hours the moon, no more than a sliver, rose over the trees. All round Kumaran bodies slept. Kumaran looked out at the invisible sea, and it seemed impossible that one living man could be out there in all that black vastness. Why had he any right to hope? Why keep the fire burning so brightly? Once he found himself praying, not for Thomas, but to him. Strange to say, he did not feel much sorrow.As the night wore on, what sorrow he did feel gave way to a vague sense of relief, of freedom.At first he felt guilty about this, but then, with a sudden vengeance, he began ticking off in his mind all the reasons he had for hating Thomas: how Thomas twisted his arm into coming with him in the first place, how he referred to the great Vanji temple as "that heathen thing," the many other infuriating things he said about the Tamils and their religion, the way he routinely embraced filthy beggars and rotting lepers but had embraced his faithful friend only thrice, most recently only a few hours ago. Kumaran told himself that Thomas was a madman and a freak. As he watched the moon rise over the strange scene around him and fought off sleep for some superstitious reason he could not quite articulate, he found himself wondering if Thomas was a figment of the imagination. But in the next instant he found himself scanning the sea for a sign of the figment and listening for a phantom voice. As the night wore on, he alone kept the fire blazing high. He began to quiver, then to pray, then to weep. Finally he drifted off to sleep.

The next thing he knew was a voice whispering his name at his ear. He opened his sleepy eyes and saw, by the light of the fire, dripping white flesh sprawled beside him on the cool sand.

It was in this fishing town, Tangasseri, that Thomas' faith took deep root in Tamil country for the first time. Nothing short of a miracle was required for it to do so, and Thomas' return from the sea was just such a miracle. Rumors abounded. Some said he was lifted from the ocean by a waterspout and disgorged on shore north of the village. Others said he rode to shore on the back of a great shark or a sea turtle fashioned miraculously by his "New God." No one said he was a good swimmer. And no one thought to ask him outright how he had managed it. Only Kumaran had asked. "I found a broken ship's mast floating in the ocean and clung to it," he said.

As if on cue, the sea's redness gave way, and once again the nets bulged with fish. Life in the village was changed—even Kumaran had to admit it. Every morning Thomas led his new flock in prayer, not to Manimekalai, the Sea-Goddess, but to the "Father Almighty." He taught them to love Jesus as their brother and savior, and Jesus' mother, Mary, in place of Manimekalai. He led them in the building of a "church" in a shaded clearing at the northern edge of the town. At first it was little more than a thatched roof fixed to four posts—posts made out of the ship's mast that had saved Thomas' life—but it served well as a meeting place. He built a large cross out of the trunk of a young areca palm and sank one end of it in the sand in front of the church. He read from his scripture about a God who had chosen a people living in a hilly, rocky, parched country far from the sea—a country different from the only one the villagers knew, a place from another world—chosen these people as his very own. He taught that all power centered in this God, that He was the world's sole creator, that it was useless to pray to any other God, and that the Father alone controlled the forces of the great ocean. Every morning he gathered the people together for "the breaking of the bread," he distributed morsels of thin rice cake, and he called the meal a "love feast." He taught several of his flock (as he called them) to speak under the influence of God's spirit—a strange, indecipherable tongue—and taught others how to interpret this tongue for all to understand. He forbade them to make images of any God, to participate in any worship service other than in honor of the Father, to consult fortune-tellers, to use magical amulets designed to catch more fish, and to swear by any God. He taught them the "Ten Commandments" and threatened them with the Father's anger if they did not avoid the intoxicating drink of the toddy palm. He applauded the chastity of the women but warned them again and again that it was not the Sea-Goddess whom they pleased with their virtue, but the Father. He commanded the wealthy men of the village to share their riches with the poor and the rulers of the people to sit with the humble as they worshipped together. He appointed a respected brahmin, a man named Kalli, once Thomas' staunchest opponent, "elder" or "bishop" directly answerable to him and accountable to God for his church. He healed Kalli's youngest son from a raging fever when the boy's life was about to slip away. And he relieved people of their various demons.

Kumaran took no joy in Thomas' success, yet he could not help feeling a certain pride in it. After all, he, Kumaran, had given Thomas his tools, so in a way Thomas' success was his. Did the old jealousies go away? Did Kumaran stop envying the attention Thomas gave other men? One might have supposed so, for Kumaran threw himself into his work with a single-mindedness he had not felt since his journey to the West. He sought out the old men and women of the village and listened for hours on end as they told their stories. All the while he took notes, sometimes not looking up from his palm manuscript for many minutes at a time, but encouraging the storyteller with little grunts. He recorded thousands of details from their lives in this way, and after two months he felt there was no poet alive who could describe the life of the fishermen better than he.

But the old jealousies had not gone away, and Kumaran was aware they had not. It made no sense to him at all. What bound him to Thomas? Not blood, not caste, not work, play, religion, spell, or debt, not the vow he made long ago on ship. He didn't know what it was, but it had something to do, he was sure, with Thomas' face—something as concrete as that, as elemental as the taste of sugar on the tongue, or the infant's cry at night for its mother's breast, or the writhing of a flashing fish caught in a net. Kumaran felt bound to him by his eyes, by his expression, by the color of his skin, by the godlike bearing of his tall, powerful, slender body, by his savagely masculine but gentle, nurturing personality. Not all the poetry in his sack or all the dreams of fame in his brain, not even the thought of his marriage to Devandi, his bride-to-be, could take his mind off Thomas. Thomas was at once his father and his child, and Kumaran felt neglected and rejected by both. He longed to get away from Tangasseri, to get Thomas away from Tangasseri, from his intimate involvement with the lives of the villagers. But Thomas kept putting off the departure, as Kumaran had earlier put off their departure from Vanji. Finally Kumaran could bear it no longer. He had finished his work and would go back home. He had his facts, the significant details of coastal culture; now he would have to put it all together into poetry.This he could do best in the comfort of his father's home. Was this good-bye forever? Thomas assured Kumaran it was not. They agreed to meet in Maliankara by the end of the next monsoon. If for some reason Thomas did not come, then Kumaran should feel free to leave for Madurai by himself.

With a lump in his throat Kumaran left Tangasseri during the height of the hot season. But as he traveled north along the coastal road, his mind turned toward home, toward the bride he would marry and the children she would give him, toward the triumphal reception of his poetry by King Attan. He wondered how he could have gotten himself so entwined in the life of Thomas. It was strange, absurd. He would forget him. He breathed the hot, stagnant air around him and imagined himself refreshed. He listened to the flute-like call of the koel in the forest on his right side and imagined himself happy."Be damned, Thomas! Good-bye and be damned by your strange God!" he told himself. His step became lighter and quicker, and not even the yellow dust kicked up by the bullock carts passing in the other direction darkened the sunshine of his new cheer.

19. The Swinging Braid, the Smell of Sweet Jasmine

"**H**oly Man of God."

Thomas, lying on burlap spread over the smooth sandy floor of his church, woke to these words. He had been dreaming, but the figure silhouetted against the moonlit sea and the hand on his arm gently shaking him and the jasmine scent were no dreams. Suddenly he was wide awake.

"Holy Man of God, you need a wife. Let it be me, Nallapennu." Her voice was earnest but not importunate. Even now she retained her dignity, which he had always admired.

He sat up, and Nallapennu's hand raised itself to his beard and nestled against it like a dove's wing.

"Nallapennu," he said. "Is it you?" He was amazed. "Nallapennu?" She was the woman who fixed his meals, prepared the rice cakes for the eucharistic feast, and in other ways assisted him. She had been working for him only three weeks. Her husband, a fisherman named Subbayya, had almost drowned when his overloaded boat capsized in a storm. He had washed ashore and been pulled out half dead. Thomas had gone to him several times and tried to heal him, but nothing helped. Subbayya lay in a semi-conscious state, unable to feed himself, barely able to swallow. Thomas had thought it odd when her oldest brother approached him and asked if she could assist him when her husband was so ill. Thomas had said he had nothing to give her except what he himself was given, but the brother eagerly pressed her upon him, and out of compassion he had accepted. Now here she was asking him to marry her! His heart went out to her in her distress, and he hated disappointing her. As an owl overhead hooted softly in the warm air, he gently removed her hand from his beard and held it in his, saying, "But you are already married, Nallapennu. What is this?"

"But Subbayya is dying, My Lord. And my two little boys, I see how you love them." She referred to her sons six and four, whom Thomas sometimes wrestled with in the sand, to their great glee.

He thought of the boys, their animated play, the way they loved to be tossed high in the air and caught. He thought of Nallapennu's shapely figure and fine white teeth that sparkled beneath a perfect nose and high forehead. But not for a moment did he forget his solemn vow of celibacy, made in the presence of Peter and the other disciples years ago. He said, "But I cannot marry, Nallapennu. I belong to God."

"I would make you a good wife, Holy Man of God," she said. She placed his hand, still held, against her breast.

He quickly drew it back and said, "You must go now."

She rose and went out, her feet squinching in the sand with every footfall.

Nallapennu didn't come back to work for him, and Thomas gave the chores to another volunteer. The growing Christian community didn't seem to know anything of what had happened, and everything went on as before. On the Sabbath the men worshipped on one side, the women and small children on the other, just as in Jerusalem. What did it matter if the stiff monsoon breeze blew spray under the eves from time to time? This large hut with the sandy floor was the house of God, the first in all India, and these were his people. He had learned to love the palms that shaded his church and the warm air that rustled through them. Sometimes he asked himself if he was getting too comfortable in Tangasseri. Shouldn't he be moving on? But then he would remember how shallow the roots of the new faith had been when he left the town the first time, and how deep they had grown because he had stayed on.

But now there was Nallapennu occupying his thoughts. He could not deny that he missed her, that he thought about her much too often, that thoughts of her distracted him while he prayed. He caught himself daydreaming about her, imagining her coming back to him in the night and taking his hand and holding it against her breast. Would he take it away? Of course he would, he told himself, and he cursed the devil that put such thoughts in his head.

It was impossible not to run into her from time to time as he went about his business, and he flirted with the idea of approaching her himself and asking her back. He spent much time debating whether or not he should do this, but he always decided against it. In time he became almost obsessed with her. He invented errands which took him by her hut, he saw her behind every corner, bent over every pond, gathering wood for every fire. When he actually did meet her, his heart would jump in his chest and he would walk on by without looking up. But then he would turn around after they had passed and watch her thick braid swing across her smooth bare back and the hitching of her hips. One time she looked back and caught him, and his heart beat like bat wings. He prayed for strength to resist her if she came, but at night as he lay on the sandy floor of his church and tried to fall asleep, he would see the braid swinging, smell the sweet jasmine.

He began to indulge a fantasy. Marriage to a Christian woman like Nallapennu would be a holy sacrament. Adopting her little boys as his own would be pleasing to God. Why not? He could still travel up and down the Coast, and that would be more than enough work for a lifetime. He could leave the rest of India to his followers. And Nallapennu, still so young, would give him his own sons, give him the sons Huldah could not. He would have heirs. Besides, what would happen to Nallapennu as a widow if he did not marry her? She would be a trouble to her brothers. No wonder they wanted her married off. He, though a foreigner, was a better catch than Nallapennu had any right to expect. He understood that they had designs on him from the beginning. He in no way resented their scheme. On the contrary, it made perfect sense to him. Why not, then? And Nallapennu was such a handsome woman, dignified and sober; she would make a devoted helpmate for life. And at times—there was no denying it—he felt so lonely.

Two nights after Nallapennu had caught him looking at her, he lay on his bed and was trying to pray himself to sleep. The night promised rain, and the wind off the sea was cool. Wrapped in his burlap, he had almost drifted off to sleep when she came. It was her scent he noticed first. He opened his eyes and saw her kneeling not far from him with the sea at her back.

"Holy Man of God," she said, "I have come to confess my sin."

He sat up. "Nallapennu!" he said. "Nallapennu!" His heart beat fast.

"I have come to confess my sin," she repeated.

"Now?"

"It cannot wait, Master."

He was suspicious. Why couldn't it wait? He wondered if confession wasn't a pretext for something else.

But he saw almost at once that she was truly contrite. She told how she had given in to her brothers and hoped to win him over by humbly serving him, and then by seduction. She wept bitterly and covered her face when she told how she had planned the seduction down to the detail, even to the bearing of her breast to his touch.

"But you did it for the good of your children," Thomas said in her defense. For he thought she was being too hard on herself.

"What does it matter? I understood your way of life."

"How could you? I hadn't told you about my vow." Then he added, "And you did love—it would not have been—you did love me, did you not?"

"Oh yes, Master!" she said with great earnestness, looking up at him in the darkness. "And I would have made you a good wife. Subbayya never complained!"

He almost reached out to touch her, but he did not trust himself. He was aware of what a monstrous thing it would have been to let her taste the fruit of a seduction she had just confessed to God. He said, "It was not so great a sin, Nallapennu. And God has surely forgiven you."

He wanted to comfort her somehow, to ask about Subbayya, but before he could she stood up and rushed out from under the enclosure into the night. He was left alone with the breeze, the crickets, and his own sense of bewildered disappointment.

Sitting on a lonely stretch of beach south of the village, Thomas watched sand crabs hunt for food and tried to understand what had happened. He noticed that the crabs constantly changed direction, jerking this way and that: a step forward, two steps backward, a side-step or two. Yet their bodies did not turn a fraction of a degree; they faced in the same direction throughout all this movement, as if entranced by something they saw in the distance. That is the way he felt. He asked the Father for forgiveness, he told himself it was granted. He let his mind roam backward into time across the Galilean hills, sideways into James' carpenter shop in Nazareth, another direction into the house where his mother had lived and practiced her unclean craft. He relived the great events of Pentecost and his travels with Bartholomew to Mesopotamia, Syria, as far as Edessa. Above all he tried to pray. But it was no use. His mind would not surrender itself to any of these things. Like the crabs, it was entranced by something else.

Now he noticed another habit of these crabs. As they searched for food, they scampered back and forth, left to right, in every direction, but never ventured far from their holes. They would find a tiny morsel washed up by the sea, lower their twin scoops, raise the morsel to their mouths. But if a crow flew high overhead, or a large wave threatened, the whole squadron would instantly disappear, each crab to its own hole. What was the focus of their attention? It seemed to be food-gathering, but a closer watch revealed it was not. Rather it was divided, divided like his own. But his enemy was not something outside, not a crow or a wave, it was himself. If he took his eye off himself for an instant, what might he do in that instant? He tried to pray, to look to the Father, but he was afraid to look away from himself. With his fingers and thumb he rubbed the ivory cross hanging around his neck and tried to converse with the Master, but he could not stop conversing with himself. "How could you have done it?" he said over and over. "What *are* you?" This last question was the one that haunted him most: "What *are* you?" He had decided he was an adulterer. Over and over he relived the last meeting with Nallapennu, over and over the undeniable feeling of disappointment when she confessed her sin. "If she had given me the chance, I wouldn't have been able to resist," he finally admitted to himself after days of denial. And he remembered Jesus' words: "If a man looks at a woman lustfully, he has already committed adultery with her in his heart." It horrified him to admit it, but it was worse to deny it. He was an adulterer, not in the flesh, but in the spirit. He vowed that if anyone were ever to ask him if he had committed adultery, he would say yes. He remembered another of Jesus' sayings, spoken to the Jewish gentry: "You are like whitewashed tombs, which outwardly appear beautiful, but within they are full of dead men's bones and every uncleanness!" Jesus' words had seared the Galilean earth like lightning, and now they seared Thomas.

From that day forward, every morning shortly after sunrise, Thomas sat under a certain palm tree on the beach and looked westward over the ocean toward Judaea. He marveled that he could have been so weak: A solemn vow taken in the presence of God and the other disciples was not sufficient armor against a common sin of the flesh. For a while he had even tried to convince himself the vow did not apply to Nallapennu, for she was no unclean woman, but his future wife. But then the word "future" did its work on his ravaged sense of moral superiority. Though he died three days later, Subbayya was not dead on that fateful night. Even if a distinction between Nallapennu and an unclean woman could be permitted, she was another man's wife at the time. In the last analysis there was simply no way to whitewash the sin. Finally, what had happened to his sense of mission? He had not agreed to evangelize the Malabar Coast, but all India. What self-ishness of spirit, what faithlessness, could have led him to forget that he belonged, not to woman, but to God?

Having seen at last the truth, an unaccustomed spirit of humili-ty settled over him, and in it he found peace. He began to read from the Psalms, meditated on each thought, let it sink down into his soul, and invited it to transform him. "You, O Lord, are a shield about me, my glory, and the One who lifts my head." God visited him, nourished him, buoyed him up, and Thomas marveled at the mercy of God which had saved him, through the powerful resolve of Nallapennu, a simple Malabar fisherwoman, from his own demons. And Jesus seemed to sit invisibly beside him on the sand.

"No more!" he promised himself. He had planted the first shoot of ivy in thick rich soil and watched it spread, even to neighboring villages and towns, even as far as Kollam; and he would watch it grow again in places far distant. He had learned his lesson, he would not fail again. Where would Kumaran take him next? To the great capital of Chera with its sophisticated city ways? That is what he had said. It would be a different kind of challenge, more ambitious, more formidable. But he, Thomas, with a new wisdom born of failure, was more formidable too. With the grace of God, he would not fail again.

20. The Game of Life

Kumaran looked at himself in the burnished brass plate and adjusted the fire-red ashoka blossoms in his hair. They were the fashion of the day, and he wanted to make the best impression on King Attan that he could. Everything had been arranged for the next morning by a fellow poet, one of the court's regulars whom Kumaran had befriended. As he stared at himself in the mirror, he tried to imagine how he would look as he paraded in state down Muziri's proud main avenue to the palace. Was it possible that he, Kumaran the pulaiyar, had an audience with King Attan? Had he actually pulled it off? But Attan would be only the beginning, he reminded himself. He let his mind wander eastward across the jungly spine of mountains that divides the subcontinent: eastward to Madurai, the capital of the Pandyan Kingdom and home of the renowned Sangam, the Academy of Tamil Poets, the great arbiter of convention and taste, the legitimate dispenser of fame and immortality. Even beyond Madurai it wandered. To the north lay the cities of the Kaveri: Uranthai, where he was born, and Puhar, capital of the Chola Empire, the great King Karikal's gift to Gods and men. Puhar lured him most of all, for it was there that he hoped to die, loved and honored by all, immortalized for his songs.

Thomas had arrived from Tangasseri on the previous day, and Kumaran's heart had leaped with joy when he caught sight of his old friend bowling with village boys in a clearing. Kumaran was surprised by the power of his feeling; he delighted to hear of Thomas' success in Tangasseri, and he made eager inquiries about the "flocks" of Christians in places like Nirnam and Kokamangalam, where they had spent time earlier. And Thomas, for his part, seemed sincerely pleased by Kumaran's audience with King Attan and greeted Kumaran's announcement of his young bride's pregnancy with a slap on the back worthy of a sailor. It was as if all the disagreements of the past never occurred.

The stage had been set for the grand day. Kumaran would pay his first visit to the court of King Attan, and Thomas would introduce himself to the community of sages and ascetics along the city's outer moat. They agreed to travel together, with Thomas accompanying Kumaran as far as the green zone on the palace grounds at Muziri's center before turning back and mingling with the sages in the hope of winning them over to his faith.

The next morning they took the ferry to Muziri. Kumaran wore his chaplet of fresh ashoka blooms, while Thomas, although declining to decorate himself in any way, donned a new robe of yellow cotton and combed his hair and beard, now beginning to gray, until he looked almost presentable. The rains had let up, and the sun beat down on the black backs of the ferrymen as they paddled across the bay to the mainland. There again was Muziri's great harbor with its tangle of masts and rigging. And there was the very wharf from which Kumaran and his strange companion, the towering yavana from the land of the Jews, had embarked for Maliankara two years earlier. What a distance they had come together! And now they would go some more.

They walked up an avenue paved with brick through a forest of palms and giant fig trees planted in rows on both sides. The uncanny cries of blue-necked peacocks haunted the forest, and tree nymphs seemed to fashion out of the ether a supernatural cool. Meanwhile a throng of people, animals, and vehicles of every description moved in and out of the city. A huge elephant still dripping from its bath in the bay lumbered along, while its driver, mechanically switching the beast, seemed lost in his thoughts. Porters skillfully guided their cargo of cane poles through seams in the traffic as they jogged past bullock carts laden with foodstuffs for the Capital. A boy carrying a parrot in a cage and alongside him a man teaching the bird to recite the Vedas passed by. A troop of the King's royal dancers, their breasts bedecked with flowers so numerous and sweet that bees buzzed around them, yawned their way out of the city toward the harbor. People from the hills carried all kinds of articles on their heads: pots of honey, sections of elephant tusks, whisks of deer hair, cardamom and pepper stalks, bunches of areca nuts, even wild hens and civet cats in cages.

Abruptly the forest ended, and Thomas and Kumaran shielded their eyes from the sunlight of the grassy clearing that greeted them next. Spread over the plain were ancient sheltering neem trees, and underneath them were vanaprasthas—older men who had retired from active life and sought immortality through philosophy, meditation, and austerities.

"This is where you'll spend most of your time over the next few months," Kumaran said. "You'll find holiness somewhere out there. 'Heathen' holiness."

They looked out at the men, and an occasional woman, sitting under the trees with manuscripts on their laps. Some of them looked back and even pointed. Kumaran thought to himself that Thomas cut a striking figure, worth the notice of even a holy man. What an irony, he mused, that they should look at Thomas rather than at the King's man! He liked that phrase "the King's man."

They came to a wide bridge over the moat. From the water below wafted a smell, not of sewage, but of fragrant oils and flowers. Scented drain water from paste factories perfumed even the crocodiles, whose knobby foreheads broke the surface among clusters of flowers as colorful as the rainbow. Beyond the moat was a narrow paved clearing, then the great gate with its symbol of Chera might, a huge black bow sculpted from a teak tree which formed an arch over the gate. On top of the walls stretching left and right were the King's guards—menacing, hardened fellows—and grotesque machines of war, armories of spears and arrows, and heaps of stones. Thomas and Kumaran walked under the high gate, high enough for the State Elephant carrying the royal umbrella to pass under.

Inside the gate a broad avenue of bricks ran alongside the walls to east and west, and in the middle of the street, directly in front of them, stood the tall teakwood column sacred to generations of Chera kings. The Victory Column, as it was called, had in time come to stand as a symbol, not only of victory over enemies, but of the hospitality for which the people of Chera were famous. Thomas and Kumaran watched men and women venerate it by ritually walking around it and touching its surface, which had become smooth and slightly concave over the years at the level of the hand. Kumaran added his touch to the millions of others, and even Thomas followed suit, though his fingers touched the column well above the concavity. Thomas' explanation surprised Kumaran as much as the deed itself had: "I will never be a Hindu or a Buddhist or a Jain, but it is time I became an Indian." It hinted to

Kumaran of a new attitude. It suggested a flexibility, a realism, perhaps even a cunning that he had not seen before in Thomas.

Moving past the column down the royal avenue paved with cobbles and wide enough for four-horse teams to pass each other with room to spare, they came upon a great expanse of land reserved for the daily marketplace. Mid-morning crowds of gaily dressed, gabbing shoppers milled around the stalls of the shopkeepers, who sold everything from fruits, vegetables, perfumes, and flower garlands to cobras and tiger cubs. Beyond the marketplace and flanking the road were the great houses of merchants often three or four stories high. Women or servants with children could be seen in their windows idly studying the two men as they passed under. Often fingers pointed at Thomas, faces became animated, necks craned. As they jostled their way forward, each block was different from the one before it. One consisted of bazaars where vessels of gold, bronze, ivory, or fine wood were crafted and sold; the next was reserved for soothsayers, astrologers, and musicians; the next for the sale of toddy, salt, and betel. The sights, the sounds, the smells constantly changed, changed every seventy paces or so. Past young foppish noblemen, past monkey-trainers who resembled their animals, peasants from the outlying villages, Buddhist monks with shaven heads, bedizened prostitutes, richly adorned businessmen, housewives carrying a child on a hip—past every imaginable form of humanity they made their way.

The smell of frying pastries, liberally applied perfumes, various foods frying in ghee, honey-scented jasmine wreaths, burning cow dung, mint growing in containers, fodder carried in carts—a hundred smells contended, each seeking to dominate all others.Drums made of stretched deer skin signaled to each other across neighborhoods in their secret codes, horses' hooves clattered against the flat cobblestones, crows called from their perches on the roofs of the city's great houses, music of the flute and the seven-stringed yal came forth from flag-decked temples, heavy doors creaked as they opened for business, a dirge wafted around a corner out of an alley, a watchman shouted the hour in a voice like thunder, a dog yapped, a bell chimed. Every emotion, every dialect, every texture and nuance of sound could be heard as Gods, men, and beasts played at the game of life in Muziri. It was exciting for Kumaran, who grew up in the great city's shadow, to be there. It was more exciting to imagine what Thomas must be feeling.

They moved through the colorful neighborhood of cloth-makers, then of fire-worshipping brahmins. Now the crowds were thinner and the vehicles more impressive as they neared the city's center. They passed the famous seven-story residence of the finance minister, the living quarters of high-ranking army officers, public halls where theater was staged and the stories of the Gods re-enacted, a hospital, alms-houses where charity was dispensed daily, a sanitarium for sick animals. Finally they entered the royal "green zone" with its public bathing ponds, canals, fountains, and groves of ancient banyan, fig, mango, and "sleeping" trees.

Thomas and Kumaran sat in two swings woven from the dangling roots of an ancient banyan tree and watched maidens, members of the King's harem, picking flowers and mimicking the strutting and preening of peacocks. Beyond them curved the inner moat and wall surrounding the palace, which could be glimpsed through the foliage.

"Kumaran," said Thomas without warning in a soft, melancholy voice as they swung side by side in the breezy morning air like court popinjays, "Kumaran, India is a big place."

Kumaran, who was nervously kicking the ground with his feet as he stared down at the ground, suddenly looked up at Thomas and smiled broadly, triumphantly.

Thomas smiled back sheepishly, and Kumaran, for the moment forgetting his anxious thoughts, felt affection for his friend, for there was something like humility in that smile; it almost seemed that Thomas was laughing at himself.

Meanwhile the harem girls continued to play. They seemed as innocent as the ducks that waddled up to receive tidbits of rice cake. Kumaran wondered how Thomas could believe that his loving God could condemn such pretty innocence to the fires of his hell. How absurd.

"Am I mad, Kumaran?"

"Quite," Kumaran said.

Thomas guffawed once under his breath. "But this is not my day, it's yours. Let's talk about you. How much time until the audience?"

"We're hours early," said Kumaran. "Why did you ask if you were mad? Tell me what's worrying you, Brother."

Thomas let his hand fall on his lap and shook his head slowly. "Those women over there. How can I reach them? They don't want to hear what I have to say." He kept shaking his head slowly as he looked down at the ground. "How can this be?"

"What be?"

"They will never know the Father."

Large green parakeets with curved orange beaks flitted about making petulant little squeaks, punctuated by occasional shrill squawks.

Thomas continued: "All those people, all those delicate fingers that will leave their marks on the Victory Column, all those millions—they will never find the way, they will never come to the Father, for they will never know Jesus."

"But no one in India wants to go to your Father," Kumaran said. "There are other Gods, other paradises. There is the eternal nirvana of the Buddhists and the merging of the soul with the Supreme Spirit or some such thing that the yogis are always talking about. Stop troubling yourself about these things. Nobody else does."

"They're all figments of men's minds inspired by Satan, Kumaran. What can I do in the face of so much confusion? Yet I've been given this impossible task, this curse!" Thomas took a deep, troubled breath. "And now I must begin again."

What a strange religion, Kumaran thought. It magnified good and evil into grotesque dimensions. It drove Thomas into excesses of every kind. It was never enough for him to befriend a person; he felt he had to "love" him—an impossible task. It was never enough for him to disapprove of another's beliefs; he was driven to find them damnable. And so on. He should have been born in Tamilakam. Then he would have been told by some yogi that good and evil were illusory. Poor Thomas. Poor fool! Yet there was something heroic about him, something larger than life. It was as if he lived his life walking on hot coals, and every step he took was fateful. But what a delusion! Well, anyhow, he was a most interesting subject. And Kumaran, to while away the time, began to think of how he might immortalize Thomas in a poem.

21. Bala Ma

On the afternoon of the same day, in the clearing between the city's outer moat and the encircling forest, Thomas approached the nearest group of vanaprasthas. This was no easy thing to do, for these venerable old men seeking enlightenment were adept at defending their respective visions. They were often brahmins; they were usually literate, could quote their scriptures extensively, and led outwardly holy lives. Yet Thomas knew the time for challenging them had come. By now he was fluent in Tamil and knew most Sanskrit philosophical terms. His plan was ambitious: He would do battle with the leader of the vanaprasthas, the one held in highest regard. If he could convince him, the others would follow. Or so he hoped.

After properly greeting the group of six men, he asked, "Who, noble sirs, among all these"—he extended his hand and brought it around in a semicircle while letting his eyes pan over the clearing—"is the holiest among you?"

The men looked surprised, then turned to each other and conferred in muffled tones.

"Many say Bala Ma," said one of the men.

"Bala Ma?" Thomas was confused. "But isn't that a woman's name?"

"Yes."

He blinked his eyes, stroked his beard, and studied the men skeptically. "What kind of woman—what is her faith?"

"Buddhist."

"But you—you are not Buddhists?" He doubted they were, for their dress, or rather undress—three were naked—suggested otherwise.

"We are Jains."

He studied their faces for a hint of levity, not knowing what to make of their recommendation.

"Where is she?" he said.

They pointed her out, sitting under a *neem* tree with a cow, a few goats, and five or six men, half of them in loin cloths, the other half in the dull yellow robe of the Buddhist monk. She herself wore the robe.

He didn't know what to expect as he approached the circle in determined strides. He had made a few brahmin converts over the course of his travels, but they weren't the "holy heathens" Kumaran was talking about. "Come, Lord. Come, Lord," he prayed in reassuring Aramaic.

He greeted her with hands folded and took his place in the circle, which moved outward to let him in. The men studied him and muttered to each other under their breath. Other vanaprasthas and idlers out for a walk or squatting under a nearby tree had noticed Thomas' approach, and they were curious to see why the tall yavana sat at the feet of Bala Ma. Figures bent their way toward him from all sides. Only the animals, grazing or resting, remained where they were.

Bala Ma sat quietly on the ground at the base of the tree with her eyes lowered. Thomas' first impression was that she carried the suffering of the world in her heart. Her shoulders stooped, her jowls sagged, her large mouth drooped at the corners, and bags of excess skin puffed over her eyes. Her whole body seemed weighed down. But when he looked more closely, looked directly into her eyes, he saw something that told a different story. He remembered Kumaran had compared the vanaprasthas to the acacia tree, which blooms after it loses its leaves.

"Venerable Ma," Thomas said, "my name is Thomas, and I am from a land far to the west."

Still wrapped in silence, Bala Ma looked up at him, smiled, and folded her hands in greeting, bowing slightly.

"Venerable lady," he continued, his feet resting discreetly on his thighs in the lotus position, "I have known a man in whom God walked, a man perfect as no other man. I have seen him suffer, die, and rise bodily from death. He wants all men to know the true God, our Father in heaven."

Thomas began, as he so often did, with this formula. Then he told her about the chosen people, the Messiah, and the approaching end of time. He spoke of eternal life in heaven for those who accepted the Messiah and obeyed his teachings, and of God's abounding love for each of his creatures who feared him. He spoke of the duty to forgive one's enemies and love one's neighbor as oneself. "But our supreme duty, the great commandment," he concluded, "is to love the true God with our whole heart, our whole mind, and our whole soul."

Throughout Thomas' speech Ma's eyes had not once left his face, nor had her expression changed. She continued to look at him after he had finished, but she said nothing.

Thomas concluded: "I invite you, venerable Bala Ma, to acknowledge the Lord of Creation, accept baptism at the hands of his humble servant, and eat of the heavenly banquet at his table."

Ma's expression changed. She looked down at the ground and smiled. Then her body began to shake while tears gathered at her eyes. She shook convulsively but made no noise. Suddenly it became clear to everyone that she was laughing, and with that a great roar of relieved laughter erupted. Just as suddenly she regained her composure. Now, as she held up her hands for quiet, there wasn't a hint of the woman who had laughed. Her face again imparted serenity, and she commanded the crowd by the quiet force of her personality. She fixed her impersonal stare on Thomas.

"Your God has taught his followers how to forgive," she said. "and that is good, for already you have something to forgive. I ask your forgiveness, for me and for all of these."

"There is nothing to forgive," Thomas said without a pause. "If fools did not laugh, then what I teach would not be true."

Bala Ma's laughter had stung Thomas. Most in the group recognized this and withheld their hisses when he returned the perceived insult. A few low grumbles, like distant thunder, sounded in the rear, but for the most part there was an uneasy silence, as when a herd of elephants and a lone tiger water from the same hole.

A shaggy old graybeard leaning on his staff broke the understood truce. "He lectures *you*, Ma!" Then followed a torrent of protest from many voices.

"His God, who has ever heard of him?"

"He is a yavana!"

"He condemns our Gods."

"I bet he denies rebirth. Ask him. Ask him about this, Ma."

"What could a yavana know of religion anyway?"

"Who has ever head of his 'Messiah'?"

"What makes him think the world will end soon? What stupidity!"

"He is a child with a child's God."

"He condemns what he does not understand—like fools everywhere."

"What's that thing around his neck?"

Finally the noise subsided, and a high-pitched, shaky voice said, "A yavana telling *you*, Ma, what is true!" Some in the crowd hissed or jeered, but Ma herself, with hands held high, implored the spectators to be quiet.

"Brother," she said in a voice now kind and compassionate, "you have been given rude treatment, but I see you not only forgive, but are strengthened. I too have known rude treatment in my day."

She hesitated, changed her position, and wiggled her toes which stuck out from under her knee.

"I too have known a perfect man, but his name was Gautama, the Buddha, the Enlightened One, and he lived long ago far to the north. In a past life I lived in the country of Gautama and was the wife of a householder. One day disease took my baby, my firstborn son, and I went to Gautama with my dead son clasped to my bosom. I had heard he was a physician, you see, a healer. 'Lord, do you have any medicine that will help my baby boy?' I said in desperation. He looked at my baby and saw he was already dead. 'I do have medicine,' he said, 'but first go collect mustard seed from a home where no child, husband, parent, or grandparent has died.' 'Very well,' I said. So I went from house to house carrying my dead baby clasped to my breast. 'Yes, we have a little mustard seed,' they would say. But then I would ask, 'In your house has there died a child, husband, parent, or grandparent?' And they would answer, 'Mother, are you serious? The dead far outnumber the living!' At every house a parent had died, or a child, or a husband, or a grandparent; at no one's house was I able to get any mustard seed. I then realized that I was not the only one who had lost a son and that all over the land, everywhere children were dying, parents were dying, husbands were dying, grandparents were dying. With this new wisdom I extinguished my love for my child and left his body in the forest. Then I went back to Gautama. 'Have you brought the mustard seed, Mother?' he said. 'No, I have not,' I said; 'the people told me, "The dead far outnumber the living."' Then Gautama said to me, 'Mother, you thought that only you had lost a son; now you have discovered for yourself that death waits on no one, that among living things there is no permanence anywhere.' Then he pointed to a lamp burning inside the door of a nearby house, for it was almost dark. 'All creatures,' he said, 'are like the flame of that lamp. At one moment it is lit, at another it goes out. Only those who have realized Nirvana are at rest. Only they are at peace. They are invisible quenchless flame.'"

Bala Ma paused for a moment, then, cocking her head to the side and looking calmly at Thomas, continued: "The whole world is on fire, O yavana. The eye is on fire. The ear is on fire. The nose is on fire. The tongue is on fire. The body is on fire. The mind is on fire. This city of Muziri is on fire. The whole world is on fire. The Buddha's doctrine can quench this fire. Will you receive this holy doctrine, O yavana, from the hands of Bala Ma?"

The tree that Bala Ma and Thomas sat under provided too little shade for the crowd that had gathered, and the sun beat down on the fringe. But no one thought of the sun as Bala Ma delivered her discourse, for the quiet force of her personality blazed brighter. No doubt several among the crowd became followers of the Buddha in the course of her speech. Even Thomas had been touched. But most in the crowd simply enjoyed the show. They waited eagerly to see the effect Ma's words would have on the strange white man. For surely his master Jesus was less than Gautama, the Illustrious One, the Buddha, just as he, Thomas, was less than Bala Ma. Surely he, even he must see this.

"Bala Ma," he began, "you are wise. You have correctly described the condition of the world. It is most certainly on fire. Yet this fire is nothing compared to the fire to come, just as Gautama is nothing compared to Jesus, the only Messiah of God. Hear me, all of you." Now he stood up and faced around to the crowd, Bala Ma on his right. "Only Jesus' doctrine can quench the fire. Only Jesus has been chosen by the Lord God to quench the fire."

But the crowd hummed and hissed so loudly that Thomas had to stop. Bala Ma motioned him to sit down, and the crowd quieted.

"Thomas"—it was the first time she used his name—"I have said nothing of any God. I have no interest in any God. The Illustrious One, Gautama the Buddha, said nothing about a God."

"I have respect for this Buddha, then," said Thomas, "for at least he has not invented a Shiva or a Murugan."

"Then where do we differ?" said Ma.

"Where do we differ? Jesus, and the prophets before him, revealed the true nature of God. Your Buddha has not done so, could not have done so, for God did not choose to reveal Himself to your Buddha. God did not choose to reveal Himself to this country. *There* is the difference, Ma."

The humming began again the instant he said "this country." But Bala Ma called for quiet.

"God, O yavana, is irrelevant to salvation. Whether such a God as you speak of exists or not is irrelevant. Such a God, even if he exists, is of no help to us. We work out our own salvation. No one will do it for us."

"But the Messiah, Jesus—" But he checked himself, stood up, bowed with hands folded in front of his face, and departed with quick, long strides.

Later that afternoon, as they took the ferry back to Maliankara, he unburdened himself to Kumaran. He had failed. Instead of letting Jesus speak through him, he had spoken himself. But he would be back the next day, and the next, as many days as it took to sprig the ivy of Christianity in Muziri.

Kumaran had news too. He had succeeded, and the King had asked him back. That evening Kumaran went off to a toddy bar across the bay and got drunk.

A strong sea wind whirred through the bright green leaves of the *neem* tree where Bala Ma sat with her company, including Thomas. As if intent on overhearing the conversation below, sea gulls as black as tar stood frozen in flight as they leaned into the wind overhead. As fluffy, hurrying clouds flew by, the sun danced into hiding, then out again, as if reflecting the mortal give-and-take of truth and error going on below.

Suddenly he understood the secret of her power. It was her face, her plain face with its baggy wrinkled flesh that attracted everybody to her. Every line spoke of a mastering compassion. Every glance told of an unearthly peace unlike any he had ever seen.

From that point on he single-mindedly sought the key to Bala Ma's secret. He wanted as much to understand her as to convert her. Where was her weakness? How could he exploit it and bring her to truth? He became obsessed by the old woman and forgot about everybody else. He told himself that if he could convert her, she would bring many with her and, in time, all Muziri. He knew there was something wrong with the path she walked, something delusive about the nirvana she claimed she had realized. Where was God in it? What meaning could eternity have without God? What good was nirvana without God?

Thomas visited Bala Ma many times. They became friends, and Thomas, although a yavana, gained the respect of the vanaprasthas. But not one, least of all Bala Ma herself, converted to his religion, although everyone found parts of it good and appealing.

When Kumaran announced one day that it was time to leave the coastlands for the inland jungle and its great mountains, which stood between them and Madurai, Thomas did not object. Muziri had become a waking nightmare. To his mind he had failed, and his mood was as gloomy and dark as the misty forest which loomed ahead. He muttered he could not understand why his Father had "abandoned" him. He stroked things with the fingers of his right hand compulsively; sometimes the object was the ivory cross hanging around his neck, sometimes a small stone cupped invisibly in his hand as it swung by his side. His fresh yellow robe had faded, and rough stitching held his sandals together. He looked like a poor man, not the yavana prince of a bygone day, not the Apostle of the New God doted on by his flock at Tangasseri. One morning he woke with a pain in his hip, and for several days he hobbled—this man who never complained of illness—on a leg that felt "tired." Scowling, his brow deeply creased, his face gaunt with sleeplessness, he looked like a deranged man in a blinkless stare. Even the children stopped tagging along after him as he drifted, like an earthbound ghost, over Maliankara's twilight byways. He had never before been so low.

Meanwhile Kumaran had won seven audiences with King Attan, and the black pulaiyar poet had served his royal patron well by describing the yavana lands of the far west. In appreciation Attan rewarded Kumaran with a young bull elephant. He sold it for fifty gold Roman coins impressed with the face of the Emperor Tiberius.

PART III: THE JUNGLE

22. Deadly Beauty

Kumaran bought a pack mule with four of his gold pieces, embedded thirty more in his leather girdle, and left the remainder with his wife. He told Devandi he would be gone for at least a year: six months in the mountain forests, six more in Madurai, a month or two in Puhar to get settled, another to travel back and fetch her.

Flush with success, he felt now all his dreams were within reach. But there was still much work to do. Rival poets at King Attan's court confirmed what he already suspected. "Too foreign and exotic," one of them had said. The criticism stung him, but he feasted on the jealousy it betrayed. For the first time he could ignore the fact that he was a pulaiyar born in the sculptor caste: He was free to do what he liked, he did it exceptionally well, and he was envied by men far above him in caste. His rivals even referred to him as the "Poet of the West," and the King could not get enough of him. Still, he knew the criticism was just. The other poets knew more about Tamil country than he did. Much more.

Kumaran made up his mind to be the best informed poet in all Tamilakam by the time he reached Puhar and King Karikal. He had familiarized himself with only one of the three kingdoms of the South. Of the five regions described by Tamil poets from time immemorial—the seacoast, the mountainous jungle, the grazing land, the fertile rice-growing delta, and the desert—he had reliable knowledge of only one, the seacoast, and a vague knowledge of one other, the rice-growing flatlands where he spent part of his boyhood.

So there was a great expanse of territory to cover before he presented himself at the Chola court. Six months in the forests seemed the minimum time needed to learn the customs of the wild mountain men. Madurai would follow; and Madurai, he had heard, was situated in flat grazing land not far from the most desert-like region of Tamil country. Then he would spend the rest of his life in the fertile rice district watered by the wide Kaveri. The three capitals, the five great land types, all would be in his grasp by the time he reached Puhar on the eastern seacoast. He would greet King Karikal, mighty Monarch of the Cholas, with nothing less than an encyclopedic knowledge of most of the world, and with no regional gaps like those found in the repertories of other poets. He might be only a low pulaiyar sculptor by birth, but he would be the best, most sought-after poet in the whole world.

Once Kumaran made up his mind to leave, he couldn't leave soon enough. He didn't care what Thomas might say; he wouldn't be persuaded to postpone his journey as much as a week. He greatly feared traveling alone, especially through the dark, dangerous jungle country that lay ahead. But he was now a "man of destiny"; nothing could stop him. Thomas would have to go along with his plans or separate.

Kumaran was greatly relieved when Thomas agreed to go. It was plain Thomas was falling on hard times in Muziri, but Kumaran had not expected him to agree without a fight. "Perhaps it's the will of God," Thomas said sullenly with a tired shrug of his shoulders. Six months seemed to him the correct length of time to stay in one place, and he especially liked the idea of traveling the whole of the Tamil country, coast to coast and south to north. He came back to his favorite metaphor: India was a giant trellis to be covered someday with the ivy of his faith. Again he explained it would be necessary only to plant the ivy in a sufficient number of places, and sufficiently wide apart; the ivy would soon blanket the whole trellis.

"How do you explain what happened in Muziri?" Kumaran asked him as they packed their belongings the day before departure.

"I made a mistake," Thomas said. "I misjudged Bala Ma. I assumed too much. I assumed the Father would take her by force, so to speak. I should have spread myself across the city instead of giving all my energies to her. If I had done that, some would have converted. Even now there would be converts, hundreds. The ivy would be growing, spreading. But I was stupid. Lazy perhaps. I wanted Bala Ma to do my work for me. But I'll come back to Muziri. It hasn't seen the last of me, Brother. I'll be wiser. I'll catch many brahmins under my net. You'll see."

"How is your leg?"

"Much better," Thomas said as he carefully placed the sacred man-uscripts of his religion in his pack.

That night, their last in Maliankara, it rained. Kumaran studied Devandi by the light of the oil lamp as she glided over the matted floor of his father's comfortable and spacious house, and as raindrops popped against the banana leaves next to the window. She was not a beautiful woman, but she had, even in pregnancy, a graceful figure and was a hue lighter than he. Her eyes pleased him with their deer-like innocence, though sometimes they betrayed what he took to be a secret sorrow.

"I will come to fetch you in fifteen months, to fetch you both," he told her, looking down at her stomach. She wept, but she had waited before. Kumaran told her it was a woman's dharma to wait.

He called her to him and they made love. When they had finished, she sat up and, without a word, gazed down at him. She did not chew betel, so her teeth were as white as the moon. But her eyes pleased him that night especially. They danced to some delightful musical riddle she had solved at last. They smiled down at him in that magical way that only a woman who has discovered what she was born for can smile: She was at once the all-receptive Mother Earth and the devouring Goddess Kali, at once adoring and triumphant. "My little Devandi," Kumaran said to her, "what has happened to that girl?"

The muddy road pitted by puddles cut through the middle of ripe yellow-green paddy as the sun, dead ahead, burned off the early morn-ing mist on their first day out. Thomas, holding the rope tied to the mule, explained once again his theory of the ivy trellis.

"Have you ever thought," Kumaran said, walking ahead, "that India's like a giant quilt of paddy, not an ivy trellis? Rice grows only where it's planted. It doesn't spread."

"No, Brother," Thomas said, "India is an ivy trellis, not a rice field."

"Is it?" Kumaran swept his arm in a circle, inviting Thomas to look around him and see what was there.

But Thomas met Kumaran's triumphant, slightly sardonic smile with a look of determined self-confidence. So quickly he had recovered from his disappointment in Muziri, Kumaran thought. What wonders he could work with a prayer. Did ever another man hope so wildly as Thomas? He was a dreamer, a mad dreamer; a child, a lovable, irre-sponsible, exasperating child. But he was also a monarch, a tall white monarch. What a paradox. He combined the authority and majesty of a king with the simple trust of a child or half-wit. Kumaran wondered if that was what made him so attractive and lovable.

"You will see," Thomas said.

"You are stubborn, Brother," Kumaran said with a smile as he looked over his shoulder, "like that animal you're pulling." And the sun broke out over Thomas' face too.

A little later Kumaran said, "I'll tell you a secret; I'm glad you failed with Bala Ma."

"Glad? Why?"

"Because I prefer her religion to yours."

"After all these months together? Brother, your heart is hardened. How long have you heard me preach the gospel?"

"Two and a half years."

Later that day Thomas asked Kumaran if he was his friend.

"Friend? You are my *brother*," Kumaran said.

"But you want my mission to fail."

"I didn't say that, Brother. I'm indifferent to it."

"Then how can you be my brother?"

Kumaran pondered the question as they walked along quietly, veering around puddles. "I want you to be happy," he said at last.

"But there's only one thing that will make me happy. You know that."

Kumaran thought some more, then said, "I want your mission to succeed, but not for its own sake. For your sake, Brother. And not like ivy on a trellis either, but more modestly, like paddy in a field."

They walked on, and their shadows stretching out behind them became shorter and shorter as the hot lowland sun rose, then longer and longer in front of them as it fell. That night they slept a good way off the road out in the open on a bund dividing two paddy fields. The moon was so bright and full that Kumaran saw a snake cross the bund a stone's throw out.

"Kumaran, before it's over, you will become a Christian," Thomas said, fingering the ivory cross hanging around his neck.

They were lying head to head on the narrow dike slapping at mosquitoes. Kumaran said nothing, and for moments at a time it was so still, between slaps, that he could hear Thomas stroking his beard. Thomas always did this when he considered a problem. Kumaran knew that *he* was a problem for Thomas, and this made him feel good, just as he felt good about the jealousy of the rival poets. It tickled him that Thomas couldn't understand why he resisted Christianity.

"Brother," Kumaran taunted, "you don't really believe I will. If you did, you wouldn't be fingering that cross just now."

"What do you mean?"

"You always finger that thing when you're unsure of yourself."

Kumaran's mind was drifting in some happy zone far removed from the hard earth at his back when Thomas finally answered. "It makes me remember. I saw the Master's resurrected body and felt the very wound in his side. Now I see this cross, I feel it. It keeps him close to me."

Kumaran wanted to taunt Thomas some more. He wanted to ask him why he fingered things almost incessantly now. Was Jesus getting away from him? Were India's Gods swallowing up his Father? It would have been a cruel thing to ask, but, after all, he, the pulaiyar Kumaran, was now a man of stature, of destiny, and Thomas was a failure. Thomas had made a fool of himself in Muziri, while he wore gold around his waist. But he could not muster the energy to put the question and instead drifted off to sleep.

They made their way eastward into the foothills. For several days the road ran along the northern bank of the wide, fast-flowing Periyar River, swollen with the heavy autumnal rains falling on the mountains ahead. When the river turned north, now narrower and swifter, it lay in their way, and they were forced to hire a large raft to take the mule across. The raft jerked violently as it docked on the other side, and the mule knocked Kumaran, who couldn't swim, into the current.

Thomas dove in, caught up with Kumaran, and dragged him to the bank downstream. Kumaran coughed up water and his breakfast. Finally his breath came in regular wheezes, and he lay on his stomach with one leg tucked under. Dazed and shivering, he stared at Thomas squatting beside him. And for a moment he thought he was looking at Murugan, the Tall God, the God of the Hills, the Child of Six Mothers, the Beautiful One—Murugan.

Thomas smiled down sweetly as he placed his hand under Kumaran's head. "I am going to Tamilakam," he said, mimicking the first Tamil phrases Kumaran taught him on the ship. "Please give me some rice. Where is your home? My name is Thomas." Kumaran smiled back as his breathing deepened and slowed. Where had Kumaran seen that smile before, that smile Thomas saved for everyone but him? In Vanji with the beggars, of course. Suddenly Kumaran understood Thomas: Thomas loved people in trouble, people who were rejected, needed help, sick, near death. He had no love for the strong, the healthy, the successful.

They spent the next two days in a hunter's settlement drying out their clothes and the parchment scrolls of Thomas' scriptures under a balky sun.

By now they were in Murugan's country. The misty jungle-coated mountains where the Hunter God lived and played rose high around them. The wind blew out of the northeast, and in the morning the women built fires to warm their families as well as to cook their meals. At night the hunters slept inside their thatched huts and hung deer skins across their doorways to protect themselves from the cool. In the hut prepared for Thomas and Kumaran, a fan dangling from a peg was covered with cobwebs. At sunrise of the last morning Kumaran saw a dancing girl warm the strings of her *yal* by rubbing them against her breast.

It was in this settlement that Kumaran first heard of Pari the mountain chieftain. Pari would welcome any poet and would be generous with gifts, he was told. Kumaran lured a man with two gold coins to guide him to Pari's capital, a week away, for it seemed the ideal place to study the mountains and their people.

On the first day they climbed east along the main road into the mountains. It was a relief having a guide, for now they didn't have to depend on grass knots at crossroads to find the right way, and Kumaran could surrender himself to the sights and sounds around him. He noted how the women, dressed in leaves and flowers, guarded their millet fields, which grew in openings in the hilly forest. He noted how they drove away parrots and other birds with shouts and by banging together bamboo clappers. Sometimes they stood on the ground, sometimes on a high platform built in a tree to keep out of the way of beasts. The mountains echoed with the rush of streams. The noise of the clear, cool water delighted the Gods and nymphs as they bathed, and Kumaran distinctly heard their celestial humming in the wind. Above this rush and hum he heard the calls of women gathering *vengu* blossoms, the thundering trumpet of a rutting elephant, the shouts of men taking honey from the wild honeycomb, the bark of hunting dogs, the yelling of a mahout freeing his elephant from the eddies of a swollen river, the grief-stricken cries of a monkey whose baby had let go its grasp and fallen to the forest floor, the dirge of a woman who had lost her husband to infection from a porcupine's quills, the shouts of boys goading cattle treading out seeds from the jack, the songs of women pounding grain, the shrieks of tipsy peacocks that had drunk wild toddy, mistaking it for water. And always there was the sound of a tight-skinned drum somewhere and the intoxicating sense that Murugan was near, that he might at any moment appear in a glorious light, his six faces looking graciously at Kumaran, his twelve arms thrilling him with their dance. Murugan! His closeness further enchanted the already enchanted forest.

Late one afternoon they camped near the junction of the main road and the road that would take them to Pari. As the guide set about building a fire and preparing the food, Kumaran asked Thomas to come with him on a walk. Although this was the hour Thomas preferred to be alone, he followed. They wound their way up a hill. A cowherd had told Kumaran there was a clearing at the top and a pillar erected to Murugan.

Kumaran couldn't remember a happier moment. Unlike Thomas, who worked at propagating his religion, Kumaran would propagate his for the sheer joy of it. It would beam out of him as spontaneously as light explodes from the sun. Or so he told himself.

"Thomas, I'd like to teach you my religion—and my art, for they are the same," Kumaran said as they sat in tall grass and looked westward at the setting sun.

"I thought you worshipped Murugan," Thomas said. "Is there more?"

"You underestimate me, Brother. My religion means as much to me as yours does to you."

Thomas looked away, blinking hard, his jawbone working.

"Look at the colors out there, Brother," Kumaran continued. "Crimson, pink, gold. Do you notice such things?"

"Notice? Of course I notice, Brother."

"But does your heart leap at the sight?"

Thomas looked out at the sunset, but before he could speak Kumaran went on:

"When I look at that, my heart leaps. 'There is Murugan,' I say, 'in all his glory!' Then I think of the Sun-God driving his seven-horsed chariot over the edge of the earth, and how he comes round from behind and rises the next morning on the other side. A world full of miracles, of Gods at play, of beauty. Such beauty, Brother!"

"Yes, it's beautiful," Thomas said, but without feeling. "But who has time to sit and admire it?"

"I do! I sit and admire and *study* it, Brother. I delight in it. I worship it! And I'd like to teach you to worship it. Will you let me try?"

"You know, Kumaran, what alone I worship. Next to God the world is a pale ghost."

"I don't believe you! I've watched you. I've never known a man who touched as many things as you."

"This is an old subject, Brother," Thomas said edgily.

"You're obsessed by the world," Kumaran said, ignoring the warning. "In your own way obsessed. Always touching or rubbing or stroking it. Don't think I'm slighting you. It's a strength. You'd make a fine poet!"

"You know why I do that," he said. "What if I told you you're always blowing mucus out of your nose? What would that prove? That you'd make a good horse?"

This was the first time Thomas mentioned Kumaran's revolting habit after all their months together. But Kumaran, though stung, recovered quickly from the insult. He was so full of himself that nothing could have deflected him then.

"A man doesn't touch ghosts," he said. "Thomas, listen to me. The world—it's what God wraps himself in. Perhaps the world is his very body—literally his body. It is to Murugan what your body is to you. . . . Have I ever seen your soul? If I am to admire you, I must admire your body, your face, your eyes. Your beauty is reflected in these. And the beauty of Murugan is reflected in his world. I revel in its beauty, I worship it. Do you think God is pleased if we don't? You're a carpenter, Brother. You should know what I'm talking about better than others. You want others to admire what you make, for you've made it as pleasing as you can. But you say you haven't time to admire what God has made. Is God happy with that?"

Thomas said nothing, but Kumaran could tell by the crease in his forehead that Thomas was weighing what he said.

"Look," Kumaran said, his voice vibrating with excitement, his right hand fluttering and wagging as if gaming with dice, "I'll teach you how to see a sunset as a poet does. And to hear it. And feel and smell it. It's not only the billowy, streaky shapes of clouds out there, or the deep purple and pink fading into the palest yellow shades; it's—listen! What do you hear? . . . Far off a lute played by a herdsman returning from the fields. And did you hear that? Some great cat, probably a tiger, snarling, perhaps calling to its mate . . . and the birds, listen, the nightingale, that noise halfway between a flute and a trumpet. And the air, what smells does it bring us? A fragrance, but of what? I don't know, but before I leave these mountains I *will* know. And note the air's chill. Not so chilly as Palestine, but chillier than you've ever felt it before in Tamil country. Did you notice this morning that you could see your breath? And the drums . . . two, no, I can hear three. Each drum is different, each has a name, but I don't know them yet. Their names are part of this sunset, Thomas, as much a part as the sun itself. . . . Tell me truly, couldn't you worship a sunset?"

"Only the Father," Thomas said quietly and without hesitation.

"But if the sunset *is* the Father, is his body?"

"A moment ago you spoke of Murugan, now you're talking about the Father." Thomas' eyes narrowed.

"Murugan, the Father, what does it matter? The sunset is the same sunset. And it's—it's beautiful!"

"It matters to me," said Thomas significantly. "Murugan is Murugan. The Father is the Father. The sunset is the sunset."

Then an inspiration—not a poetic one, not the usual kind that Kumaran cultivated, but one alien and unbidden—struck him. He looked at Thomas with an excited, beseeching expression. "Brother, Murugan and the Father are *one*! Don't you see? They're *one*!"

"What do you mean?"

"They're one, don't you see? Don't you have two names? Aren't you both Thomas and Judas? It's the same with God. Don't you see?"

"That's nonsense. You don't know what you're saying. I've never had the feeling your religion went very deep. It's something you play at. It's like your poetry. It's entertaining, it's not serious. Stick to poetry." He got up and headed for the path down the hill.

Kumaran was furious. He got up to run after Thomas. He wanted to spin him around and strike him on the face. He ran down the path, but just before he reached him, Thomas jerked to a stop and let out a faint, shuddering cry. A king cobra rose and hissed in front of him with neck dilated and poised to strike. Thomas and the snake faced each other eye to eye.

Kumaran's stomach heaved in terror and almost constricted his throat. "Don't move! Don't even blink your eyes!" he blurted somehow. He looked around in the twilight for a stick, found one, and moved to the side of the snake. He reached out toward it with the stick, and the snake rotated its head, looked quickly back at Thomas with its beady lidless eyes, then shot out at the stick. Kumaran threw it down and bolted down the jungle path with Thomas almost running him over behind.

That night they celebrated their escape from the cobra with snake stories from their past, and the memories of their dispute seemed distant. But as they coiled themselves around the embers of the fire, Kumaran couldn't resist saying, "You should think about what I said, Thomas. God might be telling you something with that snake."

On the final day of the journey before reaching Pari's capital, it rained in torrents, and sometimes they walked in mud and water up to their knees. Even if the sun had shone, it could not have penetrated that dense jungle. Thunder rumbled around them, and Kumaran prayed to Murugan to protect them from the demons and giants whose stares bore down upon them out of the misty shadows of great trees, and from the snakes and great cats that lurked everywhere. Except for the staccato reports of cane trees crashing together in the wind, they could hear nothing over the rain and thunder. Completely exhausted, cold, hungry, but protected by Murugan, they reached Pari's jungle capital as darkness fell.

The days and months that followed were prosperous for Kumaran, and up until the last days they were prosperous for Thomas as well. "Don't try to displace their God with yours; put yours *alongside* theirs," Kumaran begged him during their first week of residence, "and in time they will choose." To a degree Thomas listened. He insisted that all should worship together as equals without regard to caste and that they should put the "New God" first, treating other gods more or less as archangels. But he made concessions to local custom when he could; for example, he agreed to wear the bright-red blossoms of the ashoka tree in his hair, even when he celebrated the Lord's Supper. As a result his "New God" was accepted by many alongside other gods, a church was built out of choice timbers, and many people came to worship, a few everyday. Thomas was a kind of God to his followers; just as everywhere else, his great height and peculiar color set him off from the race of mortals. He became a new force in Pari's capital, Kurinchi (named after one of the trees of the forest)—not the equal of Murugan's chief priest, but powerful enough to arouse this priest's envy.

In the meantime Kumaran did his best to get used to this new country with its strange foods, exotic flora, ever-threatening animals, and chilly climate. Even Murugan was in some ways foreign to the Murugan he knew, and a few of their Gods he had never heard of. The people themselves—Maravars they were called—spoke Tamil, but with an accent that was peculiar, and with the addition of many words strange to Kumaran; and there was almost no Sanskrit in their tongue. They were a friendly people, but so frank as to offend against civilized niceties, and Thomas, being like them in this respect, was in some ways more at home with them, Kumaran had to admit, than he was. As for Pari, he prided himself on his liberality. Well did he understand that a poet's praises carry renown and immortality throughout all the five regions of Tamil country. And immortality was all that Pari lacked, for the booty taken over the years in wars of conquest fought against other mountain chiefs had swelled his treasury to bursting.

Kumaran lived in one of Pari's guest houses almost from the time he arrived. On many an evening Kumaran would enter Pari's home— with its thick rugs of bear, its tiger skins stretched across the floors, the tusks of giant elephants and the great bows that killed them mounted on the walls—to read his poetry and otherwise entertain the Chief and his wives. Sometimes Kumaran would read about the mysterious lands to the West, sometimes he would describe a hunt or a skirmish with a neighboring chieftain or a wedding or even a sensation, and sometimes he would read elaborate panegyric with Pari himself as subject. On one occasion Kumaran praised Pari for the mercy he showed captives taken in war, and Pari, while duly appreciative, corrected him: "Please, generosity, but not mercy! What will my enemies think?" Kumaran judged Pari, whose short stature, refined features, and almost delicate build might have tempted his enemies to underestimate him, one of the shrewdest men he had ever met. He greatly admired Pari, and Pari, judging by the gold lotus as large as a human head that he gave the poet in appreciation of his verse, seemed to return the admiration.

All together Thomas and Kumaran spent seven months in Kurinchi. Kumaran learned to tell the *thattai* drum, whose sound resembled the grunt of a bear, from the *pathalai*, a wide-faced drum with only one side and a sound like thunder. He went on hunts and watched dogs hunt down large iguanas, prized by the hunters as food. He learned to enjoy the rich meat of the deer and even the flesh of the porcupine; he ate so much meat that his teeth became blunted—or so he wrote in his notes. He drank toddy made from ripe wild rice mixed with honey; also the juice from the *vyavi* vine when water was scarce. He watched women worship snakes, especially the cobra, but also the huge-bodied python which could swallow a pig—or a human baby—in one long gulp. He learned to recognize the special stones planted at trail junctions to commemorate warriors who took their own lives after surviving a war which was lost. And how numerous and brilliant the flowers! He once saw an eagle swoop down and seize fallen petals from the fire-red *kanthal*, no doubt mistaking it for flesh. And the beasts! The older men could tell him whether a jungle grunt belonged to a tiger or boar or bear. They could even tell by the sound what the animal was doing: "That is the sound the heron makes just before its death."

Sometimes Kumaran saw things that horrified him. Once his hunting party came upon a tiger attacking a pregnant elephant. The elephant's blasts of agony as the tiger ripped open her belly to get at the baby bothered him for days. Sometimes the hunters themselves would suffer the tiger's fury; sometimes they would even set out to test it. Too often the special songs sung to a mutilated hunter by his wife turned into a dirge: it was said that there were four women in Kurinchi for every three men.

Thomas and Kumaran had arrived in Kurinchi at the height of the autumnal monsoon, and eventually they agreed to stay until the end of the summer monsoon, a total of nine or ten months. But the grim jungle demons had other plans.

23. Ordeal by Fire

Thomas' mistake was not so much that he required his converts to bury rather than burn their dead, or that he made them sit in church without regard to caste or rank, or that he ate with women or failed to ritually purify himself following an act of pollution such as anointing the dead. Nor was it, not really, that he knew little Sanskrit or that he failed to show deference to the Vedic deities. His real mistake was that he succeeded.

For several months his converts had tried to tell him that Murugavelan, Kurinchi's chief priest and only brahmin, was jealous of him. But Thomas, busy building a church and translating the Law of Moses into Tamil, ignored the warnings. When Kumaran came and told him that Murugavelan "had the Chief's ear," Thomas became concerned for a day or two but forgot about it when nothing further happened. Now Murugavelan had formally accused him of "breaking up families and committing defiling acts." And Pari wanted him to leave Kurinchi, not out of any hostility to him personally, but in order to keep the peace and mollify his chief priest. Pari sent Kumaran to talk to Thomas.

They sat at the front door of the church while women cleaned inside and masons plastered a section of the floor.

"Kumaran, he's lying," said Thomas. "I don't ask wives to leave their husbands, I *forbid* it. And who is he talking about? *Whose* family is breaking up? I haven't heard about it!"

"I understand your anger," said Kumaran. "But I'm telling you your life is in danger if you stay. It's time to go, Brother."

"Go? And leave my people to Murugavelan? What do you think would become of Christianity here?"

"Thomas, I hate him as much as you do, but—"

"I don't hate him."

"All right, you don't hate him!" Kumaran shook his head and rolled his eyes in exasperation. "We've been here over six months already—"

"And we agreed to stay until the monsoons were over. I've *work* to do here!"

"Don't be a fool. If you won't do it for your own good, then do it for me. You are putting *my* life in danger, too, if you stay!"

Thomas looked at Kumaran and tried to be patient. "For you? For you? Give up my church and the three hundred souls I've worked so hard to save—for you? Kumaran—I don't know what to say." He looked at Kumaran in utter disbelief. "Why is your life in danger anyway?" he said as an afterthought.

"Because I brought you here."

"Brought me here? We traveled together! You didn't bring me here. What are you saying?"

"The Chief thinks I brought you here."

"Then tell him the truth! And tell him his chief priest is lying!"

"But you can't deny you anoint the dead and pollute yourself, and that you refuse to honor the rites of purification prescribed by Murugavelan. And—" Kumaran paused and looked down at the ground, reluctant to say more.

"And what?"

"He implies you—you're an adulterer."

Thomas was beside himself, he did not know what to say. Finally he sputtered, "I cannot obey a priest whose gods I don't recognize! Doesn't Pari understand that? You tell me the Chief is shrewd. Then he must understand *that*." Thomas held his head with both hands as if to keep his head from vaulting off. Then, with his eyes narrowed and his brow lined with anxious sincerity, he looked up at Kumaran and said, "Adultery. Kumaran, look at me. I have *not* committed adultery. Will you tell Pari that? Will you tell him that his high priest is lying?"

"Thomas, Murugavelan is the guardian of the Sanskrit Vedas. He lives by the Vedas, every iota of it. Your word would never stand up against his. Murugavelan is revered by everyone. Without his rituals Kurinchi would fall to its enemies in a week!"

"God help you if you believe that!" said Thomas, getting up and starting to pace.

"That's what people believe here, you know that. Thomas, even if Pari believed you, what could he do? Thousands follow Murugavelan, only a few hundred you."

"My God! He is the Chief! Does he care nothing for justice? Let me talk to him! Tell him, Kumaran. Ask him. Ask him to talk to me. Will you do that? Or will that endanger your life too?"

Kumaran got up slowly. "I'll tell him."

That afternoon Kumaran came back to the church just as a marriage was being concluded. "You see," said Thomas, "I *make* families; I don't divide them."

"Pari won't see you," Kumaran said glumly.

"What?" Thomas squatted and let his head fall into his hands. For a moment he slowly shook it back and forth as he prayed, "Maranatha, Maranatha," the prayer that kept him going when all seemed lost. "Then I'm at the mercy of Murugavelan?"

"I have defended you, Thomas."

"You?" Thomas looked at Kumaran as if he found the very idea hilarious.

"Yes, me," said Kumaran, undaunted.

Thomas could not help smirking. "And what is the result of your defense?"

"You detestable bastard! I have put my life at stake and you make fun of me, you, you—you vile . . . !"

"Forgive me, Brother." With dumbfounding quickness Thomas' demeanor changed from disdainful to earnestly contrite.

Kumaran glared at Thomas, his rage unabated.

"Forgive me, Kumaran. Forgive me. I was wrong, utterly wrong. You risked your life for me and I ridiculed you. I am ashamed. Forgive me, Brother." He reached out and touched Kumaran lightly at the elbow and waited for him to regain his composure. Then he asked: "What did Pari decree?"

Kumaran, confused as always at Thomas' instant contrition and reversal of mood, stared at him for a moment. Then he answered the question, slowly, as if all feeling had been crushed out of him: "If you don't go, you will be put to the test. If you pass it, you can stay, and Murugavelan will have to make peace with you. If you fail—Pari didn't say."

"Test? What do you mean?"

"Ordeal by fire. A white-hot iron bar the size of a man's stiff penis."

Why couldn't he find peace? It must have been after midnight, and still he hadn't slept. Had he no faith in his prayer? "Father, deliver me," he had prayed over and over. "But let your will be done." Yes, that was the problem. It seemed such an easy thing for the Father to do, but Thomas knew the Father's will defied prediction. Besides, the Father answered prayers in the strangest ways. Thomas knew it was God's will that the true faith take root in Kurinchi, but he felt less than certain that he would be able to carry the white-hot bar. But it was absurd to doubt this. For if he didn't succeed, Christianity in Kurinchi was doomed, that was certain. So how could he doubt that God would work this "little miracle" for him? Logic pointed to faith.

But still he worried. He had a presentiment he had overlooked something.For a chilling instant he wondered if God was overlooking *him*. Recovering his sanity, he let himself imagine the worst. Already three of the original twelve disciples of Jesus had been martyred. Martyred. The word sounded so full of promise and glory. He could be martyred, that would be the worst that could happen. And to be martyred for Christ carried distinction. So what was there to fear? What was there to lose sleep over? Why didn't he rejoice? The worst that could happen would be that he would go to the Father and sit with the Lord at the heavenly banquet table. He tried to think of the heavenly banquet, but instead he imagined the charnel ground where criminals and enemy soldiers and the possessed were left unburied. He remembered the sickening stench and the vultures that pecked at the festering body of a thief. And martyrdom did not seem so appetizing.

"No one will know," he told himself lugubriously. "When Christians ask what happened to Thomas, they will only say he disappeared in India. There will be no story of Thomas the martyr. Thomas the doubter will be all they know." Immediately he put a stop to this unseemly meditation. As if it mattered. Wasn't he doing the will of his Master? Wouldn't they know in heaven? What did it matter if *no one* knew? His job was saving souls. Had he forgotten?

He tried to pray. "Father, receive me. I thank You and bless You for my life. You have favored me and I thank You." His heart stalled, then ventured further. "I love You, Father." But the sentiment somehow felt less than convincing, and Thomas was determined that his prayer be utterly sincere on this night. "Do I not love You, Father?" He remembered one of Kumaran's poems comparing Murugan to "a diamond rotated under sunlight." And Thomas found himself applying the metaphor to the Father: "You are my creator, my sustainer, my goal. You have all blessed qualities in unimaginable fullness. You are like a diamond rotated under sunlight."

With that prayer he beat back the doubting demons inside him and fell asleep. In his dreams he saw one face after another call out to him. The spastic orphan boy, the beggar who moved about on his back like a turned-over crab, the victims of palsy and leprosy and smallpox, the blind, the stream of lonely widows, the unhappy and despairing, the hardy seekers after life's meaning, the skeptics who wouldn't let themselves believe. In their midst Kumaran suddenly appeared, and with that Thomas woke up. He remembered the hot-iron bar, and the old fear corkscrewed through him. But what was Kumaran doing in his dream? He remembered how Kumaran accused him of pretending to love his followers without being able to truly love them. Thomas weighed the charge carefully. What did he really feel for all those people who depended on him? Love? Or did he instead love the power he had over them, the feeling of leading them to salvation? Thomas prided himself on his ability to get to the bottom of things. Always he understood what motivated him just as Kumaran never did. He could be remorseless when he spied something in himself he didn't like. And this was one of those times. Had he been fooling himself all these years? Always he had presumed that India needed saving. Now he wondered if there were something about him that needed saving. What was it? What unsettled him, what tugged at him and told him he wasn't ready to die, wasn't ready to go into the presence of God? Suddenly he remembered Nallapennu and the broken vow. What right did he have to be bitter over Murugavelan's charge of adultery? If he died, he would be getting what he deserved. He would be suffering a just fate, what all India called karma. You can escape your karma for only so long; then it catches up with you; that is what India believed. Did he believe it too? With a shudder he realized he did, that even Jesus taught something like it. Whatever consolation he had been nursing went howling into the night.

Holding the ivory pendant in his left hand, Thomas made the sign of the cross with his right. "Give me strength, Jesus my Brother, and may your will be done," he prayed as he watched the bar glow like the sun. The swollen river rushed by on his left, while on his right, lining the bank, clinging to vines and trees and shrubs, crouched hundreds of spectators, including every Christian man, woman, and child of Kurinchi. He could see them talking back and forth to each other, their faces tense and hopeful. Over the rushing of the river he vaguely made out one of the hymns he had taught them. A group waved at him, their faces bright and encouraging and full of love. He understood: They had

come to see their new faith and their new God and their high priest
formally accredited. They would never have to be ashamed of their
faith in the presence of Murugavelan and his more numerous followers; not only would they be heirs of heaven, they would be people of
consequence in their lives here and now.

Thomas studied the diagram that Murugavelan had drawn in the
sand in front of him. Two parallel rows of four circles each awaited the
fall of his feet. At the head of these circles was a ninth, where he was
to drop the bar. Eight steps with the bar in his hand, that was all. The
ninth circle, which was filled with sacred *darbha* grass, would burst
into flame at the first touch of the bar, and he would have to show that
his hands were unhurt by rubbing unhusked rice between his palms
until the grain separated. The ordeal would be passed.

Murugavelan purified each of the nine circles by smearing them
with cow dung and scattering over the sacred grass. Then he took up
a silver bowl containing water, rice, and flowers. Facing east, he held
the bowl aloft as he intoned in Sanskrit, "Glory to the three worlds!"
Successively he gave glory to eight of the Vedic deities, turning forty-five degrees after each incantation. This was followed by a prayer
addressed to the Fire God Agni: "Agni, you are the four Vedas, and as
such I offer you sacrifice. You are the countenance of all the Gods, you
are also the countenance of all learned men. You take away all our sins,
and that is why you are called pure and purifying. Purify me from all
my sins, and if this man who is about to undergo this ordeal is truly
innocent, do him no harm."

Then Thomas was made to step up in front of the circles. "O Agni,
come near! Come near and stay here! Stay here!" the priest chanted.
Then with tongs he took up the bar, glowing red orange at the blunt
end and white at the tip, and said, "O Agni, you know the secrets of
men! Reveal the truth to us now!"

With a prayer for help whirring through his head, Thomas held out
the hands that earlier on that same morning had broken the bread of
Jesus' body and healed the sick bodies they prayed over. As he cupped
them together, outwardly strong and steady, so very much the hands of
a priest, he tried desperately to place all his trust in the Father. Murugavelan dropped the bar.

Thomas took one step, two, three, then wildly threw his hands apart
and screamed from the bottom of his throat. He ran to the river and
almost threw himself in hands first. He lay on the sand and moaned
pathetically, his hands stretched out in front of him in the rushing cold

water. Not even the agony of seared flesh could silence the agony in his heart: his church, his mission, all his hopes doomed. He had failed God. As warriors with spears led him away, he wept bitterly.

The next day at dawn ten men led him away clad in only a loin cloth. Women lined the path out of the city and wailed as he passed. One ran up and hung a wreath of flowers around his neck. Another knelt shrieking and pulling her hair in front of him and had to be removed by the soldiers. A third gave him a few palm leaves—a letter— wrapped in a rag. He looked at those who loved him and waved feebly with his bandaged hands. Where he was going he did not know, but he hoped it was home to be with Jesus. He was not cut out for this world.

The warriors with their bows and arrows and machetes at the belt led him deep into the jungle. He didn't know why they didn't just put him to death where they were. The clouds hung low and thick over the mountains, and he had only a vague idea which direction they were going in. They forded streams and followed tiger trails across ravines and over ridges. They walked all day, stopping only to eat and drink. Several of the soldiers cursed Thomas as they crashed ahead through the tangle of creepers and brush or slipped on moss off the path into a swollen stream. Again he wondered why they didn't kill him at once. He asked them, but they wouldn't say. He didn't care anyway. The people he loved had been taken from him. Their new faith, just on the point of taking hold in their hearts, would be uprooted and their souls lost. The sacred scrolls of the Bible that kept his religion, his sacred home-land, and his people fresh in his mind would be burned like chaff. The palm leaves on which he was translating the Torah into Tamil would be inserted into a crack in someone's roof to repair a leak. No, he didn't care anymore, or so he told himself. But as the day wore on, and still he lived, faint bat squeaks of hope echoed through the black despair in his heart, and his mind turned to Madurai. He wondered if God might not yet be done with him. Perhaps he was wasting precious time among the tribesmen; their influence would not travel far, whereas Madurai was the hub of an empire. Was the Father freeing him from a lesser duty so he could assume a greater? He began to hope again.

But a new darkness enveloped him as the afternoon progressed. He had been naive once—at Muziri—but no longer. "Thy will be done," he prayed with numbing monotony. What else could he pray? But even as he prayed, the words had no real meaning. The truth was that Thomas feared God's will as much as he loved it. It mocked his own will, which he thought he had given to God. If the world were run according to

God's answers to his prayers, the sun would rise in the east one morning, in the west the next. There was no discoverable law that governed that thing called "God's will." It was a wild beast, a will-o'-the-wisp, a forgery. People everywhere used it to excuse their treachery. It mocked the saint's most earnest prayer.

Late in the afternoon, as the clouds cleared off and thin shafts of sunlight cut through the dense tree cover, they came to a stone marker on the path. The soldiers picked Thomas up, swung him back and forth, and threw him with curses into a thorny clump of wild lantana on the other side of the marker. As he lay in the middle of fragile pink and yellow blossoms, they warned him never to set foot in Pari's territory again or he would be slain on sight. As they turned to go, one of the men, the last, furtively threw him a chunk of boar meat.

Thomas lay for a moment in the prickly bush and hardly breathed. Were they really letting him go? Would life really go on? He waited until he heard only the usual jungle sounds—the squawks of birds, a monkey squealing, a boar grunting. Suddenly he felt a kind of savage joy that he was still alive. He tore at the meat and ate it in six swallows. For a moment he felt an inexplicable love for the jungle with its beasts and trees. All were beautiful and lovable because he was alive. A primordial passion for life filled his breast. Then for some reason it gave way to a different emotion: He was once again a little boy roving the Galilean hills, the intimate, benign hills of home, with his dog Mitzvah, a gift from his mother, the whore. But reality set in again, and he couldn't escape thinking of the people he had failed, who had trusted him, who were certain he would come through the ordeal in triumph, who depended on "God's will" to be done. Then he noticed that the ivory cross that had hung around his neck since his Parthia days was missing. In a panic he looked around him in the lantana bush. He pushed aside several of its prickly branches and looked more closely. Nothing. He tried to remember when he last noticed it around his neck, but couldn't. Had he lost it back in Kurinchi? He had received blows. Had someone ripped it off his neck? He realized it was lost, gone forever, and a feeling of desolation overcame him. Still clutching the letter the woman had placed in his hand, he pried his way out of the lantana bush.

He made his way to a hunter's hamlet, and there he was clothed and fed and sheltered for the night. A servant was even called in to salve his hands with an herbal concoction. In a room with three children he slept through the night without waking once. The next morning he found the way to the main road leading to Madurai. As he set out through the jungle with only the hunter's instructions to guide him and only enough food to get him to the next village by nightfall, he remembered the letter on palm leaf he still hadn't read. He was still holding it. He knew what kind of a letter it was, and he was sure he knew who wrote it: The widow Rangamma, devout Rangamma was the only one of his converts who could write. He took it out of his pouch, braced himself against the bitterness or desolation he expected to find, and untied the string. The message was scrawled across two leaves in large letters, but the hand wasn't Rangamma's:

Wait for me where the road to Madurai crosses the Vaigai. I will bring your baggage on the mule. You will survive. Do not lose heart. There are other worlds to conquer. Kumaran.

He couldn't believe it. He had assumed he would never see Kumaran again. He had barely thought of him the past two days, and he was amazed that Kumaran should be thinking of him in his disgrace. Kumaran still with him? It was too good to be true. Never before had he realized how loyal Kumaran was. He would not have guessed it, but there it was. It braced him. It seemed almost Christian. And the thought of his Torah scroll, the translation project, the words of Jesus that he wrote down when he remembered something the Master said so long ago, the Tamil-Greek dictionary he had begun—the whole thick wad of palm leaves weighing as much as ten coconuts—all safe with Kumaran! He could hardly believe it.

He came upon a small herd of deer at the next turn of the path. They jumped clear, and he walked on with a bounce in his step.

By sunset of the fifth day he reached the Vaigai snaking through the foothills just above the great plain spread out below. The first thing he recognized was the mule, and his heart jumped with joy. Then he saw Kumaran in the middle of a troop of minstrels—someone was playing the *yal*. "Kumaran! Brother!" he yelled. Except for Jesus on that miraculous dawn in Jerusalem twenty-eight years before, he had never been so glad to see anyone.

"Thomas!" Kumaran shouted. He jumped up from his seat on the ground, ran to Thomas, and looked him over. His liquid eyes danced, and his laughter was a titter of nervous excitement. "How like a Maravar you look!" he said. "You lack only a bow and quiver! I knew you would survive. I knew it!"

"How could you be so sure?" Thomas was laughing and pounding Kumaran with rough affection on the arms just below the shoulders as Kumaran laughed his high-pitched, rakish laugh. "It is good to *see* you! How goes it with you?"

But Kumaran didn't answer. Instead he turned around to the minstrels and said, "Didn't I tell you? Pay up! Pay up!" Then he turned back to Thomas and said with an impish grin, "They doubted your God's power."

"They what?" Thomas stared back without understanding.

"I bet you would make it," Kumaran tittered. "I bet on your Father! Do you see how much confidence I have in him?"

"Your confidence wasn't misplaced, you lovable old heathen," Thomas answered with happy tears welling up in his eyes as he playfully patted his old friend once on the cheek. "And are my manuscripts safe?"

"If only you had half so much confidence in my Murugan!" Kumaran teased. "How like a Maravar you look!" he teased again as he looked Thomas over. "Look at you! And, yes, I have your manuscripts. Would a poet forget those?"

"Kumaran! I love you! I do love you!" He had never seen Kumaran so beautiful and charming, and all his work was saved.

That night Thomas submitted to the detailed inquiries of a professional storyteller: Kumaran insisted on knowing everything. And Thomas told him the whole story: the march through the jungle, the warrior throwing him the piece of boar meat, the lost medallion, the overnight stay with the woodsman's family, the surprise at reading Kumaran's letter, the long, hungry walk to the Vaigai.

Kumaran listened to it all with acute attention. But it was the letter that interested him most. "What did you feel when you read that letter?" he asked.

"Disbelief."

"And were you pleased?"

"Very pleased."

"Why?"

"Why? Well, of course, because we would be reunited."

"Not because of the manuscripts?"

"Well, that too, Brother."

"But the thought of being reunited really pleased you?" Kumaran persisted.

"Well, of course it did, Brother! After what we've been through together? Of course it did!"

"And it pleased you more than the thought of the manuscripts?"

"Brother, what is this that you say?" Thomas laughed as he reached out and touched Kumaran affectionately on the arm.

Kumaran sighed and seemed satisfied.

PART IV: MADURAI

24. Ascetic and Debauchee

Madurai, home of the Sangam, the great and ancient acade-my of Tamil learning, was for Kumaran what Jerusalem was for Thomas. Its high priests of taste and convention were as powerful and dominant as the priests, rabbis, and elders who made up the Sanhedrin in Jerusalem. Madurai was a city with traditions so ancient that its symbol was a fish, an artifact from the legendary days when the Pandyan capital stood on the seacoast. It was here that Kumaran meant to make a name for himself among his fellow poets; their admiration and acceptance were as important to him as the King's.

Thomas and Kumaran crossed the flat bushland west of Madurai, their eyes riveted on the spot where they had last seen the city's out-line through a clearing in the low trees. Kumaran vented his expansive mood. "They'll marvel at the strange places I've seen. And now I know the jungle. They can't hold that over me!" But at the same time he won-dered if he had the technical skills to please the great Sangam's arbiters of taste. If not, then he would stay in Madurai until he mastered every scintilla of convention and good taste. "Your mission be damned—I'll stay forever if I have to!" he told Thomas playfully. But not too play-fully. Kumaran was as determined as ever to immortalize his name in the Land of the Gods. He even wondered out loud if in the next life he might become a god worshipped by later generations of poets.

Thomas, leading the ass laden with Kumaran's baggage, including the gold lotus given Kumaran by Pari, followed behind. Kumaran could tell there wasn't much cheer in Thomas' heart as they approached the famous city with its high ramparts and waving standards. But Kumaran saw in Thomas' eyes the same determination as of old, only quieter, more pensive, perhaps less burning, certainly humbler.

"I've learned from my mistakes," Thomas said earlier in the day. "Madurai will not be another Muziri. Or Kurinchi."

Kumaran realized his friend had put his failures behind him.

"I'll live outside the walls with the hermits and sages. My outward life will be like theirs, even excel theirs. I'll be indistinguishable from the most superstitious brahmin. They won't be able to find fault with me. Then they will listen to me. You'll see. They will listen."

In his own way, Kumaran thought, Thomas, too, was trying to perfect his style, his technique. The difference was that Kumaran's medium was the words he wrote, while Thomas' was his life.

"I haven't worked hard enough," Thomas went on. "I haven't sacrificed everything for God. I haven't taken up the Master's cross. Now, at last, with the grace of God, I am ready."

But Kumaran could tell Thomas was apprehensive all the same; he was afraid of a new failure. And well he might be. There were obvious difficulties with the plan.

"You'll have to cook your own food, Brother, and according to all their rules, hire a brahmin servant. Do you know what you're letting yourself in for?"

"Ah, I hadn't thought of that," said Thomas in that strange new humble tone of his.

For a while longer they walked along as the city got closer. "Don't worry, Thomas," Kumaran chuckled, "I'll come over and clean your house from time to time. A pulaiyar is allowed to do that!"

But Thomas didn't laugh at Kumaran's joke, for he was hatching a new plan. Less than a mile outside Madurai's walls, as they began to mix with the carts and palanquins and elephants going in and out of the city, Thomas told Kumaran he would pass himself off to society as a member of the raja caste, the political caste, just under the brahmin, and follow all their customs. He knew many of the great sages had been rajas, even the Buddha. "Besides," he said, "my step-father, Joseph, was descended from King David, the greatest raja of Israel. Brother, I can call myself a raja in good faith." He wore a look of bemused satisfaction. And for once, Kumaran thought, Thomas was shrewd. Very shrewd.

Though the sun burned down from straight above them when they reached the gate, Kumaran set out to earn merit and the blessings of the Gods by circumambulating the city. On the way he learned that a certain landmark off in the distance was the famous Mount Podi-yil, home of the great Agastya. In his childhood Kumaran had heard of this immortal sage who was born in a water jar, wrote some of the Vedic hymns, swallowed the ocean, forced the Vindhya Mountains to prostrate themselves in front of him, and civilized the South. His flesh tingled as he imagined Agastya meditating under Podiyil's groves. For a moment he thought he saw a purple light glowing on its summit.

As he came up on the swollen Vaigai flowing along the city's north-east boundary, he saw where Thomas would be living. There in a spa-cious grove of great *maruda* trees between the moat and the river lived the brahmins who chanted their Vedas and kept their fires going, the Buddhist and Jain monks who lived and taught the dharma of their re-spective religions, and the vanaprasthas, including a few rajas, bent on eternal release. Under each tree stood two or three makeshift thatch huts or lean-tos. Chipmunks, each with three stripes, the gift of Rama when in the dim past the great God stroked one with his fingers, scur-ried over the sand and grass.

But all was not well in Madurai. As Kumaran completed the circuit past piers where flat-bottom boats, used as ferries during the rainy sea-son, were tied, then on past a beautiful garden district studded with elegant, high, copper-colored mansions and ponds and coconut groves full of birds, a humped bull urinated in three streams directly in his path. The bull looked at Kumaran with a dirty eye that trickled, and Kumaran thought he saw in that look a demon. He hurried around the bull and tried to put it out of mind, but he had the uneasy sense he had seen some omen of great evil, either for the city or for him personally.

But that evil, whatever it might be, was quickly forgotten when Thom-as and Kumaran passed through the Western Gate emblazoned with Lakshmi, Goddess of Fortune. The plan of the city reminded them both of Muziri: the same noble houses, the same market scenes, the same displays of military might. Even here, far from the sea and the great yavana boats, yavanas guarded the King's palace, just as in Muziri. But the foliage, the customs of dress, and the climate were different. Com-pared to Muziri's lush terrain, Madurai's was almost barren. The rainy season was at its height, and the wide river, swollen with rains from the mountains, snaked along the city's edge. But the trees grew much less densely than in the mountains, and the paddy fields around the city were nourished mostly by river water passing through irrigation canals rather than local rainfall. But the dress, the sophisticated hair styles, the decorative facial paint, and the very carriage and expression of the women suggested a culture which lacked nothing, neither materially nor artistically. Many maidens wore red veils—Kumaran found them seductive—embroidered with flowers around their hips, and even the lower castes aped the aristocrats in their coiffure, which consisted of five braids down the back. As in Muziri, the wives and children of the rich sat on the high terraces of their cliff-like mansions, but there was less hubbub and noise on the streets below them than in Muziri. As for the men, their custom was to wear garlands of *neem* branches with their tiny, sweetly scented cream-colored flowers, and not the gaudy red *ashoka* so popular in Muziri. Kumaran thought this symbolic of Madurai's greater refinement and subtler pleasures. A peculiarity of the city was its protective deity. Called simply "the Goddess," her half-blue, half-golden body, fish-shaped eyes, and coral lips over shining white teeth greeted the visitor at almost every intersection. Otherwise the Gods were the same, with Shiva and Murugan more prominent than Vishnu, Balarama, and numerous others.

During their first few weeks in the city, Kumaran followed Thomas' transformation with interest. Thomas began almost at once to live the outward life of an ascetic, a sannyasin, apparently renouncing the pleasures of the world and making a bee-line for eternal liberation in the Indian manner. He built a crude hut out of sticks and palm leaves and called it his hermitage. Every week he plastered the floor with a concoction of water and cow dung, just as any high-born Tamil might have. He wore only a scanty orange loin cloth, symbol of voluntary poverty, and sandals to prevent his feet from being defiled. He adorned his forehead with red sandal paste and hung drab copper rings from his ears, which he had pierced. For a while he even wore the sacred thread of his new caste—a single strand of flax looped over his left shoulder and tied together at his right thigh. This he modified by attaching to it a small wooden fish, one of the symbols of his faith (but also of the Pandyan Kingdom), at the level of his chest. He carried a bamboo staff of seven joints and acquired a water gourd and an antelope's skin. He was careful not to sit on his haunches while he ate or to allow his eyes to rest on a woman. Although it troubled his conscience, he avoided all contact with outcastes, for there would have been nothing more defiling in the eyes of the brahmins than that. He gave up meat, fish, and eggs, and ate only one meal a day consisting of rice, milk, and vegetables—always on a banana leaf, and in such immense quantities that Kumaran dubbed him "the rhino saint." Since he didn't know how to cook approved curries, Thomas hired (with donations from curious pilgrims) a brahmin cook for several weeks until he learned. When he drank, he was careful not to touch his lips to the gourd for fear of contaminating it with his saliva. After finishing his meal, with his scarred left hand—the one that held the scalding bar longest—he poured out water from the gourd onto his right to wash it. In every way, except the color of his skin—and even this gradually became brown under the fiery sun of Madurai's balky summer monsoon—he blended in with the community of ascetics on the banks of the sacred Vaigai.

He was the talk of the city from almost the day he arrived. People did not now come to the ascetics' quarters to see the blind sannyasin who stood without moving for hours staring at the sun, or the penitent chained for life to a tree, or the saint who had taken a vow to keep his hands outstretched to God for the rest of his life and had to be fed, or the man buried alive with only a small hole and a hollow reed connecting him to life, or the pilgrims who had journeyed to the banks of the Vaigai on their bellies and resembled crabs as they navigated over the sands. They did not come to see the devotee who lived in a tree and hopped about in imitation of Hanuman, the monkey-God, and whose spine (it was said) had begun to protrude at its base as if growing a tail. They came to see, as Kumaran wrote in his notes, the "yavana sannyasin."

Although nearing thirty when he and Thomas walked through Madurai's gates for the first time, Kumaran felt like an innocent, big-eyed boy. Only with difficulty did he think of himself as a man in the same way he had thought of his father at thirty. Kumaran supposed the seeds of manhood had been planted in him, but they hadn't matured. In a way he hoped they never would. Life had been festive from the time he met Thomas on the boat in the Great Sea. Such buoyancy he had never seen in his father except when he was drunk, but he, Kumaran, the "Poet of the West," was drunk on something else.

Not even the birth of his daughter, announced in a letter that awaited him at the Sangam, impressed him with the sober duty of manhood. Perhaps it would have been otherwise if the baby had been a boy, but it was not; so Kumaran postponed going back to Maliankara to fetch Devandi and the baby. Maruthanar, an accomplished pulaiyar poet who rented him a room in his house in Madurai's jeweler's district, told him he was making a mistake. "No one can remain chaste in this city," he warned. But not even the memory of Devandi's bewitching smile on that last rainy afternoon could lure Kumaran away. So he delayed, and delayed some more.

Meanwhile the poets at the Sangam were turning his head with their attention. Many of them were better stylists than he, but they did not seem to mind, for they were hungry for his knowledge of the West. Seminars were set up, and he became a kind of guru. Within six months of his arrival he was a celebrity, and almost every night he read his poetry and told stories in the great houses of the city. He was paid with fine jewels: cloudless green emeralds, cat's-eyes mounted on gold frames, rubies called "red lotuses," pink and white pearls from Korkai, sapphires, crystals, opals, even jades from some place named Cathay. One day an invitation from the King arrived.

Maruthanar again warned Kumaran: "No king is faithful to one wife, but King Nediyon is another matter. He is a voluptuary through and through. And he will like nothing better than to make you one too. Take care, Kumaran!"

Two Greek bodyguards as tall as Thomas led Kumaran past turbaned ministers and dandies with wreaths in their hair into the very bedroom of the King. Kumaran's first sight of him was on a mammoth bed buried in brocaded pillows and festooned with flowers. Strings of pearls hung across his bare chest, and a fresh green garland of *neem* leaves crowned his head. He wore bracelets and golden rings inlaid with sparkling gems, and above his bed was the sacred emblem of his reign, a stainless white parasol, as if to suggest his throne was his bed.

And so it was. As he conferred with his counselors and made the weighty decisions of state, charging his generals to form a confederacy with the Cheras or discussing tax policy with his Chancellor of the Exchequer, young women spread out in various postures across the bed chattered and cooed among themselves like contented pigeons. None was older than twenty, yet they were all fully nubile, with fair skin the tint of mango shoots, glittering ear pendants hanging low, beauty marks of sandal paste on their breasts, and red dye painted on the bottoms of their feet. King Nediyon, Commander-in-Chief of the Pandyan Kingdom, Controller of the Weather, Fructifier of the Soil, Beloved of the Gods! It was a preposterous and bizarre sight, this mixing of statecraft with the intimacies of the bed. Kumaran was astounded.

Still standing in the door awaiting announcement, Kumaran studied the King's eyes as they moved under debauched, half-closed lids. He noted the oily complexion, the over-large mouth and puffy cheeks, the belly bulging under a crimson tunic. Kumaran decided he looked like a beast he had once seen in the Roman amphitheater—a hippopotamus.

If the contours of a noble lineage had ever marked his face, they had not survived the ravages of a steady diet of feasting and sex.

"Is that the poet?" he said suddenly, looking up and pointing to Kumaran? One of his counselors was in the middle of a sentence, but Nediyon was not to be distracted for a second from his pleasures. Resembling a vulture which has just discovered a fresh, especially piquant piece of meat, he grinned hungrily at Kumaran: "So you are to entertain me this morning? You are the famous poet from the yavana lands? Come closer, do not be shy, boy. Leave me, everyone, you bore me!" Cheered by his rudeness, he cackled.

Everyone left except the "pigeons"—seven of them—who eyed Kumaran discreetly and tittered as, at the King's command, he climbed stealthily onto the gold and crimson bedcovers and took his seat at the foot of the great bed. He had brought his collection of palm-leaf and parchment manuscripts in a pouch, and the bodyguards had placed them on the bed beside him before leaving the room. He began to read.

"Read some more," the King said testily after a description of the Parthenon in Athens.

So Kumaran read some more. And some more.

"Marvelous! Marvelous!" the King interrupted as Kumaran described the slaughter of the Roman games.

When Kumaran finished, the King clapped his hands vigorously, and the women put down their fans and clapped too. The King called back to a caged monkey, and the little beast started turning flips in its cage.

Throughout the reading the King had stopped Kumaran and questioned him not only about the subject matter but the metaphors and poetic technique. This totally unexpected turn of events delighted Kumaran. Had he misjudged the King? Was Nediyon really as boorish and dissolute as he looked? Was it possible everyone misunderstood him? Perhaps here was a man born to be a poet himself, a frustrated artist laden with throne and scepter. Of all the poets who listened to Kumaran read his poems—everyone resident in the Sangam—only Maruthanar, his friend and fellow pulaiyar, had admired his metaphors and similes as much as the content. And now it was the King who paid him this compliment. When pleased with a metaphor or sound, his eyes blazed out of his puffy face as if he were a resuscitated corpse, and he sat up on his cushion with his spine as straight as a novice yogi's. His face was almost handsome. Had Kumaran misjudged him?

Kumaran became a regular visitor to the King. During one of these visits near the onset of the hot season, when Kumaran had been in

Madurai for nine months, he departed from his usual themes of love, the affairs of state, and the strange lands of the far west. This time his theme was none other than Thomas—not Thomas the missionary of an awkward, misfit religion, but Thomas the exotic yavana adventurer and miracle worker.

"Stupendous!" the King exploded the moment Kumaran finished. "This Thomas, this yavana—he is a real person?"

"Yes, Sire, he's an ascetic living on the banks of the Vaigai," said Kumaran, relieved the King had enjoyed the experiment.

"Our own Vaigai? Here in Madurai?"

"Have you ever heard of the one they call the 'yavana sannyasin'?"

"*That* fellow! The one who swam all night in the ocean?" The King's eyebrows climbed halfway up his forehead.

"The very same."

"You must *bring* him to me, Kumaran. Do you know him well?"

"Rather well."

"Kumaran, beautiful boy, of all the poems I have heard you read, this pleases me the most, I swear it by the Gods! But did he really swim in the ocean all night? You made this up!"

"No, I swear it on oath. I was awake when he dragged himself onto the beach. Besides, he never lies, and that is how he tells it."

"Never lies?" The King looked at Kumaran with incredulity. "Never?"

"Not that I know of," said Kumaran sheepishly, shrugging his shoulders.

"Well, then, he might make good sport for us, heh heh." The King fidgeted. Perhaps he felt threatened by the prospect of so much virtue keeping company with so much manhood. "*I'll* get a lie out of him!"

"I'm certain you will," Kumaran lied.

"Well, I'll have to meet this yavana sannyasin and welcome him to Madurai officially," said the King. "Can you bring him to me?"

"I—would be delighted to—but—he might not come," Kumaran stuttered. "And if he does, you will get an earful of his religion. That is all he cares about."

"He would dare lecture *me?*" The King began to cackle again in that deranged way of his, then played at being indignant. "Surely not, my dear Kumaran. Could he be that stupid? But then he is a yavana. Who can say what a yavana will not do? Religion, you say? How tasteless."

"He would dare to lecture anyone, Your Majesty."

"Then throw him to the dogs!" said the King in his grandest style, a broad lascivious smile replacing his frown. "Who needs him? You are here. You, my dark pulaiyar boy! You and your stories. Is the world ever so good in reality as you make it out to be?"

Kumaran looked at the King uneasily. There was something profoundly sinister and crazed about Nediyon's expression. Half of his face smiled while the other half did not: his mobile mouth and flabby lips were pulled back in a ridiculous grin while his eyes stared at him with the gravity of an executioner.

"Kumaran, come . . . come to me. Sit beside me. Here," he said in a hushed, secretive voice.

Kumaran's mind went blank.

"Come, come, dear boy!"

His head swimming, Kumaran crawled across the great down mattress and sat next to the King of the Pandyan Empire under the Royal Parasol. The King's hand stole over Kumaran's shoulders and gripped his bare elbow.

"How you delight me, Kumaran! Do you know that?" he purred, his body sweating as it gave off a scent of perfume blended with its natural odor. "Will you stay with me in Madurai—stay with me forever? I don't intend to die, ha ha ha!"

He laughed deliriously, then kissed Kumaran with that horrid mouth of his, that great hippopotamus' mouth that could swallow you from nose to chin. He did not kiss his prey, he ate them. He was as carnivorous in love as he was in battle. Kumaran shuddered.

If there was ever a time for Kumaran to leave Madurai, to go back to Maliankara and fetch his family, this was it. He had a ready excuse, and not even the King could have objected. But he did not go. He found the King repulsive, but he continued to let himself be flattered, to read to him, to accept his gifts, and, yes, share the pleasures of his bed. He dreaded the times when he was his pleasure, but much more often there were women, and on these occasions Kumaran got, as a reward for a good reading, one of the "pigeons."

For a long time the mother bird of Kumaran's karma had not left her roost, and the eggs of his destiny were warm with her brooding, but not yet hatched. A little more time, a little more time, and then? Does karma have a shape, as the Jains say? Is it sculpted by the Gods out of some invisible ethereal substance? Is its shape even recognizable? Or is it not quite visible in the dim candlelight of our soul's still center—is it something so close to us that it both defines us and obscures us from ourselves?

These were a few of the thoughts that Kumaran toyed with in his spare time. Looking back over the last three and a half years, he felt there was something inexorable about the march of events since he met Thomas. At first he told himself he might have at any point altered his destiny by a simple yea or nay—so it would seem to an outsider. But was it really so? If he had never met Thomas, his whole life would have been different, of that he was sure. If he had said no to Thomas on the great boat, again it would have been different. The same could be said about every other decision he had made since. Or could it? Or could it? Was the precise predicament in which he found himself the fruit of chance encounters or the collective fury of the Gods? And if the latter, how could he be said to be free? He looked into the dark corners of his soul, he strained to see; but all he could see, glimmering and ominous, was Thomas' brooding face. There was only one way to escape its censure: He told himself he did not become, in Madurai, what he was. Instead, what he already was, though long hidden from himself, simply became apparent. There was nothing he could do to alter his destiny.

But then the King gave him Madari, a kidnapped fifteen-year-old brahmin virgin. Could the Gods have conjured a liaison so bizarre and improbable? What action in a past life could have produced such a karma? Wasn't life merely a chance event, a senseless dice throw on a warped gaming table? It seemed so to Kumaran on the first anniversary of his arrival in Madurai.

25. The Trial

Thomas' hut stood at the base of an immense dogbane tree branchless until halfway up the trunk—a tree shunned by other ascetics because it had no holy associations and provided so little protection from the sun's fierce rays. Under this tree, either within or outside of his hut, Thomas spent much of his time. Sometimes he sang hymns about Jesus or his Father or what he called the "Religion of Truth"; he always sang in simple Tamil and in the correct meter. Sometimes he composed sermons while seated in the half-lotus position in the doorway of his hut. A sketch in the sand announced the time of the sermon and asked for quiet as he worked. At other times he received guests, and they would sit under the tree in front of the hut and ask about his religion or recommend their own. Always he told them he came from a royal family in faraway Judaea, a land that none of them had heard of, and that for some time now he had been living the celibate life of a sannyasin. He accepted gifts, in the Indian manner, as long as they weren't defiling. He taught what he called the "special Veda": God is one; He is creator and sovereign (Thomas used the Sanskrit term "Sarveshvara," "Lord of the Universe"); He is the loving Father of all men, of the lowly pulaiyar as well as the brahmin; He sent Jesus the Christ, the Savior, to lead all men to Him; He does not demand super-human stints of yoga or brutal austerities for salvation; He holds out salvation after a single lifetime to any who love Him, accept Jesus as Messiah, and live the gospel of love, forgiveness, and purity taught by Jesus. About hell, Thomas had learned to say nothing.

The people who heard the yavana sannyasin were impressed by his mastery of their language and the depth of his knowledge. Even brahmins who at first spat as they passed by the "barbarian pretender" or said a prayer to protect themselves from a bad omen, now came to hear him speak. He began to baptize several disciples at a time, first only pulaiyars, then their families, then a fellow raja. This raja, Shivabala, was the first member of a high-born caste that Thomas baptized in Madurai. Thomas did not ask Shivabala to change his name, drop his caste, or remove the ash from his forehead and chest. He sought only a change of heart, and Shivabala gave him this. Gradually Thomas became widely acknowledged not only as the "yavana sannyasin," but as the "raja sannyasin," white skin and all. Some people addressed him as "Aiyer," "Master of the House," and referred to him as "Tattuva Bodhakar," "Teacher of Reality." Others called him simply "the holy man." He had not only been accepted; by many he had come to be revered—some addressed him as "Guru." Others knelt at his feet as they greeted him, and Thomas, understanding the custom, did not discourage them.

Thomas had no contempt for any man. He was largely free of the prejudice that marks the high-born Indian. But at first he kept aloof. Then, as he grew to be accepted, he dropped his aloofness and began to mingle warmly with the people, even accepting invitations to their homes. As his Master had taught him, he laughed with those who laughed and wept with those who wept. This was unheard of for a holy man, for whom the world's joys and sorrows were supposed to be as insubstantial as mist. But Thomas wanted souls for Christ more than a reputation for holiness, and he knew how practical a virtue compassion was. It was not that he did not really feel compassion for the sheep of his steadily growing flock; he did feel it. But his zeal to save souls towered over every other emotion, even love. He pictured many Vaigais, many cities; and all of them—all races, castes, and language groups— were thronged with Christians singing praises to the True God, breaking and eating the body of the risen Master, loving their neighbors and forgiving their enemies. He saw the ivy of his faith spreading north in a great V with Madurai at the base, spreading and spreading until it covered the whole of India. He was secretly thrilled by his success.

One day three brahmins jealous of Thomas broke in on him as he preached under his tree to a small group of disciples, including one of their own caste. The men waved the crowd away, took their seats without observing any of the courtesies of greeting, and began to question him.

"Do you believe," said the first, tall and lean and wearing a scowl across his velvety bronze face, "that God resides in all men or in only a few?"

"All men may know him," said Thomas as his pulse quickened, "the Indian as certainly as the Jew, the pulaiyar as certainly as the brahmin."

"Why are some men born in low castes and others in high?" said the second, a saintly looking man with a body that bent over and twisted at the waist.

"The reasons are beyond knowing," Thomas said with proper formality. "Consider the human body. It consists of many parts. Each is necessary, although some are higher than others. So it is with men. Kings are like the head of the body; artisans and farmers are like the hands; the lowest classes are like the feet."

"And brahmins?"

"They are like the soul."

"It is said you know Sanskrit and study the Vedas, yet you are only a yavana. Do you not consider this blasphemy?" said the third, an erudite toothless man with a long sideways scar on his throat which suggested someone had once tried to cut it.

"I am a raja, a member of a twice-born caste, and you are brahmins. We are equally God's sons. God wants us to discover truth wherever we may. Where in the Vedas does it say a raja should not read scripture? Is it not true that some of the greatest Vedic teachers were rajas? Even the Buddha?"

The three brahmins huddled and whispered to each other, then turned back around to Thomas. "What constitutes a good work?" said the tall man. "What kind of act merits heaven?"

"Good works," Thomas said, "are of two types. There are those performed by people who do not know God. These acts are good in themselves but do not merit heaven, for God does not take notice of them. The same works performed by one who knows God do merit heaven, for God notices these works and is pleased with them."

"Do you believe," asked the second brahmin, "that pilgrimages to the Ganges, baths, anointings, giving alms to brahmins, and all the other ceremonies sacred to brahmins are pleasing to God?"

"In themselves they are of no value at all."

The brahmins had heard enough. Each got up without looking again at Thomas, and the tall one spat contemptuously on the ground. Thomas took no offense.

Several days went by, and Thomas continued to teach, to baptize, and to study the Vedas under the direction of a brahmin named Nakkirar.

As yet, none of Madurai's brahmins had received baptism; most of Thomas' followers were pulaiyars. But his tutor, the young brahmin Nakkirar, had come under the spell of the new religion. He said he was deeply impressed by the clarity and simplicity of Thomas' faith. He was hungry for baptism.

Then one day the three brahmins walked up to his hut. "You are summoned to stand trial for insulting the holy caste of the brahmin priesthood," said the tall man, their leader.

Nakkirar had warned him this might happen. Thomas knew if convicted he could be exiled from the city, have his eyes gouged out, or be put to death. Madurai's brahmin community had the authority to pass sentence without applying to the King.

"I welcome the chance to tell you about my faith," he replied bravely."You will not get the chance. Nakkirar will defend you."

Thomas stared back at the tall brahmin as if undaunted and wished them Godspeed, then withdrew into the shadows of his hut. Nakkirar? He thought of his pupil's weak voice. Nakkirar? But with God all things were possible; how many times he had heard Jesus say that. But Nakkirar? Thomas looked at his hands and saw the scars from the hot iron bar he had carried for three steps in Kurinchi. Would Madurai be another Kurinchi? Would all his precautions, all the sacrifices he had made come to nothing? The old ghosts of doubt and despair numbed his bones, and all he could do was repeat, for hours on end, his Aramaic mantra, "Maranatha, Maranatha."

Over five-hundred brahmins gathered round a low platform under an ancient blooming tamarind tree in the assembly ground at the center of Madurai's brahmin quarters. All except those who were crippled sat in the lotus position, some in the shade under the tree, some on the outer edge in the sunlight. Each brahmin was naked from the waist up except for the sacred cord, a thin triple strand of white cotton that hung over the left shoulder and gleamed against a bronze torso. Each had shaved his beard and head except for a thick wad of hair gathered up at the topmost point of the head. Each dangled a water gourd over his shoulder for drinking and cleaning, held a bamboo staff to defend against evil spirits, and wore sandals to protect his feet from defilement. Some held umbrellas over their heads to accentuate their dignity and keep the sun off.

On the outskirts of this assembly of God-chosen men, cows lay about and lowed languidly in the heat. In every corner of the square, black-skinned pulaiyars gathered to wait on the pleasure of their brown-skinned brahmin masters. Laughing children scampered about wearing necklaces of monkeys' bones; some of the boys still had long curls while others wore their hair in tufts. On balconies chaste brahmin wives stood about in their colorful attire, their breasts covered by silk or cotton cloths which draped over their shoulders. They wore earrings, golden anklets, and flowers in their hair. They chatted among themselves or called out shrill orders to their children below, who somehow managed to play games with balls and dibstones in the crowd.

Kumaran, dressed incognito in an ordinary loin cloth, stood in a group of pulaiyar servants waiting in the shade of a "sleeping tree." Thomas picked him out of the crowd and saluted him with a glance. He marveled that Kumaran, the King's favorite poet, should be in attendance at all, much less as a lowly servant. He wondered what was behind Kumaran's loyalty. "Why is he drawn to me? Why not to my religion?" Thomas did not know. But he did know he was glad to see Kumaran. His eyes moistened as he recalled their first meeting, the language lessons on the Nile, the times in the desert sleeping under the moon. But then he looked around him at the crowd, the brahmins seating themselves, all the things that told him he was on alien ground. He pictured his daughters back in Galilee and tried to imagine the grandchildren he had never met. He wondered if he would ever meet them. He reminded himself everything hung on the will of God. But that thought brought little comfort, for God's will had decreed his disgrace at Muziri and—he looked down at his hands—Kurinchi. Though he had never put words around the feelings in his heart, he had learned to fear that thing called "God's will." What was the use of praying for something? Wouldn't events turn out the same whether one prayed or not? More and more "Thy will be done" had become Thomas' only petitionary prayer; what other prayer made as much sense?

At last everyone was seated in his proper place, the Gods invoked, and eight pieces of the *villi* tree dipped in a mixture of butter and rice thrown into the sacred fire as an offering to the Goddess of Virtue.

"Read the charge," said the chief brahmin, an indignant, forceful old man who sat straight and cross-legged on a low stool at the back of the platform near the tree's trunk.

One of the three brahmins who had examined Thomas was the plaintiff. This man, the tall one who had spoken first to Thomas, was named Pippalada; he sat to the right of the chief brahmin facing the crowd. Defending Thomas was the timid Nakkirar, Thomas' tutor and disciple. He sat to the left of the chief brahmin.

"Let it be known to you, O brahmins!" Pippalada began, "that in this city there lives a yavana who claims that he is a raja, a member of the ancient raja caste of rulers. Moreover, he calls himself a sannyasin, when in fact he is—you can see for yourself what he is!"

Pippalada pointed at Thomas, and a low murmur stole through the crowd.

"But it is not his color that condemns him," the plaintiff continued. "It is the following blasphemies that he spoke before me and our brothers Bidagdha and Ushasta, and in the presence of his tutor, the witless brahmin Nakkirar, that condemn him. First he said that he, a vile yavana, is entitled to read the Vedas. Second, that a raja is higher and nobler than a brahmin. Third, that giving alms to a brahmin and going on pilgrimage to the holy sites on the Ganges confer no merit. Fourth, that the reasons one man is born a brahmin and another a pulaiyar cannot be known. And last, that only he and those who believe as he does can be finally liberated from the round of rebirths—in other words, that he alone knows God, and that we brahmins cannot be saved. This fivefold insult against our most holy caste and sacred priesthood, and against the eternal truths of the Vedas, is false and perfidious. Not only did he insult me and my two brothers who listened to these outrageous boasts and calumnies; he has insulted all of you here, every brahmin in Madurai. Worst of all, he threatens to undermine our caste. With his lies and promises of easy salvation he seduces the masses into following him. It will not be long before a brahmin, perhaps your own son, succumbs, as Nakkirar has, to the madness that this impostor preaches.

"To prove the truth of what I have said, I call on the yavana's defendant and tutor, Nakkirar, yes, Nakkirar himself! to bear me witness. If what I have spoken is not true, then may my tongue be cut out! But if I have spoken truly, then let the yavana be punished according to the wishes of this assembly."

After Vidagdha and Ushasta attested to the truth of Pippalada's accusations, the presiding brahmin asked Nakkirar to defend Thomas against the charges.

Nakkirar bowed to the presiding brahmin, then to the assembly. His glance fell for an instant on his father, who sat trembling in the convocation. Nakirrar realized he was not only fighting for Thomas, for the truth as he understood it, for the Father God that he had come to accept, but for his entire family's standing in the community. After reminding the assembly that he was a young man, and asking its indulgence for any inelegance in his speech, he began his defense.

"Learned and holy brahmins, I have listened carefully to the claims of the worthy brahmins who accuse the raja sannyasin. I do not believe they are lying, but I am certain they are mistaken."

Nakkirar spoke in his peculiar way: a near falsetto both urgent and soothing at once. The large, regular, and somewhat heavy features of his face contrasted oddly with the almost feminine texture of his voice. It was this voice, Thomas realized, this feckless sparrow's voice and over-earnest face, that stood between him and the collective wrath of the brahmin community. In spite of the heat, a shiver went up his spine.

"First," continued Nakkirar, "the accusers say the raja sannyasin is of low birth because he is white; but by the same argument I could argue that all of you who are brown, and not wheat-skinned as befits a brahmin according to the holy Vedas, must be of low birth. In our country men are often of the same color but of different castes. Why should it not be the same in the raja sannyasin's native country? What right do we have to suppose he is as debased as the King's yavana guards merely because he shares their color? It is true that until now Madurai has never seen a yavana saint. But neither has it seen a yavana raja. And Thomas is a yavana raja, descended from a yavana King named David, who once ruled over an ancient Western land unknown to any of us.

"The accusers next condemn the raja sannyasin for reading and thereby defiling the holy Vedas. I ask you, fellow brahmins, did you condemn our former King for reading the Vedas? Did you condemn him because his guru taught him to read the Vedas? Did you not rather applaud him for this excess of virtue and reverence? But Thomas is a raja no less than the King was! Is it reasonable to praise one raja and condemn another for the same act?

"The accusers next condemn the raja sannyasin for saying a raja is higher in nobility than a brahmin. The raja sannyasin did not say this. What he did do was compare the raja caste to the head of the body and the brahmin caste to the soul. Now it is true the Vedas compare the brahmin caste to the head and give second place to the raja caste by comparing it to the shoulders. But consider what the raja sannyasin intended by the analogy. He meant to suggest only that we brahmins are under the protection of and are subject to the King and his ministers—as indeed we are. Besides, what is nobler, the head or the soul? It is true the Vedas make no mention of the soul in this analogy. But what of that? Is the raja sannyasin on trial because he does not know the Vedas? He has honored us all by comparing us to the soul, the best part, the only permanent part of any of us. It is for *that* the accusers would punish him!

"The accusers next say the raja sannyasin insults our caste by teaching that giving alms to a brahmin and going on pilgrimage to the Ganges confer no merit. What the raja sannyasin meant is that these things are of no value for the man who does not know God; they are of no value *in themselves*. Do the plaintiffs wish to plead that such actions are meritorious in themselves? Where in the Vedas do they find such a teaching? This teaching is a law imagined and invented by the plaintiffs. It implies one can be saved without knowing God—a damnable, vile teaching unworthy of a brahmin!"

Thomas was amazed. He understood crowds; he knew how to read them. Nakkirar, despite his timid, almost effeminate manner, was winning the crowd over like the cleverest of magistrates. No sound except Nakkirar's increasingly forceful voice could be heard; no baby prattled or cried; even the sparrows ceased their twittering. Bewitched, scarcely daring to breathe, Thomas listened as Nakkirar continued: "The accusers next charge the raja sannyasin with rejecting the law of karma, by which each of us is allotted our place in society by the deeds of our past lives." Fellow brahmins! Which of you can point to this or that deed performed in a past life and say that *there* is the reason you have been born brahmin? Which of you can point to the aggregate of your deeds performed in all your past lives and say that *there* are the reasons you have been born brahmin? Never has the raja sannyasin taught that the reasons one man is born a brahmin and another a pulaiyar are not known *to God*! They are knowable—they are known. Known by *God*, not by us!

"The accusers next charge that the raja sannyasin teaches only he and those who believe as he does can know God and thus be saved. The raja sannyasin *does* teach this doctrine. But he does *not* teach that no brahmin can be saved. He teaches that anyone, from the most despised outcast mleccha to the most high-born brahmin, can worship the True God and be saved. Nor does he ask any of his converts to leave their castes. A brahmin convert may continue to wear his thread; he may keep his tuft of hair and wear sandal paste on his forehead; he may retain his name and honor his ancestors. The waters of baptism wash away his sins, not his caste!

"The raja sannyasin respects all castes, including ours. He has never insulted any brahmin. If he is to be punished, then it must be for teaching a new religion. But the Tamil country has always permitted all religions to exist in harmony side by side. It is said that the yavanas in distant Western lands persecute each other because the other's religion is different. Are we to follow the example of these barbarians? Surely one more religion can comfortably take its place on the banks of the holy Vaigai! All over the Tamil country, throughout each of the kingdoms—the Pandyan, the Chola, and the Chera—all religions are permitted to exist in harmony, side by side. If we banish the yavana for his religion, then we must banish the Jains, the Buddhists, and the Ajivakas for theirs. Which of you is prepared to do this?"

At that Nakkirar bowed to the chief brahmin, indicating that he was finished.

Nakkirar's defense of his new guru astounded everyone. His outer features and personality had hidden the brilliance of his intellect; no one until now had guessed it. By the time the convocation drew to a close, the assembly and judges had swung over to Thomas' side. The last question addressed to Nakkirar came from the accuser himself. Probably Pippalada had originally meant to use it as the climactic finishing stroke, but now he asked it in desperation:

"It is well known that this yavana religion is open to everyone, that all mingle together and 'break bread,' as they say. Do I need to tell you how defiling this practice is to a brahmin? How can a brahmin keep caste if he eats with pulaiyars and—I shudder to think of it—pig-eating outcasts? Answer if you can, Nakkirar!"

Nakkirar's gnat-like voice pounced on Pippalada's question with the lethal intent and incisive grace of a tiger: "When have you seen a brahmin worship with any of these? When have you heard the raja sannyasin talk of brahmins breaking bread with pulaiyars and outcasts, or even vaishyas and rajas? The raja sannyasin respects our customs. He has decreed that brahmins will be given precedence, that they will worship and break bread apart from the others. Pippalada! Do you see this ant crawling in front of us? . . . It eats up every scrap of food in its way. Pippalada, the white sannyasin is like the white ant, and your calumnies are like the scraps!"

Nakkirar accomplished two things with this curious analogy. People everywhere began referring to Pippalada as "White Ant," and he was so disgraced that he gathered his family and left Madurai for good. The other result was that Thomas was obliged to give his brahmin converts the precedence that Nakkirar invented for them in the heat of battle. Thomas himself had never thought of the problem that Pippalada proposed.

Nakkirar's ingenuity not only delivered Thomas from the proud Madurai brahmins; it made his religion less contemptible to them. It planted a tiny sprig of ivy in new soil.

Nakkirar himself was the first Madurai brahmin to convert. By then the white-hot cloudless sky had reduced the Vaigai to a wide sandy waste spotted with puddles that almost boiled under the fierce sun. To the trumpeting of wild elephants which had come to the river's farther bank to drink, Thomas, on the last day of Vaikhasi, Thomas triumphant, and with hundreds attending, immersed Nakkirar in the hot waters of baptism.

26. Madari

adari had nothing in common with the other concubines and ladies-in-waiting who dallied with the King on his bed, pollen grains sprinkled over their silken breasts. Sex with him was their chief object in life. When the bodyguards opened the door, the women would come in eyeing the King seductively, scarcely noticing Kumaran. The King would assign one of the ladies-in-waiting, as distinguished from his concubines, or "wives," to Kumaran, while the rest, both concubines and ladies-in-waiting, would wait for the King's pleasure. When he invited one to him, the others would cuddle up against the couple. They kissed and fondled the King up and down the length of his body, and often they caressed each other. To Kumaran they all seemed, at first, part of a single grotesque organism with a single vile purpose, a single pulse, but he was so drunk with his own importance, his own incredible fortune, that he failed to listen to either his conscience or to Maruthanar's warnings.

But Madari reawakened Kumaran's dazed conscience. She felt a revulsion for the King from the moment she crossed the threshold of the bedroom and laid eyes on the "monster," as she called him later. New to the harem and still a virgin when she made her fateful first entry, she was the daughter of a brahmin from a village on the northern border which had sided with the Cholas against Nediyon. Her grandfather, the village elder, had made the mistake of condemning the King for his dissoluteness. Nediyon punished him by deporting his fifteen-year-old granddaughter with skin the color of gingerbread to the royal harem.

When she entered the bedroom the first time, she understood her duty. But she hated the King for what he had done to her family, not to mention herself. As luck would have it, the King was drunk, and he didn't even notice her; nor did he remember to appoint one of the ladies-in-waiting to go to Kumaran. Horrified by everything the King represented, she gravitated to the slight man with the poet's eyes as the lesser of two evils.

Kumaran knew none of this when he made love to Madari on that first meeting. He did not even know she was a "wife" rather than a lady-in-waiting.

He learned to love Madari with the purest passion. She consumed his thoughts to such a degree he no longer lived for his poetry, but for the weekly visit to the King's bedroom. He told the King about his love for Madari, both in his poetry and in conversation, and the King always assigned her to him, though sometimes with a frown.

Kumaran noticed the frown and understood it. Once the King said to him privately, "But she's a wife, not a lady-in-waiting. What if she should have a child—by you?" He looked at Kumaran and suddenly began to laugh. His broad mouth parted almost to his ears, as if he wore a mask, and the laughter gushed out until his eyes watered. Then he sobered. "Yes, that would be a problem," he said. And a chill ran through Kumaran.

On one occasion, after Madari had been in the harem for three months, the King complained Kumaran was writing too much poetry about Madari, and this nettled Kumaran. The King, sensing the annoyance, decided to test his friend.

"Kumaran, I will have her this time; you entertain the rest. I must see what it is you find in her."

Kumaran looked blankly at the King's wily, drunken face. He was speechless.

"Maiden with golden earrings, come to me, let me see what it is that a poet loves."

"Please, please—" Kumaran stammered in a faint voice. But he stopped. What could he say? Madari was one of the King's wives.

"Come, child, come. Girls"—the King's voice had been tender and peculiarly reverential as he addressed Madari, but now it became contemptuous and odious—"girls, go to Kumaran, show him your stuff."

Madari began to shake all over. She was wearing hollow anklets with stones in them, and they began to jingle. Her golden earrings glittered as they jumped and revolved under a few runaway strands of hair. Pearl-studded armlets worn round her upper arms dropped to her elbows. She looked at Kumaran in despair.

"Your Majesty, please, not for my sake, but for the girl's," Kumaran said, his right hand flopping back and forth on his wrist.

"What is this, child? You dislike me?" said the King in a sweetly seductive, even musical, but unmistakably threatening voice.

With eyes as big as sunflowers she crawled over to him, while the others crawled over to Kumaran. Kumaran lay listless against the pillow and turned the other way. Even the concubines, as if understanding Madari's depredation in a way they could not their own, lay around Kumaran murmuring quietly to each other or trying to reassure him.

Kumaran could not forgive the King this act, although it was never repeated; from that moment he hated him and resolved to get revenge. But still he read his poetry and shared the pleasures of Nediyon's bed, though no longer out of a desire to be close to the throne. What kept him coming back was Madari. Shortly after Madari's rape—that is how Kumaran thought of it—he tried to meet her in one of the palace storerooms away from the King, but the plan was discovered. The King left him no choice: The only way to see her was to visit him. Sometimes he whispered to Madari he considered himself her slave, and he promised to return her to her father's house. Sometimes she whispered back that she was no longer a brahmin but an outcast, and she was *his* slave.

"If I were ever to marry a brahmin, and my husband found out about us," she told him, "I would have to ride through the streets of my village on a black donkey facing backwards, my body smeared with butter and my head shaved. I saw this happen when I was a little girl. I would rather die!"

She never asked Kumaran if he were married. And he never told her he had made up his mind to kill the King, though he implied it. "I'll bring you to your father," he told her. "I'll find a way. I've already *found* a way. It won't be much longer."

Meanwhile Kumaran studied at the Sangam and gave lectures by day, though far fewer than before, while at night he secretly studied the art of poison. In the early days he visited Thomas in his hut on the Vaigai three or four times a week, but lately they had less and less to say to each other, and the visits had become less frequent. About Devandi he thought only with regret. How could he ever find her desirable again? If only he were free to marry Madari. It was a preposterous idea, but one that he clung to in his fancy. He could bring her to King Karikal's court in Puhar, where she would impress all who knew her with her grace and beauty. Most of all, however, he simply wanted to be with her.

One day Maruthanar told him his life was in danger. "They are saying the King is insane, they are saying he lets you sleep with his own wives. They are saying the Gods will destroy the city, for the mixing of castes is abhorrent to them." Maruthanar was too timid to ask if the rumors were true; perhaps he found them unbelievable, for he didn't ask Kumaran to leave the house. "You should have heeded my warning, Kumaran!" he said.

Kumaran knew Maruthanar was correct, but he was willing to risk anything for Madari. He lived to be with her. He loved her smile; it didn't begin at her lips but, as he wrote in one of his poems, in the marrow of her soul. He loved the color of her golden skin. He loved her eyes: round, noble, otherworldly yet passionate, sometimes red with tears and smeared with black kohl which she put on her eyelids. He loved her thick hair, its five plaits perfumed with paste made from the musk deer. He loved her body, as firm and slender and lithe as the woody liana vine which wraps itself around the trunks of jungle trees. He loved her little hands, laden with bracelets; her dainty feet, their bottoms painted with red lac and resembling a dog's tongue; her rounded thighs decorated with ornaments, always different, always worn to please him alone, and the painted beauty spots on her hips. He loved her because she loved him back and because her pedigree was the noblest in all the world. It showed itself every time she spoke: Though she could not read, her idiom and formal speech patterns told of a refinement that could belong only to a brahmin. What strange, contradictory deed in a past life could he have performed? A lowly pulaiyar, a menial, a servant to brahmins—loved by a pure brahmin girl! And what improbable karma fated Madari's fall? Though Kumaran only half-believed in the notion of karma anymore, they talked of such things under the King's muslin bedcovers. An invisible curtain separated them from the profane bedlam on the other side of the immense mattress. They ignored it as best they could.

What he could not ignore was a certain tedium—actually it was something deeper, something more oppressive and less easy to define— he felt in the presence of Thomas. Their values, the things they loved had never been the same, but they had shared so much and confided so much to each other that their differences, though mutually painful, could be overlooked. And besides, Thomas was at once a beloved master to whom he felt indentured and a dear friend whose presence sometimes nourished him and made him happy. And always Thomas was his brother. But now, though never challenged or chastised, Kumaran began to feel uneasy in his presence. Had Thomas heard the rumors that Maruthanar heard? Surely someone must have told him; but then Thomas tolerated no gossip.

In spite of his allegiance to Thomas, Thomas began to weary him, for he could tell him nothing about Madari, and that was almost the only subject that interested him. Instead he had to pretend he was continuing to master the conventions of Tamil poetry, which he was not. Indeed his poetry, except when Madari was the subject, had become as sterile as any other clever libertine's. The receptions and invitations had dried to a trickle. He was increasingly resented, then hated, especially by the Queen, who abhorred him for joining with her husband in his infidelities, and by her oldest son, Nedunjeliyan, the Crown Prince, a man of sober disposition. Not a word of any of this did Kumaran breathe to Thomas.

That year the clouds, as if doing penance for the treacheries of men, did not drink the ocean's water, and the autumnal monsoons failed. The Vaigai flowed, but it did not swell, and hence the irrigation tanks did not fill. Travelers brought news from all over the Pandyan Kingdom, always the same: The rains had been light. Priests offered sacrifices to the Gods. Astrologers looked for portents. Soothsayers warned of famine. Many blamed the King. They blamed him because his conduct had offended the Gods, or because he had failed to build and stock an adequate number of granaries, or because he had not listened to the priests' interpretations of portents. Everywhere there was talk of signs. Some people had seen ants' eggs on water, or crows' nests on temples, or inauspicious cloud formations at twilight, or a crescent moon lying on its side like a rocking cradle with its southern tip slightly raised. All these signs portended drought. Others found bloodier signs. There was much talk of a dark streak cutting the solar disc in two at sunset, an omen portending the murder of the King by one of his own ministers. Others whispered the sun had been struck by lightning at sunrise, a portent the King would die and an invading king would be installed in his place. And everyone talked about a certain stone statue that shed tears when the King deviated from justice.

On the seventh day of Margali, the cool month, as the entire Pandyan Kingdom slept, the King's bodyguard discovered Nediyon dead in his bed.

27. Love-Behind-Things

As the moon rose and passed its meridian, Judas Thomas, the world's first Christian sannyasin, meditated on the bank of the burbling Vaigai, far from his home half a world away. He felt that a Love-Behind-Things at the heart of the universe beamed down and bathed the earth in its perfect, impartial light. It was as cool and still as a summer night in Jerusalem. What did it matter that a king had died the night before? Kings came and went. A thin, unflickering flame glowed in Thomas' heart as he poured out thanks to the True God who loved him without change. He was at peace.

It was close to midnight when he got up from his meditation, and the drums of mourning that had beat all day and into the night were quiet. He finished his ablutions, lay down in his hut to sleep, and with eyes closed turned his mind to Jesus. He thought of Jesus' face on that ghostly night so long ago, the gentle, loving eyes. He remembered the joy, the feeling of confidence, the amazement. Jesus had defeated death. "Come, Lord," he prayed. "Maranatha, Maranatha, Maranatha."

All seemed to be going well. He was teaching Greek to Nakkirar and two others. New missionaries would be arriving someday not too far off; he had written Jerusalem for them to meet him in Puhar in the sannyasins' quarter. He had overcome the temptation to go home, even if it meant never seeing his daughters again, even if it meant dying in India. He had embraced the life of the cross, and God had rewarded him by putting all India within his grasp. All he needed was twenty or thirty more years.

He gave thanks to God and fell asleep.

28. The Great Sati

The news had fanned out over the countryside as far south as Cape Cormorin. The great families gathered, their hair hanging down in mourning, their public lamentations lifted to Murugan, Shiva, and the other Gods, even as they secretly thanked these same Gods. Bullock carts carried load after load of sandalwood to the cremation ground along the Vaigai. Outcasts so polluted that the proximity of death could not pollute them further dug a pit, a huge pit. Then the rumor began. There would be a Sati. Not only the Queen, but—

Kumaran told himself it could not be. It was unthinkable. He tried to cajole his way into the palace to see Madari, to see what she could tell him. "The harem is quarantined, no messages in or out," said the guards. He offered bribes, but the guards held fast.

A huge crowd had gathered around the pit—thousands, tens of thousands, perhaps a hundred thousand. The firewood had been heaped into a pyramid well above the rim of the pit. Everyone would be able to see.

The retinue of elephants, horses, soldiers, relatives, and ministers processed through the street, passed under the northern gate, and turned toward the pyre. There was no place for Kumaran in the cortege. Did no one remember the King's love for his favorite poet, his partner in play? For an instant he felt sorry for himself, but then his thoughts turned again to Madari. He barely heard the trumpets and drums and wails of the crowd as he imagined the worst. To be so close to achieving his goal, planned and executed with such consummate skill. And now this unthinkable, this—but it was all rumor. Who could say what was really going to happen? He let himself hope.

Armed soldiers followed by musicians marched out of the palace gates. Then came the King's corpse in a scarlet jeweled palanquin. Kumaran saw through the window the face he had loathed in life and finally murdered. For an instant he imagined the face opening its eyes and staring at him with a vengeful leer as it condemned him to a long stay in some burning, snake-infested hell. Then he felt sorry for the King and regretted his deed: it was one thing to kill a man, another to see him dead. But he thought of Madari and felt glad; he noted the corpse's golden diadem intertwined with *neem* flowers and felt contempt for the face.

Nediyon was accompanied by his court, his chief ministers, and his nearest relatives, including the prince, soon to be crowned "Nedunjeli-yan the First." Next came the Queen riding in her carved teak palanquin paneled with jade and splotched with so many precious stones that it took eight porters to carry her. Following her on foot came the dead King's "junior queens," his courtesans, with their attendants. Kumaran jumped up and down, searching this jewel-laden group for a sign of Madari. Around him the surging crowd lifted their hands toward these forty or fifty "queens"; a few isolated, spasmodic shrieks knifed through the low hum of the crowd. No one knew what would happen at the pyre, for Sati was a custom only recently introduced with the full-scale worship of Shiva. But there had been a multiple Sati at Kanchi to the north a few years earlier. Would Madurai, pearl of the Pandyan Kingdom, allow herself to be outshone by rival Chola Kanchi? The crowd hoped the courtesans would join the Queen in the fire. What a spectacle that would be!

As the courtesans passed in front of Kumaran, several women in the crowd broke through the rope barricades. They wanted to hear their fortunes told, for they had heard a Sati was prescient. Or they wanted to receive a small coin or trinket or even a piece of betel leaf from the hand of a Sati, for they had heard there was magical power in this.

Kumaran saw Madari at the back of the retinue, and a desperate plan took shape in his mind in case the worst were true. His senses grow felinely alert: An inner voice whispered to him that this was Madari's only chance. He pushed his way through the crowd, ducked under the rope, and ran after Madari, who was dressed in only a plain ocher-colored dress the shade of an ascetic's loin cloth.

"Madari!" he cried as he caught up to her.

162

She looked up at him with frightened but hopeful eyes.

"Come with me!"

But as he grabbed her arm and tried to burrow into the crowd, a soldier rushed at him and prodded him at the throat with a spear. Kumaran froze.

"Let go of her!" said the soldier, digging the point of the spear into his neck just below the chin.

As the crowd yelled, "What's he doing?" and a stray voice or two cried, "Kill him!" Kumaran let go of Madari, lurched sideways, ducked under the crowd which buffeted him with fists and elbows, and fought his way backward. He tasted blood from a wound in his mouth as he fought free of the crowd and ran into an alley. He looked around, but no one seemed to be interested in him. His courage returned and he ran by a circuitous route to the site of the pyre. He rounded the corner of a building and saw the crowd swarming and packing together. He faltered, not knowing what to do. He decided he would have to work his way to the front. More curses fell on him as he burrowed his way to the front against the retaining rope. Those around him cursed him some more, but he didn't care. He squatted and waited.

The pit was a man's height deep and eight paces square. The pyre itself rose out of the pit to the height of a second man. The King's sons and other close male relatives were placing his body on top of the pyre, which was flat, when Kumaran arrived. The Queen was performing her final ablutions in the shallow Vaigai out of his sight. Brahmins stood around; three held torches while the others guarded jugs of ghee or nursed the three sacred fires. Soldiers squatted inside the retaining ropes. A cow lay inside the makeshift earthen sanctuary. The junior queens waited beside the pit; they seemed to huddle together, and Kumaran studied their faces for signs of fright. Madari stood aloof, talked to no one; her eyes were closed and lips moving. The sun split the morning air like a chisel, and jewels gleamed from every ankle, wrist, neck, finger, ear, and nose. Bright orange, green, and white flags bearing the Pandyan fish waved from hundreds of posts built along the Vaigai's banks. Every nearby tree drooped from the weight of spectators. The balconies of distant houses bulged with sightseers, and their roofs were lined with still more. Even the city's more distant ramparts bore its share of the curious.

Every kind of speculation wormed through the crowd. Some people bet all the queens would jump into the fire. Others argued they were merely honored spectators and only the Queen, as in the past, would join the King in death. "Look at their wrists," they complained, "they haven't even broken their bangles!" The desperately curious even shouted questions at the queens: "Will you jump?""Are you Sati?" Everyone studied their faces for hints. "You see how she nodded? They're all going to jump," said a woman behind Kumaran in an undertone. A dire but excited consensus seemed to form: They were all going to jump. The people could hardly bear to wait. Would the Queen never get back from her ablutions? Why was she taking so long?

When she showed, a tense murmur rippled through the crowd. Wet all over and dripping, she began circling the pit the required three times. She walked alone, never faltering, her expression grave and composed. Then, assisted by her sons, she climbed up a ladder to the top of the pyre and lay on her back next to the King.Meanwhile the officiating priest exorcised the demons that haunt cremation grounds with the words, "Get away, leave this spot!" Again and again he repeated this formula in Sanskrit. Then it was time to sacrifice the cow. One of the brahmin assistants brought the dagger down as prayers were chanted to the Gods, and the beast, gushing blood, groaned and quivered, then lay still. The priest cut up the carcass and placed its heart, kidneys, and other sacred parts on the appropriate parts of the King's body, all according to ancient Vedic rite, and gave a final instruction to the Queen. Her embroidered white dress lay spread out in lumps across the pyre, a breeze fluttering its edges.

The Queen signaled to the brahmin by touching the hand of her dead master. The head brahmin sprinkled the couple with holy water, chanted more mantras, and motioned to his assistants. Almost before anyone realized what was happening, the fire began to crackle. A silence fell over the huge crowd, and those close by heard the Queen call out, "Shiva, Shiva!" as she stretched her arms up toward the immaculate blue sky. Then there was a shriek, short and tentative, followed by a guttural scream that made Kumaran shiver. A moment of uncanny silence followed, then, as if on cue, a hundred thousand voices rent the heavens and waved whatever they could in salute to the new Goddess who had taken her place beside her husband in Shiva's paradise.

What now? The fire climbed higher and higher, it whooshed and crackled. Everyone studied the faces in the King's harem. Kumaran began to sweat as the women drew together and clung to each other— all of them except Madari. With glassy unseeing eyes staring ahead and her right hand fingering beads, Madari stood alone on the warm sands of the Vaigai.

Without any warning or fanfare, one of the concubines started to walk around the fire. Once, twice, three times: she completed the triple circuit. The spectators, their lust for death at fever pitch, shouted every kind of advice, every epithet of adoration. One voice would whine, another would roar, and the effect of all those thousands of voices raised to a frenzy was like the roaring, howling wind of a cyclone. Kumaran recognized the woman, as well as most of the others. She had been the King's favorite. She squeezed off the bangles she wore round her wrist and threw them on the ground. She took off her finger ring, which if left on would hinder the egress of her soul, and gave it to one of the priests. Finally she stood still, her hands hanging loose by her sides, and looked straight ahead at the fire as her breasts rose and fell. In all her finery—her best jewels, her softest red silks, her braided hair bobbing in the breeze, her perfumed face with darkened eyes and voluptuous reddened lips—she studied the leaping flames. Prepared in every exquisite detail for the glorious reception that awaited her in heaven, she eyed the flames that would engulf her and restore her to the presence of her master, now a god. Lifting her folded hands to the sky, she invoked the name of Shiva and the King. She looked back down at the flame, took a single deep breath, called out the name of the King one more time, and rushed at the fire. Did she hesitate as she got to the rim? Kumaran's poet's eye picked up that last staggering step as her courage failed. But her momentum carried her into the flames. If she suffered the agony of a lifetime condensed into a single second, no one had a hint of it. The roar of the fire, the howls and cheers of the crowd, the drums—these were the only sounds that anyone heard. Now the Queen had a rival in heaven, just as on earth.

All morning the women, not only the King's mistresses but their ladies-in-waiting, threw themselves into the fire. Some staggered into it. A few lost heart at the last instant and had to be dragged. Several forgot to break their bangles and take off their rings. Sometimes, especially near the end of the spectacle as the fire died down, screams rent the air. At one point a peasant woman carrying a baby broke from beneath the rope and threw herself and her child on the pyre. Periodically the priests added wood and consecrated the flames with more ghee. If a girl seemed to lose heart, they would grow impatient and threaten her. If another fainted from terror as she circumambulated the fire, they ordered servants to prop her up and carry her around; then they doused her with water to wake her. One girl tried to run away, but the priests dragged her back; two of her companions grasped her under her arms, and the three of them, the girl screaming and resisting up till the last second, went into the fire together. But these were the exceptions. Most of the Satis carried off the ordeal courageously.

Frantic, lunatic thoughts raged in Kumaran's brain as he squatted and watched, all but lost in the gawking, shouting throng. He must do something. He decided to try again to capture Madari, then bolt through the crowd and hide out until night. But he could not get her attention, neither by calling nor by waving: Like a tortoise she had completely closed herself off from the crowd. What then? He would have to work his way along the rope to the other side of the pit near to where she squatted. He would lure her to him when no priest or guard was looking, then disappear into the crowd. For many minutes he stayed on the verge of doing this, but the more he ran the plan through his head, the more certain it seemed he would only end up himself in the pit with Madari or someplace worse. Then let it be, he told himself. He would end it all, he would go to his death with her. He would *choose* it. He would run up to her when it was her turn—and that could not be far away now—and go in with her, their hands entwined! But when he smelled the stench of burning flesh in the air, the thought of flame against his skin horrified him. Suddenly life seemed precious. Still, he had to do something. He remembered how he'd saved Thomas in Kurinchi. He had argued, made an eloquent plea. Why not again? Why not? He had plenty to bribe with if necessary. Yes, he would appeal—appeal to the priest. The priest, of course! The priest was of the brahmin caste, and so was Madari!

He got the attention of one of the priests, and the head priest approached, though not too closely.

"That girl, in the ocher dress, the Sati, she is only a child!" Kumaran shouted, waving his finger at Madari. "And she is a brahmin, captured by the King and dragged into his harem. She is a *brahmin*!"

The priest, fingering his sacred thread, looked at Kumaran as if he were a madman.

"Don't let her die! She despised the King in life. Must she join him in death? It would be monstrous!"

The priest's smoothed-down eyebrows contracted in contempt as he grunted something and shuffled away.

Kumaran grew more desperate as the ranks of the courtesans thinned. He called out to the head priest again, "She is a brahmin!" But the priest pretended not to hear, and Kumaran screamed all the louder: "You're murdering a brahmin! You're all murderers! Murderers!"

166

The head priest turned and looked at Kumaran. "I know who you are," he said menacingly. Then he called to one of the guards. But Kumaran backed away cursing and sobbing and, like a mole moving through earth, disappeared into the crowd.

He did not see Madari begin her circuit around the pit. He did not see the look of otherworldly detachment on her face as she stood at the edge of the pit for a moment and studied the pyre, by now a pile of fiery embers below ground level. He did not see her fall into the fire as naturally as an otter drops into water. From a place well behind the huge throng, he heard the peculiar rise of excited voices that meant still another had jumped. He knew this time it was Madari. She was the last of ninety-three.

Many in the crowd walked in single file three times around the fire. When they left, still in single file, they took pains not to look back. They walked to the Vaigai and washed away their pollution. The Sati was finished.

Kumaran looked on from a distance while standing under the balcony of a house facing the burning grounds. He held his hand over his mouth as if he were about to be sick and muttered Madari's name over and over, as if he were crazy. But he was far from crazy. He was facing reality in a manner rare for him. He realized that *he* had killed Madari, that she would be alive if he had not murdered the King. He, Kumaran, her lover, was her killer. Then a thought almost as ghastly struck him. He remembered Maruthanar's telling him it was rumored he was sleeping with the King's queens and there was concern the King's blood line might be defiled by pulaiyar blood. Six of the queens had been pregnant, and how could anyone be sure who the father was? Is that why they all had to be killed? Staring across at the smoking pit, he wondered if his karma was saturated with the blood of a hundred innocent women. Was he a mass murderer?

As he looked up toward the smoke rising into the sky and felt the enormity of what he had done, Murugan's terrible consort, the Goddess, sprang up in his imagination, and she accused him and all men of terrible crimes against her sex. Her blood-stained mouth of crooked pointed teeth gaped open, and her green bulging eyes penetrated his heart with their rage. She wore long snake-like earrings which scraped against her breasts of venom, and she held in her hand a fetid black skull whose eyeballs she had just gouged out and eaten. Blood dripped from her spear-shaped fingernails as she danced—danced to the drumbeat of Kumaran's heart. "Oh, Madari!" his heart screamed forth.

"You're under arrest!" A gruff voice belonging to the face of a wolfish blue-eyed devil with a spiky, short-cropped beard shocked Kumaran out of his nightmare. The man was armed, menacing, and surly, and Kumaran recognized him; he was one of the King's yavana bodyguards.

29. Kumaran's Hole

Two soldiers led Thomas toward a corner of the garrison yard where the abandoned well stood. Thomas was not the usual sort seen on the dusty parade ground. The orange cloth that hung from his waist down to his knees and the stitched sandals that flapped against his heals as he walked bore no resemblance to the military issue of the Pandyan Empire. Had Thomas' mood been lighthearted, he might have laughed at the incongruity of his appearance. But his thoughts were filled with Kumaran, and Kumaran, everyone said, would be dead within a week. It troubled Thomas when he realized Kumaran for months had been keeping secrets from him. It troubled him that he hadn't sensed something terribly wrong with Kumaran. Hindsight revealed hints; why hadn't he noticed them at the time? It troubled him most of all that his old friend might die without baptism.

Maruthanar, the poet, brought Thomas the news. The new King had imprisoned Kumaran in a dry well at the royal garrison for "crimes against the state." Would he, Thomas, be kind enough to visit the prisoner? The prisoner begged to see him.

Thomas looked over the parapet down into the darkness of the well. "Kumaran, it's me, Thomas. Are you there?"

A noise below sounded like rats scrabbling.

Thomas turned to the guards. "May I go down?"

"Go down?" The guards looked at him in disbelief. "In *there?*"

Thomas nodded his head, and the men, guffawing, fetched a long ladder and lowered it into the hole.

Thomas had noticed the smell as soon as he reached the parapet; as he climbed down the ladder, it blasted him. Kumaran had been living in his own excrement for a week. The pit also served as a latrine for any soldier who felt inclined to add his own form of torture.

"Kumaran, it's me. My God, man, my God! . . . Here, let me lift you up." Thomas' head reeled as he lifted Kumaran out of the sewage and sat him up. "I've brought bread, look. . . . I didn't dream it would be so bad!"

"Look, Brother," Kumaran said in a strangely excited voice.

Kumaran held something up in the half light, and Thomas strained to see it. "What is it?"

"Magic."

"What are you talking about? Here, have some bread." Thomas unfolded the loaf and broke it in two.

"Feel it, Brother! Here, feel it!" Kumaran grabbed Thomas' hand, and the bread dropped into the mud and excrement. "It's a monkey's head. See? It's connected to four monkey bodies. One hangs down from a branch, another is sitting, one is walking from the right, another from the left. But they all have the same head. It's magic, Thomas! It's magic, don't you see?"

Thomas was appalled. "Kumaran—"

"And look at this!" Kumaran put the monkey piece down and picked up something else. "Do you see? Look, if you look at it one way, it's a bull. If you look at it another, it's an elephant. They share the same head. The elephant's tusks are the bull's horns, and the bull's hump is the elephant's snout. It's magic, ha ha ha ha ha! I'm carving it for the soldiers. So they won't piss on me!"

"Brother. Oh, Brother, Brother!" Thomas put his arms around Kumaran's filthy body and held him close. "Kumaran, I love you." He spoke slowly and with great gentleness, as if he were soothing a baby. "God loves you. . . . Jesus loves you, Brother."

"So thirsty. I'm so thirsty. Help me, I'm so thirsty."

Thomas let go of Kumaran and called up to the guards for water.

"Not allowed," they called down. "Just once a day."

Thomas began to work his mouth and tongue back and forth. "This will hold you for a little while," he said. "Open your mouth."

Kumaran opened his mouth, and Thomas spit in his saliva.

Thomas learned from one of the officers the new King had forbidden the soldiers to help the prisoner in any way; with the drought, food and water were scarce enough anyway. King Nedunjeliyan knew all about Kumaran' antics with his father. Any other sovereign would have sent Kumaran's soul packing off to hell without a second thought. But Nedunjeliyan, the officer said, was a man of piety; he followed his mother's rather than his father's example. In particular he respected a man's karma: as much as possible he preferred to let nature take its course. So he decreed that Kumaran would rot in his hole until he died; if someone, an outsider, a friend (if he had any left) brought him something, then the prisoner could receive it; that would be the fruit of his good karma. If not, then death would come quickly. One thing the King made clear: Kumaran would never get out of his hole alive.

Everyday Thomas, with an assistant or two, came to the garrison with food, drink, a brass pitcher of water for bathing, and an earthen bowl to serve as a toilet. Thomas would go down the ladder and minister to Kumaran while the assistants waited above. It was tedious and difficult work, and Thomas prayed hard that Kumaran would receive baptism and then be taken to heaven without further suffering. Meanwhile Kumaran's life dragged on. Week followed week, and the conversion, though sometimes seeming within Thomas' grasp, did not happen. The hot season approached, and at noon Kumaran's hole turned into an inferno of light for a fraction of an hour as the sun stood poised on the pit's edge and beamed its fire straight down before passing on.

Thomas thought sometimes of "God's will." He remembered Jesus' words one rainy day above Capernaum: "What man, if his son asks him for bread, will give him a stone? Or if he asks for a fish, will give him a snake?" Was Jesus wrong? That was impossible, but sometimes it seemed to Thomas the inexplicable God, his Heavenly Father, had given him many a stone or snake instead of bread. He prayed fervidly for Kumaran to accept baptism, but Kumaran showed no interest. How could it be God's will that Kumaran *not* receive baptism?

But Thomas had no doubts about God's will for himself. Jesus had made that plain in many a sermon from hilltop or field or orchard or synagogue or porch, up and down the length of Galilee's lake-district and across Jerusalem's hills and vales. Thomas could hear Jesus' voice, "for I was sick and in prison and you did not visit me," ringing out from the Mount of Olives; and he could hear the sequel, "And they will go away into eternal punishment." Thus Thomas seldom missed a day seeing Kumaran, and when he was forced to miss, he sent a replacement with the day's provisions.

Down into the hole Thomas would go, about fifteen feet; there would be bathing, Kumaran would eat and drink, sand would be spread over the excrement, they would talk, then up the ladder to the business of the day. Although it couldn't have been more clear to Thomas what his Christian duty to Kumaran was, he couldn't help feeling resentment. He had so many things to do: supervise the building of a church, attend the dying, instruct the catechumens, organize the new community, study the Vedas so he would know how to combat the brahmins, continue the translation project, train Nakkirar to lead the church as Madurai's first bishop, and all this sandwiched between stints of silent prayer and meditation twice a day, when he communed with Jesus and his Father in heaven and gained the strength to continue his work. The duties, as always, were endless. And there was much too little time for it all, too little time to plant the ivy and train it up the trellis; and he had already stayed in Madurai too long anyway, almost two years. But he knew he could not leave Kumaran alive in that stinking hole. "Please let him die, Lord," Thomas caught himself praying one day, forgetting to mention baptism. "Let him die!" For there was Puhar ahead, and he had to get back to Muziri, and he was nearing fifty, and the old feeling that he should make at least one visit home before he died to see his daughters and grandchildren hounded him. And there was all the rest of India to tend to. And Nakkirar had told him that ships from places far to the east regularly sailed into Puhar's harbor. So India was not on the eastern edge of the world after all! How was the great work to be accomplished in time?

But first there was Kumaran, and Kumaran refused to die. Thomas became more and more resentful of him, for he had despaired that the ivy of his faith would ever take root in that hole of excrement. Yet he descended into its filth almost daily, for Jesus had taught that visiting the imprisoned was a sacred duty of all who followed him. Jesus had even said he was *in* the prisoner.

30. A Reluctant Baptism

The indescribable filth of his hole and his own body, the stench, the grievous heat of the dry season which worked its way down like the head of a drill around noon, the brutality of the guards, a few of whom continued to urinate into the well in spite of Thomas' pleas, all this had reduced Kumaran to a half-wild pariah dog. Sometimes he remembered that a year ago he entertained rich patrons, conducted seminars at the Sangam, and collected what was for him a small fortune. He remembered only three months separated him from the sheer muslin of the royal bed. And he remembered Madari, but only as an event that happened to someone else. At most she seemed like someone he had met in a dream a long time ago; not even the contours of her face were clear. She took her place, along with his travels, wife, successes, ambition, in the twilight of an unreal past. His only world now was what he called "the anus of Madurai."

During his first days in the "anus" he mentally recorded the particulars of his experience for some future benefactor. He compared himself to an earthenware bowl hardening in the fierce dark heat of a smoldering kiln, but as the weeks went by he lost interest in metaphor-making, and the palm leaves that Maruthanar brought him during the first weeks had long since disappeared under the mud and sand. The great King Karikal and his capital, Puhar—Kumaran lost interest even in them.

Sometimes he dwelled on what he might do when free: he would go back to his father's house, raise his family, live contentedly as a humble pulaiyar sculptor. But such imaginings were merely a diversion; they were like the yarns he embroidered to flatter rich patrons; they were not real; he felt nothing for them. What kept him going? Only the wood in his hand that he carved and out of which he brought forth "magic." That and Thomas. Thomas was a pool of clear water, and Kumaran was an exposed root twisting down over bare rock to that water. Thomas and "magic": They were the only hedges against insanity and death he had, the only things from his past that didn't disappear in the shadow of his hot stinking hole. Sometimes Maruthanar would come, but he would stay just long enough to drop down some more wood to carve, and to take away Kumaran's latest creation to be sold in the market to someone who fancied it for his lavatory. Maruthanar's nose was not as durable as Thomas'; he would always leave after a few whiffs, and Kumaran would sit staring up at the bright opening with its dreadful silence where the voice of his friend had been.

Kumaran had confessed everything to Thomas: the depravity of the royal bed, the poisoning of the King, the death of the queens that followed. Thomas told him several of the cooks had been accused of poisoning the King; no one suspected him of the murder. But Kumaran was incapable of feeling guilt on their account. He wished he could have wept, cursed, cried out, but he was numb. He felt no more remorse than a sleepy time-caller feels after missing an hour. In his true heart he feared he was destined for the deepest hell, followed by rebirth as a belly-crawling reptile or something worse. Such presentiments gave rise to dread, but dread did not give rise to repentance, only to more dread. This dread was not something that Kumaran could have pointed to. It was largely unconscious; or rather it was so prominent a part of his consciousness, never relenting for a moment, that it engulfed him—like the drone of an army of crickets, whose sound no one hears because it never varies or stops. But the dread did have a useful purpose: It kept him clinging to life.

"It's not enough to confess. You must repent," Thomas said.

The day was early, but it was already warm. Thomas had come shortly after sunrise to escape the heat.

"We've been over this before," Kumaran said dolefully.

"But you can't go around killing people. God will deal with the sinner. What the King did to Madari God will punish. Don't you see? It's not *your* place to do the punishing, Brother, that's all."

"Don't 'brother' me! I'm glad I killed that pig! May he burn forever in your everlasting hell of crap!"

For a moment Thomas squatted in stunned silence, then stood up.

"Don't go! Don't go!" Kumaran pleaded. "Please don't go!" His voice clucked in a strange staccato whimper while his hands dithered back and forth in front of his face.

Thomas slowly squatted back down.

"I'm going out of my mind. I don't know what I'm saying. Help me, Brother. If only you knew how glad I am to see you! I don't know what I'd do if—I don't know." Kumaran's voice trailed off into a dismal yowl.

"I don't know how to help you," said Thomas with exasperation. "I've tried everything. I've offered the Father's forgiveness and eternal life. I've read to you from the Psalms, brought you bread and water, bathed you, covered your waste, even carried some away in the bucket. What more can I do? Who else would do as much? Who else loves you as I do? And what is the secret of this love? It's the truth of the gospel, of the cross. If it weren't true, I couldn't possibly love you this way! I couldn't possibly! It's my faith that empowers me. Don't you see?"

"Get out of here with your stinking love, your professional charity! Go away, go away, go away!"

Thomas did not go away, but instead picked up Kumaran's latest creation, which lay off to the side on a raised mound of dry sand. "What is this?"

"It's a medallion, a cross I made for you," said Kumaran more quietly.

Thomas picked it up and examined it. "Oh, Kumaran," he said, shaking his head. "Kumaran, what am I going to do about you? You rave like a demon one moment, and now this." In the half light Thomas fingered the sculpture, its four arms carved in intricate whorls. "It's beautiful," he said. "I shall treasure it, Brother."

"I made it to replace the one you lost in the jungle."

"Dear Kumaran, how could you—? Brother, I think I've never loved you so much as at this moment. Thank you. Thank you!" Thomas held up the cross so he could see it better in the gloom, then said: "That you should be thinking about me down in this hole! I am—I am—touched." He looked away from the gift and back at Kumaran. "Ah, but if only I could share my peace, my joy with you, the peace and joy of this cross. I would do anything to bring you to Christ!"

As Thomas slowly shook his head and caressed the cross, Kumaran felt something strange and new quietly explode inside him. Suddenly, inexplicably he wanted to stop fighting, stop hating; he wanted to put an end to his misery. It was true: Thomas *was* filled with peace and joy and love. Why had he only scoffed at Thomas' truth? Now it all made sense. Thomas *was* at peace because he'd found the truth.

Yes, it made sense; it was so obvious. Besides, what was there to lose? What had Murugan done for him? Where was Murugan anyway? Kumaran realized that Thomas' God actually seemed more real to him than Murugan. Murugan's bright images, the stories of his exploits, they all seemed like fairy tales. They were for the bright world above the pit. Yes, he would repent. He would give up his proud hatred. He already had—it had melted away. Even King Nediyon seemed less than despicable. And what peace he felt! It was as if a hot ball of lead long stuck in his chest dissolved. Yes, why not? And it would make Thomas so happy. And Thomas really seemed to love him.

"I repent," Kumaran said.

"You do?" said Thomas, looking up.

"I repent, yes."

"What do you mean?"

"Brother," Kumaran said with emphasis, "I want you to baptize me!"

"What?"

"Baptize me. Do it now."

Kumaran felt Thomas' eyes scrutinizing him in amazement, and he could not help smiling.

"Kumaran, if this is a joke—"

"It's not a joke, Brother!"

"Baptism? You are ready for baptism?" Thomas' voice quavered.

"I will never be as ready again."

"But it usually—well—" Thomas was speechless. "Kumaran! You accept Jesus as your Lord and the Father as the one God over all?"

"Yes, yes! I am ready, Brother, I tell you, I am ready!" Kumaran's voice vibrated with almost hysterical impatience.

Shaking his head, Thomas looked around and picked up the water pitcher lying on its side empty. "May the Lord be praised," he said in almost a whisper. "But we are out of water."

"A few drops will do. That's all I'm worth anyway."

"Kumaran!" Thomas embraced him

"Get on with it, Thomas. Get on with it."

"Yes, yes!" Thomas picked up the pitcher, blessed it with a sign of the cross, and closed his eyes in prayer.

Kumaran gazed up at the light streaming down into the hole.

"I baptize you, Judas Kumaran, in the name of the Lord Jesus." As Thomas said the words, he poured the few drops of water left in the pitcher over Kumaran's forehead. They rolled down his cheeks, like tears. "Kumaran, you are now part of Christ's body. Jews and gentiles, black and white, slaves and freemen, male and females—we are all one body. We are heirs of heaven."

Thomas put the pitcher down, then placed his hands over Kumaran's head. "Receive the Holy Spirit, Judas Kumaran." Thomas closed his eyes and prayed with his lips moving silently, and Kumaran remembered the demons that Thomas had expelled from Philetus on the ship in the Red Sea in what seemed like another life.

"Praise God, Kumaran! Praise God!" said Thomas, opening his eyes.

"I do praise him," said Kumaran shyly.

Thomas embraced him again, kissing him once on each cheek, as one kisses his son. "Welcome, Brother. Now you are my true brother, my spiritual brother. In the end there is no other kind that matters!" Thomas' voice swelled with gladness. Then, still holding Kumaran, he broke down and wept. He wept for a long time at the bottom of that hot stinking hole, and Kumaran wept with him. It was one of the happiest moments of Thomas' life.

"But why Judas?" said Kumaran finally.

"Judas. I have always saved that name for you, dear Brother. *My* name. Now we are one."

"But there was that other Judas. Wasn't he a traitor?"

"Judas Iscariot, yes. You aren't planning to follow his example, are you?" They both laughed, then wept again, but only briefly.

"There won't be time for that," said Kumaran after a moment. "I can't last much longer, you know that." He reached out to the side of the pit and touched it, and the angels of brightness that had gathered around seemed to scatter.

There was silence between them for a while. Then Thomas said, "Don't give up hope, Brother. I just thought of something. Why haven't I thought of it before?"

"What do you mean?"

Thomas didn't answer right away. "I can't say. Nothing might come of it. But don't give up hope. Not yet. Give me a little time. A little more time. Now, more than ever—oh, much, much more!—I must get you out of here."

That same evening, soon after sunset in the world above, Kumaran, sitting in his black hole, mulled over what he had done and what logically followed. He had confessed, even confessed killing the King, and Thomas had told him his sins were forgiven. No more karma to worry about. No more incarnations. No more rewards or punishments between incarnations. In place of Murugan's bright, playful, compassionless aloofness, an all-forgiving, all-loving Father God who had accepted Jesus' death as a bloody sacrifice to atone for the karma of all men. But wasn't all this too good to be true? Wasn't this a lunatic's God? Wasn't a man's karma inexorable? And did he really feel remorse for killing the King? Was it really a sin to kill such a tyrant, such a monster? Wouldn't it have been cowardice not to? He thought of Murugan and how Murugan despised cowardice. Yet he, Kumaran, had felt remorse. Or had he? Anyway, he had confessed. He remembered how he used to scorn the simple fools who let themselves be deceived into believing Thomas' teachings. Now he was one of those fools. Had he been seduced by Thomas' bewitching maternal concern, that thing called "charity," that dutiful form of service that only succeeded in enslaving its victim without feeling any affection for him? Never mind. He would accept Thomas' love in whatever guise it took. He fell on his knees and tried to rivet his heart on the Father. "Have mercy on me," he prayed. "Have mercy on me." But the words seemed to belong to someone else.

He thought of Thomas' mysterious words about not giving up hope. Oh, Thomas! Kumaran knew that Thomas was a fool in worldly matters. He knew that getting out of his hole was as likely as Thomas' converting all India. Yet he clung to those words. He let himself be bewitched by them; he relived them over and over just as Thomas spoke them; he treasured them, played with them, tried to guess what Thomas might do. And he let himself crave once again the bright world above his hole.

31. Thomas Strikes a Bargain

A s the hot season wore on, as all Madurai baked once again in the incandescent air that dried the Vaigai to a sandy waste and choked men's mouths with its yellow dust, Thomas carried through with his plan.

"Let me win his release, O Father! Oh, let me win his release!" he prayed as he waited to be brought in before the King. He felt the cross Kumaran had given him. It hung around his neck from a thong just like the other one. The sun had been up for less than an hour. The usual business of state hadn't yet begun.

A eunuch attendant led Thomas into King Nedunjeliyan's private receiving room. Seated on his dais and crowned by the usual wreath of fresh *neem* leaves, the King studied Thomas from underneath his Umbrella of State. At the King's feet a plum-colored cushion with the Pandyan emblem, the fish, sat on a rug with an ornate orange and blue floral design, and Thomas supposed that was where he should sit. But the King surprised him by getting off his throne and sitting on the cushion himself.

"I wouldn't insult you by offering you, an ascetic, a place beneath us," said the King.

Thomas bowed without a word and sat down in the lotus position on the rug. He liked the King at once. Though his eyes were small and the flesh around them slightly puffy, they didn't reflect treachery or a mean spirit.

"You are the yavana ascetic we have heard so much about, the apostle of that new God," said the King in a voice formal and self-possessed.

179

"Of *Sarveshvara*, the God of all. Not at all new. Very old, without beginning," Thomas said, declining to use a title of respect while addressing the King.

"We have room for all Gods in Madurai," said the King. "What brings you to us on this warm morning?"

"I come to ask for the release of the prisoner Kumaran."

"Kumaran? Our father's playmate? That corrupter of the royal blood line? He is still alive in that hole, you say?"

"Only barely. I have kept him alive all these weeks."

The King paused each time before he spoke, as if weighing his words carefully. This time he paused longer than usual. "What is your God's interest in our prisoner?"

"My God is a God of the widowed, the orphaned, the enslaved, the poor, the oppressed—and the imprisoned," Thomas answered respectfully but coolly.

"What does he have against kings?" Nedunjeliyan said, this time without a pause, and with more animation.

Thomas paused. "Political power is not the personal property of a king. It is a trust from God, to be used to further the divine purpose."

"Well spoken. You speak our language well, holy yavana. Not like our bodyguards. Who taught you?"

"The man you hold prisoner, the poet Kumaran."

The King frowned, then changed the subject. "Yogis can see into the past, can even relive past lives. And they see the future unfold in front of them as if it were the present. You are a yogi, are you not?"

"A yogi for Christ, yes," said Thomas.

"Tell us, Yogi for Christ, whoever he is, why you do not address us as other people do. As, 'Your Majesty,' and so forth. We are not offended, merely curious. Does your religion forbid it?"

Thomas didn't immediately know the answer. As he lowered his eyes and looked for the reason, the King, taking the opportunity, came to the point that interested him: "Never mind. Tell us, Yogi for Christ, tell us how my Pandyan army will fare against Karikal's Chola legions. Tell us if you can."

Suddenly Thomas understood Kumaran's freedom would come at a price. The King wanted him to see into the future, and if the vision pleased him, then Kumaran would go free. Not a word of this was spoken, but both men understood the barter as if it had been written down in a contract.

Thomas didn't have the least idea how to answer the King's question. He knew nothing of politics and almost said so. But then he thought of

Kumaran rotting in his hole. "Maranatha," he called out to God under his breath with eyes closed. "Maranatha." He opened his eyes and said, "Do you mean there will be war?"

"Our people are hungry," said the King, lowering his voice so none of the attendants would hear. "The people on our northern border are dying. Their fields are parched. We need to push our borders to the Kaveri and tap into her waters. Our kingdom used to extend that far at one time."

Thomas was touched by the King's concern for his people. Here was no potentate greedy for empire. He merely wanted to keep his people from starving.

"What do you see, Yogi?" said the King.

Thomas felt he should cooperate for Kumaran's sake. He closed his eyes, asked for God's help again, emptied his mind until it was as still as a pond on a windless dawn, and waited, holding the cross against his chest.

He began to see a series of images, and he heard himself begin to speak: "A butterfly, large and beautiful, black with green spots. Another, smaller, just as beautiful, black with a large yellow mark on each wing. Flitting around each other, attacking each other. And I see men, a water brigade. A man takes a bucket from his fellow, walks a few strides, hands it to the next man. And that man in turn carries it to the next. They look like puppets, they move as if asleep—no, as if dead. Such a long line. I can't see the end in either direction. Back and forth each man treads, bucket after bucket, the same ground over and over. I look inside a bucket. It is—empty. They are all empty. Now I see a lone man walking—walking away from me, toward Madurai. He is sickly, bent over, as thin as a stick. One arm is bowed and stiff, the other swings slightly. I feel sorry for him, run to catch up, to give him a coin, a coin, a large gold coin—with a great tiger in the center, a tiger surrounded by a small bow and fish—"

"Stop, Yogi," said the King. "You see only what is upon us now. This is not the future, it is the present. Our people are thirsty *now*."

Then the King, who had been sitting in a relaxed position on his cushion, jerked forward. "Wait! You were saying something about a coin—just before I interrupted you."

Thomas looked up at a man transfigured. The self-possession and formality had fled.

"Go back to that, Yogi, go back to that. Something about a tiger, a tiger—what did you say?"

"A tiger, yes, in the center," Thomas said, his eyes now open and looking at the King.

"Something to do with a coin, you said?" said the King, his eyes intent and anxious.

"Yes, in the center of the coin."

"And it was surrounded by—by what?"

"A fish, and a bow."

Nedunjeliyan stood up and began to pace, tense lines on his youthful copper-colored brow. "I—we—interrupted you—you were saying something about a—a beggar, or—go back to that if you can."

"Not a beggar, but a stick-man; I was about to say the stick man—was you."

"Me?" The King's eyes opened wide. "If I—we—did not know of you by reputation, we would think you were a spy. What's that thing around your neck? *Are* you a spy?" As soon as he asked the question, he turned aside and waved the thought away. It was a ridiculous inquiry, and he knew it. Recovering his aplomb, he dismissed Thomas, holding out two gold coins.

"I am grateful to the King, but only one gift will please me," Thomas said.

"What is that, Yogi?"

"The poet Kumaran's freedom. He has become a Christian, he has repented, he abhors what he did with your father. And he would leave Madurai at once if freed. You have my word as a yogi on that."

The King studied Thomas for a moment, then said, "We will consider it."

"One other thing," said Thomas. "The cooks did not murder your father. They are innocent."

"How do you know this?"

"I cannot say how I know it."

"I order you to say!"

"I cannot. Even if it costs me my life. I am not at liberty."

"Tell me this, yes or no. Was Kumaran the assassin?"

Thomas only looked down at the floor.

"It doesn't matter," said the King after a moment. "Whoever killed him saved us all from ruin."

Thomas bowed slightly. The King called to the next room, and a eunuch came in and led him out.

"You will say nothing of this to anyone, on your life," the King said as Thomas passed through the door.

Thomas went straight from the King's palace to Kumaran's hole. Perhaps Kumaran would understand the dream that so agitated the King.

"The meaning is obvious," Kumaran said in a weak voice. "The tiger is the totem of Karikal's Chola Empire. The bow is the totem of the Chera. The fish is the totem of the Pandyan. The King was upset because the coin showed the tiger at the center and the bow and the fish on the edge. And the tiger is large while the bow and the fish are small. And the stick-man is the King. And he's walking toward Madurai. He's been defeated, Brother. And the water brigade stands for all his subjects. They're thirsty, they're suffering, they're dying. The meaning is clear." He paused, then added, "I never knew you could see into the future."

"I'm as surprised as you," said Thomas. "But what about the butterflies?"

"Nothing I can make sense of, except in a general sort of way. The big butterfly is probably Karikal, the littler one Nedunjeliyan. They're battling, that's all. Now will you tell me why you had an audience with the King?"

Thomas had hinted at some great good news from the time his feet touched the floor of Kumaran's pit. Now he placed his hands on either side of Kumaran's shoulders and stared at him hard in the face. "Judas Kumaran, I asked the King for your freedom."

For a moment Kumaran was speechless. Then he asked with quiet fervor, "And did he give it?"

"He said he'd consider it. But you must tell no one."

"Tell no one? Who would I tell?"

"Maruthanar, perhaps? But you must not."

Kumaran looked down at the ground and picked up the piece of teak he was working on. He felt around for his knife, found it, and started whittling. Then he dropped the knife and began to sob.

"Come, Brother," said Thomas, taking Kumaran in his arms. "Come now. Come, come. Stay alive a little longer. We have so much more work to do. So much work. It's just begun."

Kumaran put his head on Thomas's gaunt but still powerful shoulder and wept like a baby.

Finally Thomas said, "What's that you're carving?"

"Murugan," Kumaran whimpered.

"Murugan?" The word stung Thomas.

"Maruthanar tells me that's—that's what's selling these days. Next month is his festival, you know."

"Ahhhhhh." Thomas slowly relaxed his arms and released Kumaran. "The King was surprised to hear you were still alive. I think he'd forgotten about you. Did you know the guards bet how long you would last? You've surpassed all their guesses. They say they've never seen anyone survive the pit so long."

"They don't even piss on me anymore."

"A sign of respect?"

Kumaran looked down at the ground, picked up his knife, and began whittling at Murugan again. Then he said, "I saved *your* life once, you know."

"You did? When was that, Brother?"

"In Kurinchi. I went to Pari and persuaded him to let you go. He would have killed you."

"You never told me that. Well then, maybe we'll be even in a few days."

Kumaran kept on whittling and said nothing. Then he said, "I wish your vision had been different."

Thomas embraced Kumaran again, then stood up and said, "The King's a just man. I trust him. I'll come back tomorrow. A few months ago I had a dream. About a snake. Maybe you can make sense of that too."

Then Kumaran said mysteriously, "Brother, I'm not good enough to be a Christian."

"None of us is, Brother. None of us is." Thomas kissed Kumaran on his oily, smelly forehead, bent down to pick up the empty pitcher, and mounted the ladder.

Thomas prayed hard and often for Kumaran's release, and one day, about a fortnight after his visit to the King, Kumaran, too weak to mount the ladder himself, was triumphantly hoisted out of his hole on a hook by three pulaiyar Christians. When he emerged into the light, he couldn't open his eyes for many minutes. But he was out, free, and the soldiers cheered from a discreet distance: They had never seen a prisoner hoisted out of the hole alive.

That night Thomas went to his usual spot on the bank of the dry Vaigai. Fleecy clouds were blowing in from the west and faintly hinted of rain, but still the air was uncomfortably hot. Sitting on the warm sands in the lotus position, he thanked God for Kumaran's release. When a breath of cooler air wafted over his bare body, he thought again of the weather. Some of his poorer converts were just beginning to feel the effect of the drought: The smell of their bodies told him they hadn't been bathing. "Let it rain, Father!" Thomas prayed, joining his voice to the millions of voices across the Pandyan Empire that prayed the same prayer to their various gods.

His head leaned back on his neck and he stared with eyes wide open almost straight up, as if trying to penetrate the dark beyond the stars. He felt like weightless spirit yearning upward and uniting with God. Suddenly everything made sense; everything was right just as it was. He was the string, and all he had to do now was let himself be plucked by the Divine Minstrel. As the hand is to the self, so was he to God.

The thought of Kumaran being lifted out of the pit brought him back down to earth. They had taken Kumaran to Maruthanar's house, but Maruthanar wouldn't receive him when he learned he had converted to the alien faith. Thomas worried Kumaran would weaken. Would Kumaran want to give his attention to serving God, or would he lapse back into writing his worldly poetry for the praise of men? As clouds of white muslin passed across the young crescent moon, dimming it, unveiling it, then dimming it again, Thomas prayed over and over, "Make Kumaran one of Yours, Lord! Make him Yours forever!" And he became convinced the Lord would.

Then his mind turned to the work he had done in Madurai. He had ordained Nakkirar bishop; the ivy had taken root and was spreading. Refugees from outlying villages driven by drought to the city would help it spread more quickly once they returned home. Now there was Puhar ahead of him—Puhar and the great Chola Empire, the greatest prize of all. And again Kumaran—but a new Kumaran—would be his companion.

PART V: THE JOURNEY

32. Drought

It took Kumaran a week to rub the smell out of his skin and another to build up enough strength to travel. He was surprised at how quickly his old but now chastened ambition returned. Yes, it still goaded him. But there was little joy in it; the dream was no longer sweet. He almost envied lesser men. They did not live in a future time that might never be, but in a humble present as real as a radish, and he suspected that most of them were happier than he. But he had fallen under a kind of curse. It was not enough that he had won fame once; he had to do it again. He told himself it was madness. But what were the alternatives? He could go back home to Maliankara and take up sculpting again, or he could help Thomas as a full-time missionary of a faith that looked more appealing from inside his hole than outside. He had the stomach for neither. Once again he allowed himself to be lured by the siren song of Puhar.

Thomas, for his part, was eager to move on. He took Kumaran's freedom as a sign from God that his work in Madurai was finished: Two years were plenty long enough for one place. Kumaran didn't notice this eagerness and supposed Thomas had become a true sannyasin, inwardly as well as outwardly. To Kumaran Thomas seemed not to care at all for anything the world offered. His loin cloth, once bright orange, was now the color of the hot dust over which the wheels of the bullock cart creaked as it turned its first revolution northward out of Madurai. His hair was short and black and rather unkempt, his beard long and streaked with silver. His shoulders seemed unnaturally broad as they sat astride his narrow chest and gaunt stomach; only his shoulders reminded Kumaran that Thomas had once been a carpenter. Kumaran was surprised to find Thomas' old habit of stroking and rubbing things still intact.

Their cart was so laden with water, food, and other baggage, much of it donated by Thomas' Christians, that they themselves had to walk. For the last time Thomas blessed his flock, almost five-hundred strong; all had turned out to see him off. In their devotion to him they ignored Kumaran, and Kumaran found himself thinking about the sloughed skin of a cobra, which the peasants said made one invisible when carried. Maruthanar and his family had waved good-bye to him from the balcony of their house, where he went to pick up his writings and riches from an earlier day; but he knew their waves only disguised the fact they were glad to see him go. How could he blame them? So he said a silent good-bye to the city that only a year before had seemed eager to immortalize him for his verse and storytelling. For all Madurai cared now, he might as well have been a needle maker. Several of the Christians called out "Kumaran" as he and Thomas struck out across the sandy wastes of the Vaigai. Their charity embarrassed him.

They walked up the tree-lined bank on the far side, teeming with refugees from the hungry outlying areas, and left the great city behind. Except for a patch of paddy here and there irrigated by hand from some nearby well, the flat land north of the river lay parched and fallow. The trickle of refugees heading south—a month earlier there had been a torrent—always asked the same question: "Is there food in the city?" They warned there wasn't a grain of food ahead, and the looks on their desperate, starving faces were proof enough of this. They couldn't understand why anyone would be leaving Madurai, where grain was convoyed in from the mountains. But Kumaran told himself not to worry. In four or five more days they would reach Kumaran's birthplace, Uranthai, in a foreign empire where the yellow-green waters of the broad, swelling Kaveri never dried up. Their cart was still heaped high with water and hay for the bullock, and at the bottom of the pile he had hid a sizable hoard of jewels and gold and silver, the loot from adoring patrons he had accumulated in better days when he was the toast of Madurai.

Near the end of the first day the cracked brown earth took on a reddish hue, and the faraway blue mountain ranges on both sides were replaced by rock-strewn, shrubby hills close in. Kumaran realized they were now in the country referred to as "desert" or "wasteland" by the troubadours and that he should carefully note the characteristics of this bleak bushland: its land features, vegetation, animals, and people. But except for the red-legged lizards that scurried over the rocks, there were few animals or men to note, and more carcasses of cattle than living bodies. Once they came to a pond, one of the last with water still in it, and saw deer and boar watering; but what impressed Kumaran most was the blinding white sky, the yellow dust that caked in the sockets of the eyes, the creaking of the wobbly wheels with their protruding hubs, the vultures tearing at the carrion that rotted on the side of the road, and the gnats that descended in swirling clouds of black dots to drive a man crazy.

That evening the road ran through a village surrounded by a thick thorny hedge that still had a few people in it. In a roadside ditch under a clump of withered bamboo, they came upon a dog which had just whelped. Three of its brood lay dead, their tiny pink bent-eared faces already swarmed over by flies, while three more, still too young to open their eyes, sucked frantically at the bitch's milkless teats. A few more minutes and they too would be free, Kumaran told himself—free for the duration of one blink of Brahma's eye, then condemned to suffer anew in some other land dictated by their pitiless karmas.

In the first house, which belonged, as it happened, to the village drummer and his family of five children, hunger had taken its toll too. A baby girl a few weeks old had died just minutes before Kumaran and Thomas came upon the scene. The mother, who was slicing raw tubers in the hot twilight outside the entrance to keep the others from starving, didn't have time or energy to mourn; but two of the older children wept quietly as they sat around the corpse of their baby sister, lying naked on the hard clay floor just inside the entrance.

Thomas peered down at this pathetic sight. "Mother," he said, "we have food for you."

The whole family looked up as if they expected to see Yama, the God of Death, playing a trick on them. Then the mother got up and fell at Thomas' feet.

"Come," he said, leading her to the cart. He took two mangos, some dried pomegranate slices, a few peppers, and scooped up four cupfuls of rice from the larder. "Take these and eat."

The woman's eyes glowed as she gazed up at the tall, pale apparition. Then she fell on the baked earth at his feet and cried out, "Master, Master, Master!" through moans and dry-eyed sobs.

"Get up, Mother," Thomas said softly. "We want to know if we might spend this night with you."

She looked at him with alarm. "But our baby—our baby has—just died, Aiyer. The house is polluted."

For an instant Thomas looked puzzled, then said, "Bring the baby to me."

The woman looked up at him with her forehead creased and mouth open, then brought him the baby.

Thomas took the body, blessed it, and put his lips to its tiny mouth, breathing in and out, as a muddy tear worked its way down his dust-caked face. He waited a minute, then drooled out spittle on the baby's forehead. "I baptize you in the name of the Lord Jesus, the Christ," he said in Aramaic. He gave the dead baby back to the mother and said: "I have taken the pollution to myself. Your house is free of it." Then he looked around. "Mother, you have mimosa trees, one on either side of the house. If we might sleep under one of them beside our bullock and cart, we would be grateful. We will pay you with food."

"You may stay," said her husband, the drummer, who had come up a moment earlier with excitement on his feverish face. He was carry-ing the dog, which he had just killed. "We have food!" he told his wife. "And there is more where I found this!"

The woman's eyes grew large for an instant, as if, once again, she couldn't believe them. Then she got up, bowed quickly to Thomas, and walked away down the main road into the village.

Soon a collection of ragged or naked bodies with encrusted, sunken eyes began to gather at the front door of the house. Each carried a dish and cup. Some tip-toed, as if not wanting to attract notice. Others were coughing. Several of the children had bloated stomachs and cracks in the corners of their mouths. One of the old women had orange hair. Some eyed the skinned dog being cut up by the drummer and the rice being fed into a cooking pot by his old-est daughter with a fierce, ravenous interest, while others seemed listless and uninterested.

When the woman came back, Thomas asked her who these peo-ple were.

"They are all that remain in the village, Aiyer," she said.

He looked surprised. "Are they your relatives?"

"No, Aiyer. They are the ones who couldn't get away in time. They are the starving."

"But your own children, there will—there will be less for them. And—" Thomas glanced at the floor where the dead infant lay, now wrapped in a rag.

"Where he is now, he will be cared for, Aiyer," she said. "The hungry—we can still help them."

For a moment Thomas said nothing, then asked frowning, "But—are they as hungry as you?"

"Oh, yes, Aiyer, some hungrier. Some of them are too weak to dig for roots. They stay alive by sleeping and eating insects, even lice. And yesterday"—she hesitated as if she couldn't go on—"my neighbor, my best friend, strangled her children, then—then bashed her head in with a rock."

Thomas studied the scrawny black woman with withered breasts hanging like empty bags almost to her waist, large holes cut in her sagging ear lobes, and a single bead in her hair. He looked as if he were trying to remember when or where he had met her before, or as if she represented some strange new species he had never before seen.

"Kumaran," he said, "we must feed these people well, feed *all* of them, until they're full. I'll get the larder. Would you bring the water?"

"No," Kumaran whispered emphatically, coming up close to Thomas. "No, Brother, we're at best just a quarter of the way to Uranthai. They'll eat up all the food. And there is barely enough water for the two of us and the bullock. There must be thirty of them. We can't allow it!"

"We can stand a little hunger and thirst, Brother. These people are dying."

"But—we'll die, too!"

"No, we won't die. You packed enough to take us all the way to Puhar."

"Not water!" Kumaran almost shrieked. "At least keep the water back!"

"We'll keep two of the jugs for us. That will be enough."

"No, it won't! You're forgetting the bullock!"

Thomas made a movement toward the cart.

"I paid for it!" Kumaran yelled.

"The Kaveri is only three days ahead," said Thomas. "We must share even if we have to suffer."

"Maybe four. And haven't I suffered enough!?" Kumaran was begging. "Here, I'll go!" He pushed ahead of Thomas. "I'll bring the stuff. You go back to the people."

So it was Kumaran who brought in the rice and the water. But he did not bring in as much water as Thomas wanted. He poured out a generous quantity for the bullock first, then carried in the jug. Then he brought in the rice.

Some of the people ate ravenously of the rice-and-dog stew, while others took only a few bites and vomited. These latter screamed and beat their bodies; they were desperate to keep their food down; they knew their lives depended on it. They tried over and over to eat, but always they vomited. They went to their houses cursing the gods who condemned them to starve even though food was abundant. Still others had no interest in eating. Their relatives or friends had to coax them to swallow the food.

Later that evening, after the last guests had slipped away into the night, Thomas, like a sliver of iron drawn to a magnet, came back to the woman. "Tell me, Mother, why did you feed them, all these people? Do you owe them something?"

"No. We have debts, but not to them."

"Why then? Please, tell me."

She looked at Thomas with wonder. "I told you already, Aiyer."

"Tell me again, Mother."

"They were starving. *I* was starving. We've always helped each other." She waggled her head and smiled sheepishly.

"But you are rewarded—in the next life?"

"Rewarded? Me? *You* are the one to be rewarded, Aiyer. You brought the food. You'll be a brahmin in your next life. . . Or—or are you now?" Her voice dropped off to almost a whisper as she looked humbly at the ground, suddenly afraid she had become too familiar.

"She's a good woman," said her husband, pulling her aside by the elbow.

The next day as they continued north along the straight, flat, deserted road, with prickly shrubs, scorched trees, and dry ponds flanking it on both sides, and the fierce white sun searing the earth, Kumaran asked Thomas about the woman. Why had he bothered her with all those questions? But Thomas would not tell him. Instead he put questions back to Kumaran. Did he know the significance of circumcision? Or the major feasts of the Jewish calendar and what each celebrated? Or how the Sabbath feast came into being? Thomas explained all these things as they walked beside the cart with the sun beating down.

"God hates sin," he said as Kumaran waved away a swarm of gnats, "and Jesus had to die. Do you remember why?"

Kumaran didn't answer. He waved his hand at the question as much as at the gnats.

"This is what I came to India to preach, and this is what you will need to preach, too."

Feeling his stomach go queasy, Kumaran looked across the bullock at Thomas, who looked back at him anxiously.

"You *will* preach this, Brother, won't you?" Thomas said.

Kumaran shrugged his shoulders and said, "We need to water the bullock."

They stopped, and Kumaran ladled out water from the second of the three large water jugs under the hay into a large metal dish. "We've barely enough water to get to Uranthai," he said. "Why do you drink so much?!" he yelled at the animal.

Thomas said after a moment, "You and Devandi must marry again—as soon as you bring her back. If you're to be a deacon, you must be exemplary. And Christian marriage brings with it a special grace. It's a covenant before God, a covenant between two people before God."

They got underway again, and Thomas wondered aloud how he might Christianize the Indra festival. On and on he went, until Kumaran's head whirred and spun like the gnats in front of his face.

They stopped that evening in a completely deserted village. Nothing moved in it except a few rags on a clothesline swaying in the wind.

"Brother," Thomas said early the next morning on the deserted road, "what is mine is yours, what is yours is mine." Thomas looked at Kumaran in that trusting, forgiving way of his. "We are brothers in Christ. What do you want from me in return for the food I gave them? Take it, it's yours."

"It's not the food. We're at best halfway to the Kaveri, and we have only one jug left. You've put us in danger," Kumaran hissed.

"Not as much danger as those people back in the village."

"They were done for! It was too late!"

They walked along in silence for a few minutes. Then Thomas said, "If you want to be reimbursed, take everything I own."

"There is nothing you own that I want!"

For an instant Thomas' eyes flashed with an anger of their own, and Kumaran checked his just in time. As the sun climbed the sky to cauterize the earth for another day, they trudged on. There was nothing ahead but parched earth; mountains on both sides stuck their purple heads up into the blinding bleached sky. How far from the Kaveri they were they did not know.

As they rationed out a little more of the water from the last jug, Kumaran was afraid. It was strange: Though there was much less reason to fear, he was more afraid of dying now than he had ever been back in his hole in Madurai, when death was almost certain.

The day was clear, but nothing on the horizon ahead of them suggested their destination. They slept in another deserted village. It was the third night.

On the fourth morning they walked along without speaking, their mouths as dry as the hot air surrounding them. But around noon, clouds moved in from the southwest, the temperature dropped, and Kumaran dared to hope. As the sun sank, they saw a green patch of earth dead ahead. They quickened their pace and came upon an irrigated millet field. They led the bullock over to a flowing canal, shouted for joy, and drank deep draughts from the last jar. Thomas' optimism had proven correct, and Kumaran didn't mind being wrong one bit. As the sun set and black clouds hovered on the horizon to the west, they came upon a sizable town full of life.

Peacocks danced on the main road as Kumaran and Thomas entered the town. Kumaran knew that peacocks announced rain with their strutting, so they took lodging in a large bungalow near the center of town in case they needed to escape the rain.

In the middle of the night the rain came, and Kumaran, sleeping outside, moved from his bed of hay beside the cart to a storeroom just inside the wall of the house nearest the cart. It made him nervous to think of the cart with all his possessions left untended, but who would go prowling about in this weather? The rain falling against the thatched roof made a soothing sound, and as he strained to hear the lowing of the bullock through the wall, he fell asleep.

He woke to shrieking and shouting. Jumping off his rope cot in the pitch dark, he felt his way to the door to see what was happening. There in the middle of the central room, lit by a dim oil lamp, knelt the householder, a large man, beating another man with a pickax as he lay unconscious on the ground. The man's skull had cracked, but the host continued to beat him. Suddenly two wild-looking men squeezed through a hole in the earthen wall like moles. With a few swift jabs they beat back the householder as Kumaran looked on in a daze, frozen to the wall and afraid for his life. One of the men then took his cleaver and with a single swipe severed the dead man's head. They fled out the front door with the head while the corpse gushed blood from the neck over the floor.

The men were members of the Kallar robber caste, notorious for their stealth and willing to take any risk to recover the heads of their slain comrades. They had slashed the forearm of the householder, but he had saved the family fortune. Thomas had just awakened, and amid great confusion and shouting he and Kumaran dragged the corpse out of the house while the women and girls cleaned up the blood. When they came back in, the householder, breathless and almost hysterical, told how he heard a sound—he called it a "clank"—out back and woke up. Then he caught the man, who had burrowed a hole through the wall with a pickax after the fashion of the Kallar, stacking up the family's gold and silver plates and goblets. He wrestled the robber, a much smaller man, to the ground and beat him to death with his own pickax.

As the householder was finishing his story, Kumaran's heart suddenly froze. What did that "clank out back" mean? He thought of the cart with all his possessions, his wealth. He asked for a lantern, and a servant got one, lit it, and gave it to him. Normally he would have been excited about the rain, which splashed down around him as he groped toward the stall in the back. But it was not the rain that he thanked God for as he spotted the bullock and the cart. He stepped up closer, confident all was well, and held the lantern over the hay just to make sure. What was that? His heart heaved as he gazed at a hole in the middle of the hay. He reached into the hole and felt for the fat skin of gold, silver, precious stones. Impossible! He must look harder. He leaned into the hole and felt down to the floor of the cart and around under the hay. Then the truth hit him, and he felt a nausea not of the stomach but of the lungs, of the very soul. It was gone, it was all gone. Then he thought of the gold lotus given him by the Maravar Chief. He had hidden it separately; surely they had missed that. He threw all the baggage out of the cart, got down on hands and knees and groveled around like a scavenging animal, refusing to believe it could be gone. But there was nothing, nothing left, not a single solitary jewel fit for the crotch of an outcast whore. He sat down in the hay where his treasure should have been and cursed every God he could think of, starting with Thomas'. He cursed them all to the deepest, darkest, foulest hell. The mansion he had planned to buy in Puhar, the silks he would dress his wife in, the servants and the nurse for his baby girl, the rich foods and Greek wines, the proper friends—all were gone. He flung himself down into the mud, blubbered and screamed like a man possessed, beat his fists into the ground, wished he were dead, deader than dead.

He became aware of Thomas squatting beside him in the darkness as the rain fell. Part of him wanted only to be left alone so he could curse the night, but another part longed to hear the words of comfort he knew Thomas had for him. Kumaran had watched Thomas weep many times for strangers, only three days before for a nameless infant that could have meant nothing to him; Thomas' compassion came cheap, Kumaran knew that, but he still wanted it, even craved it. Thomas was his friend, his companion of almost five years, his student and teacher, his sworn brother.

But Kumaran didn't see tears well up in Thomas' eyes as Thomas led him back into the house. Thomas' voice said something about being "fortunate." Twice Kumaran heard the phrase "danger of riches." He had the strange impression that Thomas was congratulating him on his loss. "The load will be lighter tomorrow," he thought he heard Thomas say at one point. "And look, they didn't take your bag of poetry." His heart was stricken with anguish and horror; he could hardly believe what he was hearing. There was almost something laughable about it. As he lay in his bed after drying off and rehearsed what he thought Thomas had said, he felt numb. The idea of living without wealth was bad enough, but Thomas' betrayal—that is the way he thought of it—was unthinkable and shocking. Sympathy, fellow-feeling? He had none at all. Thomas might as well have been talking to an apprentice cartwright about how to repair a wheel. Kumaran's heart pounded in the dark like a blacksmith's hammer, and each stroke fell with the thud of hatred.

The next day as they splashed their way around puddles, Thomas told him again, "Brother, what is mine is yours, and what is yours is mine." Kumaran wanted to lash out at him, to hit him, to smash his teeth into his face, to spit at him, but some obscure grace, or perhaps exhaustion, held him back. Here was a man, Kumaran told himself, who wept tears for strangers, but for his own brother he had only advice, a sermon, an edifying discourse about what it means to live as a Christian. "I lost some things too," Kumaran heard him say. It was true, but he had not lost what he valued most: his manuscripts and writings, which he had in the house with him at the time of the robbery. "Brother, did I ever tell you about the rich man we met outside Jericho? When he asked Jesus what he had to do to be saved—"

"Stop!" Kumaran screamed, his eyes squinted as they glowered at his persecutor, daring him to say another word.

"I only—"

"I've heard it a thousand times!"

They looked like executioner and victim as they crossed the border into Chola country with Uranthai in sight.

33. Hatred

Early the next morning, the sixth day since leaving Madurai, Thomas and Kumaran walked into Uranthai, with its massive jutting rock next to the broad, ever-flowing Kaveri. Kumaran had planned to go back to his old neighborhood, the sculptor's street where he lived until he was twelve, and visit old playmates now grown. He found his old house, but much else was changed, and only a few faces seemed at all familiar. He lost heart just as he was about to venture an introduction.

Early the next day he traded the bullock and cart for a small boat, no more than a skiff, while Thomas bought rolls made of millet, various fruits and nuts, and implements for writing. They loaded their baggage, much reduced since the attack, took up pole and paddle, and pushed out onto the dull blue-gray waters of the Kaveri. Kumaran felt sad as he watched the city pass by on his right. It was here he had been loved by his mother; it was here he watched her body borne to the ghats bordering the river and consigned to flame. These very waters flowed over her bones.

By the time the two halves of the stream joined again into a single mighty current, he had recovered. Sitting at the front of the boat and paddling only so much as necessary to keep the boat parallel to the current, he surrendered himself to the spirit of the unfailing river. For hours he and Thomas said nothing, and that was the way he liked it. He almost imagined himself happy—happy to be alone in that boat with only the river, happy to have forgotten his great loss and Thomas' oppressive presence. Such is the balm of Mother Kaveri that it can cast spells and induce illusions.

Thunder rumbled over distant fields to the south where dark sheets of rain fell, but it was hot and sticky where they were; they moved in the direction and at the speed of the breeze.

"I understand your poets and saints for the first time," Thomas said from the rear of the boat as he broke the long silence. "I'm beginning to understand how they can worship rivers, make pilgrimages to them, even deify them."

Anything Thomas said might have annoyed Kumaran, but he couldn't help feeling mildly curious about this unexpected disclosure.

"This river," Thomas went on, "it's immense, it seems to have a personality all its own."

"Every bend is a smile, every cataract a frown," Kumaran said in a humdrum tone of voice, quoting an ancient proverb.

"We too have a sacred river, the Jordan. That's where Jesus was baptized."

Kumaran resented the way Thomas used Tamil country to evoke memories of Galilee and Judaea. He found such comparisons tedious and demeaning. But he held his tongue.

"Compared to this it's only a brook," Thomas said, "but its waters wash away sin."

"Is it worshipped?" Kumaran said, sensing an opportunity for the thing burning in his breast.

"No, no!" Thomas laughed, trying to sound more cheerful than Kumaran knew he could feel.

Kumaran knew Thomas' tricks, and he wouldn't let himself be charmed by his personality, still less by any strategic show of tardy compassion. No, it would be a long time before Kumaran let Thomas think he was forgiven. Instead revenge smoldered in his throat. "Perhaps if it were larger," he said, trying to get under Thomas' skin.

"No, Brother!" Thomas said. "Size doesn't make a river holy." Then after a pause he continued: "Do you know what the Vedas say about a river? One of the yogis on the Vaigai told me this. A river flowing into the sea is like the soul shaking off all names and forms and uniting with Brahman, God, the Universal Soul."

"That offends you, doesn't it?" said Kumaran, who hadn't turned around once to look back at Thomas.

"Why should it?" Thomas said. "The oneness we agree with. Not all Indians worship many gods, I've learned. But the nature of the oneness—that's where we differ. The Indian yogi sees God as one with everything. We see him as the creator of everything. Yet we both acknowledge his holiness. And since meeting that woman back in that starving village, I have to admit both ways work. Both ways—both ways can transform lives."

"Sometimes you surprise me," Kumaran said after a moment. "By the way, why did you question that woman like that? You never told me."

Thomas said nothing, and Kumaran finally turned around and asked in a rude voice, "Did you hear me?"

"Yes," Thomas said quietly, as if to himself, as if lost in his own thoughts. "No one in India has taught me as much as that simple woman." Then in a louder voice he said, "Kumaran, have I ever told you the story of the sheep and the goats?"

"Too many times, I'm sure."

Taking no offense, Thomas told the story: "When Christ comes again to bring time to a close, when he comes down to earth in all his glory, all the angels with him, and sits on his glorious throne in Jerusalem, all nations, all people living, or who have ever lived, will gather before him. And he will separate all of them into two groups as a shepherd weeds out the goats from his sheep. The sheep he'll place at his right hand, the goats at the left. The sheep he'll carry up with him into the Father's eternal Kingdom. The goats he'll—"

"Yes, yes, yes, and all that other rot," Kumaran said.

"Ah, Kumaran, when will you stop fighting me? When, Brother?" asked Thomas in an injured tone. Then he added, "Forgive me for—for not feeling your—your loss."

Kumaran only scorned Thomas for being so predictable. Thomas, he told himself, didn't really feel sorrow; he forced himself to feel it. Kumaran decided to ignore the peace offering and said, "This Christ—I suppose you mean Jesus, the carpenter you grew up with, your humble step-brother? He has the power—did I hear you say he has the power to bring time to a close? Time? Do you know what you are saying?"

"Why do you ask this, Kumaran? You know exactly what I am saying. You accepted baptism into his flock."

"Quite a fellow, wouldn't you say? Perhaps he'll be deified some day. Indians deify their rivers; you Israelites deify your friends."

"That's not my point," Thomas said darkly, as Kumaran sensed with malicious satisfaction that a volcano was about to explode. But Thomas put his open hand against the cross hanging around his neck, the cross Kumaran had made for him back in Madurai, and said, "The point is— what do you think qualifies a person to be a sheep?"

"And get into heaven, you mean? What?"

Thomas forced his spirits back up, and he began to speak in that oracular way of his that was so effective in debate but that Kumaran had come to detest. "I hear the Master's voice as clearly as if we were sitting on the Mount of Olives outside Jerusalem. 'Come, blessed of my Father, inherit the Kingdom prepared for you from the foundation of the world! For I was hungry and you fed me, thirsty and you gave me drink, a stranger and you welcomed me, naked and you clothed me, sick and you visited me, in prison and you came to me.'"

"So *that's* why you came to see me in prison," Kumaran said.

Taken aback, Thomas hesitated. Then he regrouped and said, "Yes, Brother, it is. At least in part. It's why you saw so *much* of me. Do you object? You didn't object then."

"Please don't call me 'brother'."

"Why not?"

"That woman, the woman who fed her neighbors, let's get back to her. Is she a sheep or a goat? By your own standards she should be a sheep, for she fed the hungry."

"That's what I've been thinking, too. I've thought a great deal about that woman."

"I'm sure she'd be honored to know that."

"I've never known a person who practiced the Master's gospel more perfectly," said Thomas, ignoring Kumaran's malice.

"Yet she had never heard the Master's gospel. You didn't tell her about it on the sneak while I was putting away the cart and feeding the bullock, did you?"

"She'd never heard of the Master or his gospel, Kumaran," Thomas said in a soft, carefully measured tone that suggested acute self-mastery.

"And you didn't pour the waters of baptism over her head while she lay helpless in a hot hole and hadn't the strength to protest—as you did me?" Holding a finger to one nostril, Kumaran blew the mucus out of the other with a great explosion. The mucus hit the river with a splat.

"If we take the Master at his word, there will be at least one pagan in heaven," Thomas said in a voice that quavered.

"Would she have the choice of leaving?" Kumaran held a finger to the opposite nostril and blew out as violently as before. "I mean, would she be happy there all by herself?"

"Get out! Get out!" Thomas yelled absurdly. "By God—!" But he didn't complete his thought.

Kumaran had turned around at last and was watching, a grin smeared across his face.

"I despise you!" Thomas yelled. "By God, I despise you!" Then he said more quietly, but with his face still contorted by fury, "Is nothing sacred to you?"

"The river," Kumaran said with a feigned, superior serenity, "is sacred."

"The river!" Thomas sputtered. "The river that you just polluted with that—that—that despicable habit of yours!" Again he had taken the bait. Kumaran watched in triumph as Thomas fecklessly slapped the water with his paddle. He had broken that impervious facade of calm that Thomas had cultivated on the Vaigai. He wanted Thomas to suffer cruelly for his pitiless, sterile moralizing in the face of his great loss. He wanted Thomas to crack, and crack he did. But Kumaran was only getting started.

"I hope you don't think she's alone," Kumaran said. "Many of us would have done the same thing. Along with killing a brahmin or a cow, or violating the wife of your guru, or passing yourself off as learned when you're not—alongside these is the sin of looking at a hungry man and not feeding him. We're all taught this from the cradle. Didn't you know that?"

"It's one thing to hear a teaching, another to practice it," Thomas said more quietly.

"And do you Jews and Christians practice it any better?"

"Yes, we do! You Indians throw all your efforts into saving your souls. You spare nothing in this pursuit. And because it's selfish, it fails. That's the irony, the tragedy—it fails. We Christians do practice the Master's gospel! You know that. You have seen it."

"So do Indians. You admit it yourself. The woman—"

"She's an exception!"

"Is she? Possibly you just haven't noticed!"

Another route of attack occurred to Kumaran. "Tell me, O wise sannyasin from the Vaigai, if this woman can enter heaven, without baptism, without even hearing Jesus' name, without ever praying a single prayer to your Father, then why are you here? The woman is saved without your help. You admit it. And she's saved without upsetting her family or relatives or caste guardians by converting to a strange religion which scoffs at most of their traditions."

Thomas didn't answer this question. Instead he said, "Kumaran, let's forget about the woman. Let's talk about *you* for a minute." He almost spat out the word *you*.

They had been so absorbed in the argument that they failed to notice the boat had turned sideways in the current. Suddenly Kumaran found himself in the rear facing backwards as the boat completed the turn. They shifted around in their seats, and now Thomas was in front.

"Look what happened to you in Madurai," Thomas began. He was looking down at the current, scoring the water in brief, futile jerks. "Do you know what's wrong with your religion? I'll be frank. We're friends—"

"Friends!?"

"May you be damned if you deny it!"

"I am already, I thought," said Kumaran with the utmost malignity.

"You've been baptized!" Thomas answered, his eyes tense with rage and fear. Then, in a voice suddenly soft and contrite, he said, "Forgive me, Kumaran." He put his paddle aside on the floor of the boat and for a moment buried his head in his hands, as if praying, or weeping. Then he looked back up, turned on his seat to face Kumaran in the back, and said in a normal voice, but with eyes bleary and red, "I was saying you don't fear God. You don't—how could you have let yourself wallow like a beast with those—those whores? And the King—I don't understand." Now his voice began to rise again as he shook his head in slow, wide sweeps: "Kumaran, Brother, what?—how could?—do you know how God hates such a sin? If you did, if you feared God, it wouldn't have happened—how could it have?—you wouldn't have dared let yourself do it. A sin so unnatural, so abominable. Kumaran, I've known you for a long time. Where does this weakness come from? I think I know. Take it from someone who knows you. Take it from a friend. Please. I speak out of love, I speak so you might be healed—"

"Ha ha ha ha ha!" Kumaran howled with laughter at this latest of Thomas' self-delusions. Then he said unflappably, "And you, Thomas, are arrogant and superior and a hypocrite!"

"Hear me out, Kumaran," Thomas pleaded, his composure beginning to slip again. "What you need—what you need—what you need," he sputtered, "is a challenging—a *strenuous* faith. And a God to match it. Tell me, Brother, does Murugan hate sin? Murugan, that twelve-armed—that twelve-armed—that—that dissolute, dancing god, that coxcomb who dallies in the forest with—with Valli the huntress or whatever she is. And what of murder? You *murdered* the King, Kumaran, you didn't just 'kill' him. Did you feel the wrathful eye of Murugan upon you as?—but no. Murugan himself would have done the same thing. So why should you fear him? But the Father—the Father is righteous and holy. And He expects all of us to live righteous and holy lives. And when we don't, and when we don't—'Fear God and keep his commandments, for this is the whole duty of man,' say the scriptures. Kumaran, you don't fear God enough."

It was true, and Kumaran knew it. But who, who besides Thomas, feared God in such a way? There was something unnatural about Thomas' fear. God to him was as real as a piece of meat held in the hand. That was the difference between him and other men. Other men might fear as much if they knew with as much certainty that there was something to fear. That was the difference. That was the only difference. That was the whole secret of Thomas' moral superiority. He feared God so much that he dared not sin. Who would be foolish enough to sin with God staring him in the face? God stared Thomas in the face.

Then a desperate thought clawed its way into Kumaran's brain. What if Thomas was a sinner like other men? What if, all along, he had been other than he seemed to be? Just now he had lost his temper and howled like a hyena. Perhaps there had been other lapses. What went on inside the homes of his Christian converts? Widows fawned on him wherever he went. What was the meaning of that? Who could say? Kumaran decided to take the offensive one more time.

"Do you mean to say you've never committed adultery?"

Thomas looked up quickly with surprise. "Adultery? Why do you ask?"

"Answer the question." There was fear in Kumaran's voice, fear he would get the answer he didn't want.

"I—no, I haven't."

"Not even as a young man? Not just once? Tell the truth!"

Thomas picked up his paddle, turned around to face the river, and began to paddle. "No," he called back over his shoulder.

There was something awkward about Thomas' answer that Kumaran might have linked to a lie or a twinge of conscience if Thomas had been any other man. But Thomas never lied, and Kumaran knew it. Suddenly he felt weary of battle, defeated, almost contrite. If he had won a concession here, if Thomas were not so different from other men, if once, just once in his life, he had slipped and fornicated like any other man and been convicted by his own self-righteous judgment, if he were not so perfect—then Kumaran could have ignored his holy wrath. Perhaps he even could have forgiven Thomas, yes, even that. But as it was, he felt like the demon crushed by Kali's weight: dizzy, suffocating, about to be devoured.

Thomas turned back around to face Kumaran. "I came to India to teach her that God, the true God, the living God, hates sin; that our bodies don't belong to us to do whatever we want, but belong to Him; that God is awesome, majestic, mighty, to be feared—"

"Stop! Stop! Stop!" Kumaran shouted, getting up out of his seat and clambering up to the front of the boat as it almost capsized. Then, in front of Thomas' face, Kumaran made an obscene gesture with his hand.

"And that he loves us," Thomas added in a whisper as he looked straight at Kumaran.

For an instant the two men stared at each other so closely that they could smell each other's breath. Then Kumaran crawled back to his seat again, and for a while they peacefully sat, paddling intermittently. The dense silence between paddles seemed to envelop them in discrete layers as if it had bulk.

"We fear the law of karma," Kumaran said later as they ate lunch while tied to a branch on the bank.

"It's not the same thing as fearing God Himself," said Thomas.

"But the law of karma is God's law. Besides, it's wrong to say we don't fear God. Look at the faces of old women as they cower in front of their deities. On any roadside shrine—"

"Kumaran, do *you* fear God? That's what I want to know."

Perhaps it was a full belly and sweet juice of the coconut that healed Kumaran's spirit somewhat. Whatever the case, his answer was civil and truthful. "Not very much. Not as much as I fear the demons."

"Then you can't love Him very much either. Men can't love, really love, a God they do not fear."

Much more was said that afternoon. More than ever before, each got to know the other as he was, stripped of polish and civility. Each learned what the other regarded as his peculiar and fatal weakness. Each grew wiser, but at a terrible price. For friendship can stand only so much truth. Kumaran did not learn to fear Thomas' God, but Thomas.

This fear was something new. Kumaran's memory rehearsed all Thomas' "treacheries": his love of the beggars and lepers at Vanji, his insults in the jungle clearing, the baptism under duress and without proper preparation, the offering of all their food and drink to the villagers, the merciless lecture about riches after the Kallar raid, and now these most recent insults, however true they might be. These were like peppers thrown into a stew already too hot. But the fear—that was something new.

Kumaran turned his attention to the countryside and his poetry. As they drifted along with the current, the river gradually turned from blue-gray to drab green, and then, by the third day, to a rich golden brown. On either side of the great stream, dark thickets of trees and brush grew out of the banks. Elephants, rhinoceros, deer, gaur, boar, sambar, even an occasional tiger could be seen watering, and every now and then a long-nosed crocodile swam close by. When they decided to stop for the night, they paddled down an irrigation canal until they reached a village or farmhouse. The land was luxuriant with rice, sugar cane, and cotton, all of it grown through the munificence of the Kaveri. White water lilies pushed up out of ponds in thick clusters. Columns of smoke rose over the fields out of ovens where sweet juice from the cane was being boiled. In every paddy field there was a watchman; mostly women by day and men by night, they guarded their golden bounty against birds, beasts, and the rare thief. The bending coconut and the bright green banana tree, the upright areca palm and the fragrant turmeric, the giant banyan, the shady mango, the palmyra palm, and hedges of ginger grew profusely around each village. Chubby-faced children wearing jingling anklets played on paths with three-wheeled toy carts and warned their elders to get out of the way. "Karikal is coming! Make way!" shouted one little charioteer. Kumaran remembered a certain poem that sang of this flat evergreen delta as a land where men sweat not from their labor, but from the ardor of their feasting. Another poem praised the rice harvest: The grain grew so thickly that the small space in which an elephant can lie down could feed seven hungry men.

And how they did feast! Not only on grain and milk and fruits, but on succulent roasted deer and iguana dripping with fat. Thomas, when he saw how plentiful and inexpensive the game was, stuffed his lean ascetic's belly until he belched like the barbarian that he was—or so Kumaran wrote in his notes.

By sunset of the fourth day the river had swollen to a prodigious width. Ahead they saw the masts of ships. On the left, behind embankments, lay Puhar, its lights already shining, its mansions seven-storied. Once again Kumaran became a child, and his heart raced. He forgot about Thomas.

PART VI: PUHAR

34. Letter to Mary

Troubled by Kumaran's insults and his own failings, Thomas wandered alone through Puhar, begging in the Tamil fashion as he went. The community of ascetics and vanaprasthas along the bank of the Kaveri, where he knew he would live, seemed oppressive for the moment. He found the parks pleasant but alien. He made his way to the beach on the great Eastern Ocean, and there he found what he wanted.

The Paradavars, as they were called, lived up and down the wide beach in houses with low-hanging thatched roofs. Outside in their yards of sand they spread their deep-sea fishing nets out to dry or repaired their boats, much as the simple fishermen of Tangasseri had done on the other side of the continent. Their black bodies were muscular, and they delighted in wrestling on dunes under ancient screw pines. They were adept at killing birds with stones shot from slingshots and at brewing toddy from the coconut. Their women dressed in garments of green leaves and prattled like happy parrots. Their children played with crabs at the edge of the sea or fashioned puppets out of sticks and rags. They always had plenty of fish and shrimp to eat, and they varied their diet with the meat of the field-turtle.These fisherfolk were despised because they killed for a trade, but Thomas did not despise them; on the contrary, he felt at home with them, and they welcomed him and offered him more food than he could eat. They were a proud people and told Thomas they wouldn't barter their prosperity for the esteem of the world.

Thomas spent his first week in Puhar, also known as Kaveripattinam, with these people. They let him live in a vacant hut, and it was there, or on top of a sand dune, that he searched his soul and wrote his letters. One of these he wrote to Mary:

Judas Thomas, missionary to India: to Mary, the mother of Jesus who is called the Christ, in Jerusalem of Judaea in the yavana lands of the Roman Empire:

Blessings to you, dear Mother. I thank God always when I remember you in my prayers, for I have derived the very greatest comfort from your love. And I love you too, as you know, and love you especially when I remember the fruit of your womb, Jesus.

It cannot be too many more years now before we come together again, either on this earth or with the brethren in heaven.

I am thinking back, far back in time. I am remembering my wedding day in Cana. Do you remember the head-band of coins you made for Huldah? Do you remember when I lifted the veil from her face and laid it on my shoulder—how she looked up shyly into my eyes—and hiccoughed, and how everyone laughed?

Do you remember the torchlit procession to the little house that Jesus built for us, and the food and the music and the dancing that awaited us when we got there? Do you remember when the wine ran out and you got upset, blaming it on Jesus since he was best man, and how he came to the rescue with those two water jugs of wine, and how everyone was amazed the best wine was saved for last? To this day I don't know where he got it. Those were happy times, Mother, were they not? Far happier times lie ahead of us!

My beard has turned silvery since I saw you last. That was over five years ago. Will Tabitha and Judith have brought sons into the world by the time you read this—sons that I could not have? And does John still take care of you, or does James now enjoy that privilege? I pray you are in good health, best of mothers.

I have just arrived in Puhar on the southeast coast of India after a difficult voyage overland. I left a city behind with 500 converts to the faith, but my heart is sad. For I have sinned against the Father, grievously sinned, and scandalized the one soul who means most to me here. Sometimes I am depressed by my failings, which seem only to increase with age, as do my physical infirmities, in particular a weak hip and dimming eyesight. No amount of prayer seems capable of transforming me. My hot temper still does me in from time to time.

There is nothing in particular that I want to say. Only that I miss you and all the others. It pains me that I have not yet received a single letter from home in all this time. Sometimes I am lonely, Mother, so lonely. I know you have tried to write, but I do not stay in one place long enough to get news of you. Or perhaps the letters get lost. Anyhow, continue to write me in Madurai. Write in care of Nakkirar, Bishop of Madurai, in the East Vaigai Brahmin Quarter, Madurai, Kingdom of Pandya, Tamilakam, South India. He will forward your letters.

Dearest Mother, what a privilege to have worked and played and wept and eaten and drunk and slept and walked and prayed with the world's Messiah, your son and my brother! Sometimes I dream we are working in the old carpenter shop at Nazareth; I am holding and he is hammering. Then I wake up and smell his sweat all around me—it does not matter whether I am in someone's guest house under embroidered silk or out in the open on a sandy river bank under the moon.

All who are with me, all my dark-skinned Indian converts, especially my bishop, Nakkirar, and the deacons and their families have heard about you. They join me in wishing you well.

I greet you, Mother, with a kiss of love. Peace be to you and to all who are in Christ. To him be glory both now and for all eternity.

To his old friend Bartholomew Thomas wrote a different kind of letter. This is how he ended it:

As I sit alone on a dune looking out over the ocean, I feel abandoned. I ask myself why I am here. The thing that drove me as recently as a fortnight ago was the belief that my services won souls for Christ, and that he alone could save them. Every convert I made was an indelible triumph over Satan; what I said and did had therefore the most tremendous importance, not only for me but for God. But I doubt all this now. I do not deny it, but I doubt it. I fear that God does not need me. I suspect he accomplishes his purpose without my help, invites devout pagans into his kingdom who know nothing of Him, nothing of the Holy Torah, nothing of the Lord's gospel, but whose hearts are ripe for the good news. If so, then what am I doing here? Sometimes I bring suffering into the lives of my converts. If nothing is gained by their conversion, then I am worse than useless. But I know these thoughts are unworthy of me, truly I do, Brother in Christ. I am feeling sorry for myself, that is all. The gospel is good news, it liberates. It makes God and the life of spirit, lived so perfectly by the Master, attractive. I must trust completely in the Master, in his gospel, in the advantage it gives the soul as it duels with the Adversary. Yes, it is all much clearer now. I needed to talk to someone about what troubles me. You are not here in the flesh, but be assured you are very much with me in spirit. Pray for me, Brother, but do not doubt that I will find a way to do the work. Do not doubt that God will use me, however humbly.

As he finished this letter in the shade of one of the pines that sheltered the beach, he remembered that only a few weeks ago he still thought in terms of converting all India. Now he doubted, doubted his destiny more deeply than ever before. In the past, a despairing sadness would settle over him until he drove it away. Now there was less sadness, more resignation. God would save whom it pleased Him to save. He, Thomas, God's servant, would do what he could do, and no more.

He thought of Kumaran and the lie he told him concerning adultery. Why had he lied? He knew why. He had lied for the Kingdom of God. He would not lie again. God would not need him to.

What *did* God need him to do? Was it enough to repeat his modest success in Madurai? Would he live the outwardly spotless life of a raja sannyasin again? Or was this imposture merely another lie? But what was the alternative? He had gotten nowhere in Muziri because he was not Indian enough. What was the key to the riddle? How could he make the gospel more attractive without violating his own nature? There had to be an easier, more natural way. But he didn't know what it was.

He had to figure it out, to act. He could not spend all his time writing letters home and quietly studying and translating. He decided to repeat the performance of Madurai, for at least that netted five hundred souls. But he would watch for some unsought opportunity, wait with anticipation, as the eagle waits for prey, fully expecting it to come along, but not knowing what it will be.

35. Kumaran Meets King Karikal

Kumaran had not been in Puhar three weeks when he decided that of all the cities he had ever seen, she was the richest and the fairest. Let other poets sing of Athens or Rome, Alexandria or Jerusalem, Muziri or Madurai. He would sing of Puhar. She was the crest jewel of the sea-encircled earth. She was the favorite garland of the Gods.

Up and down her broad brick-paved avenues stood rows of flowering shade trees that cooled and perfumed the breezes. At the center of the city was a spacious grassy park with groves of trees and long crescent-shaped ponds whose loamy banks sparkled with flowers—"like moons surrounded by stars in a cloudless sky," Kumaran wrote in one of his poems. Along the shore rose dunes of shining sand shaded by groves of flowering screw pines. Inland along the Kaveri stood shapely thickets of rustling cane. Aloft from every building—from the boulevard lining the harbor to the most northern suburb—waved flags so large and numerous that their shadows shut out the setting sun.

Puhar's seven-storied mansions were patterned after heaven, whose six lower paradises are but stepping stones to the supreme bliss of union with God. Each mansion was studded with eye-shaped windows and surrounded by layers of verandahs reached by ladders. At any time of day you could look up and see women glittering in jewels at the windows of the upper floors. They might be daydreaming or praying or calling down to someone at street level. They might be sifting through the crowd in search of someone. Or they might be practicing the flute or lute or receiving instruction from their guru.

Puhar's waters were as holy as the Ganges. Where the Kaveri mingled with the salt water waves of the ocean, pilgrims from all over the South bathed to cleanse themselves of sin. The city's kitchens dispensed so much rice in alms to hermits with matted locks that the drains flowed white with cunjee. Goddess Lakshmi's auspicious picture was painted at regular intervals along the city's high walls, and the temples sparkled with bright-tinted sketches out of the great epics *Ramayana* and *Mahabharata*.

But in spite of the city's piety, pleasure fetched a higher price than religious merit. Goods flowed from every land into her docks and markets, and just as abundantly they flowed back out. Her harbor was so deep and spacious that high-masted ships approached her wharves at full sail. While coolies shouldered exotic burdens from as far away as Cathay, these ships strained at their piers like rutting elephants tethered to stumps. Meanwhile the streets near the harbor overflowed with riches: horses that had come by sea, bags full of black pepper brought in by cart, gems and gold dug out of the northern hills, sandalwood and *agil* cut from the western mountains, pearls from the southern sea and coral from the eastern, foodstuffs from the Kaveri and from Lanka, goods of every kind from Burma and the Ganges valley—all of these stamped with the tiger mark, emblem of the Chola empire. Goods were also piled high in fenced yards and warehouses, where bulls prowled freely to frighten away thieves. It was said that if Puhar played host to the whole world for one month, her hospitality would not fail.

People of every country, tribe, and caste lived in Puhar. Along the Kaveri outside the city's southern wall but inside the dike lived the ascetics. Hindus, Buddhists, Jains, and Ajivakas dwelled in huts of mud and straw or out in the open. With faces sunken and wrinkled, noses long and beak-like, eye sockets hollowed and eyes as red as drops of wine, earlobes distended, and jaws jutting out like plowshares, these yogis and monks brought their rounds of rebirth to a close. Inside the walls stood the city's great houses. The most magnificent of these belonged to the Vanigars, a vegetarian caste of merchants as ancient, some said, as the brahmins. These merchants were celebrated for their generosity in dispensing alms. They guarded the rights of others as jealously as they did their own and spoke the truth when trading. They never exacted an unfair price. Their just hearts were as steady and immovable as the pin in the middle of the plow's yoke. Their women mixed in society. They visited temples, attended and participated in public debates, read and wrote poetry, went to the theater, and even took part in sacred dances. They dressed like peacocks in silk and muslin, modestly covered their perfumed breasts even in the hottest weather, and adorned themselves with gold pendants and wreaths of jasmine.

The lower castes lived in their own neighborhoods. Goldsmiths, tailors, oil pressers, mat makers, potters, bangle sellers, cotton carders, water carriers, leather workers, washermen—each group thrived at its respective trade. Even the bhangis dressed colorfully as they herded their pigs and cleaned the city's latrines. Only the Sinhalese slaves building dikes along the Kaveri's banks appeared hopeless, but even they were well-fed.

Kumaran was surprised by the large number of yavanas who lived and prospered in Puhar. Most of them worked as stevedores, dock loaders, seamen, or merchants, and a few of the merchants were as rich as any Vanigar. The wealthier yavanas were not only entertained in the houses of the gentry; they were ogled by women of all classes, who found their pale faces and "red" hair arresting. Even the common yavana sailor was sometimes admired for his beauty. The only yavana that was suspect was the Jew. The Jews lived together on one street and refused to mix with their "heathen" hosts. It was hard to say who disliked the other more, the Jew the Tamil or the Tamil the Jew. Yet even the Jew was tolerated. He could practice his religion with the blessing of the King; he had business contacts; he owned land; he could get rich.

Puhar's heart was the royal palace. As large as a small city, it was enclosed by a series of moats and walls. Watchtowers rose at regular intervals; each flew a tiger standard, usually white on red or blue. Massive gateways faced the four cardinal points. On either side of the chief gateway, which faced east toward the sea, a sculpture of a springing tiger warned the would-be enemy. One tiger was plated with gold, the other with silver. The upper portion of the gate itself was ornamented with an immense ivory bas-relief of a tiger, while the lower portion was studded with stout iron spikes to keep enemy elephants from battering it in.

The palace grounds were divided into two sectors: the public, which was accessible to anyone, and the private, which included the King's own quarters, his major political departments, and the harem. The public grounds resembled a giant chess board, with elegantly designed buildings, often massive and high and colorfully painted, occupying the dark squares; and brightly tiled courtyards shaded by trees and ornamented with splashy flower gardens, artificial hillocks of cropped grass, gurgling rivulets, and even miniature waterfalls occupying the light squares. Some of these buildings comprised the royal granary. Others were flat-roofed raised pavilions where theater or dance or even cock fights were staged, and where philosophers of the different schools did public battle. The most expansive building, surprisingly, was an aviary. A huge fresco showing the saintly vulture Jatayu struggling to save Sita from the archdemon Ravana was painted on the facade, with Ravana on one side of the door and Jatayu on the other. The courtyard behind the aviary was a tiger compound. All day long throngs of people gaped through cracks between high fence posts to get a glimpse of these beasts, each a symbol of the Emperor Karikal's might and prowess. A number of buildings made up the royal stable. Riding horses for the King's cavalry and draw horses used to pull war chariots were quartered there. The King's hundred war elephants and a large number of cattle, many with painted or gilded horns, were domiciled in other buildings. Along the circumference of the public sector stood long lines of sheds housing chariots and carriages. A favorite pastime of the Puharis was to watch the King's charioteers practice their art in their brightly painted bigas or quadrigas. In full battle array a charioteer would maneuver his horses with shouts, reins, and a whip while the archer standing in the lotus-shaped chariot shot at moving targets. The jangling harnesses with their bells, the neighing, snorting steeds, the whip cracks and choking dust suggested to the awe-struck spectators the conditions of actual battle, and all went away after the show confident they had nothing to fear from the ever-preying kingdoms of Chera and Pandya.

The private sector of the palace was enclosed by an inner moat and two rows of thick, pointed timbers reinforced by a wall of earth between the rows. For a few hours every morning the public was allowed inside the moat to look through tunnel-like peepholes piercing the walls at the sights within. The grounds were much like those in the public sector, but the buildings were much more extravagant. At the center was the King's residence rising eleven stories, a glittering Mount Meru holding up the universe. The arsenal, the treasury, the meeting halls, the ministerial offices, the catering department, the guest houses, and other buildings, while imposing, were dwarfed by the size and elegance of Karikal's residence. Its towering shiny whitewashed walls, crystal windows bordered by sparkling gems, steep gilded roof, and immense height inspired awe in all.

When Kumaran first saw this building towering above the horizon, saw it as Thomas and he floated into the city in their boat, he wondered what it was and whether he might someday view it from the inside. When he first viewed it through the public peephole in the inner wall, a tidal wave of ambition swelled over him. He vowed to himself that he would enter its most intimate chambers, however that might be accomplished. He looked at that glowing gilded roof jutting into the great bowl of deep blue sky and knew, somehow knew that he was staring at his destiny.

As fate would have it, less than a month had passed when he was ushered by a porter through the massive gate leading into the private sector and into the King's very presence. Two poets whom he had known in Madurai during his early months there insisted on introducing him to King Karikal, and Kumaran was quick to accept. He was amazed to discover that the King had known of him—the "poet of the yavana lands" he was called—for many months. The King was all the more delighted because his spies had told him Kumaran was dead, yet here he was with his satchel bag of poetry

What everyone had told Kumaran of Karikal was true: poetry, not his queens, was his passion. He composed it almost as well as the poets themselves, and his appetite for it was insatiable. This dreaded warrior who wore anklets made out of the gold of conquered kings' crowns, this eagle of a man who had never known a minute on earth when he was not King—his father had died when he was in his mother's womb—this canny statesman and ruthless builder of an empire: Karikal frolicked with his children as if he were their nurse and joked with his poets as if they were his brothers or cousins! Kumaran was astonished, for he had heard the King had only a few friends and slept in a different chamber every night. The first attempt on his life was made when he was nine. Thirty-seven years had taught him to be cautious.

Kumaran's first meeting with him was unforgettable. He was half-conscious of airy light and crystal and gold and ivory and jewels and silks and scents of flowers and music of the *yal* as a guard led him into the hall. He failed to note any of this specifically but remembered it later as a kind of heavenly haze. A great door was opened, and there was Karikal seated on a raised chair covered with a tiger pelt. Kumaran and the other poets greeted the King with deep bows and sat on cushions set randomly on the floor in front of him. Some of the poets— there were eight—obviously felt comfortable with the King, for they lay back against their pillows and propped themselves on their elbows. As

Kumaran noted the crimson paste smeared over the King's chest, he thought of all the blood this man had spilled. As the gems embedded in his girdle gleamed, he thought of the slain chiefs whose crowns they had once studded. As he noted the simple wreath of fragile white *atti* flowers threaded into the coils of his hair, he remembered how one of the poems he had studied at the Sangam described him before battle: "Adorned with a thick wreath of many blossoms, he looks like a hill overgrown with shrubs." As Kumaran looked into his eyes, which were alert, mobile, and proud, he thought of Murugan. But he also detected a look of longing, a look suggesting that even the King of the Chola Empire had missed true happiness. A God, a hawk, a widow in mourning, a squirrel—there was something about Karikal's expression that reminded Kumaran of each of these.

Following the introduction, the King began putting questions to Kumaran about Madurai. Satisfied Kumaran was who he claimed to be, the darling for a day of the Sangam, and not a spy or an assassin, the King settled back and invited him to read. As female attendants kept the warm air in the wide-windowed hall moving with their fans, Kumaran sang of Athens and Rome and Jerusalem. As he read, the King leaned farther and farther forward in his chair. Kumaran could tell that the King was immensely pleased. At one point as he read about Jerusalem, embellishing impromptu the description with his knowledge of the Jews he had gotten from Thomas, the King stopped him and told an attendant to bring in his Guru. When the Guru entered—he was a gray-haired brahmin with a peculiar growth on the back of his neck shaped like a stupa, and reminded Kumaran of a humped bull—the King told him to start over "at Jerusalem." When Kumaran finished, everyone, led by the King, applauded with tremendous fervor.

During the discussion that followed, Karikal did not ask about meter and metaphor—as King Nediyon had—but about the subject matter. In particular he asked if the Acropolis in Athens was as tall as his palace, and Athens as grand as Puhar.

"The Acropolis," Kumaran said, "is higher than any feature in Puhar, and the Parthenon with its columns is the most beautiful building in the world"—here he paused for an instant, then added emphatically—"next to your palace, Your Majesty!" As everyone cheered and congratulated the King, Karikal motioned to his Guru, whose name was Charishnu.

"This Jerusalem," the Guru asked Kumaran perfunctorily, as if willing to pretend interest to please the King, "it is the place where the Jews who"—he paused, then went on, his eyebrows arched sarcastically as he drew the next word out—"grace our city come from?"

"It is their holy city," Kumaran said, "their Varanasi. For them, God dwells there. It is where God and men meet."

"Interesting," said Charishnu.

Then the King asked, "Did you get to know any of the Jews in their, shall I say, own setting? Do they all wear those queer flowing beards and earlocks? And are they all as—well, let us not mince words—are they all as nasty as the ones we have here?"

"I knew, or rather know, one well, Your Majesty—"

"Be at ease, poet, no formalities."

"But, but he dresses like one of our sannyasins," Kumaran stammered, suddenly feeling awkward.

"What? In Jerusalem?" said the King.

"No, Your—he is—he is here in Puhar."

"A Jew dressed as a sannyasin?!" said Charishnu, showing interest for the first time.

"Something stranger still, not just any Jew, but a Christian Jew."

"What is that?" said Charishnu.

But before Kumaran could answer, the King said, "Is he intelligent?"

"Yes, even learned."

"Does he speak our language?" said one of the poets.

"Yes, even that."

"Speaks our language? Not just the gibberish of the market place?" said Charishnu.

"Yes, he speaks the language well, even eloquently."

"Who taught him?" said the King.

"It—I—I did," Kumaran stammered.

"*You* did? What a surprising man you are! Can you—can you bring him to us, to one of our sessions?" said the King. Then, turning to his Guru, he said under his breath, "It should be good fun, quite a change of pace."

Charishnu grunted.

"Bring him!" thundered the King, laughing. "We will throw him into the ring with the others!" Suddenly his voice became serious, and like a suppliant he asked Charishnu, "You will permit it, Guru of my Father? Please excuse my irreverence."

"If it pleases you," said Charishnu. "Yes, of course."

The poets dutifully applauded, and even the fan-girls smiled.

"And *I* will participate," added Charishnu in a grand manner. And now even he, the bull with the hump, smiled.

Everyone applauded, even the King.

Kumaran sat behind his desk next to his caged parakeet and idly looked out the window at monkeys chattering and romping in the fig tree in the dusty courtyard of his narrow Bard Street apartment. He marveled that King Karikal should be interested in Thomas, and marveled still more that he, Kumaran, should be the one to bring them together by an offhand remark. Why didn't Thomas just fade away? Why did he keep re-entering his life? What brought them together? Kumaran began reliving the major events of his life. He had traveled to strange lands that his countrymen had never heard of. He had become intimate with a white Jew who called himself a Christian and had saved this man's life. He had slept in the bed of a king and shared his concubines, even one of his wives. He had murdered this king. He had been the direct cause of a historic Sati. He had rotted in prison. And somehow, against all odds, he had managed to stay alive. But no, that was not correct. He had not managed it. Nothing he had done could explain it. The events of his life were symptoms of something much deeper, more rudimentary, but hidden—something that governed the ebb and flow of his life like an invisible tidal force.

Kumaran had become convinced again that this force was karma. But where did Thomas fit in? Kumaran reminded himself how contemptible Thomas was. Then why had he mentioned him to the King? Why did his mind incline in Thomas' direction at all? Why, if Thomas was so contemptible? Was it because Thomas had saved his life back in Madurai? But that was in the past, and, besides, he had saved Thomas' in Kurinchi, so there should be no question of a lingering debt. But then he remembered how Thomas had saved him from drowning in the Periyar River.

Kumaran thought he had finished with Thomas when he left him on the banks of the Kaveri after selling their boat. But evidently not. That night, in his private notebook, he wrote that they were like tree and creeper. When you cut away the creeper from the tree, it always grows back. Up the tree it climbs again. They are alien to each other; their natures are different; they have nothing in common except the same space.

It seemed that karma was about to dictate that they occupy the same space again. But this time the space would be no fishing village or jungle guest house or ascetic's hut. It would be the inner palace of Tamil country's greatest monarch.

He wrote bravely that he would put Thomas out of his thoughts. He would make the creeper die, not by hacking it back, but by not watering it. In time it would wither and die. He would create a new karma to nullify the old. In the meantime he would go back to Maliankara and fetch Devandi. The King had given him access to the palace and twenty gold coins, so he could afford to travel. Yes, it was time to fetch Devandi. Devandi and his little daughter. What did Thomas have to do with him anymore?

36. Puttaswamy

Four months had passed since his arrival in Puhar, and Thomas resided in the ascetic's quarter on the banks of the Kaveri. The work went forward more briskly than at Madurai, and already fifty or more converts broke bread with him on the Sabbath. One of them was the six-year old son of an elephant driver in King Karikal's cavalry. Little Puttaswamy—that was the boy's name—was won over to the new religion in an unusual way. It was his habit to come to the river early in the morning with his father's huge elephant to wash it. The beast would lie down on the bank, and Puttaswamy would swab it down. On one occasion, Thomas, who had been meditating nearby, walked up to the elephant and began washing one of its white tusks with a wet rag. From that day forward Thomas and Puttaswamy were friends, and Puttaswamy soon asked Thomas to baptize him. Not long after, the boy's father accepted the new religion, and then other cavalrymen began taking instructions.

Thomas soon learned to love Puttaswamy like a son, the son he never had, and the love he felt for the boy, and received in return, left him changed, though he hardly realized it himself. It had a warm tactile quality about it; it enveloped him in a kind of sweet, tranquil haze. He went about his duties as faithfully as ever, but now the source of his strength was not only an exalted sense of God's presence in him but a new rootedness in God's creation. Simple people felt that he belonged to them, that he gave them all his attention. They felt his gentleness and compassion; they began coming to him, not for religious instruction, but with their problems. It did not matter what God they worshipped; all day long Thomas received them, received them all. Sometimes he shared his faith with them, sometimes he did not; but he always tried to help them with their problems. He quickly became known as the "people's sannyasin."

A neglected wife nursing a baby approached him one day. "Look at me," she complained. "My garment smells like ghee and curry, and underneath my nails there's lampblack. My armpits stink from carrying my baby all around and feeding him at my breast. And what does my husband do? In his best clothes he dashes off to the street of the harlots! What can I do?"

Sometimes the problems were trivial. Once a twelve year old girl rushed up to him on a whim. "That boy over there," she said pointing, "he kicked over my sand castle with his foot and stole the garland from my head. Now he has my rag-ball. Please get it back!"

At other times they were weighty. A sick woman with breasts like wrinkled bladders sat down at his feet with tears hanging on her lashes. In her arms a dying baby boy chewed on a dried up nipple, crying feebly. She wanted to know what Thomas could do for her.

He thought often of Bala Ma's story of the woman carrying her dead son on her hip to the Buddha, and how the Buddha helped her get over her suffering. Now he too was a spiritual physician. One time a woman came to him distraught over her daughter, who had eloped. As the woman talked, he saw she was inordinately attached to the daughter and had made it impossible for the lovers to marry. The woman was wearing a string of white pearls along the parting of her hair. "Mother," Thomas said, "where did those pearls on your head come from?"

"Why, from the sea," said the woman.

"What use would they be if they had remained there?"

The woman began to blink nervously. "I don't understand," she said.

"Your daughter is like those pearls, Mother. She must go where she is highly prized. And isn't that scent you are wearing sandalwood?"

"Yes," said the woman.

"The sandalwood tree grows in the mountains. The mountains are its home. Suppose it had stayed there. Of what use would it be? Your daughter, Mother, is like the sandalwood tree."

With parables like these he won converts to the new religion in droves. He did not court the brahmins or any other group. The people came to him, and whoever came, he wooed. He was careless about his diet and ate whatever was given him. If a leper served him food with her own hands, he did not hesitate to eat. If an untouchable butcher dropped pork into his bowl, he ate. He ate what was offered.

He didn't always meet his people on the Kaveri's sands. If they asked him to go with them, he went. On one occasion a seamstress wept because she had lost her prize needle. He found out where she lived, and when he got the chance he went to her house to help look for it. Another time a demented man told him a snake lived in his house, and Thomas agreed to go with him to get rid of it. He felt nothing was beneath him.

During the daylight hours little Puttaswamy was never far away, and Thomas thanked his Father in heaven for sending him the little "son" he and Huldah had never had. He couldn't remember ever before being so calmly content, so indifferent to spiritual conquest, so free of dogging ambition. He didn't worry anymore about what God expected of him. He didn't even miss the letters from home. He knew he was doing the humble work Jesus had done, and he knew Jesus was with him.

One day a man dressed like a dignitary came to see him. Earrings bearing rare stones dangled from both of his lobes, and black cosmetic lined his eyes and enhanced their beauty. Thomas stood up and received the man.

"Are you the 'raja sannyasin'," the man asked?

Thomas hadn't heard that name since Madurai, and he wondered how the man came to hear of it. "Yes, some call me that," he stammered.

"I am the King's Emissary. The King requests your presence at the next Philosopher's Debate. Will you accept the invitation?"

"You must forgive me," said Thomas, wondering if the man were playing a joke on him, a joke instigated perhaps by Kumaran, the only man in Puhar who could have known the name "raja sannyasin." "I have not lived in Puhar long. I have not heard of this debate. What is expected of me?"

The man looked as if Thomas had insulted him but then seemed to understand he was telling the truth. "You will present your dharma in the the Hall of Philosophers, then be prepared to defend it," the man said. "There will be four others, each representing a different dharma. Keep your presentation brief, a small fraction of an hour. No more than a thousand words. You will answer the question"—the man pulled out of his pocket a scrap of parchment and held it close to his eyes—"the question: What is the nature of the world, and what constitutes salvation from it?" Then he looked back up at Thomas and said, "After each man presents his side, the debate begins. It can be quite—fun."

"Fun?" said Thomas, beginning to trust the man.

"You are liable to hear anything from the crowd. It can get boisterous. It goes on all night. The winner becomes famous."

"There is a winner?" said Thomas as a flutter of excitement ran through him. "Does the King choose him?"

"Not for the last six or seven debates. The Queen usually chooses."

"The Queen?" Thomas was amazed.

"I can tell you haven't heard of her either," said the man, raising his eyebrows significantly.

"Who will be present?"

"The King, the Queen, many of the ministers, a few generals, members of the great houses, servants, guards, some from the lower castes. Even a dog, I am told."

"A dog?"

"A dog."

Thomas hesitated, then said, "I accept."

"The second to last day of Kartigai. Be there at sunset or a little after. And, with due respect, take a bath. You smell like a rabbit's pelt," said the man, wrinkling his nose.

Later in the day Thomas inquired about the debate and learned that the man had spoken truly. That night he bathed in the Kaveri, as if ratifying the agreement by that act. His imagination leaped ahead as he lay out in the open under a full moon high overhead. What if he were to win? "Famous," the man had said. And the Queen was to judge. He had always been more effective with women than men. What if the Queen chose him? Might it be possible to win all India after all? For months he had not even been tempted to dream the old dream, for he knew he was not up to the task. He had grown almost comfortable in his new role as the servant of the humble. Had he grown too comfortable? Was God now about to jerk him up by the scruff of his neck and throw him back into the fray? Was God ticking off the final days until Jesus' return, and would the great miracles of conversion begin to happen simultaneously all over the world? He dared to think this might be so, for what other explanation was there for this utterly improbable invitation? It was as if God materialized the debate to forward his divine purposes. And wasn't that just like God? He was always full of surprises. No sooner did you give up trying than He came to your assistance whether you liked it or not! It had always been that way with Thomas. The harder he tried, the greater his failure. The more he relaxed, the more likely his success.

He had forgotten to ask what dharmas the other four participants represented. He was certain one would be a brahmin, and that meant more study of the Vedas; he would have to brush up on his Sanskrit. And surely there would be a Buddhist. Thanks to Bala Ma he would not be at a loss. His mind raced ahead into the great hall, and he saw the thousands sitting around, the King and Queen high on their daises, beautifully dyed curtains parted at the window. It would be cool by then, and he must think with a cool head. He began to imagine the debate as it might unfold. Argument after argument took shape in his heated brain. The moon reached its zenith, and still his mind whirred on. Not even with a hundred "Maranathas" could he shut it down to sleep.

37. The Debate

Thoughts of Thomas wisped out of Kumaran's mind like tremulous waves of heat rising from the desert floor. Had he been hating a phantom for the past half year? Was Thomas really the villain he imagined him to be? Was it really true he didn't miss Thomas, as he told himself again and again? What disquieting surprise might await him as he watched Thomas in action at the debate? These were his thoughts as he and Devandi, newly fetched from Maliankara, walked down the stairs of the residence where the King housed his Imperial Poets, and where Kumaran had been living for less than a month. Like a suspicious mouse hesitating in front of the baited trap, but in the end deciding to risk the danger, Kumaran tugged at the cheese.

The debate was scheduled to begin an hour after sunset when the Guardian of the Hours struck the drum twice. Long before this hour the gentry of Puhar had begun to gather. They had heard the King himself would attend, and they thrilled at the chance to share anything with him. Others had heard that a "yavana ascetic" was to participate, and this extraordinary anomaly helped to swell the crowd even more. This is not to say that no one in attendance was interested in philosophy for its own sake. Many were, none more so, Kumaran had heard, than the Queen, who never missed a debate, and often, it was said, chose the contestants. But this time the King had chosen them, and his choices promised a much livelier skirmish than usual. His selection of the well-known scoffer Nalli, who never went anywhere without a brutish dog on a leash, was guaranteed to provide fireworks, and the addition of Thomas was so daring and so novel—Kumaran overheard a Vani-gar call it "grotesque"—that no one could predict with confidence what would happen. It was rumored that even the Buddhist, whose name was Ashvaghosha, was no ordinary monk; visiting from the north, he was supposed to represent some new school of Buddhism known as the Mahayana; he did not speak Tamil, only Sanskrit, and his views could be learned of only through an interpreter. Truly this was no or-dinary gathering.

Devandi, wide-eyed and clutching Kumaran's arm, walked beside him toward the open pavilion in the public sector where the debate was to be staged. The air was mild and windless, the night moonless, starlit, and as soft as Devandi's silks which soothingly rubbed together as she walked. Throughout the palace gardens stood single columns, torchlit and topped with a platform, to which peacocks were tied. Sometimes one would mount its platform and spread its beautiful tail feathers—a symbol of Puhar's beauty just as surely as the tiger was the symbol of her might. Kumaran saw all this through the eyes of Devandi, who was newly installed in Puhar, as if for the first time and was ravished by the ambient pomp and glitter. As the couple drew closer to the pavilion, the quiet of the night gave way to the sounds of the royal orchestra.

After winding their way up the S-shaped stairs of the balustraded entrance, they seated themselves with other courtiers near the front of the raised stage. Kumaran looked around at the crowd of faces, many beautifully groomed, decorated with flowers, bejeweled, sweet-smell-ing with the most costly unguents, talking excitedly or quietly wait-ing, admiring the exquisitely decorated coffered ceilings lit by torches attached to each column. Some of the women held painted fans, and the air whirred to their movement even though it was far from hot.

Preceded by blaring conches and clanging gongs and cymbals, the King with his Queen and retinue promenaded up the stairs into the building. A gigantic male assistant taller than Thomas carried the royal parasol over his head. Then followed three female assistants carrying his sword, his sandals, and his flywhisk. Next followed Queen Adimanti. Almost as legendary as the King himself, she was everywhere revered for her wisdom and virtue, and by many for her beauty, which would have been peerless were it not for an unusually long neck. Her dress, cosmetics, jewels, and coiffure set trends for the empire, although on this night her attire was extraordinary. Wrapped in a long high-necked green dress with matching bodice, she wore not a single piece of jewel-ry—she whose tinkling, pellet-filled anklets were celebrated by all the poets who visited Karikal's court. The lobes of her ears, ritually pierced when she was but a child and gradually enlarged by increasingly thick cylinders made of fish-bone, hung limp and flabby, austere holes their only ornament. Her hair, normally studied and imitated by a whole empire, was tonight neatly combed back and braided into a single pigtail, peasant fashion, which hung down to her waist. Many in the audience had never seen her like this, including Kumaran, and more than a few were aghast when they first saw her. Kumaran guessed she dressed in this way to honor the ideals of the holy men on stage. Everyone bowed deeply as King and Queen passed through the crowd and took their seats on cushions in the royal box to the right of the stage, where each of their gestures would be registered by adoring subjects.

Finally the contestants themselves were led in. Again the crowd bowed, but this time the King bowed with them. After the courtesies of friendship and civility were exchanged, the participants took their seats on cushions arranged in a straight line facing the crowd. On one end, to the audience's left, sat Ashvaghosha, the visiting Buddhist, his head freshly shaved, his garb a simple full-length yellow-brown robe. The delicacy of his slender, perfectly proportioned body, the quiet dignity of his bearing, and the gentle, austere beauty of his face were a sermon in themselves. Next to him was a white-haired Jain monk named Rishabha who lived in the ascetic community on the Kaveri. He was beardless and completely naked except for five dots of sandalwood paste on his forehead, neck, stomach, and both shoulders, and a piece of gauze which he wore over his mouth to keep from inadvertently destroying the life of an insect when breathing in. In the center sat the stout Charishnu, the Imperial Guru, representing orthodox Shaivism. He wore a bright new red-orange loin cloth embroidered at its edges with green silk trim. On his head stood the characteristic hair tuft of his proud caste. His forehead was marked with red sandal paste and, along with his chest, was smeared with sandal ash; his beard was white and impeccably barbered. Across his flabby chest and ample stomach hung the triple thread of white cotton, the most sacred emblem of the brahmin. On Charishnu's left was the extraordinary Nalli, representing the Charvaka, or Materialist school, with his curled mustache and his dog. Nalli's deep blue tunic with its scarlet girdle dripped with gems, and his fingers bulged with rings. On his head was a thick wreath of delicate white *atti* flowers. Kohl darkened his eyelids, and sandal paste reddened his lips and cheeks. On his left sat the dog snapping at gnats—no doubt, alas, killing some of the very insects the Jain monk had taken pains to preserve. Finally, at the opposite end, next to the dog, came Thomas, who looked to Kumaran the same as always in his simple, but no longer frayed, orange loin cloth.

There were only four rules governing the contest. First, each contestant would be allowed to answer the question without interruption. Second, long sermons or harangues would be cut short; all statements had to be concise. Third, each contestant was to be given the chance to say all he wanted to say by the conclusion of the session. Fourth, the King or Queen could interrupt at any time and would decide the winner.

Queen Adimanti, addressing the audience of over a thousand, asked the question in a ringing voice: "What is the nature of the world, and what constitutes salvation from it?" Then she turned to Ashvaghosha and repeated the question more softly. The well-favored, gentle Buddhist from the distant north, speaking through a translator but relying on no text, said the following:

"All things in their fundamental nature are unknowable and inexplicable. They are subject neither to transformation nor to destruction. They are all part of the great, all-inclusive, eternal Whole which is called Suchness. From this Suchness nothing is excluded, to it nothing has to be added." The monk went on to describe how men lose sight of their innate Suchness and how they can save themselves from the suffering of endless births and deaths and realize nirvana.

When Ashvaghosha and his translator finished, Kumaran jotted down on palm leaf, "It was as if the moon glowed by itself in a starless black sky." Kumaran couldn't have said why the speech impressed him, for he understood very little of its content. He heard someone sitting behind him predict that Buddhism in Tamil land would never be the same again from that day forward.

The audience heard the Queen put the question next to the Jain: "Reverend Monk, what is the nature of the world, and what constitutes salvation from it?"

Rishabha took off his gauzy mouthpiece and spoke in a raspy voice devoid of passion about the nature of persons in general. He then said:

"What makes us appear different from each other is the body that each of us is bound to. Your body is your bondage for a lifetime. My body is my bondage for a lifetime. What causes this bondage? It is your karma, which attaches itself to your soul like a thin but poisonous fungus. You experience it as ignorance, as feebleness, as sorrow, as doubt, as pain. Your karma, which is material, obstructs and obscures your perfect nature, which is spiritual. This karma is the link between soul and body. It is the glue that keeps your spirit in slavery to first one body, then another, then another, throughout the ages."

Rishabha went on to say that salvation was the freeing of the soul from its karma and that "omniscient bliss for all eternity at the top of the universe was the result." He said he followed Mahavira, "the great Teacher of our age" who prescribed penance, meditation, and self-restraint as the path to spiritual freedom. Rishabha concluded:

"After practicing the twelve successive degrees of meditation and resolutely denying your body everything that might attach your soul to it, there will come a time when you are free from passion. You will be able to live without food for weeks straight and never miss it. You will become insensible to heat and cold, to dust and rain. You will scarcely even notice the calls of nature. You will feel indifferent to everything, indifferent to the splendor of a king or to the filth of a bhangi. You will take no account of the doings of any man, be they good or bad. Your feelings, your attention will have turned away from the world, and the glue attaching your spirit to the world will dry up and crack. One day death will come and with it the full blaze of omniscience. You will have become a Conqueror."

If Ashvaghosha was a brilliant moon in a starless sky, then Rishabha was a leper congratulating himself on his disease, and holding out his naked pussy sores for all to kiss: At least that is what Kumaran wrote. Kumaran shrank back from monkish Jainism with its loathing of every pleasure—he had heard this speech before. But many in the audience inclined toward the doctrine, not in its extreme monkish form, but a modified version of it. They approved its clear-cut division of the world into perfect spirit and degenerate matter; it fit their experience of things. And they agreed with its emphasis on self-control and generosity. But Kumaran was not alone in his detestation of this doctrine.

The Queen put the question next to Nalli: "What is the nature of the world, and what constitutes salvation from it?"

Tamils delight in training parrots to talk, but Nalli had trained his dog, for the dog let out a howl as soon as the Queen finished asking the question. Most in the audience found this an unspeakable affront, the very sort of vulgarity one might expect from Nalli, whose hobby seemed to be twitting any man who took anything at all seriously. But the King was immensely amused and almost choked as he tried to stifle laughter. Soon the entire audience began to twitter, then to laugh boisterously as the King finally exploded. At last the hall quieted and Nalli began:

"The beast speaks my mind precisely. The question offends him. Salvation? Give him a dish of fried fish and, lo, salvation is his! He sniffs, he eats, he drinks, he plays, he sleeps, he copulates, he scavenges, he shits, he hunts, he fights, he enjoys my company. You do enjoy my company, you beast? You see? He wags his tail. There's salvation!"

The dog deliriously wagged his tail, which turned up at the same angle as his master's mustache, and came forward to receive a pat on the head. Then Nalli continued:

"I'll be happy to tell you about the nature of the world. Happy, yes! Never do anything that doesn't make you happy, that's what I say. Right, Shiva? Yes, his name is Shiva. I hadn't planned telling you that."

As Nalli grinned impudently, an undercurrent of embarrassed whispering stirred. He ignored it and continued:

"The world? It's the color of the peacock, the taste of the kayal fish, the song of the cuckoo, the smell of jasmine in the evening, the zing in a stiff cock. Who makes all these good things? Nature, I say! And what's Nature? Earth, water, fire, air—that's all. These are the ultimates of the sweet-tongued Charvaka. Everything else—the body, the mind—all secondary. Take the mind. What's consciousness but a chance expression—an effusion, I would say—of the mixing of these four elements in a certain way? The mind's like the intoxicating power of toddy. And who do we have to thank for the toddy? You say the Gods? They're but an effusion of an effusion! No, not the Gods, but Nature!

"My poor beast, look how he broods and drools! He must be thinking about the speakers who went before me. See how sad his eyes look and how dejectedly his noble head rests on his paws.

"Pleasure and pain, that's all he knows. That's all any of us know. Heaven, hell, karma, final liberation, the Gods, the demons, the ancestors, the soul—they're all fictions. The four Vedas—they were written by buffoons and knaves. The ceremonies for the dead—they're means by which priests get fat."

Nalli looked boldly at the scowling Charishnu, then went on:

"The four castes, the ascetic's staff, smearing yourself with ash, sacrificing a beast in the Jyotishtoma rite, offering shraddha for the dead—they're social conventions for servile fools.

"Nalli says: While life remains, let a man enjoy himself, let him eat ghee even though he goes into debt. Pleasure in life is the sole aim of man, it's his only salvation. The only final liberation is the rotting of the body.

"Don't believe these mangy monks. Their bodies are rotting before they're even dead. Fly for refuge to the compassionate doctrine of the Charvaka, that's what Nalli says. Shiva!"

At Nalli's command the dog yipped its approval, but this time the King did not laugh. Catcalls, hisses, and hums greeted Nalli from all sides, but he also had a few followers who applauded and cheered. Kumaran wrote down, "Nalli, evening's entertainment."

The Queen held up her hands. The audience quieted and looked at Thomas.

"Apostle of the Yavana God," said the Queen, "what is the nature of the world, and what constitutes salvation from it?"

Of all the people in the world whom Kumaran had heard speak, there was none, he realized at that instant, whom he more anticipated hearing than Thomas. He was done with Thomas, even detested him, but he relished the prospect of hearing what he might say. His anticipation wasn't that of the teacher who looks forward to what his prized student might say in the hope of basking in a borrowed glory; that he had done once, but those days were gone forever. Now his anticipation was of another sort. He remembered with mortification how Thomas made him promise to follow him all over India and to pray to his God, and finally coaxed him into baptism. How would Thomas' words affect this crowd of sophisticates? Would any of them be seduced, as he had been? This was a spectacle Kumaran would enjoy. However it went, he would relish it. For if the old tricks failed, then Thomas would go home defeated. But if he succeeded, then he, Kumaran, would have other fools for company, and he could gloat knowingly at their error. He would listen with the fascination of a deflowered maiden who overhears the seductions of her former lover. Would the new maiden succumb? Would she succumb to the same blandishments and promises? Or would the lover's approach be different? And if so, what would be its effect?

Thomas bowed to the King and the Queen on his left, then spoke without a text:

"I must begin by correcting Her Majesty the Queen. I am not an apostle of the yavana God, but of the universal God, the true God, Sarveshvara."

Sarveshvara, hooray! Kumaran had seen that strategy before back in Madurai. An excellent strategy it was: Sanskrit for a cultivated audience. Everyone except Charishnu was immediately impressed. It was extraordinary enough that he should speak impeccable Tamil with only a slight accent, but Sanskrit! Heavens, he might even quote from the Vedas.

Thomas continued: "What is the nature of the world? I will tell you a story. A man was going up from Madurai to Puhar, and he was attacked by robbers. They beat him and stripped him and left him half dead. Now by chance a brahmin was going down the road, and when the brahmin saw the injured man he passed by on the other side, for the man was a pulaiyar. Then an ascetic with his staff and begging bowl came by, and he too saw the man, and he too passed by, for he was meditating on God. But a wretched outcast mleccha, as he was out gathering wood, came to where the man lay. And when the mleccha saw the man, he had pity on him, bound up his wounds, and propped him up on his bony bullock. Then he brought him to a nearby house and nursed him. As night fell, he handed over all his firewood to the housekeeper and said, 'Take care of him; whatever more you spend, I will repay you when I come back.' Now I ask all of you, which of these men is more precious in the eyes of God Sarveshvara? The brahmin who guarded himself from pollution by not touching an outcast, the ascetic who refused to break his concentration on God, or the despised mleccha who showed mercy to his neighbor? Each of you in his heart knows the answer. Try as you might to shut out the truth, each of you knows the mleccha is more pleasing to God, that it is he, O citizens of Puhar, he whom you despise and shun, he whose very shadow when it passes over you defiles you, it is *he* who is closer to salvation."

Kumaran eyed the Queen as Thomas told this quaint story. At the question, "or the despised mleccha who showed mercy on his neighbor?" she jerked into a stiff upright position on her seat, brought the tips of her fingers together in front of her chin, and knit her brow in fierce concentration as she stared at Thomas.

Thomas then described the human condition at its worst with a series of metaphors. He compared clannishness and caste hatred to mucus, for example. Kumaran thought Thomas was better when he stuck to his stories. In trying to play the poet he served up a diet that was over-ripe and a bit disgusting. But no one seemed to mind. Most were enthralled by the pale man who spoke their language so skillfully and so edifyingly. But they had not yet heard what he came to say, and Kumaran chuckled to himself and prepared to watch their faces fall.

Thomas continued: "What is salvation? the Queen asks. I will tell you. For the Christian, salvation is a right relation to the one holy God through his Messiah and beloved son Jesus the Christ." Thomas explained that the Messiah was the Jew named Jesus, a kind of avatar sent by God for everyone's salvation.

He concluded: "Happy are they who listen to my word and, having listened, follow it! This word was not intended for yavanas alone. Christianity is no yavana religion. All of you are invited to embrace it, everyone of you, from the King to his most humble subject. If you do, you will go to your reward, after this very life, as surely as the waters of the wide Kaveri flow to the great ocean."

Thomas finished powerfully, but the enthusiasm of the crowd minutes earlier had been replaced by murmurs of confusion. Was he calling the audience to convert to a new religion, a new God? A mere yavana asking even the King to convert? Unthinkable, yet it seemed so! Kumaran could see their thoughts in their bemused faces, in the nudges they gave each other, in their frowns. It tickled him to think Thomas had learned so little in five years. The peasants might eat the rough millet of his new religion, but the gentry?

But he had done better, Kumaran thought, than he deserved. Kumaran would have to wait until after intermission, when everyone talked over what they had heard. Then the real scandal of Thomas' religion would surely come out. In the meantime, there was the King's Guru.

With the loftiness of his caste and his royal position, Charishnu delivered his carefully prepared speech, written out in meticulous script and replete with quotations from the Vedas translated into Tamil.

"It is not enough" he began, "to speculate about the nature of the world as these fellows who have spoken before me have done. Nor is it enough to quote some human authority. Only the eternal Vedas, revealed and infallible, can settle the issue.

"The holy Upanishad known as Shvetashvatara says, 'Now it is to be understood that *Prakriti* is *maya*,' that is, that Nature, the world in which we live, is a projection, an artifice, a kind of magic show fashioned by a magician. And who is this magician? The Upanishad says, 'Maheshvara, the Great Lord, is the *mayin*.' So it is God who has fashioned this world of *maya*, God is the magician, the creator. The Upanishad continues: 'This whole world is pervaded with beings that are parts of Him.' What does this mean? The holy Mundaka says: 'As a spider emits and draws in its web, so from the Imperishable does everything here arise.' So we see that everything that exists comes from Brahman, is fashioned out of his very substance, and participates in his being. This is the meaning of the Mundaka when it says, 'Fire is his head; the moon and sun are his eyes; the regions of space are his ears; his voice is the revealed Vedas; the wind is his breath; the planet itself is his heart; the dirt of the planet is his feet. Most certainly He is the inner self of everything.' Yet God, Brahman, is much more than the universe. Brahman is neither identical with the universe nor exhausted in it. For it says in the holy Brihadaranyaka, 'He who, dwelling in all things, yet is other than all things, whom all things fail to know—He is the inner controller of all these things.'"

Kumaran could not follow Charishnu, so he let his mind drift. He heard only bits and pieces. Something was compared to a fig tree, and something else to the tiny seed of that tree, but Kumaran was not sure what. There were several other metaphors that interested him, but for the most part he found the talk windy, overly abstract, and long. He perked up only at the end, when Charishnu cast a deprecating eye at Thomas:

"These instructions," he concluded, "apply only to the twice-born male. Pulaiyars, mlecchas, and yavanas must wait for a more auspicious rebirth. In the meantime they must worship God, do their respective duties, respect the Vedas, and support and revere all brahmins. In this way they will gain access to an auspicious womb and, with effort, gain eternal release. Failing at that, they will enter, as the Chandogya says, 'a fetid womb, either the womb of a swine, or an outcast, or a dog.'"

Responding to a sudden jab from its master, Nalli's dog protested in a long tenor howl. The timing, Kumaran thought, was hilarious, but the King did not laugh. One did not laugh at the King's Guru.

It was intermission, and people stood up and stretched or chewed betel or talked or mingled with their friends or even approached the royal couple. Meanwhile four male attendants massaged the King, who had slouched back on cushions. The Queen, sitting erectly, shifted her arresting eyes back and forth between the man she was talking to and Thomas, who talked to a dozen or so inquirers. At one point Kumaran thought Thomas stared straight at him, but there was no look of recognition. Then Kumaran remembered Thomas' vision got fuzzy when indoors at night, when candles or torches provided the only light. A quick bleat of tenderness sounded through Kumaran's heart as he thought of this little infirmity of his old friend and former brother. He caught himself, however, and muffled the voice. He gave his attention back to the group of poets he stood with.

After intermission many frictions developed. Charishnu began by condemning all who challenged the authority of the Vedas. The Buddhist and the Jain argued over the nature of karma. Nalli called Charishnu's doctrine of Brahman "unintelligible sleight-of-hand." Charishnu countered by labeling Nalli's materialism a "counsel of despair with no hope beyond this life" and "transparent hedonism which reduces all men to swine." Nalli ridiculed the eminent Buddhist monk visiting from the Ganges with a humorless but outrageous doggerel about "Suchness and out-of-touchness." It was not until these clouds of dust had been kicked up and settled that Thomas spoke.

Charishnu drew Thomas into the discussion. After attacking yavanas in a general way, he turned his attention to Thomas. After all, this yavana upstart had challenged the privileged status of the brahmin caste. Charishnu gave the impression of someone who relished the attack he was about to launch.

"Yavana ascetic," Charishnu began, "we have never seen pale skin in an ocher loin cloth before. And we have never before heard such words. Tell me, are you saying that the King"—Charishnu looked significantly at Karikal in his sequined red tunic—"cannot know salvation until he becomes—what do you call yourself?"

"A Christian," Thomas answered in a ringing voice, no doubt so the people in the back could hear; meanwhile Kumaran leaned forward with a manic grin.

"Until he becomes a Christian?" Charishnu said, completing his question.

"I did not say that," Thomas answered. "I said only that if he becomes a Christian, he will surely gain salvation at the end of this life."

"And if he does not?"

"Then he must live like the good mleccha in my story."

"Live like a mleccha?! *The King?!*" Charishnu looked at the King in mock horror as nervous laughter rippled through the audience.

"Like the *good mleccha in my story*," Thomas calmly corrected.

"How can a king live like the mleccha in your story?"

"I have already said how. It is clear to anyone who has ears to hear. Surely the King is not without imagination."

"Then *I* must be," warned Charishnu, "for it is not clear to me!"

"As you say," answered Thomas.

The audience was stunned by this meek rebuke of the King's Guru, and Kumaran chuckled under his breath as he watched the agitation on Charishnu's face. Charishnu composed himself enough to say, though in words dripping with menace, "Tell me, yavana, what will happen to the King if he does *not* live like the mleccha in your story?"

"Well, he may at any time decide to."

"But if he does not, what will happen to him—when he dies?"

"Are you saying the King does not already live like the mleccha in my story?" asked Thomas with the cunning of a court eunuch, a cunning Kumaran had never seen before in him during all their years together.

"I am—I am not—answer the question!" said the infuriated Charishnu.

"I ask because I have heard the King plants shade trees along the royal roads, builds reservoirs and dikes to contain the Kaveri at flood, maintains a huge almshouse near here, raises rest houses for travelers, digs wells at intersections, and in other ways works for the good of his subjects. But if you insist on using the King as an example—"

"I do *not* insist! Let us use me as an example!" the flustered Charishnu interrupted.

"Very well. If you do not live like the mleccha in my story; if you instead treat men with contempt, putting yourself above them, lording your rank over them; if you neglect charity until some profit comes of it; if you ignore the sick and the dying and the feeble; if you calculate gain from every good act—if this is the way you live your life, then at death you will be thrust into the fires of hell, or Naraka, as you call it, where there will be weeping and grinding of teeth."

"Are you saying that I, a brahmin, the Guru of the King, my father the Guru of the King's ancestors—are you saying that I am liable to the tortures of Naraka—to the fire, the snakes, the insects, the savage beasts, the birds of prey, and the stench? I, Charishnu, the high priest who placed the crown on the King's infant head, who daily offers the fire sacrifice—I?"

"I, too, venerable brahmin," Thomas said.

Charishnu could not let this insufferable, although unintended affront pass. *"You?! You?!* You put yourself at my level!? I am to take comfort because what could happen to me might also happen to you?!"

"Or to the King, or the Queen, or anyone else," Thomas went on calmly as the audience held its breath. "We are all called to the same life, a life of service to each other, of resolve to do God's will. There are no exceptions. None is privileged at death."

What thinking man could deny this last statement? Some of the braver poets even wrote poetry to this effect for their royal patrons. Kumaran, intensely excited, thought of Aiyaticciru's famous lines: "Good-hearted kings who have ruled this great earth surrounded by the black sea so that not even one *utai* leaf belonged to someone else—even they have gone to the ground of burned corpses as their final home, more of them than there is sand heaped by the waves." So far Thomas had gotten the best of Charishnu. The yavana barbarian had cornered the royal brahmin, and the crowd sat as still as stone as Charishnu, scratching his chin through his close-cropped beard with a single finger, sought a way out of the trap.

"And if I should go to Naraka, how long would I stay there?" Charishnu said with a sly look on his face that suggested he knew how to throw his adversary off guard once again.

"Everlastingly," said Thomas.

"Everlastingly? Everlastingly, you say?" A sudden, ominous murmur gusted through the building.

"For a very long time at the least." Thomas seemed to squirm.

"Not when my evil karma is exhausted?" asked Charishnu.

Thomas did not answer.

"Speak up, man! Would there be any hope for me?"

"God is your judge, not me," Thomas said.

"Tell me this, yavana: If I should build up *good* karma, and go into heaven as a result, what would happen once I had exhausted my good karma? Would I not then be reborn?" Charishnu sensed a kill. His eyes glistened with revenge.

"Jesus, my Master, the anointed Messiah of God, did not teach rebirth."

"So there is *no rebirth?!* You say no one here has ever lived before or will ever live again on this earth?"

"It—I did not say that. My Master will live again on this earth. And those who have died will come back to live in his kingdom."

"But what about those who do *not* follow your master?" Charishnu sneered.

Thomas hesitated, closed his eyes briefly, then said, "As I said before, unless they live like the mleccha, they will be lost."

"Aaahhh!" Charishnu suddenly looked up at the ceiling, put his palms together, and said, "Oh Shiva, why did you not reveal this to me sooner?" Many in the crowd laughed at Charishnu's antic, while others, until then rooting for Thomas, didn't know what to think. Charishnu, a minute earlier almost reduced to laughingstock, sensed the shift in the mood and kept his peace.

Thomas might not have been heard from again were it not for the royal prerogative of intruding in the conversation. The Queen regularly exercised this prerogative at debates, sometimes to such an extent that she ended by moderating them. Kumaran had heard there was no one in Puhar fairer or more skillful than she at guiding discussion, and the Puharis adored her for this ability. On this night she had held her tongue, probably in deference to her husband's Guru, who might have taken offense if she had opposed him on some point. But late in the evening, for whatever reason, she entered the debate, and Thomas was drawn back in.

Rishabha, the raspy-voiced, white-haired, imperturbable old Jain monk, and the outwardly jolly but mean-spirited Nalli, were debating the wisdom of forming attachments to things.

"The world," said Rishabha, "is transitory, evil, full of suffering. There is nothing in it that commends it to a discriminating man. It is not to be clung to."

"Tell me, monk," said Nalli, "have you ever in your long, tortured life, have you ever, just once, clung to the narrow-waisted body of a Chola maiden?"

The expressionless wrinkled face of the monk registered no response to this shockingly impudent challenge.

"If you had," Nalli continued, "you would know there was at least one thing in this world you despise that's worth clinging to."

"The body of the most beautiful woman," said the monk, "decays as quickly as a stray dog's. It will become loathsome to smell, infested with worms, full of pus, swollen, discolored, and then a hollow-eyed skeleton. While it is alive it is little better. Out of each of the nine holes—the ears, the eyes, the nostrils, the mouth, the anus, and the vaginal opening—trickles a foul substance. The body is only a machine composed of the four elements. There is your Chola maiden."

At this point the Queen broke in and said, "I believe we understand each of your positions." She courteously looked first at one, then at the other. "But how is one to decide who is correct? Let us hear a different, a fresh point of view. Let us hear what the yavana sannyasin has to say. What say you, visitor from the West?"

Thomas, surprised he should be asked to speak, groped for the right words: "It is obvious to me that—I would say that neither—it is not a matter of one of them being correct. Or rather, both are partially correct—yes. We Christians have a scripture of our own, a "special Veda"—you Shaivas, Vaishnavas, Buddhists, Jains, Ajivakas, you are not the only ones with scriptures. And it says in our Veda that when God created the world, he saw that it was good. So it is not right to hate the world, not right to renounce it, as the monk does. The world is good and of value because—because God made it and loves it. Yet this—how do you speak of Nalli? I would use the word *nastika* to describe him, for he denies the existence of God and the spiritual world—this nastika, this nihilist—I would agree with the monk this nastika is foolish. For he will lose everything he ever valued when he dies, if not before. He will be—he will be *forced* to renounce by death, but he does not know how to renounce. His life will surely become one of misery; he has only to live long enough. But the monk, he certainly knows how to renounce, but his renunciation is based on—on a—on a misunderstanding, a self-deception. He has convinced himself there is no good in the world, nothing to value. He has convinced himself a wise man can only hate the world. And why? Because we might become attached to what we love, and our attachment will eventually cause us pain. But I say, I believe—that to live without attachment is to live without love, and to love, to love each other, to love God—this is the very thing that God commands us to do. This is our very fulfillment as God's children. So—both the monk and the nastika are wrong."

Thomas shifted his legs, looked with fierce concentration down at the floor, and held up a single finger as if to focus the crowd on it alone. Then he let his hand fall to his lap and began again. "Let me explain it this way. We should love each other, love the good creations of our Father in heaven, yes. We should hold the world close to us, but with—I will give you a paradox—with open arms. Hold it, yes. But hold it with open arms. Hold it, hold it tightly, press it close to your bosom! But hold it with open arms."

"How do you propose to hold the world close to you, but with—as you say—open arms?" said the Queen. "Explain this riddle if you can, smooth-tongued yavana."

"I mean we should love the world but not cling to it. We should love it, but we should be ready to let it go when it's taken from us."

"But how can you let it go so easily once you have held it so close?" said the Queen. "That is no easy matter. The Jain has told us how to let it go, but you have not. What do you say, smooth-tongued yavana?"

"The Jain," said Thomas, "lets it go by hating it. I let it go, not by hating it, but by loving God *more* than it. I have daughters, I am attached to them, it is right and good for me to be attached—"

At this point Charishnu interrupted: "You claim to be an ascetic, you dress like an ascetic, and you have attachments? You even defend the right of an ascetic to have attachments? Surely this is hypocrisy! You are but another Nalli in disguise!"

"I am not a Nalli!" Thomas shot back. "Nalli will suffer without hope when he loses his lover—or his health. I will not. For I know that those I love will not be lost to me forever. They will be taken up by God to his

Kingdom, where I will soon join them or they will join me. As for my health, I guard and value it while I have it, but when it's taken away, I do not grieve. An incorruptible body, a spiritual body is waiting for me when I enter the Kingdom. But Nalli, Nalli, with no hope in the Kingdom, will suffer without hope when his body—the only one he will ever have, he believes—begins to fail. How am I like Nalli?"

"I still fail to see," said Charishnu sourly, "what you have *given up*. Why do you dress like a sannyasin if you have not given anything up?"

"Because I have renounced everything that is not approved by God, everything that comes between me and Sarveshvara, my true Father in heaven—that is why, Guru of the King. Whatever tempts me to love it more than God, I renounce. I do not hate it, I do not say it is without value, but I renounce it anyway. And that which does not come between me and God, that, O brahmin, I allow myself to love."

"Can you speak less abstractly?" interjected the Queen.

"Forgive me if I am less than clear," said Thomas, "but I have not thought this through before now. It seems—it seems to me, as I look back over my life, that I have allowed myself to *love people*, and *renounced things*."

"But your God said the *world* was good," said the Queen. "By 'the world' I thought you meant—did you mean only persons?"

"You have listened well, gracious and beautiful Queen," said Thomas.

At that instant the Jain monk looked up and over at Thomas, and then at the Queen in her box, as if he saw them for the first time, while Charishnu's face twitched and shook in violent agitation as he exclaimed in a muffled but still audible voice, "Outrageous! Outrageous! Now he will say it is the sannyasin's place to flatter!"

"But Reverend Guru of my Husband, does he not—does he not, by his own logic, have the right, even the duty, to admire the good?"

"And the beautiful," said Thomas before Charishnu could answer. "To desire to *possess* the good—that for a sannyasin is a sin. To *admire* it—that is a virtue. I was not flattering the Queen. Yet I apologize to the King"—Thomas looked over at the King—"if I have been too familiar."

The King signaled to Thomas, with a single waggle of his head and a wave of his hand as it dangled over his knee, that the very idea of taking offense was ridiculous.

"Summarize your position, holy man from the West," said the Queen, who seemed touched by Thomas' exposition. "Or rather, let me try to summarize it myself as I understand it. You say you are different from the reverend Jain monk because he does not see the world as good, whereas you do. And you are different from the *nastika* because his attachments will be finally and hopelessly disappointed and defeated when he loses what he loves, which is inevitable, whereas you—how would you phrase it?"

"Whereas I," said Thomas, "because I love God above all else, and trust in his goodness, can rejoice when those I love are taken from me. That is what I mean by 'holding with open arms.' I love my friends devotedly, as ardently as Nalli, but because I love God and trust in his goodness, I can bear to let them go. I hold them, as I say, with open arms. And why not? God will take care of them. They will be better off in God's Kingdom than here with me. So why should I cling to them when they are called? I do not cling. Thus I do not grieve when they pass on."

"As Nalli would," said the Queen, who looked quickly at Nalli to see if he objected. But his dog remained quiet.

"As Nalli most certainly would, by his own admission," said Thomas.

"So you have devised a means of escaping suffering without first hating what you want to escape from," said the Queen.

"How well you understand!" said Thomas. "Except that *I* have not devised it. Anyone who knows the Father, Sarveshvara, will be able to love the world without grieving when it is taken from him. He too will be able to hold with open arms."

Suddenly the Queen looked at Charishnu and said, "But that is, in different language, what Shaivism teaches. Is that not correct, Guru of my Husband?"

Charishnu looked back at her for an instant, grunted something, then looked down at his lap and shook his head.

The Queen waited hopefully for a moment, then looked back at Thomas, who continued:

"The mistake of the Jain is that he believes he can escape pain only by hating what will be taken from him. Sometimes I think he is worse off than the nastika. The nastika at least holds on. But the reverend Jain ascetic, he is like a man without arms at all."

"Reverend Rishabha," the Queen broke in, "defend yourself if you care to."

But Rishabha only remained imperturbably silent.

"Reverend Rishabha, the Dharma of the great master Mahavira has been impugned," said the Queen. "If not for yourself, then for the rest of us defend what you value!" she exhorted.

Queen Adimanti had completely taken over. Now Kumaran understood why all Puhar adored her. Such power, such a mind, and in a woman! He had never seen the like. She was even able to get Rishabha to speak once more.

"The Dharma of the Great Master needs no defense," the old monk began. "Everyone, even this yavana, will one day discover the truth for himself in a future incarnation. I cannot hurry the process. Fools will be fools whether they be Tamil fools or yavana fools. But since you ask me, I will speak. The yavana's philosophy is based on a God. Yet the yavana has never seen or heard or in any other way perceived this God. Nor is he able to infer by argument that this God exists. He has only a strange, unknown scripture, a yavana scripture, which speaks of these things. And what could this scripture be worth? The best that can be said about his God is that *only in a certain sense* does he exist, whereas in another sense he does not. Even if he does exist in a certain sense, it would be impossible to describe the sense in which he exists. Yet the yavana speaks of this God in absolute terms. He seems to know exactly what this God commands his followers to do, and exactly what it means to describe this God as 'good.' But how can he know these things? In addition, there is a contradiction. If his God created the world, then he must have *needed* to create the world. And if he feels a need, then he would lack the necessary perfection to be considered supreme. There is no such God, and the world has always existed. If you would find God, then look to yourself. When your inherent powers have blossomed fully, you will find all the divinity you will ever require. This is the final truth."

"How, Sir, do you answer the noble monk?" said the Queen, looking at Thomas. "On what do you base your knowledge of God?"

"On scripture," said Thomas.

"But there are many scriptures," said the Queen.

"On my Master's testimony. And my own experience. God has shown his power to me, He has worked through me. To doubt his existence—I would just as soon doubt his existence, his power, his goodness, as the howl of Nalli's dog."

"And the argument against God's creating the world?"

"Yes, that argument. God has no needs, I agree with the monk. God lacks no perfection. But He loves—He loves without tiring, in every direction. And out of this love, out of his goodness He creates the world—not for Him, but for us. It is *because* He is perfect that He creates.

"It is *because* He is perfect that He creates," the Queen repeated, as if to herself. "I see." At that she relaxed her straight back and held her peace.

Suddenly a man in the back, where the low castes were grouped, waved his arms and shouted: "The reverend Rishabha disqualifies himself!" A thick growth of gray hairs bushed out of his chest, and a wreath of flowers bounced on his head as he looked around at the audience, looking for support.

"He will not allow his opponent to speak in absolute terms, but listen to the way he himself speaks!" the man went on. "'There is no such God, the world has always existed, look to yourself and find all the divinity you will ever require,' he says! What are those but absolute dogmas of his own Dharma? The truth is we all speak in absolutes. The Jain is no exception. It's a pretense, a trick he uses to embarrass an opponent! That's all!"

"What say you, good monk Rishabha?" said the Queen.

"This ignorant man maligns the eternal doctrine of the Conquerors," said Rishabha. "Woe unto him!" Rishabha spoke with a passion he had not shown before. Then he said something that startled everyone in the crowd: "And woe to this city and this empire! Even now kings plot how to overthrow the ravenous Chola tiger! The Kaveri will flow red with the blood of her warriors! Rice grown in the battlefield will forevermore have a red hue! Wise men of Puhar, look to the doctrine of the twenty-four Founders, ending with Mahavira, or be crushed and born again as slaves!"

Kumaran knew the oracle of a holy man, of whatever religion, is more reliable than the best of omens by a soothsayer; thus he was not surprised when Charishnu, at a signal from the King, closed the evening with a hurried benediction, even before a winner was chosen.

Most in the crowd dispersed quickly, but twenty or more gathered around Thomas, including the low-caste man who denounced Rishabha. The King had stood up and was talking to two of his ministers with obvious displeasure. But the Queen had not stirred. She sat with a long finger placed pensively over her mouth and stared at the crowd round Thomas. Or was it Thomas she stared at? Kumaran could not say with certainty, but a feeling of envy jabbed at him. Not once had the Queen shown any curiosity about his poetry; she had not even attended one of his readings. But she stared at the white barbarian as if he had some special potion that would take away all her ills.

As Kumaran escorted Devandi out of the Hall, his mind drifted back to Madurai and down into that terrible hole. He remembered the feeling that had settled over him as the dirty waters of baptism rolled across his forehead. For a few weeks he had actually believed in

Thomas' loving, karma-canceling God. What if the Queen should believe? What if Puhar should follow her lead in this, as it did in so much else? It occurred to him for the first time that Thomas' religion might spread like ivy after all. Would he, Kumaran, be part of it? Suddenly he felt the other aspect of Thomas' God, the wrathful, damning aspect, the aspect that hated sin so much that it threatened damnation. As he moved through the door of the Hall, he was filled with misgiving, and he shivered for an instant as the cool night air closed around him.

38. The Queen

Thomas sat on top of the dike and dangled his feet over the edge. The river flowed quietly by, its shadowy shore a long stone's throw out. The cool dry evening air buzzed with the secret codes of crickets and frogs, drowning out whatever noise the gently lapping waves made. Thomas relived the previous night's debate. His heart was split—at once grateful to God he had done well, but regretful he hadn't done better.

"Sir," a voice behind him said.

Thomas turned around and saw a man holding a lantern.

"Sir, are you the yavana sannyasin?"

"Some call me that," said Thomas as he rose to receive his guest, whose face glowed golden in the light of his lantern.

"Her Majesty the Queen wishes to see you."

"The Queen?"

"Yes, the Queen wishes to honor you. I am told she wants to speak with you."

"The Queen? Do you mean the Queen of the Cholas? Queen Adimanti?"

"None other," said the man.

"Why?" said Thomas, as his heart pounded. He wondered if the man was playing a joke on him. But why would he do that? And he did speak with the formality of an official.

"I don't know the reason," said the man. "If you will come, I will meet you here tomorrow—at this very spot, let's agree—an hour after sunrise. I will take you to her. Do you agree?"

Thomas stared at the man for a moment in utter disbelief. Then he stammered, "Of course. Of course. I—I am at the Queen's command. Tell her I would be honored."

"Good evening, then, Sir. Until tomorrow."

"Yes, until to—tomorrow."

The man turned and walked away, carrying his lantern. Thomas stared at him for a long time, until all he could see was the lantern in the dark distance. Then he turned back to the river and sat down again. "What could this mean?" he prayed aloud to Jesus. He let himself dream—dream he could win the Queen over to the new faith. "Could it be?" he considered. He looked for a clue in the questions she had asked him at the debate. "No!" he finally concluded. And he laughed at himself, laughed at his silly reverie. "No, Master, your gospel is not for the great of this world. Not yet anyway." He mastered the impulse to let himself dream some more, then turned inward where he found God waiting. "We will let what happens happen, Heavenly Father. It's enough that you use me as your instrument."

For a while he listened to the frogs and crickets drone their ageless symphony of praise to the Creator; then he fell asleep on the Kaveri's cool sands between clumps of reeds.

Queen Adimanti greeted him in a wine-colored muslin dress that came up to her neck; she almost looked like an Israelite woman, except that her breasts were vaguely visible through the thin gauzy bodice. As before at the debate, she received him without jewelry in deference to his high and holy calling, except for the amethyst permanently lodged in her nose. He wore only his faded ocher loin cloth and the cross around his neck that Kumaran made and that he sometimes draped over his left shoulder in the style of a high born Indian.

"I have wanted to speak to you privately since the debate," she said as she rose to greet him on a second-story verandah at the rear of her residence, which looked out onto an exuberant, sweet-scented forest of trees, shrubs, and flowers in the courtyard. "I am grateful to you for coming," she said, bowing slightly from the waist and holding her hands together. "You are called 'Thomas,' I believe. May I call you that?"

"Yes," he said, "and how do I call you?"

Apparently taken aback by his self-possession and directness, she needed to think a moment. "I am at heart a simple woman from one of the Velir tribes in the Western Hills," she said. "You may call me Adi, as my brothers do to this day."

"Why have you honored me with this invitation?" Thomas said.

"I want to ask you, Thomas, to be my guru. Will you accept me as your shishya, your student in sacred matters?" She bowed deeply, then turned to a table behind her and picked up a white satin pillow with a bright new ocher loin cloth on it. She held it out to him with a look of deep respect, almost homage, on her face.

"But you—barely know me," Thomas stammered in surprise.

"But I do know you. I heard you speak at the debate. Do you not remember?"

"But—" He was stunned; he couldn't believe, couldn't comprehend what had happened. But he quickly came to his senses. Staring down at the gift she held out to him, he suddenly imagined a fish or a cross in every village, the breaking of bread in every caste. He imagined grape vines imported from the West growing on hallowed ground outside every town, and he saw Jesus bless the wine and say, "This is my blood, O India, take it and drink it." A single woman, a queen, an Indian handmaid of the Lord—he and she—he and she together would capture India for Christ. A second Pentecost. All of India Christian. The dream, the dream! It was alive after all.

"I am honored," he said, controlling his excitement, "and humbly accept you as my shishya." He reached out and took the pillow from the Queen.

Then the Queen got down on her knees and bowed to the floor. A few wisps of loose hair brushed against the tops of Thomas' feet and sent a thrill through his entire body, which broke out in goose flesh. Inadvertently he let the loin cloth unfurl to its full length, and its ends grazed the Queen's back.

In Madurai he had to start from the bottom, in isolation, with enemies all around. Now it would be different. He had a sponsor, he would build from the top; everyone who was the Queen's friend—and she was universally loved by her Chola subjects—would want to be his friend, too. This time he would succeed—succeed in a mighty way.

When he first decked himself out in his shiny new ocher garb in his tumble-down hut by the river, he thanked God in ecstatic prayer. He even let himself indulge a careless fantasy: Jesus was Israel's Messiah, he would be India's. Still they were twins! Twin Messiahs! But as quickly as the thought arose, he banished it.

At their first formal meeting she told him that Charishnu had been her first Guru, as was only natural, but that she had learned to disrespect him. She had turned next to two holy men in succession, one a Jain, the other a Buddhist. But she had grown up loving Murugan as

Lord, and they did not offer her a God to adore. It was then that she discovered Noni almost under her nose. Noni—a brahmin woman who had been taught the Vedas by her father, who lived in a village on the Ganges not far from Kashi—was Charishnu's wife and a devotee of Shiva. She spoke Tamil with an odd accent, but the young Queen was deeply impressed by the unassuming learnedness and bosomy warmth of the woman and ended, following Noni's example, by taking Shiva, Lord of the Universe, as her Lord. In time she came to treasure Noni as mother, guru, and best friend, all at once; and as her love for Noni deepened, so did her love for Shiva. When Noni died suddenly, the Queen couldn't imagine taking someone else as her guru—that is, until Thomas, the "yavana Guru," entered her life.

Twice a week they met. He taught her the Lord's prayer. He told her about his Master, the Messiah of God's chosen nation, Israel, who now sat at the right hand of the Father. He taught her Jesus' gospel of love, forgiveness, service, and joy. He illustrated Jesus' teachings with the same homely parables Jesus used. He taught her the end of time was approaching, that Jesus would judge all the nations, and that he, Thomas, he and she, the Queen, were the instruments of India's conversion and salvation. He told her about the rewards of the just and the punishment of the wicked and faithless. He showed her the fingers that slid into the wound of Jesus' glorified body.

She had much to teach him also—not about her religion, at least not at first, but about herself. She told him that as a girl she climbed into the upper boughs of a wild mango tree that stood at the edge of the forest behind the village. From her invisible perch in the thick clusters of leaves she watched the comings and goings of people and animals on the ground and imagined them to be her subjects. "Queen of the World" she called her private game, and at night she sometimes continued the fantasy in her dreams.

She told him about the brahmin hired to teach her brothers and how it was discovered she had more aptitude than they. She told him about an ugly, toothless old woman in her village who had never married but could hold the villagers spellbound for hours at a time with her stories, and who once took her aside and told her how "the last would be first"—the very words Thomas used at the debate. She told him a strange story about her sister-in-law's sister, a young woman who died when she was bitten by a krait and who appeared as a ghost to her sister-in-law a few days later and made her promise to ask Shiva that the next child she bore be her reincarnated spirit, and how the baby the sister-in-law bore grew into a young woman who exactly resembled the dead sister.

When going about his daily chores Thomas often thought of Adimanti. He imagined her noble long neck, her straight small bones, the long-fingered hands that moved with the precision of a dancer's, her narrow out-turned feet as they glided beneath her robe, the bow-harp she placed beside her when sitting and sometimes played when she sang religious songs for him. He thought of her crystal-like eyes, which seemed to him the most beautiful he had ever seen, and at times almost took his breath away with their indefinable spiritual luster. He thought of her aristocratic bearing and voice, which struck him as incongruous with what he took to be her humble origins. He carried with him her laugh, which seemed to him curiously gracious and energetic, as if perhaps to compensate for a sense of humor that did not know how to delight in the simple earthy things of life ordinary people laughed at, but felt at home only with what was sublime, ethereal, or abstract.

They always met in the same upper room, which looked out over a garden. Bright scenes of reposing gods and their busty goddess-consorts were freshly painted on the walls; with their calm unwinking eyes these goddesses oversaw the passionate pursuits of foolish men below. No furniture stood in the room except for thick mats on the floor and a Shiva *lingam* at one end. The windows on both sides of the room were large and reached down almost to the floor; it would have been a dangerous place for children to play, for they could have easily bounced out one of the windows.

But the Queen had no children. She had gained the adoration of her people, even of the King's lesser wives, who named their daughters after her. But she had lost the love of her husband. Many years ago she had defied Charishnu by seeking out a low-caste priest and having herself branded on her lower abdomen with the symbol of the bloodthirsty Goddess Mariamma in the hope of having a child, but nothing had come of this act. She told this story with serenity, but Thomas knew she was not unmoved, for her voice quavered at the mention of her barrenness. He had seen her with other women's children and noted how she loved being with them and they with her. Yet she would never have any of her own. What was behind her self-mastery? How many tears had gone into its making? Thomas could not hold back tears of his own as he listened to Adimanti's tragic, all-too-human tale.

By the time she finished her story he felt a powerful desire to hold her close, to comfort her, his dear shishya, his new and best friend. But he did not dare. What held him back was not the fact that such familiarity with the Queen could merit death; it was that underneath his loin cloth there was a slight throbbing movement that was inconsistent with the vow of a passionless sannyasin. The movement alerted him to a danger, a signal from a faint yesterday that had all but passed out of existence. So he kept his distance. But he didn't harden his heart as he might have. Instead he let himself savor the strange mingling of passion and compassion the Queen inspired in him, a feeling not quite like any other he had ever had.

She invited him to live at the palace, and he accepted on condition he could minister to all castes and come and go as he needed to. Rumors of war abounded throughout the city, and Thomas had already made up his mind to accompany his Christian converts in the King's elephant battalion to battle. The Queen not only agreed to Thomas' stipulations, but promised to accompany him—and of course her husband—in the event of war. So there was an excellent understanding all around.

39. War

In the sixth year after Kumaran's return from the yavana lands, in his thirty-second year, as the cool month of Tai gave way to bright mild Masi, war broke out. King Attan of Chera, King Nedunjeliyan of Pandya, and eleven semi-independent Velir chieftains allied themselves in desperation to fight against and slay the great Chola Tiger before it devoured them all. Karikal's spies informed him the enemy forces were already marching toward Puhar; they were laying waste the winter rice just harvested by his farmers.

Kumaran was both disturbed and thrilled when he heard the news. War was the only significant human activity he had not witnessed. In both Madurai and Puhar the hallmark of his poetry was its originality. His meter and rhyme were not the best, his word choice was sometimes excelled, but his subject matter was unique, and his metaphors were so celebrated they were imitated everywhere. But had anyone noticed he seldom wrote of war, that almost obligatory subject among Tamil poets? Had anyone noticed that on those rare occasions when he did, he relied on conventional themes? Kumaran sometimes suspected this lack had been noted and that all Puhar whispered about it behind his back.

The community of poets, especially the elite Imperial Poets, had other reasons for loving war. If Karikal won, they would have much to praise him for, and he would reward them lavishly with the spoils: not only gold and silver and jewels taken from the bodies of fallen soldiers, but tracts of fertile land abounding in water, and handsome chariots pulled by four horses abreast.

But the poets feared war as much as they rejoiced over it. Several who had known previous battles were especially chary of this new war. Kumaran listened carefully to what they said. The danger was much greater than he had imagined. Not only would he be expected to observe and chronicle the war; he would have to rally and inspire the warriors as they fought. For the first time he heard the story of the poet who died in battle as he exhorted a squadron of foot-soldiers to fight, and of the hero stone that marked the place where he fell. One night Kumaran went home and tried to capture his fear in words: He described the Kaveri's flow on the eve of battle as supernaturally slow— as if the River Goddess herself were holding her breath in horror over the impending slaughter.

As for his sympathies, he found himself in a strange position. He was one of the few men in the world, perhaps the only one, who had actual dealings with each of the three kings. He of course hated Nedunjeliyan for what he had done to him in Madurai, but he had loved gentle King Attan, King of Chera, when the King rewarded him with the bull elephant which he sold for fifty gold coins. And for another reason it seemed unnatural to be fighting against Attan. Kumaran had come into manhood in Chera country: He thought of Chera Maliankara, not of Chola Uranthai, where he was born, as his home. He even imagined his own brothers fighting in Attan's army. But events had conspired to tie him to Karikal, his new lord and provider. Perhaps he would soon learn that such scruples over loyalty, whatever their merit as one put on his armor, were a gratuitous luxury in the thick of battle. At least that's what one of his friends told him.

Once Karikal's spies brought him news of the invasion, the preparations moved at lightning speed. Karikal the statesman and poet became Karikal the commander-in-chief. Within three days a huge army of elephants, chariots, cavalry, and infantry gathered from all over the empire in a vast staging area northwest of the city. Early on the evening before setting out, the King worshipped at the altars of Kotravai, Goddess of War, and the Sun God, controller of the weather. Then, in the courtyard of the torch-lit Shiva temple on the palace grounds, the King, urged on by the thunderous roar of hundreds of two-sided drums, danced the *veriyatal* in tiger-skin armor. His clan and harem, his commanders and specially picked warriors, the brahmins and poets connected with the palace, and many others watched as he twisted and jerked and gyrated. His entranced eyes became frenzied as the power of the Gods entered into him, their regent on earth, then burst out and spilled over into the ecstatic crowd. The soldiers in battle array with their wooden shields covered with skin of the tiger or wild boar felt a superhuman energy and confidence. The women, jewelless and already mourning their husbands' absences, shouted encouragement while their round-eyed children clung fearfully to their legs. As toddy was passed around and drums covered the earth with their din of solid, rhythmless sound, all felt themselves transported into a new, entirely different world.

Finally the king fell face-down, and the swelling voices of the crowd drowned out even the drums. As he lay on the ground exhausted, his subjects, especially his soldiers, felt mystically empowered by the energy he imparted. The collective passion and excitation left the spectators feeling they could not rest until they had utterly defeated the invading army. So intense, so bloodthirsty was the ardor of Karikal's warriors that two young officers, their shields fouled with dried human blood and remnants of flesh left from earlier campaigns, offered their heads to the Goddess Kotravai and their King. The thunder of the raw-leather drums rose again as the men bent their heads over the altar. The sacrificial priest looked questioningly at the King, who had just risen, for such an offering was unusual except during Indra's annual festival. The King nodded, asked for his sword, then handed it to the priest. Torchlight glinted off the upraised steel. . . . A head fell on the altar. . . . Then another. The crowd's roar again drowned out the drums, but not for long. Again the frenzied drums thundered into the night. "Accept, O Great Goddess, our lives which we offer to Thee in sacrifice for our King!" they seemed to say as they rent the air.

The next day finally dawned. Woe to any astrologer who might have warned the King the time was inauspicious for marching! More potent than the God of Death he looked as he sat high on the back of his great elephant. The Guardian of the Umbrella, seated behind him on the howdah, propped the sacred emblem high over Karikal's head, decked out in the traditional wreath of *atti* blossoms. The Queen rode behind him in her palanquin carried by eight men, her first lady-in-waiting seated behind her. Close to the royal couple—on horseback or riding in chariots or even walking—were the King's Guru, his top generals, his chief ministers, priests, soothsayers, jesters, messengers, poets, even the chief cook. And walking somewhat apart from the rest—at first Kumaran couldn't believe his eyes as he looked down from his horse—was a freakish sight, Thomas.

For seven miles the army stretched out along the highway along the northern bank of the Kaveri. Three-hundred elephants, hundreds of mules and pack horses, countless bullock carts carried the impedimenta of slaughter: weapons, armor, tents, tools, drums, conchs, flags, gold and silver to pay the soldiers, official records, kitchen utensils, wardrobes for the dancers and jesters, musicians' instruments, images of the Gods, a great variety and quantity of food, even a few volumes of Kautilya's manual of warfare, the *Arthashastra*, translated into Tamil for Karikal's commanders. At the head of the column were several hundred laborers armed with machetes, spades, axes, saws, spikes, and rope. They walked quickly, hacking away brambles that encroached on the road, smoothing out bumps, filling in washouts, cutting detours—in all ways expediting movement forward. Behind them came the elephants, as useful for crossing rivers and making earthworks as for charging the enemy in the field or battering the gates of his forts. Then came the son of Ilaiyon, the mighty King himself, Karikal, as jealous of the welfare of his elephants as of his human subjects. Strewn out behind him along miles of dust-choked road were the sometimes handsome, sometimes weedy chargers of the cavalry; the infantry composed mostly of pulaiyars carrying spears, swords, pikes, maces, sling shots, or razor-edged discuses; gaudy war chariots pulled by teams of two or four horses and jingling with bells; conveyances carrying baggage; strings of milk cows; and every conceivable kind of camp-follower: tradesmen, carpenters, blacksmiths, prostitutes, religious mendicants, pickpockets, seamstresses, doctors, conjurers, professional pillagers, even blind men. Twenty-five thousand souls, it was estimated, marched with Karikal.

The King's chief preoccupations were interpreting omens and deciding when and where to cross the Kaveri. From time to time a dust-covered spy would gallop back to the King with the latest news of the enemy's movement. Every other business was immediately put aside when this happened. After one of these messages—delivered on the afternoon of the third day—Karikal went into consultation with his generals. On the next day, the fourth, the crossing began.

Kumaran found out that the Queen had taken Thomas as her guru, and his amazement knew no bounds. Racked by envy, Kumaran studied his old nemesis from a distance. He watched as Thomas would run ahead and disappear for half a day. Where did he go? Then suddenly he would reappear walking next to the Queen's palanquin, sometimes talking to her, sometimes not. Kumaran was extremely curious about Thomas' new position, but of course he would not let himself speak to him. And he was vexed to discover that buried under all the hate was something else, something like its opposite. For why else would he follow Thomas' humble movements with more interest than the King's? Why else would he catch himself looking back—back to Maliankara to the man bowling with the children, further back to the Red Sea to the man who cast two demons out of Philetus, all the way back to Alexandria to the man who carried a broken oar off a ship so he could master a new language? For whatever strange reason—he wished he could have denied it with thirty oaths—Kumaran still felt bound to Thomas in some peculiar way. Even then, even after the betrayals of friendship—or rather what he told himself were betrayals, for it was becoming less clear to him they amounted to much—a part of him wanted to run up to Thomas, embrace him, and get the latest news of him. On several occasions their eyes met, and Thomas would always nod in recognition. But Kumaran kept away, and Thomas did not force a meeting. So Kumaran ignored the intimations of forgiveness and friendship that nibbled at his heart. He covered them over with thoughts taking him in the opposite direction. He let himself dwell on the way Thomas and the Queen seemed to enjoy each other's company. Could it be that she, like many other of Puhar's indolent aristocratic ladies, favored the yavana's white flesh after the decadent fashion of the day? Kumaran simmered with envy. If with a part of himself he secretly loved Thomas, the larger part of himself, or at least the conscious part, hated him with a malevolence that could not be measured.

Kumaran had other reasons to envy Thomas, for it was not only the Queen with whom Thomas dealt, but the King. On one occasion, as the column moved south beyond the Kaveri across rice fields through village after village filled with waving well-wishers, a strange keening sound reached the King's ears.

"What is that?" he said in a voice full of portent.

Everyone stopped moving and listened. Kumaran thought it was some kind of animal giving birth, as did others.

"Charishnu, what do you say?" said the King to his Guru.

"It sounds like a dying animal, Your Majesty."

"A dying animal? What kind of an omen is that?" said the King.

"It is not a good one. Perhaps you should halt the march, at least temporarily," said Charishnu.

"Let us see what it is first!" said the King hotly.

Karikal dismounted and, with everyone following, walked down the lane the noise came from. There, under a grove of tamarind trees, was the explanation. Two bullocks hitched to the axle of an oil press walked slowly in a circle; and as they walked, wood creaked against wood, and the high-pitched groan came forth.

The operator fell on his knees when he realized who his guest was, and a few small boys whose job it was to drive the bullocks gazed with their mouths open until the operator shouted at them to kneel. Everybody was relieved, and many laughed at the boys as they fell clumsily to the ground and bowed with the grace of calves learning to walk.

But the King was not satisfied. "Charishnu, what do you say now?" he said.

"I can make nothing of the oil press. But the sound—the sound is still like that of a dying animal. I still say it is ominous."

"What do the rest of you say?" said the King, looking about him on his high horse.

But no one said anything, for who would dare contradict the King's Guru?

Then it occurred to the King who might. "The Queen's Guru, that yavana—is he here?"

"Do you mean that Christian, Your Majesty?" Thomas said firmly, holding up his hand at the edge of the circle.

"I mean the Queen's Guru!" shouted the King in a fury. "Speak up, you barbar—!" But he checked himself before he pronounced the insult.

"I see nothing but an oil press, Your Majesty," said Thomas calmly. "Why make an omen of it? No doubt the press will moan in the same way next year as it did last. But"—he paused slightly and fingered his beard in the usual way—"it is odd . . ."

"*What* is odd?" said the King as he glowered at Thomas.

". . . that the operator carries on as if nothing is going to change. He does not fear invaders, that is obvious. If I were looking for an omen, I would look to that. That, and the fact that he works under a tamarind grove."

Everyone looked up and noted the dusty green leaves and ripening seed pods of the auspicious shade tree.

"So you see good in the omen?" said the King, his voice suddenly chastened, surprised, but most of all relieved.

"I do," said Thomas.

For the next several days the King kept Thomas near his side over the quiet protests of Charishnu, his own Guru. Once as the King was standing by the Kaveri after backtracking to oversee the fording operation, he saw a boy dive from a tree branch into the river, stay under a long time, then surface downstream holding up a handful of sand. When the King asked Charishnu for his interpretation, the brahmin answered that whereas the water of the Kaveri was holy, the sediment at the bottom was not. "It is a symbol of evil overcoming good," Charishnu concluded in his most peremptory brahmanic tone.

"What says the Queen's Guru?" the King snapped, glaring at Thomas.

"I see nothing but a boy diving into a river and scooping up some sand from the river's bottom," said Thomas. "Why make an omen of it?"

"But if one chose to?" said the King.

"Well, did you note the look on the boy's face?"

"He was smiling," answered the King.

"Yes," said Thomas, "he was smiling. He was smiling because he had accomplished something difficult. He had triumphed."

And so had Thomas. Kumaran, spying from a discreet distance, wondered at Thomas' new-found guile. How had he come by it? Kumaran was sure Thomas owed it to him. He owed him that and much more, but he never acknowledged it, any of it, perhaps never even realized it. Yet look how well it served him. Look where it took him. There he sat on a horse beside the King! Kumaran felt cheated. The old resentment built and built until his chest throbbed with a squeezing pain he had never felt before.

Thomas didn't always say what the King wanted to hear, but always he began by asking, "Why make an omen of it?" and then gave the least fanciful interpretation he could think of. Next to Charishnu's inventive, often specious readings, Thomas' seemed plodding and commonplace, but also more robust. It was the King's pleasure to choose between the two royal Gurus. He always chose the more optimistic, leaving Charishnu fuming.

The column marched south until it reached a village named Venni. Beyond a line of trees ahead, all could see smoke from the enemy's fires and hear his drums and horns. Kumaran forgot about Thomas.

The flags flying the fish, the bow, and the tiger standards were so numerous as they flapped in the morning breeze they cut up the sun's warm rays. Roaring drums, blasts of conch shells and long horns, jangling bells hanging from the necks of war elephants and from chariots, clanging cymbals—all of this noise was set off by the remorseless rhythmic booming of Karikal's immense shaggy-sided war drum. The formal, rather silly insults had been delivered: "If we defeat you, you will be disgraced as much as if you lived on cow's flesh!" Karikal's spies, too, had done their work: "Did you hear the alliance between Chera and Pandya is breaking down?" they whispered up and down enemy lines. Now there was nothing left but to fight. Karikal advanced on his quadriga pulled by four white steeds with red manes and shot the traditional arrow just short of the chariots of the two enemy kings, and they did the same to him. A swaggering ultimatum, "Surrender now or die!" was shouted back and forth. A short gallop back to their respective armies, the mounting of each King on his war elephant, a final order: The two forces, each a quarter mile wide, approached each other like two massive clouds with flashing lightning and doomful thunder.

The elephants in the front line began their charge across the flat dry field. The ground shook. Carrying a shield, Kumaran, still more the poet than the warrior, thought of Adishesha, the Serpent God bearing the weight of the earth on his coiled back; it was as if the great serpent himself trembled. Suddenly arrows began to fall ahead of him like rain, and the screams of men made him forget about poetry.

He pulled up behind his battalion of reserve infantrymen armed with swords and spears and cowered, shivering, behind his shield. It was then he heard the first guttural screams of men in their death agony. Only out of the mouths of trapped jungle beasts had he heard cries of terror like these. But soon they were drowned out by trumpet blasts of wounded elephants. Before long a single violent, screaming, sky-rending din of slaughter floated across Venni's dusty plain. Wounded men limped or crawled through the clouds of yellow dust as they fled the slaughter. Trunkless elephants bellowed in agony and charged blindly in any direction. Riderless horses bleeding from deep dripping gashes or from arrows still stuck in their sides dropped on the ground and expired in front of Kumaran's eyes. Several men in his battalion began to panic and had to be restrained by their officers from fleeing.

"Advance! Advance!" came the order. As snakes cowered in their holes beneath the pounding footfall of men gone mad, Kumaran's battalion rushed into battle. Now Kumaran could hear sounds more distinctly. The terrifying zings of notched arrows, the clicking and clanking of swords and spears, the dazed dying whimpers of a warrior crushed by a chariot and lying at his feet—all of this, every syncopation of the slaughter he heard, even the gulps of goblins drinking the blood gushing from human carcasses.

Now he could see better. Through the dust, diminished by the blood which had spilled everywhere, he saw horses stand on their hind legs and rush at huge elephants with their hooves. Noblemen of the warrior caste fired arrows at point-blank range from their invincible armor-plated perches on top of their chariots. Roaring elephants with dozens of arrows dangling from their thick colorful caparisons charged at enemy foot-soldiers. Men on horseback, retaliating with long pikes or swords, swiped and gouged at their vulnerable trunks. The once parched soil had turned into a shallow black-red mud and was cluttered with corpses. Infantrymen armed with spears stood on piles of bodies or on the flanks of fallen horses or elephants to gain the advantage of "high ground." At one point something powerful and snake-like slammed against Kumaran's ankles and sent him sprawling on top of his shield into the gore: It was an elephant's severed trunk, a sudden monstrous creation of war with a brief agony all its own.

In mid-afternoon Karikal's forces broke through. This happened when a suicide squad of sappers slew the war elephant bearing King Attan, who was shot with an arrow in the back as he made his escape. With the parasol mounted on the elephant nowhere in view, and rumors of Attan's death fanning out over the battlefield, Attan's palmyra-wreathed warriors disengaged and retreated. When Karikal saw what had happened, he swung his newly freed forces round and struck Nedunjeliyan's army on its left flank. With tiger shields protecting them and wreaths of *atti* blossoms waving on their heads, Karikal's forces charged. Cavalry, elephants, and chariots fell upon the enemy. Kumaran watched as the proud fish-emblems of Pandya began toppling over, and somehow a metaphor worked its way up out of his dazed mind: "Like brittle stubble in a hurricane the enemy standards fell."

But as his battalion of foot-soldiers pushed nearer the combat, their shouts sanguine with the expectation of victory, a fresh rain of arrows fell from the sky with their terrifying whizzing sound. With a "chock!" one bit into Kumaran's shield, and all around him men began screaming and falling and stumbling over each other. Horrified, Kumaran peered out from behind his shield up at the sky, as if by careful scrutiny he might see the arrow aimed at his heart and dodge his destiny.

"Thomas! Oh, Thomas!" Kumaran cried out. He felt an arrow sticking out of his shoulder near the neck, sticking out of both sides, and in his terror he wanted only Thomas. But Thomas was walking across the field with a large brass water pot balanced on his head, another under his arm, after the fashion of a woman. "Thomas!" Kumaran cried, beginning to run after him. But Thomas took no notice as he walked under the serene palms of Maliankara where Kumaran grew up. Maliankara! What were they doing there? Kumaran felt a throbbing pain in his shoulder, and there was Thomas getting ahead of him, disappearing into the deep shade of the coconut palms. "Mother, Mother," Kumaran called—called these very words to Thomas, for Thomas was both Thomas and Mother at once, though Kumaran had no idea how this could be. Suddenly Kumaran saw the old house, the house he called home. And there was the glistening canal, the green backwater, the trees as tall as a mountain. He ran after Thomas, ran toward the house, faster and faster. Why did they not get any closer? And what was wrong with his shoulder? "Mother! Mother!" he shouted again. He reached up in the direction of the pain and felt something sticking out of his body. With a start he realized where he was, and the sounds and sights of the battlefield closed in on him again. Then he lost consciousness.

He awoke at night to a throbbing pain in his left leg near the knee. He thought back, remembered the arrow, tried to lift his head. He felt more pain, this time in his neck and shoulder.

"What happened to my leg?" he asked a man in the shadows who offered him water from a cupped palmyra leaf. The man did not know. Kumaran curled around on the mat and looked at the leg in the torchlight. He tried to move it, but the pain was unbearable. He settled back down on the mat and whimpered into the dark. Something was terribly wrong with his leg, that was all he could think of.

Later that night the King came to see him. "We beat them, Kumaran," the King said as he bent down with torch in hand and peered into his poet's face. "And you will get well and write about it—as only you can."

Kumaran's eyes swam with tears as this God in the flesh whispered his name and touched his cheek with a finger. Then the God went away, and all that night Kumaran drifted in and out of consciousness. In his delirium he thought of Thomas and tried to cry out to him. At one moment he felt a great love and yearning for Thomas, at the next he hated him because he would not come. He had come before—in the pit—but where was he now? When the pain let Kumaran sleep, he had nightmares. Headless corpses danced on their own heads to the sinister beat of the devil dance, and demoness cooks stirred a human soup made of blood and entrails with ladles that were the arms of kings.

Many weeks later Kumaran wrote the poem the King asked for. He told of enemy warriors so frightened they fled the battlefield disguised as mendicants or musicians, of horses sick with wounds and twitching their ears in pain as they refused to eat, of elephants clogging the canals around Venni with their huge dark carcasses, of King Attan so disgraced by the wound in his back that he vowed to become a Jain monk and ritually starve himself to death, of heroes invited by celestial hosts to join them in heaven. He told of King Karikal's glorious

capture of the enemy kings' parasols and war drums. He told of Karikal's subjugation of the whole of Tamil country and of the betrothal
of his oldest daughter, Princess Mandi, to his vassal, young Attan II,
the new regent over Chera country. But of the tears as numerous as
the sands of the Kaveri, tears shed by wives and mothers and sons and
daughters and servants from Cape Cormorin in the south to Kanchi in
the north, from Muziri in the west to Puhar in the east, of all the broken bodies and embittered hearts and smashed dreams—of all these
things, the things that lay most heavily on Kumaran's heart, he wrote
nothing at all.

He survived. He came back home on a crutch and with a shiny new
scar at his shoulder—two scars actually, for the arrow had come out
the other side. Devandi told him he should be proud.

Kumaran went about the usual business of a Court poet: He feasted
and dallied; he attended concerts and plays; he honored the Gods in
the appropriate ways and at the appropriate times; he wrote and read
his poetry. He kept himself fashionably dressed and bejeweled, freshly barbered, massaged with scented oils, wreathed in a garland of sea-
sonal flowers. But his leg was disfigured, and he limped with a lurch
that left no one thinking he was handsome or pretty anymore. He had
always loathed disfigurements of any kind, and now he was forced
to loathe his own body. Even his face seemed changed for the worse.
When he looked at the mirror, he saw a certain haggard quality he had
not noticed since Madurai—since the day he was released from his pit
and got the first look at himself after five months of incarceration. He
wrote in his diary he was "tired of the burden of quietly, motionlessly,
weightlessly being me." He did not walk on solid earth, as he wrote in
another entry, "but on cumbersome piles of bodies."

Sometimes he saw Thomas, and three or four times he couldn't avoid
running into him and exchanging a greeting. He felt a deep disquiet following such meetings. What caused it he couldn't have said, but it had
something to do with the fine figure that Thomas cut, with his tall, pale,
upright body and smooth, dignified gait. Or perhaps the eyes: they had
once burned with intimidating conviction, but now they reflected something new Kumaran did not understand: a softness, perhaps a sadness,
something that made him more human and less like a God. Had Thomas
found love, whereas he, Kumaran, only the chariot wheel that rolled over
his leg as he lay unconscious on the battlefield and left him bent forever?

Kumaran wondered why Thomas hadn't come to see him while he
convalesced. It would have been like Thomas to come. At least it would

have been like the old Thomas, the Thomas who prided himself on healing the sick. Kumaran told himself that of course he wouldn't have let Thomas in, but Thomas hadn't even given him the chance. Or perhaps he would have relented and let him in after all. Perhaps he would have been cordial. Perhaps he would have told Thomas he missed him terribly and loved him like a brother, a father, a friend, a . . .

No! Kumaran cringed at the way his thoughts betrayed him when he wasn't careful. He reminded himself Thomas was contemptible. Never again, never again would he let himself be fooled. How many times would he have to remind himself of that?

In his imagination he saw Thomas' determined, long, straight-bodied stride, and hated him.

40. A Dangerous Play

Thomas had survived that day of human slaughter, when Venni's irrigation canals turned from an oily olive-green to a dark gluey red. Never before had he valued his faith so much as when the arrows and spears whirred around him. He had gone into battle with the elephant battalion during the first charge. He had been fearless, for he felt God wasn't done with him yet. He had acted as a body-bearer, a physician of sorts. This wasn't what he had planned; he had thought he would minister to his converts as they fell. But he couldn't keep track of where they were in the confusion of battle. He had been wounded in three places by arrows and distinguished himself for his bravery. At the height of the battle he led a wagon of wounded and dead back to the rear area, where a physician discovered an arrow dangling from his thigh and pulled it out. He would not even wait for his wound to be bound before going back for more of the wounded. Even the King heard about Thomas' bravery.

Thomas' wounds had been superficial, but several of his converts had not been so fortunate. Four Christians had been slain and more than a dozen seriously wounded. Puttaswamy's father was among the dead. His elephant was found stiff and bloated on the battlefield with its trunk severed, spears sticking out of its hide, and vultures already gnawing at its stomach.

Back in Puhar life was getting back to normal, but it was a new normalcy for Thomas. Now the boy Puttaswamy followed him like a shadow, often spending the night with him in his palace apartment.

Everyday the Queen came to see Thomas if he didn't come to see her first, and she developed a great liking for the boy and couldn't resist bringing him little gifts. Puttaswamy returned her affection and playfully called her "Auntie Queen." Once it occurred to Thomas he might be able to be happy living in an obscure village with Adimanti for a wife and Puttaswamy for a son.

Meanwhile the work of conversion went forward briskly. He had been in Puhar only eighteen months, but already two churches stood. And Valluvar, the low-caste man who had struck out at the Jain monk Rishabha at the debate and fallen at Thomas' feet afterwards, was doing the Lord's work in Mayilapur, a city to the north. The ivy of Thomas' faith was indeed growing.

But it was not growing fast enough for him. For this to happen Queen Adimanti would have to convert publicly. She wore a wide ivory bracelet on her wrist with a large cross and scenes from the story of the "good mleccha" carved on it, but she resisted baptism. What had gone wrong? Had he let her get too close to him? He had thought friendship would make conversion all the more probable. But theirs, after all, was no ordinary closeness. All the Court knew about them; had their reputations been less than spotless, the gossip might have turned malicious. As it was, Thomas was the only one who found fault. He told himself he was too intimate with her; she knew his soul inside and out; she saw his faults. He urged himself to keep a greater distance from her. But as soon as he found himself in her presence, his resolve broke down: not so much out of weakness but because reserve seemed unhealthy and unnatural when they were actually together. He loved her as his dearest friend. She went to concerts with him, she listened to him mumble his little complaints and hold forth on his little successes, she sometimes swept his room and tidied up his manuscripts and bedding, she was his partner in bringing up little Puttaswamy. Did one "keep a distance" from such a friend as the Queen? Even if it were advisable, how could one? Her presence was so sweet to him, so essential, that he couldn't bring himself to keep her away. So she remained his shishya and friend at once.

They sat on cushions and looked out the dark window of Thomas' apartment at the torchlit pathways three stories down. People came and went from one pleasure to another in the still sultry air of the early evening. Couples hung on each other's arms, children chased each other like happy monkeys, men stepped eagerly toward home and a delicious meal complete with servants to fan them as they ate.

They were alone, guru and pupil—and whatever else they were to each other. Somehow the conversation came around to Karikal. She began admiring and praising him as she'd never done before in Thomas' presence. He tried to listen with sympathy: It was his responsibility always to listen. It was usually his pleasure too, but not this time.

"I remember when we were newly married, he was not quite eighteen," she said. "He put on a gray beard and presided over a difficult case. My Karikal is very clever!"

In spite of his studious detachment, it stung Thomas to hear her use the words "my Karikal."

"He is wiser than you think," she went on. "He has his junior queens, but he knows pleasure is fleeting. He loves to conquer new territory, but for him it is a game."

"But he takes the game so seriously," Thomas interjected, "and it's such a bloody game." Suddenly feeling ashamed of himself for speaking with such severity, he tried to turn the conversation away from the King. "So many men died," he said, speaking of the great battle.

"Men have always died, Master," the Queen said. "And what better way for a warrior to die than in battle? I do not think that kings want more territory as much as they want an excuse to fight. Men love war. I am sure it is a game for him. Karikal knows the pleasure of victory passes quickly. He is more ready to die than you suspect."

Thomas scowled. "So you think he is ready to die? And what would you do if he died?"

"I would join him on top of his pyre, of course," she said without hesitation.

"So you could be his queen in the next world?" he said.

"No," she laughed, "but because it is expected. I would do it for the good of the Kingdom."

"And if it were not expected?"

Then she said with a giggle: "Well, Thomas, friend and teacher, I would marry you and take you back to my village. I would wash your feet and serve you simple food on a banana leaf and say, 'Here is your food, my Lord! May you be pleased to eat!' What do you say to that, sannyasin?" And she giggled at the unprecedented boldness of her joke.

He didn't know what to say, but his heart leaped with excitement even as his mind rebuked it. She looked quietly out at the night. He could barely make out her face, a black silhouette against a dark background. He felt a sudden impulse to touch her, to let the tips of his fingers brush her soft cheeks. But he checked himself.

"All those men out on the battlefield who died," she said after a while, changing the subject. "What do you suppose happened to them? I will tell you what we say." Her joined index fingers pressed against her chin as she looked, not at him, but up at the infinite sky with its numberless stars. "A few went to God forever. Their souls were liberated from the game of life and death. Tell me, I have been wondering, if you were to die today . . ."

She stopped herself in mid-sentence and looked intently into the night as if in mystical communion with it. "I can almost see all those thousands of souls rising like wisps of vapor to the heavens," she said with an air of wonder. Then she looked at Thomas and said in her normal voice, "If you had died at Venni, how would you have chosen to come back, Master? As a yavana or a Tamil?"

"But I don't believe we come back," he said.

"I know, but pretend." Then she added before he could answer, "Such a strange belief! One life, one destiny forever and ever. A soul is jolted out of its body by a well-aimed spear. To think it is on its way to everlasting bliss or torment. Everlasting! On the basis of what? You say on the basis of eighteen, or twenty, or thirty short years. What could the soul have done in so short a span to deserve such a destiny? What kind of God would hand out such a destiny? Tell me, friend and Guru"—she lowered her voice to a whisper and leaned forward with her intense round eyes staring up at him, even though he could not see them clearly—"what do you think would have happened to my husband if he had died?"

Thomas didn't answer.

Suddenly she seemed annoyed. "Well, if Karikal goes to hell, then so do I!" She paused, then added, but now more quietly, "I would despise the God who sent him there. I would not want to be anywhere near such a God." She shook her head, clicked her tongue, and continued: "I have known children born of lepers. They catch the disease from their parents by the age of eight and live out their short lives in destitution. Then there are those of us who are more fortunate. On what basis does God assign us our destinies? The leper child his, me mine? Is God arbitrary? Does He have favorites even before He creates?"

Thomas waited for her to continue.

"But if we have lived before, then that would explain our different destinies. Do you not see this, Master?"

"The doctrine has no basis in my scripture, and Jesus didn't teach it," he said, "and besides, why don't we remember our past lives? It's such a strange doctrine, being born more than once—don't you see this, my Queen?"

"Strange?" she said, "why strange? The miracle is that we were born the first time. Twice is no more mysterious than waking up after a long sleep."

"Still," he said, "it makes no sense to believe we have lived a life we can't remember. If we can't remember it, how can we say it's ours?"

"But we *will* remember it once we die. We are sleeping now. When we die, we wake up. Then we remember all our lives—as much of them as we want—just as we remember all our days when we wake from sleep."

Thomas felt suffocated—tantalized too, but most of all suffocated—by the Queen's argument. The truth was he no longer quite knew what he believed about the resurrected life. He wished he were in Jerusalem so he could lay aside some of his doubts. He was confident Jesus did not teach reincarnation, but did he forbid it? Thomas could not remember. And now the Queen, so close to making an announcement of conversion, was making an argument for this pagan doctrine. And all India acted as if the doctrine were obviously true. He told himself he needed to get away, get back home, before he was swallowed up. "Maranatha," he cried out in the dark of his soul.

But the Lord did not come. And like the crow's single eye which, it was said, rolls from one side of its face to the other, first peering out of the left socket, then the right, then again the left, his mind returned to Venni, then to the doctrine that both repelled and tantalized him, then back to Venni, then—

"What a blessing we do not remember our lives," he heard her say. "Some men do terrible things. They do something terrible, and people condemn them up until the day they die. People never forget. Death and rebirth, death and rebirth—this is God's kindness to us. This is his way of forcing us to forget. He gives us disguises, new bodies, as many as we need. We are so well disguised that we fool even ourselves! We forget our own past treacheries. We get fresh starts, over and over we get fresh starts. No one condemns us for our past sins. We do not even condemn ourselves. Such a mercy, don't you think? Do you not see, Master? Will you not accept from me a crumb of wisdom this one time? You have given me so much. I would like to give you this in return."

Thomas remembered how difficult it had been to deny Jesus anything he wanted. It was the same with Adimanti. She was completely sincere. She could cast a spell over anyone who succumbed to that sincerity. Was he in danger of succumbing?

Then he remembered he was the teacher and she the student. He said, "You ask if I would want to come back as a yavana or a Tamil. I wouldn't want either. I want to live with the Father and Jesus in their everlasting kingdom. Even if I could return, I wouldn't choose to."

"Neither would I!" she said, apparently delighted to find him in agreement with her. "That is what draws me to you. You are tired of the games we play on earth, and so am I."

Thomas wanted to tell her she had jumped to the wrong conclusion, though what exactly it was he didn't quite see. He wanted to tell her not to be seduced by rebirth. Instead he said, "Then how do we differ from Karikal? He is also tired of the game—or so you said."

"I did not say that," she replied. "I said that he *knows* it is a game, not that he is tired of playing it. Karikal *enjoys* the game, he enjoys it much too much to wear the ocher robe."

"Suppose he should die," Thomas said, "and you missed him. Wouldn't you be playing the same game yourself? Wouldn't you be enjoying it too?"

For a long time she stared silently out of the window into the night. Meanwhile Thomas thought back to Venni and relived the sounds of the battle. He could hear the conchs blaring, the swords and spears clicking and clacking, elephants trumpeting, men bellowing and screaming. These were the sounds of "the game." Birth and death and rebirth, then death again. And again and again. This was the game. This was the assumption he met in almost all Indians, this was the doctrine that united them all, however their faiths might divide them in other respects. No one he had ever met in India thought as he did. The doctrine of a single life followed by heaven or hell was the greatest scandal of his religion for the people he tried to convert. It cost him thousands of converts. And here he was—not even sure what the Master said on the subject. He thought again about the soldiers dying on the battlefield. He was sure he knew the fate of his converts. But what about all the others? He realized he was less than certain.

"Thomas," said the Queen after the long lull, "I think he *will* die."

"Who?" said Thomas, roused from his reverie.

"The King."

"The King? Why do you say that?"

"No special reason. It is just an intuition I have. And I think he suspects it too. Teacher and friend, I will tell you a secret. Last night he visited me for the first time in over a year. I know you think of him as an adulterer. But in Tamil country it is the King's prerogative to take more than one queen. The Chola people do not see him as an adulterer.

True, everyone would prefer him to have only one queen, that is the ideal; but no one really expects it. Especially since—I can't give him an heir. But I wonder if he expects it of himself. He is not irreligious. Perhaps, on the eve of his death, he is returning to virtue."

Thomas did not know what to make of the Queen's hunch, but he was not deaf to the wing flaps of jealousy in his own heart at her mention of the "visit." Was it possible that Adimanti still loved the King? It weighed on his heart to think so. "But let's return to my question," he said, changing the subject. "Would you miss him?"

"Thomas," the Queen said, "I would not stay in the world long enough to find out. Let me remind you that I would join him on the pyre!"

"I wish I could persuade you not to do that," he said distractedly, his mind still dazed by the thought she might still love the King.

"Why?" she said.

It was at that moment something in him snapped. He said what he had no right to say, say even in jest. He said what he had been tempted to say, in one way or another, for several months but knew he could never say, never say as long as he lived. Perhaps the thought of the King's "visit" left him unhinged. Or perhaps he had been in India too long. Or perhaps the long denial of his passion had left him exhausted, and a demon entered him. Whatever the reason, he said it: "Because then you wouldn't be able to take me back to your village. You wouldn't be able to wash my feet. You wouldn't serve me simple food on a banana leaf and say, 'Here is your food, my Lord! May you be pleased to eat!'"

Adimanti had been gazing out across the treetops silhouetted darkly against the moonlit sky. Now she turned to him and reached out. Her hand fell lightly and chastely on his. It was the first time she had ever touched him intentionally. "You are my true friend, Thomas," she said. Then she drew her hand away.

The moon had just risen above the treetops. It was round and full and bright.

From that day forward Queen Adimanti permitted herself to wear jewelry in Thomas' presence.

41. Wife against Husband

For a few weeks Thomas had been conducting meetings in a grove of camphor trees on the palace grounds. People from a variety of castes and occupations connected with the running of the palace and its ministries attended the meetings, for everyone knew Thomas was the Queen's Guru, and that gave him an authority he wouldn't have had otherwise. But most of the crowd were women, and most of them members of a service caste.

Once Kumaran spied on one of the meetings from behind one of the trees off to the side. He couldn't hear distinctly, but he could tell that Thomas' approach was quieter than before, and he suspected his position as Queen's Guru had everything to do with his success. That and his fashionable white skin.

One day Devandi told Kumaran she had accepted baptism into Thomas' faith. She said she had never forgotten the things he said at the debate and couldn't resist the temptation to hear him again. She had gone to hear him, and on that very day, after the meeting, the "Holy Spirit" had descended upon her and she had been baptized a Christian.

Kumaran flew into a rage. "You didn't consult me!" he screamed. He tried to make her renounce the faith, but she wouldn't. He slapped her in the face and kicked her with his crippled leg; but he only succeeded in losing his balance and fell down stupidly.

"But he said a time would come when husband would turn against wife and father against son!" she screamed at him even as she helped him off the floor.

It was all so familiar. For the sake of a convert, Thomas thought nothing of turning a family upside down. Kumaran threatened to kick Devandi out of the house if she went back, but nothing he said or did changed her mind. She even brought their daughter and baby son along.

A sense of burning, a bilious constriction in his chest threatened Kumaran's well-being every time he thought of Thomas and Devandi. It was as if he had swallowed a jagged stone that wouldn't go all the way down.

42. One God, Many Names

It hadn't gone as Thomas planned. Like a scavenger deciding what to take and what to leave behind, the Queen would accept one doctrine and reject another. She rejected any teaching that forbade her to call God by the name Shiva, yet she endorsed the idea of God as "Father" and was getting used to calling Him that. She rejected the notion of Jesus as a single Messiah for all nations, but wholeheartedly embraced his moral teachings. She accepted the idea of resurrection following death but resisted any scheme that didn't include a series of births for each being. She dismissed any mention of an approaching end of time with a waggle or two of her long neck. She frowned at any mention of an everlasting hell. She told Thomas that Jesus was not the only man seen following his death, and that some of India's greatest yogis materialized themselves after death to their closest disciples. She even asked if he cleaned his hand after feeling Jesus' wound—and he remembered, with great puzzlement, that he hadn't. "He materialized himself for you; it was not the actual corpse come back to life," she said matter-of-factly.

Thomas had endured months of Adimanti's picking and choosing and was growing more and more anxious about his prize disciple. He was willing to baptize her though, if only because she revered Jesus' gospel of love, humility, and equality and because she was the key to his plans. But it was she who balked when the subject of baptism was brought up. He felt almost desperate when he thought a whole empire might be lost to Christ because he failed with her. So he decided to dispense with his homely parables and lessons from Scripture. He would follow the dangerous course of philosophical disputation, the manly science of reason. He would overwhelm her with logic, analogy, and argument. He would ask her to list her beliefs one by one, then dismantle them piecemeal. He would gouge them out of her mind like a dentist digging out an abscessed molar. Then he would substitute God's truth. He hated what he was about to do; it seemed unfriendly and intimidating; it didn't at all seem the way to treat the person he loved most in the world. He vacillated, worried for weeks about it. He might lose her patronage or even—what was much worse—her friendship. But what else could he do? The stakes were high, very high. He would have to risk it.

He decided to reintroduce some formal structure into their meetings. Wasn't it in her own best interest to look up to her teacher? By nature he was egalitarian; he felt uncomfortable with hierarchies, from greater India's caste system to the apostolic pecking order back in Jerusalem. As a young child he had lived at the bottom of Nazareth's society, for he was a *mamzer*. As an apostle, in spite of his unique gift with languages and privileged relationship with Jesus, his "twin," he could never quite forget that he was the "Doubter" and therefore flawed. Wasn't that the reason he felt on an equal footing with the Queen even though she was a woman and called him "Master"? When they were together, he did not think of her as the Queen of the Chola Empire; she was only his dearest friend. Never mind. All that would have to change.

So they met in the same upper room they had met in during the first formal session many months ago. The same stylized murals of gods and goddesses covered the walls. On the floor lay the thick mats of bamboo, with two cushions carefully placed at the center not too close together. There were no couches, and the whole effect was not only formal but slightly austere, in spite of the bright paintings. At one end of the room stood the Shiva *lingam*, representing the Queen's ancestral faith, at the other a single large water jug, representing Christian baptism.

The investigation began with God. The Queen brought the joined tips of her index fingers up in front of her chin, as was her custom when she became engrossed in some matter of the intellect. "Shiva," she said, "Shiva is formless spirit, the Supreme Being, like the Father you worship. Since He is formless, He can dwell anywhere, He dwells in the hearts of those who love Him, He dwells in my heart. I *am* Shiva. I—"

"Stop!" Thomas said. A tentative, apologetic smile settled over his face. "You just said Shiva was the Supreme Being. Now you say you are

Shiva. That would make *you* supreme. Not even a Queen would want to maintain that." He gave her a conciliatory smile. "It would also make you eternal. What do you say?"

"I *am* eternal," said the Queen simply. "I am his image."

"Ah, but it's one thing to be made in God's image, another to *be* Him."

"But we *are* Him," the Queen said. "We are particles of his Infinite Spirit. Each individual soul is a tiny sliver of infinite Being."

"Then each soul is eternal. Do you really mean to say that?"

"The substance that makes up each soul is eternal, yes. But its existence as an individual, as a sliver cut off from the infinite Shiva Himself, had a beginning in time."

Thomas stroked his silvery beard and scowled as he weighed what the Queen had said. "You were telling me about Shiva. Please continue."

"You look so unhappy, Master."

"No! Not unhappy. Please, please go on."

"Well, He is the Creator and Destroyer of all the worlds. The world is his toy, his amusement, He dances it in and out of existence. His body is covered with ashes—"

"His body?" Thomas interrupted again. "But didn't you just say he was formless?"

"Yes," she said with an infectious smile and hands that danced in front of her body, "but we delight in giving Him form anyway. In reality He has no form, but you would not guess this from reading the stories about Him in the holy books. The forms we give Him are symbols—symbols of his power. His body is covered with ashes because He is a penitent, the Great Yogi—"

"But didn't you just say that he is a dancer, that he amuses himself? Now you say he is a penitent too? That would seem to be contradictory."

"Every perfection is his," she said; "would it be proper, would He be God if He lacked either of these perfections? His yoga is so fierce that He could burn the universe up with a single glance of his third eye. And his delight is so great when He dances that the world sometimes quakes with his cosmic energy. And these are only two of his attributes. As many perfections as we can conceive, He has these and many more."

"And you love this god?" Thomas asked, taking a new tack. "You really love this god with four arms, body covered with ashes, snakes hanging from his ears, and eyes so round he seems to be in a constant state of fury?"

"I do," she said. "Oh, I do!"

"And that—that stone phallus," he said, pointing to the lingam at the far end of the room, "that lingam over there. Do you approve of Shiva's worshippers kneeling before it and adoring it?"

"Not it, Master," she said, "but Him *in* it. It symbolizes his creative energy. And it is midway between form and formlessness. It is a simple smooth column tapering at the top. It is a form, something we can see and grasp, but it is the simplest of all forms and therefore comes closest to God's true, formless Self. Yes, I do approve of its worship."

"But do you not see," he said, "that it appeals to the baser senses—and you, noble lady, you of all people, celibate and high-minded—well, nearly celibate—that you should approve of falling down in front of this idol and—"

"And worshipping God?"

"And worshipping stone, I would say."

Adimanti then fixed her eyes on the cross that Thomas wore around his neck, the gift from Kumaran he still wore. "And why do you wear that cross, good teacher?"

He looked down at it. "To remind myself of the man who died on it."

"For a similar reason," she said, "the devotee worships in front of the lingam—it reminds him of God."

"But the cross is a sacred symbol. It stands for the sacrifice that Jesus made of himself to God on our behalf."

"No less sacred," she said, "is the lingam to the devotee. It stands for God's infinite life and energy."

Back and forth they went like this, and Thomas began to suspect he had never met a mind, in either man or woman, quite like hers. She defended vegetarianism, image-worship, the eventual salvation of all creatures from the lowest salamander to the great god Brahma himself, with as much skill as she defended Shiva. Her way of arguing was different from the artificial tricks of some of the brahmins he had known on the Vaigai. Their strategy when cornered was to obscure the issue by quoting a text from their scripture that was irrelevant; they thought they had carried off an argument if they succeeded in sidetracking their opponent. But Adimanti kept to the point, she did not lose the sense of what was relevant. So cogent were her reasons and so lovely her person that it was not too long before he actually began to understand things from her point of view. And with that, a dangerous new truth began to dawn on him.

Two months later they found themselves in the same room, and Adimanti as usual was answering Thomas' questions while he was dissecting her answers. It happened to be the first anniversary of their guru-shishya relationship.

"Good Queen," Thomas said, "do you remember taking me as your guru?"

"Forgive me," she pleaded, "I have been talking too much." She lowered her beautiful eyes and touched the floor in front of his feet with her broad, shining copper-colored forehead.

"Tell me truly, Adi," he said, allowing himself to get familiar, perhaps in honor of the occasion, "why did you take me as your guru? You are not progressing in the dharma I teach. You know that."

"Oh, but you are wrong!" she said. "Your teaching has completed my religion. I have added your Christian dharma to my own. I have become in my heart the very mleccha who stopped to help the beaten man. Jesus has captured me with his gospel of unselfish love. He showed me—you showed me—that God is best found in the service of my fellow man. What a new thought! I have learned not to hate the world, but to love it. And you have taught me *how* to love it—with open arms. I used to think Shiva's dance was selfish, but now I see that love motivates it. He does not create the universe for sport, as I used to think, but out of love. You have taught me all of this, good Thomas—not in these exact words, but you planted the seeds. Besides," she said with a curiously mischievous twinkle in her eyes, "you are a yavana, and I confess that you have always fascinated me: so much wisdom between pale cheekbones! And you say you have not taught me your dharma! If you only knew! Do you know what comfort there is in realizing there is one person in the world who prays to the same God I pray to?"

"What is this?" Thomas said. "The same God? Are you—are you sure?"

"The same God, yes, of course, the same God," she said.

"The same God? Explain what you mean."

"How do they differ, except in name?"

"Explain what you mean," he repeated.

"The way we conceive them is the same. They are both spirit, supreme, holy, demanding; they both love their devotees, show mercy—"

"Love their devotees? But surely you see that Shiva's devotees are different from the Father's?" said Thomas.

"I see no such thing, Master!"

The Queen's luminous eyes sparkled with round incredulity as she lifted her head back off the tips of her joined fingers which had propped up her chin. "Do you believe that one God approves of you, and another of me?" She found the notion so absurd that she could not stifle a laugh.

Her voice trailed off into a high-pitched sigh, and Thomas thought of the call of the long-necked peacock.

He had almost told her that whereas the one true God approved of him, no one approved of her, for in all the vast starry heavens there was not one Shiva. Wouldn't that have been the logical thing to say? But something bubbled up from deep inside him that told him otherwise. It was the same dark truth that had tried to break out into the open on top of a jungle hill when Kumaran claimed years ago that Murugan and the Father were the same God. He had not been ready to listen to Kumaran, but Adimanti was not Kumaran.

43. The Indra Festival

On the day of the full moon in the month of Chitrai at the start of the hot season, Puhar celebrates the annual Indra Festival. Indra, who rules the lesser Gods and rides on an elephant and has the thunderbolt for his weapon, enjoys a special relation with Puhar. Many generations ago the God sent a great spirit to help the ancient King Muchukunda, a distant ancestor of Karikal's. That spirit, called simply "the Buta," is Puhar's Guardian Deity. King Karikal spared no effort to honor properly, not only Indra, but each of the other four great Gods: the beginningless Lord Shiva, the dark-faced Krishna, Krishna's brother Baladeva with the complexion of a white conch shell, and the six-faced red God, Lord Murugan. To help celebrate, Karikal invited Gods and men from all over India, as far away as the remote Himalayas in the north. At the climax of the festival, which lasted four days, one-thousand and eight chiefs from villages all over the Chola Empire would bear on their heads golden jugs filled with pollen-scented water scooped out of the Kaveri at the point where it joins the sea, and ritually wash the thousand-eyed Indra with his strings of pearls, while the Buta and all in heaven looked on joyfully.

Throughout the city there is music, dance, poetry, drama, feasting, and love-making. It is said that the pleasures of Puhar's Indra Festival rival those of the Nagas, those serpent deities who live in the City of Pleasure under the earth.

Fourteen months had passed since the Battle of Venni, and it was clear to everyone that this was a far happier Festival than the previous year's, when a pall of grief hung over many of the Empire's great houses. This year virgins with skin as soft as flower petals danced the *Rasa-lila*, the Dance of Lust in honor of Krishna, with an abandon unlike anything the city had seen before. The seductive seven-holed bamboo flute, the low-voiced *mridanga* drum, the various kinds of stringed *yals*, the passionate quavering voice of the singer—music of every kind pulsated from the emerald-studded balconies of the mansions on Merchant Street. At the entrances of these same mansions, cloths embroidered with colorful sea dragons and other auspicious symbols made from inlaid coral and pearls were hung. Along all the major streets of the city, golden pitchers filled with water for drinking were laid out as if for a marriage feast. Metal lamps shaped like maidens lit up these same streets and revealed golden flags flapping in the warm night air. Festoons of flowers hung from fences bordering public parks.

The moon was round and high. It was late, but the crowds still buzzed and laughed and reveled in the city's markets, streets, and parks. Kumaran reached under his gaudy red tunic and felt his passport to pleasure. "Come with me," he said in his sweetest voice to a girl of no more than fifteen, one of those who had danced the *Rasa-lila*. The maiden looked Kumaran over with wide frightened eyes, and he pressed into her hand the poem he had written for whomever struck his fancy on that sacred but dissolute night. She studied him some more, smiled sheepishly, then read the poem. An absurd little thing, but typical of its genre, it said:

Terrified of Rahu, who swallows her on nights of the eclipse,
The Moon Goddess ran away and hid.
Where did she go? Ah, there!
Shining out from under the black clouds of your hair.
None other than your pretty, glowing face!
Look how she chases away the hairs dangling over your cheeks.
Look how she paints those black fish-shaped eyes on your fair face.
Look how daintily she places the narcissus, your lovely nose.
O girl with coral lips, luminous maiden!
Even the swans hide themselves among the shadows of the pond,
For how can they compete with the graceful movements
Of your gliding figure with wasp waist and honey breasts?
What foolishness has draped you with jewels? You,
With face of golden hue, you unadorned are the fairest jewel of all!

The girl was probably a virgin, but since the war the virgin girls of Puhar, even some of good family, had begun succumbing to the frivolous talk of gallants armed with a verse or two. The virtuous citizens of Puhar prayed to the Buta to put an end to this calamitous sin which, they said, foreshadowed the destruction of the Empire, but the Buta had not yet taken any action. Kumaran had no mind to help him.

He asked her to walk with him to the beach. "My name is Kumaran; I'm one of the King's poets," he said as they started out.

"The famous poet of the yavana lands!" she said, her eyes wide and eager to pay homage. I am—"

But she didn't finish the sentence. Kumaran could tell she noticed the way he lurched when he walked, and he followed her eyes as they looked down at his disfigured leg. Her lashes fluttered. Just then two tall yavana seamen, one fair-haired and blue-eyed and the other the color of Thomas, and each with a girl, walked by babbling to each other in Greek. Kumaran saw the girl look at them. Suddenly she dropped the poem at his feet, darted away like a frightened doe, and disappeared into the crowd.

Kumaran tried to console himself: "You are the famous Kumaran. Who is she? Just some baggage in red sandal paste! My own Devandi is as handsome!" And it was true. But it was not true Devandi was as cultivated, as literate, and, above all, as seductive—seductive in the way dancers and actresses were. He grew enraged as he thought about the rebuff. He imagined her in the arms of one of those human gewgaws, the yavana seaman. He hated all yavanas, hated the girl, hated his simple pulaiyar wife, hated his limp, hated all men who were young and strong and straight and spraying their seed about with the artlessness of a heavy-pollened flower shaking in the wind.

Blindly tumbling along in the crowd, he came around a corner and almost ran into someone. Looking up, he found himself—by what extraordinary whimsy of the Gods he did not know—face to face with a tall masked man who turned out to be Thomas. Kumaran would not have guessed his identity if the man had not helped him."Kumaran!" the man cried out impulsively.

"Thomas?" Kumaran wanted to get away as soon as he could.

"How is your family?" Thomas said.

"They are well."

Kumaran noticed then that Thomas had company. A woman wearing a mask stood beside him, and Kumaran could not resist saying with a hint of a sneer, "And you, the sannyasin, are not alone?"

There was an embarrassing pause. "Would you like to come—come along with us?" Thomas stammered finally.

"No, no!" Kumaran said, horrified at the idea. "I'm on my way to the Indra Temple, going in the opposite direction," he lied.

Kumaran knew well Thomas didn't want him to come along. It was Thomas' religion that compelled him to invite him—his stupid, hypocritical religion. "Poor Kumaran," the question implied, "with no companion on this most festive night!" It rankled him that he might be the object of Thomas' pity.

Kumaran and Thomas wished each other well and said their goodbyes, but not before Kumaran realized who the woman was. He had looked her up and down and noted the rings on her toes, the jewel-studded anklets above her red-dyed feet, and the parallel lines of pearls set in her blue silk girdle. He had noted the diamonds and dark rubies on her fingers, which disappeared under rings shaped like fish-jaws, and her fine gold bracelets. He had been fooled at first, fooled like the rest of the world that would have deplored her being with any man but her husband on a night like this, until his eyes fell on the exquisite necklace of bright red coral hanging around her neck. Not even the purple mask, which covered her face from just above her eyebrows to below her chin, could disguise that extraordinary neck. It was the Queen.

Suddenly it occurred to Kumaran that Thomas had an altogether different motive in asking him to come along. Was it possible Thomas felt compromised at being caught with a bejeweled woman by his side and wanted to demonstrate his innocent intentions? What better way to do this than to invite him to come along? But of course Thomas knew that was the last thing he would do.

Kumaran walked a dozen or so steps, then wheeled around. There they were, still in sight, walking side by side, a slight distance between them, she looking up at him, he down at her, no doubt smiling behind their masks. With a heart suspicious and bitter Kumaran started to follow them. They disappeared in shadow, emerged again under the glare of the next lantern, disappeared in a crowd, reappeared. Four or five times they stopped for one reason or another, but they did not speak to anyone else, and no one recognized them. Past ancient spreading trees standing in flower gardens they wandered as Kumaran, hobbling along, stalked his prey. On and on they went as the crowds thinned. The twin lighthouses marking the mouth of the river came into view, then the lamps of the fishmongers along the beach.

Kumaran's heart beat with malevolent anticipation as he followed them out onto the beach, the narrow strip of sand where the river weds the sea. They passed canvas tents; girls were singing and dancing inside. A pleasure cove—a sandy stretch of beach surrounded by fragrant pandanus shrubs and equipped with beds and movable screens—lay just ahead. Aha! But Thomas and the Queen walked past it without seeming to notice, walked to the very edge of the sea and sat down. For a long time they just sat. Then they lay back, lay down on their backs, their feet pointed at the sea and the warm wind. In the bright moonlight Kumaran could see their dark bodies against the pale sand or the glowing silver of the next wave. He waited for those two dots to come together and merge into one, waited for the evidence that would confirm what he suspected and hoped with all his heart: that Thomas was a complete fraud.

As Kumaran cowered behind a bush, his knee began to ache and he cursed his deformity. He thought of the yavana seamen with their girls and remembered how one of them had been tall and straight and looked like Thomas. By some preposterous trick of logic he found himself blaming Thomas for his misfortune: Hadn't Thomas coerced him into coming to Puhar, and therefore wasn't he to blame for all that followed, including the deformity? Kumaran thought of Thomas' absurd religion with all its lofty ethical pretensions and detested him for his power over Devandi and the Queen. He cursed Thomas' friendship with the Queen, a friendship he, Kumaran, would have given anything to have, but which Thomas had not even sought. What right had Thomas to be on such easy, intimate terms with the queen of an empire, to walk with her through its capital at the height of its most sacred season? Kumaran hated Thomas because at Venni he had escaped serious injury. Why had he been spared? Why was he always so lucky? Most of all Kumaran hated Thomas for his self-righteousness: "You're weak, Brother . . . take it from someone who knows you. . . . You murdered the King, Kumaran, you didn't just 'kill' him! . . . Murugan, that dissolute, dancing god! . . . I DESPISE YOU!" The memory of these words made Kumaran almost frantic. His brain had become a spider web, and Thomas' words were the spider. Back and forth and up and down the spider crawled, its pale bulbous body growing fatter by the day off the dung of Kumaran's soul.

Kumaran thought of the dutiful, cheerless visit that Thomas had paid him a month ago. "Forgive me all my sins against you," he had said as he sat on a cushion in Kumaran's workroom. His voice had been bleak, astringent, as taut as a hawser straining at its dock. He had forced himself to do what his God demanded of him, he had done it, and he had felt better. That was all there was to it: he had felt better. Kumaran remembered Thomas' face in the boat going down the Kaveri, how his mouth had twitched, his eyes had narrowed, his whole head had shaken to the beat of his hating heart. For years Thomas had buried his anger, and then like an earthquake it had erupted, and his contempt toward Kumaran's religion and his country had flowed out. "I forgive you," Kumaran had lied as he eyed Thomas slumped on his cushion. So Thomas had supposed all was well, and no doubt he went about his pious, self-righteous business with a soul as carefree as a baby's, not even the dust of his sin's karma to dim its natural luster. What a fool! What a delusion!

And yet, and yet—there he was, lying at the side of the Queen of the Chola Empire. Was that the way God dealt with a fool? Well, Kumaran knew how to deal with one. So he waited, waited and watched as the spider in his brain crawled up and down, back and forth.

But he was disappointed. Thomas and the Queen suddenly got up. Kumaran could see the Queen put her mask back on from where he crouched behind his shrub. Nothing had happened. As swans in the lotus ponds of the city's parks called out the dawn, he slunk back to the palace.

44. God the Inaccessible

Thomas' tall figure towered over the eager faces of his flock. His silvery beard ended at the tops of the heads of the women. He was a snowy Mount Meru among dark wooded hills.

It was the Feast of Tabernacles, and the Lord's Supper had been celebrated. He had preached on the bountifulness of God, and now he was passing out some bounty of his own. The night before he had asked the Queen for sweetmeats and syrupy cakes, and she had responded liberally.

The simple fisher folk laughed and exclaimed and smacked their fingers. Joy was written across their faces as the sweetbread slid down their gullets. Joy and gratitude. Gratitude to their Thomas, their Aiyer, who brought them good news and good things.

But there was not much joy in Thomas, though no one outside the new church on the beach guessed it. Who could he tell his doubts to? All his friends were converts or catechumens, and he had to set a good example for them. It would certainly not do to tell them he had doubts about a few of the very truths he taught!

But this was no time to mope. There were instructions to give and quarrels to settle. There were the sick, the endless stream of the sick and the dying who would want some sweetbread too. "Come on," he cried out to Puttaswamy. "And bring Sidda if he wants to come."

Of course Sidda wanted to come. Sidda the Cripple was ten years old and had only a stump for one of his legs. Thomas loved Sidda because the boy brought cheer wherever he went. He had suffered from lice since anyone could remember, but no one could have guessed this from the buoyancy of his personality. Hopping about on his crutch, he scrambled after the rag ball or played tag with the agility of a spider monkey. The other boys never even noticed he was lame. Instead they followed him. Sidda was their leader.

So all Sidda's playmates tagged along with Thomas because Sidda came. They had a mission to perform, and each carried his little bit of sweetbread through the back alleys of Puhar with the pride of a sword-bearer carrying his master's manhood. The requirement to practice charity was one thing Thomas never doubted. He wanted to show the boys how it was given and the joy it brought the sick who received it.

Lately he had become obsessed with the question, 'What is the one thing in life most worth doing'? Up until a few weeks ago he had thought it was bringing in converts.Now he doubted this. It seemed instead that charity might be that one thing. And what was charity but the expression of selfless love? And selfless love came in other forms besides preaching the gospel of Christ. It came in the form of living it. It meant listening: listening to hardened hearts bent on revenge, listening to repentant hearts hounded by guilt. It meant giving counsel, sometimes even interfering in people's lives in order to stop the resentment and hatred that trickled through the cracks in men's souls everywhere. It meant giving food, bathing worn-out or leprous bodies, expelling demons, laying hands on ulcers and boils, picking out lice, giving comfort, cheer, and sometimes nothing more than one's mute company. Of all the little boys who hovered around Thomas, Sidda the Cripple was the best equipped to give this kind of love. Was the snakebite that took his leg four years ago when he was six the cause of his compassion? Or was he compassionate by nature? Several times Thomas asked Sidda about it, but Sidda didn't know what he was talking about. It puzzled Thomas all the more because Sidda was the only one of the boys not baptized. He was not even a catechumen. Thomas had never met his parents. Sidda said they were devotees of the snake-goddess Manasa and they forbade him to convert.

The warm, overcast night buzzed with the sounds of crickets, frogs, and owls as Thomas sat alone on the roof of his apartment. A year ago his heart would have swelled with love for God's hidden creation on such a night. His life was simpler then, and his will had been swept along by a single surging tide. But all that had changed.

He tried to pray in a new way. He wouldn't let himself think he was special to God just because he was Jewish or Jesus' twin. He rejected the impulse to regard himself as a member of a "chosen" race, as he had been taught since his boyhood. He realized he could never pray again, "There but for the grace of God go I," when he looked upon a pagan. He was determined to tear out by the roots the slightest presumption of superiority. He would be a universal man, not an Israelite. And his God would have no favorites.

"You are like a diamond rotated under sunlight," he prayed into the dark. "You are the abode of all conceivable best perfections." But his heart did not respond to such abstractions. The God he grew up with walked in Eden and appeared to Moses as a burning bush. He spoke with thunder through the Prophets and in a still small voice to Elijah. He manifested Himself in a pillar of cloud or fire. With his might he broke the tablets of the Law and ground the golden calf to powder.

But that was the God of Israel, and now Thomas wouldn't let himself address a God so narrowly conceived. For years he had listened to Indians speak of their gods' exploits with as much conviction as any Jew speaking of his. Indians believed Krishna chastised the serpent demon Kaliya by dancing on his hundred heads, killed hordes of demonic giants, and suspended a mountain in mid-air. There was no end to Krishna's miracles. And there were just as many stories about Shiva.

Two days before, as he organized his thoughts for a letter home to Bartholomew, a letter he never got around to writing, an inescapable conclusion forced itself on him: If he believed in the stories about Yahweh's great deeds but rejected those about Krishna's and Shiva's, that was only because he had been born a Jew and not an Indian. The form of his faith depended on an accident of birth.

He had been running from this truth for several years. Back in Madurai when he began to call God Sarveshvara, "God of All," he had an inkling of it. When it finally dawned on him in its full force, he was shaken to his foundations and forever changed.

He vowed from that moment on to think of God in a way at once intimately personal but neither Jewish nor Indian. He was committed to the loving Father preached by Jesus, but he would give up everything else that might identify God as belonging to one people but not another.

Seated in the lotus position on the roof, still warm against his buttocks even through his loin cloth, he ventured forth. "You are like a gentle wind looking for a place to rest, and I am that place."

But God—the newly conceived God, the unfamiliar True God, the inaccessible God-As-He-Is-In-Himself—did not rest in Thomas. Instead of a gentle wind there was a noisy, dislocating whirlwind. He felt like a man who has been sailing for years down a river with well-defined shores to a well-known destination at the river's end, but who, when he reaches the ocean, is asked to keep on going.

The crickets and frogs sang to God their hymn of the universe, but Thomas only wondered where God was hiding. No Milky Way with its vaporous stardust lit up the night. No moon shone through the trees overhead and traced on the earth its bright script.

45. A Tamil Dog

Charishnu often complained to the King, and to anyone within earshot, of the Queen's Guru, for he detested Thomas. Kumaran was well aware of Charishnu's loathing and knew if ever he had a mind to get rid of his old "brother," it would be through this man. It would be difficult to imagine two men more opposite than Kumaran and Charishnu, but their common hatred of Thomas made them allies. Charishnu had never known such public humiliation as on the night of the debate at Thomas's hands, and to this was added the insult of the Queen's taking him as her Guru. As for Kumaran, he had more reasons to hate Thomas than he could keep track of.

If Kumaran had witnessed the slightest indiscretion on the beach on the night of Indra's Festival, he would have told Charishnu. If Thomas and the Queen had so much as touched each other, he would have felt it his duty—so he told himself at the time—to report it. But, of course, he never caught them in anything. He held his tongue, but he didn't forget.

At the beginning of the monsoon, as if in imitation of the clouds, which rumbled with faint, premonitory thunder, he decided to talk. Two events conspired to loosen his tongue. The first was the conversion of Devandi. The second, though less dramatic, was decisive.

Charishnu was again complaining about Thomas to the King, this time in front of the poets: "My servant happened to see him answer the call of nature. Disgusting! Disgusting!" Tiny flecks of spit flew out of Charishnu's mouth as he spoke. "Has he ever heard of the *Nityakarma*?

'He must chew nothing, have nothing in his mouth, and hold nothing on his head.'"

Charishnu was always quoting some authority; the practice usually bored Kumaran, but this time he listened carefully.

"My servant reported that the Queen's Guru was chewing betel as he squatted," Charishnu continued. "Outrageous! But that was only the beginning. It seems that he is unclean. For on another occasion he did not wash his private parts the required number of times, and he did not use the prescribed mixture of water and clay. And when he rinsed his mouth, he did not do it the required eight times, and he spat straight ahead of him."

Kumaran was certain Charishnu himself, rather than his servant, had been the spy. He knew, as much as any man knows, to what insane lengths a hater might go.

"'When he is doing this last act,'" Charishnu continued, again quoting, "'he must take very great care to spit out the water on his left side, for if by carelessness or otherwise he unfortunately spits it out on the other side, he will surely go to hell.' So states the *Nityakarma*. In countless ways this yavana barbarian masquerading as a holy man offends the Gods!"

"I am not always so careful myself," the King said, trying to be conciliatory.

"You are a busy monarch. But this, this Thomas"—Charishnu snarled out the name—"pretends to be a teacher. He wears the ocher robe. He claims to be the descendant of a king. He is the Queen's Guru. His conduct should be exemplary. Instead he disgraces decency. Why do you defend him, son of Ilaiyon?"

The hour had come. Like Charishnu, Kumaran had convinced himself Thomas was a menace to the Kingdom. He broke up families, created dissension in the castes and guilds, preached a false religion, offended public taste by associating intimately with the Queen, and now insulted public decency. As regards this last charge, Kumaran was as lax as Thomas, but still, Thomas in his carelessness had been *observed*. Besides, Kumaran was a mere pulaiyar while Thomas—Kumaran no longer knew what he was. All he knew was that the time to act was now. Thomas was a menace, a menace. The word *menace* drummed through Kumaran's brain over and over. He thought of the proverb, "Be like the heron when it is time to be patient, and like it strike when it is time to act." He had been patient long enough; now it was time to strike. So he followed Charishnu after the gathering had broken up and found him just inside the gate of his villa.

"Reverend Sire, Guru of the King of the Cholas—"

"Yes, yes, what is it?" Charishnu said. He looked at Kumaran painfully, as if he feared Kumaran might get too close and pollute him.

"As you may know, I am Kumaran, one of the—"

"Yes, I know," said Charishnu peevishly.

"I have something to report about the Queen and her Guru."

"That odious man! Yes, what is it?" Charishnu suddenly seemed to forget that Kumaran was a black-faced pulaiyar. He turned and faced him, bending forward as a man does who deals habitually in the currency of whispered slander.

"But I must ask you to swear an oath that you will never divulge the source of this report," said Kumaran.

"What?! An oath? To whom do you think you are talking? I am a brahmin. You have my word! That is enough!"

Kumaran fidgeted with his hands, then decided to go ahead and risk it. "During the last Indra's Festival—I saw them together—"

"*Them*? Do you mean the Queen and—him?"

"Yes, Your Reverence."

"Well?"

"They were lying side by side on the beach—just lying there—it was late, and dark, and there was no one around—"

"Lying, you say? Side by side? Are you sure? On the beach, you say? Did you see them yourself?"

Kumaran and Charishnu were standing in the courtyard of Charishnu's palatial residence under an avocado tree laden with shiny ripe green fruit. Charishnu straightened, bent his head back, and looked up into the tree. Then, like a hungry monkey snatching at a nut, he grabbed the lowest fruit and snapped it off.

"Yes, I saw them myself, just as you, I mean your servant, saw—"

"They were lying there?" said Charishnu, fingering the avocado and looking off to the side. "And then—did they—surely they—well, man, speak up!" Charishnu turned back around toward Kumaran and thrust his head out turtle-fashion to receive the news.

"They just lay there," Kumaran said sheepishly, suddenly feeling ridiculous.

"But there was touching, surely. And kissing. And—but it is too horrible to think about. But you must tell me everything you saw. Every detail. Did they—copulate like dogs in the marketplace?"

"I—I do not know," Kumaran stuttered, his ears beginning to burn. "It was dark. I can't be sure."

"But surely you saw *something*! Is this all you've come to tell me? Do you know who I am? Are you wasting my time with this?"

"Well, yes. I mean no!"

"Come on, man! Speak it out. I'll protect you. Don't be afraid."

"Well, yes, they—it might be safe to assume that they—"

"Are you saying you *saw* them?" Charishnu said, looking off to the side with a look of wolfish malice that made Kumaran shiver. "*Saw*, poet!" Charishnu spit out, turning toward him again and leveling him with his stare. "That is what I must hear if he is to burn!"

The word "burn" startled Kumaran; it brought home the seriousness of the charge he was making. He was not playing chess with one of the courtiers; this was no game. But he was more frightened for his reputation and career than for Thomas' life. What might Charishnu do in retaliation if he did not tell him what he wanted to hear? Kumaran felt he had to go all the way, he could not stop now. "Yes, yes, that's what I am saying."

"You *saw* them copulate on the beach? Do I have it right?"

"Yes, I saw them."

Charishnu suddenly seemed to remember the fruit in his hand. He held it out in front of him and studied it. Then, with a grimace and a violent jerk of his arm and hand downward, he squashed the avocado. The slimy fruit oozed out between his fingers.

In all the lands that Kumaran had traveled, he found that dogs were cursed animals. In yavana countries, however, as well as in Tamil country, rich people sometimes adopted them as pets—as bizarre a practice as Kumaran had ever known. He had even seen dogs treated as if they were heirs to the family fortune—the example of Nalli came quickly to mind. But for the most part they stayed in packs and lived by scavenging. And always they cowered, they slunk away when confronted by men, who predictably beat and kick them. But never in the West did Kumaran see dogs slink as they did in Tamilakam—he was certain he was not imagining this even though he had never written a word about it in his notes. When he left Charishnu after informing on Thomas, he slunk away, not like any old dog, but like a Tamil dog.

46. Prison

First he was conscious of something in the air stuffy and slightly fetid. Then he heard the soft patter of rain falling on the roof and, from somewhere overhead, a faint squeaking. "Bats," he thought to himself. Opening his eyes, he vaguely made out the shapes of shadows; faint daylight eked through openings under the eves.

He heard crows squawking. Then a cuckoo, a solitary cuckoo, sang its clear, flute-like melody. Thomas had always found pleasure in the call of the Indian cuckoo. This plain black bird could fill a whole sky with its ascending notes—piercing, mysterious, pure. There it was again: "Whoop, Whoop, WHOOP, *WHOOP!*" But on this morning the bird's call reminded him of a bird in a cage.

This was the sixth place he had been taken to in two weeks. Always the guards transferred him at night. He was a prisoner.

Why? He could only guess, but his suspicions kept coming back to Charishnu. Twice before, jealous brahmin priests had tried to destroy him. He told himself it did not matter. But it did matter. It mattered intensely. What must Adimanti and Puttaswamy think? He had been taken in the middle of the night as Puhar slept. He hadn't had time even to scribble a note and leave it on his desk. His heart ached for Adimanti and broke for the boy. And there were the three thousand souls who depended on him for spiritual direction. What might they be saying? He had simply vanished without a trace. He was desperate to get a message out.

He heard shuffling and clanking on the other side of the door, then voices. The guards were changing. He waited for the unfriendly night guard to go off, then called out, "Is that you, Mahadeva?"

"Yes, Sire. Just come on duty."

"Did they give you permission to break the silence?"

"No. I'm still under the strictest orders to say nothing about you. They told me my life depends on it. The same with the other guard."

"My God, my God!" he called out quietly into the darkness. After a moment he asked, "Are we still on the palace grounds?"

"Yes, we're on the park."

Thomas had the impression of spaciousness even though he knew there was a lot of clutter in the room. He had bumped into it in the darkness when they brought him in.

"Mahadeva, did you happen to see the Queen about?"

"No, but I asked about her as you asked me to. Someone saw her with a little boy going someplace in a hurry."

Puttaswamy! He was with her! Oh, thank God! He imagined the little boy to be Puttaswamy, though it could have been one of her nephews. Eventually they would be allowed to visit him. Surely they would. Unless he got out first. In the meantime—he told himself to be content to wait. Wasn't he healthy and breathing Puhar's air? And didn't Mother Kaveri pour her wealth out across the rich rice plains and feed him. "Don't be ungrateful!" he told himself.

The rain had stopped, and the sun shone through cracks in the windows in needle-thin shafts. How slowly time passed. Thomas began to explore his latest prison. Where was he? He noticed that light entered in larger streaks from under the eaves. Light, he wanted more light. The shutters. Did he dare? He would have to be very quiet. He tried to unlatch one of them, but it was stuck. . . . Ah, there! . . . The air was still thick and cool. Below him spread the park. He looked down and across in both directions. Yes, now he recognized the building where he was, though he had never been in it before and didn't know what it was used for. He looked out again over the park: the lush flowering trees, the artificial ponds covered with sweet-scented lilies and lavender hyacinths, the hedges and clusters of flowers of every color and type, the fountains and zigzagging canals, the bridges of carved teak, the hillocks covered with cropped grass, the flagstone paths, the benches and swings, the island of *neem* trees with its pleasure house at the center—all so familiar. Then he turned around and looked at the room, clearly visible now for the first time. A huge eagle, a Garuda with fierce claws was painted on the wall opposite the windows. On either side of the Garuda were more paintings, some showing astrological symbols, others the various gods and heroes so dear to India. All were covered with cobwebs, and their gaudy colors had faded. Statues and busts were strewn about the room. Some were chipped or missing a limb, others crumbling. Who were they? He decided to open more shutters. Now the light poured in. He saw sculptures and furniture stretching from one end of the room to the other—a great clutter of discarded objects. He looked out again onto the park. How high he was!—level with the top of that mango tree. He looked straight down at the outer wall below him—ledges at intervals, but otherwise a sheer drop. No way out.

He looked back into the room. Several wooden backless benches sat about—he discovered the one he used for his bed. He decided to walk from one end of the room to the other and measure it. . . . twenty, twenty-one, twenty-two. Twenty-two paces he counted as he picked his way through the maze of clutter. He studied the statures and busts more closely. Some were of the gods; some of men, not former kings, but probably their gurus, for their dress was austere and sacerdotal; some of *apsarases* with their bulging breasts and tiny waists. And what was it he had laid his head on last night? . . . A footprint of the Buddha—carved out of teak. The Buddha . . . Bala Ma . . . A picture of the old Buddhist sage of Muziri flitted through his memory. Bala Ma. He felt at home thinking about her. He wished he could see her one more time.

He turned his mind to the letter he received with great joy from Simon Peter a month before—one of several in a small bundle, the first word ever from home. "There is no other name under heaven given among men by which we may be saved," Peter had written. Why did Peter write him that? In Jerusalem, in Antioch, Corinth, even Rome, that is what they were teaching, Peter said. "No other name." Thomas was sure that if he hadn't been in India so long, he would be teaching it too.

He walked over to the inner wall and sat down facing the open windows. He tucked his feet under his haunches, straightened his back, closed his eyes, and tried to pray: "Jesus, my brother, you, only you know what I know now."

His mind began to range over the past. He saw Venni's battlefield and heard the shrieks of mutilated elephants ringing in his ears. He watched King Nediyon's hundred queens and concubines jump into the fire at the Great Sati. He felt the fishermen grab him under the shoulders and throw him into the Western Ocean with its monsters. He watched the Kali that Kumaran carved on the great temple at

Vanji take shape. Kumaran. Suddenly he wondered what had happened to Kumaran?

"Sire, your breakfast!"

Startled, Thomas looked up at Mahadeva, who came in smiling and carrying a wide tray full of food laid out on banana leaves. Would Mahadeva scold him about the opened shutters? Did he even know they had been closed? Thomas studied the genial guard for hints of irritation. But there were none. Then he turned his attention to the food. His spirits lifted as he saw rice cakes in milk, pulp from the jack, palmyra fruits, a bunch of sweet yellow plantains, and several sauces.

"Where did you get this?" Thomas asked, surprised.

"Don't ask too many questions, Sire."

"I'm grateful—so grateful." Then he fell at once to eating, almost attacking his food, beginning with the rice cakes.

"Very, very good!" he called out once. He ate with the concentration and thoroughness of a squirrel eating a nut. When he finished, he washed his hands in a bowl; then he tilted his head back and held a copper cup over his lips, as Kumaran had taught him years ago, and poured water into his mouth. He gargled the prescribed twelve times and spat each time into the spittoon Mahadeva had brought in with the food. He swallowed a few leaves of basil, thereby insuring good digestion, but passed up the betel. In every outward respect he ate like a Tamil; one might have assumed this white yavana from Judaea sought the blessings of his household gods before he ate, and that he reverently addressed the local sage Agastya as he swallowed the basil.

"I will cry out like the swallow and meditate like the turtledove!" he suddenly sang out, quoting a random scriptural passage that floated into his mind from somewhere. How well things were going all of a sudden. Good food, but most of all the open shutters. Up until now he had been cut off entirely from the outside world. A new hope, a plan began to hatch in his brain.

He stood up, rubbed his stomach, and watched Mahadeva as the guard took the tray away. An old clepsydra caught his eye. "Ah, Mahadeva, friend, if I may call you that, before you go—do you see this old water clock?"

Thomas picked up a dusty brass basin and inspected the large copper cup resting inside it. "How much time does it measure?"

Still carrying the tray, Mahadeva examined the tiny hole bored through its bottom. "Two hours, I'd say."

"Two hours. Would you fill the basin for me?"

"Of course, Sire. Here, put it on the tray."

Mahadeva wound his way through the clutter to the door and closed it behind him.

The water clock triggered in Thomas a meditation on time. Sixteen days—was that so long? Yet at times it seemed interminable. He wondered if he might spend years in prison. He wondered if he might die in prison. How many more rooms would he be taken to before . . . before what? Perhaps the King would decide he should be executed. Or perhaps the King just wanted to teach him a lesson. But for what? He had no idea what he had been charged with. He only guessed it had something to do with the Queen and that Charishnu had instigated it. Oh, not to know! To know nothing! But what could he do? His mind came back to the subject of time and how precious it was. He thought of the elders, the deacons, the workers in the orphanage, the pariah carpenters building the new meeting hall in the Widow Nalini's back yard. So much work to be done, so much to do! What would happen to his church? And to Puttaswamy? And there was unfinished business with Kumaran. And there was the Queen. Always his thoughts came back to her.

Feeling desperate, he got up and began arranging the clutter. He cleared a weaving path down the long axis of the room. He began to stalk, wondering, "Is this your revenge, Charishnu? Did you ask the King to put me here? With all these broken busts of dead men to pass the time with? Does it amuse you? Is this your little joke? Lord, help me not to hate him!"

Mahadeva came back in with the basin full of water and placed it on a low table. Thomas picked up the cup and put it in the basin. The water began to trickle into the cup through the hole. In two hours it would sink.

"Now we'll see how fast the vessel fills," Thomas said. "I wonder if it's broken." "It probably is, Sire. They wear out at the aperture."

Mahadeva went out, and Thomas stared at the cup sinking imperceptibly lower into the basin as water trickled in. "Father, Father, are You with me in here?" he said in a quiet voice. "I see Vishnu over there on his Garuda, over there Shiva dancing, in the corner Yama—Yama, god of death. Is Yama waiting for me, Father?"

Back and forth he paced as the sparrows chirped their matins outside. "Why did You send me to India? You know how I fought You after I drew the straw. 'No, Peter, I won't go!' But that night You sent Jesus to me in a dream, and I knew it was all right. So I went. And now this."

His eyes swept over the long musty gallery. He looked out the window at the trees glistening under the sun. "Tell me, Father, is there room for You in India? Is there room?"

Up and down the length of the room he weaved his way, gradually working himself into a quiet resentment. He thought of the Indians, the thousands of Indians he had baptized, the presbyters and deacons he had ordained. He was an apostle, was he not? He was a man of God. So why was Peter telling him what to preach?

Just then Thomas heard again the cry of the solitary cuckoo through the riot of sparrow talk.

He sat for a while and watched the morning darken as a cloud passed over the sun. The bats, which had been squeaking and flapping their wings as they hung from a beam high overhead, quieted. They hated the light—like so many men he knew. He thought of Kumaran. Did Kumaran hate the light too? As the sun threw a final assault at the bats, an old memory surfaced. He remembered that Kumaran had saved his life in Kurinchi.

"Mahadeva!"

"Sire?"

"I really, I *must* see the poet Kumaran. Can you tell the Chief of the Guards I *must* see this man? Please. Do you know him, the court poet, the poet with the crooked leg? He is very close to the King. It's a personal matter."

"I know who you mean."

"Please. Do what you can do. It's very important."

"I'm nobody, Sire. But I'll pass on your wish."

"Nobody? You brought me that breakfast. If you can arrange that, you can do anything."

"That's what they say about you, Sire."

"They do? Who?" But Mahadeva did not answer.

Thomas got up and began to pace again. "Haieeee!" he called out at the bats, waving his hands. "Haieee!" One by one they uncoiled their wings and flew out the windows. Back and forth he paced along the inner wall. He fixed his thoughts on Kumaran, saw his dancing eyes as they looked in the old days, his gleaming poet's eyes.

"Mahadeva, it's raining again," he cried out as fresh drops pattered down.

"Is it?"

Through the steady drumming of the rain Thomas heard a dull clank. It was the water clock; the cup with the hole in the bottom had sunk to the bottom of the basin. There were a few ripples on the water's surface over the cup.

He walked over to the clepsydra, picked the cup up out of the water, emptied the water back into the basin, and set the cup afloat again. He watched as the first tiny stream began once again to trickle in through the hole. Kumaran. Yes, why hadn't he thought of him before?

47. Kumaran's Visit

For an instant Kumaran sized up the pale, bearded, austerely dressed man with the cross around his neck, the very cross he had fashioned. He remembered their meeting on a galley in a faraway harbor in what seemed like another life. They had not talked to each other for six months.

He had come because the King commanded it. "Get underneath the facade of that guru-shishya charade," said the King one day after Kumaran read his poetry. "Between the two of us, I have reason to suspect them of—. Get him to confess it, Kumaran. You know him well. Get the dirt—you'll find it if you look hard enough. I will reward you handsomely. And tell no one about any of this. If you slip up, as much as I esteem you..." The King gave Kumaran a look that no one could mistake. "Keep your tongue tacked down when you drink toddy or wine. Better still, don't drink at all. You can't afford to. Not anymore."

Kumaran had been greatly relieved to discover that Charishnu kept his word. Obviously the King did not suspect his favorite poet of informing on Thomas. On the other hand, one could never be too confident, for the King was as clever a dissembler as ever lived.

Kumaran had both dreaded and looked forward to the visit. He was greedy for a sight of Thomas in his ignominy. He wanted him to suffer for all the mischief he had worked in people's lives, especially in his own family. He told himself there was no fate too harsh. But Kumaran only half believed this. Just below the surface he felt a profound disquiet over the harm he was doing Thomas.

Thomas didn't extend his arms and grasp Kumaran by his shoulders as he used to, nor did he call attention to their former fraternal bond. "Kumaran," he said through a hesitant smile, "it is good to see you."

Kumaran jerked his head—the only greeting he offered—as the guard locked the door behind them.

"You are my first visitor," Thomas said. "The King let you come?"

"Yes. But I'm in a hurry. I'm dining with Kadyalur, the court musician."

"Ah. So that explains your dress."

"Actually, no. I dress this way all the time now."

"Ah, then you've realized your dream at last. I congratulate you, Kumaran. Did you buy that house? . . . And how is your family? . . ."

Kumaran didn't answer either question.

"Sit down, sit down! Anywhere you can manage."

Kumaran bristled at the word *manage,* then sat down slowly on the floor where he happened to be standing. His lame leg, bent in at the knee like a cracked bow, stuck out at an awkward angle.

Thomas began by asking Kumaran if everyone on the outside knew his plight.

"No. I didn't know myself until yesterday when the King told me," said Kumaran without feeling.

"Did you by any chance find out what the charge is? No one has told me."

"No, it's all hush-hush," said Kumaran, deciding not to risk the truth. He cleared his throat, then said with a hint of impatience, "The King said you wanted to see me."

"Kumaran, what has happened to us? We were once brothers."

Kumaran hesitated, then said, "We were brothers when it was to your advantage."

"How can you say that?"

"Why did you ask me here?"

"Kumaran, that is not true! It hurts to hear you say that!"

"Why did you ask me here?"

Thomas recomposed himself, then said: "For all I know, I might die."

Kumaran looked back at Thomas impassively.

"I want to assume the worst. If I am to die, then there are some matters we need to clear up." Thomas shifted on the floor where he sat. "I would also like you to help me. If you would."

"Help you? How?" said Kumaran. He felt like laughing out loud. What a fool this Thomas was!

"Once before you saved me from a king. From Pari, the Maravar Chief."

"And you want me to risk my reputation to help you again?"

"Forget it, Kumaran. I asked because I—"

"You dare to ask me to help you after all that's happened? You're unbelievable! You don't live in the world of men!"Kumaran felt an implacable contempt for Thomas.

"I—I thought that if you told him I was innocent, he would believe you."

"Innocent, you say? Innocent of what?"

"Of whatever I'm accused of."

Kumaran let out a muffled giggle and shook his head. He squirmed in his seat and fidgeted with his hands. He didn't know what to feel or think. "That's not what I hear," he flung out.

"But I—" Suddenly Thomas glared at Kumaran. "But a minute ago you said you didn't know what the charge was."

Kumaran stammered, "Oh, no, I don't. I—just know that people have accused you—of—"

"Of what, Kumaran? *Of what?*"

Kumaran was badly flustered, and the truth slipped out. "Of adultery."

"Adultery?! With whom?!"

"Whom do you think?"

"For the sake of all that has passed between us, Kumaran, tell me!"

"With the Queen."

Thomas pressed his thumb hard against the cross hanging around his neck. He shook his head in wide, exaggerated motions. "So it's as bad as I feared," he said in a solemn voice looking down at the floor. "So I'm to die." Then he looked up at Kumaran and asked with alarm, "What about the Queen? What has happened to her?"

Kumaran let his gaze roam across the room. He got up, stepped to his left, and picked out of the clutter a terra-cotta statuette, about a cubit in length, of a *yakshi*. The *yakshi*, naked except for necklace, armlets, girdle, and anklets, had the usual bulging breasts, tiny waist, and exaggeratedly wide hips. She carried a bird cage and stood on a dwarf.

Sitting back down, Kumaran began stroking the *yakshi* with his thumb. Then he looked across at Thomas and said, hoping against hope: "And are you guilty of adultery?"

Thomas riveted Kumaran with his intense dark eyes and slowly shook his head.

Kumaran withered under Thomas' piercing stare, looked down at the floor, and stroked the *yakshi.* Then Thomas gave him an advantage that not even the cleverest strategy could have produced.

"I did lie to you once," he said.

Kumaran stopped stroking the *yakshi* and looked up.

"This is one of the things I wanted to clear up with you." Thomas's voice was now soft and vulnerable. "I don't want to die with a lie between us. It was on the boat going down the Kaveri. I should have confessed this to you a long time ago, I've always meant to. But it mortifies me to say it. Just to think it. Do you remember asking me if I had ever—if I had ever committed adultery?"

Kumaran looked at Thomas in speechless surprise.

"I lied, Kumaran, I lied. It happened on the seacoast, in Tangasseri. Her name was Nallapennu. Maybe you remember her. She was my helper. It happened only once. Not that it matters, but it was a sin of intent, and . . . well . . . I lied to you."

Kumaran's heart swirled with contending emotions. "Why did you lie?"

"At the time—God forgive me, and may you forgive me, too—I thought it necessary to make a point with you. We had been arguing; we were talking about fearing God, and—do you remember?"

"I remember," said Kumaran very deliberately. "I remember it well. . . . So you lied." Kumaran looked out the window and marveled. Thomas human after all. Thomas just like other men. Weak and hypocritical. A dissembler. Then he felt anger beginning to build. Anger was not the only emotion he felt; he also felt something like love. But he preferred the anger. He decided to give it play, make it grow. He felt a rage beginning to build. He imagined the rage to be genuine, and by the time he finally spoke, it was. "So, you made your point with a lie. You beat me over the head with a lie! You proved I was worthless with a lie! I hate liars! You—you condemned me to your stinking hell with a lie!"

"Yes," said Thomas as he cowered before Kumaran's rage. "And I ask you now from the bottom of my heart to forgive me."

"You called my religion 'not strenuous.' Do you remember? Did you ever think that my religion might be strenuous but that *I* am not? And look at you! How strenuous are you, liar? You're a liar and a hypocrite, like the rest of us! I've hated you ever since that lie. And I've felt guilty for hating you. And it was all over a lie, over a *lie!* And now you want me to believe you're innocent. And to help you. Why should I? You were seen next to the Queen, lying beside her, on the beach. During the last Indra's Festival." Kumaran suddenly turned off the torrent of words as he remembered the King's warning.

Thomas' face flushed. He said weakly, "Actually it was not a sin of adultery in the flesh, but in the spirit."

"What is that supposed to mean?" Kumaran snarled.

"It means —it means I would have—I would have committed adultery with her if she had given me a chance."

"Look, either you did or you didn't. Which is it?"

"You are right. I did."

Kumaran could hardly believe his ears. Here was a fool so advanced that he thought he'd committed a sin when he didn't really! Momentarily thrown off the trail by this strange confession, Kumaran had to discover another pretext for his rage. He found it in the very confusion that Thomas' asinine confession had aroused in him; he found it in the fact that Thomas wasn't guilty after all in spite of what the stupid fool himself thought. Kumaran looked back down at the *yakshi* in his hand, then up at the wooden cross hanging around Thomas' neck that he had lovingly carved in his hole. He lunged at Thomas, tore the cross off his neck, and, with a look of hatred, jammed the end of the cross against the *yakshi*. "Did you do *this* to the Queen?!" he hissed. *"This?!"*

Thomas could only stare in dumb shock at Kumaran jamming, up and down, the sacred piece of wood against the statuette.

When Kumaran next spoke, he sounded as if he had a bone stuck in his throat and could barely get his breath, and yet the effect was that of a snarling beast. His bulging, hating eyes wept, or rather sweat, as he said, "You've used me! You despise me! And now you want me to help you. I will watch you burn. And I will despise *you*. I made you this cross because I loved you. I loved you! I would have given my life for you. But you only despised me in return. You never even told me, not once, you liked my poetry. You never even asked me to read it! You gave all my food and water away, you made light when I lost everything. You insulted my God. 'Dissolute—dissolute coxcomb,' you said. Why does Murugan let you live another day? 'Weak,' you said. After I had killed that filthy tyrant! 'Weak!' Is that 'weak'?! I put up with your stupid religion while you condemned mine every chance you had. Tell me, tell me, did you do *this* to the Queen?!"

Again Kumaran began pounding the end of the cross against the *yakshi*. Then he let his hands fall slackly on the floor in front of him and wept bitterly. Finally, in a paroxysm that seemed to issue from his bowels, he took a deep, shuddering breath, looked up with wild, frightened, blurry eyes toward the light, and with a look of unbelievable fury flung the cross out the window. It arced against the vivid blue sky, the green of the trees, then disappeared below the window ledge.

Thomas had managed to keep some semblance of composure as he listened to Kumaran's shocking disclosure, but when he saw the cross used to such a vile purpose, and then watched it sail out the window, he wanted to murder Kumaran. With all his carpenter's strength he wanted to fling Kumaran's deformed body down against the brittle ground and see it splatter like a bird's egg. But he had controlled himself with his Aramaic mantra, "Maranatha," which he silently screamed over and over in his head.

After a minute of quiet during which neither man moved from his position, Kumaran looked at Thomas with a demeanor strangely out of place. It was as if Kumaran had been possessed and now for some reason the demon had fled. Looking up at Thomas, he said in a brotherly, almost intimate way, "Tell me, have you ever—been tempted? The Queen is a beautiful woman."

Thomas looked suspiciously at Kumaran and said nothing.

"She reminds me of Madari, the way Madari might have looked if she had lived, and matured, and grown wise. But she doesn't tempt you? She would me if I were you," Kumaran went on.

Thomas didn't know how to respond. Suddenly and inexplicably Kumaran was talking as if he believed he and the Queen were innocent. Fighting back the sense of outrage that had consumed him, Thomas forced himself to be polite. "She attracts me," he said. "But she doesn't tempt me. Not really. Temptation is possible only when the will wavers."

"But I've found the will does waver," said the transformed Kumaran.

"Only when you let it," said Thomas, still feeling blasted, but recovering his equilibrium.

"'Only when you let it.' What does that mean?" said Kumaran. "A man and his will: Are they two different things? And the difference between sin and virtue—what is it but a slight wavering of the will? That's all: an ever-so-slight wavering of the will. That's how it was with me in Madurai when King Nediyon invited me to his bed. My will wavered. A tiny, fragile thing—with what crushing results!"

Thomas didn't know what to make of Kumaran's return to decency; Kumaran was actually rational, even humble. Thomas said, "Yes, but the will doesn't have to be a fragile thing. Jesus' will wasn't fragile at all. It was like a huge wave sweeping everything out of its way. Or like an arrow speeding toward its target."

"And your will, is it like Jesus'?"

At that moment it occurred to Thomas that Kumaran, the transformed Kumaran, the new, gentle Kumaran, might be willing to help him after all. Thomas paused, then answered Kumaran's question. "No," he said, "but with respect to the Queen, yes."

"I have to go, but one more thing," said Kumaran calmly. "Your Jesus was condemned unjustly, wasn't he?"

"That's right."

"But he didn't try to free himself—at least that's what I've heard you say a hundred times."

"That's right."

"Well, why don't you follow his example?"

"Me?"

"Yes, you." Now there was about Kumaran's voice a hint of contempt.

"Because—because there is so much that still needs to be done," said Thomas edgily.

"But don't you see that Jesus could have said the same thing?"

Thomas looked down at the floor and scowled.

"Don't mistake me," said Kumaran. "I'm not suggesting you do nothing. It's just that you're always holding up your Jesus as an example."

Having said that, or rather in the middle of saying it, Kumaran lurched up and began to weave his way through the clutter toward the back of the room. "What a strange place this is!" he said. When he got close to the back wall, which consisted entirely of an ivory bas-relief, he said, "It's out of the *Ramayana*. There is Sita in her hermitage, and there is the ten-headed Ravana disguised as a holy man. Do you know the episode?"

"Vaguely," said Thomas, not knowing what to make of Kumaran's digression in the face of his own impending execution. He remembered Kumaran had referred to it as "burning." Was he really to be burned?

"Over there is Rama, God in the flesh. Maybe your Jesus was God in the flesh. Did you ever think about that, Thomas? Maybe your Jesus was an avatar." Kumaran tossed these last words jokingly over his shoulder while looking back at Thomas, but now he turned again to the sculpture and said: "Next to Rama is his brother Lakshmana. And there is the deer with an arrow stuck in its heart. And there is the fiend Maricha rising out of the deer. But the technique! The technique! Who *was* this sculptor? If I could learn to carve like him, I would be tempted to give up my poetry! The technique! And to think this just sits here—in all this bat shit!"

It was incredible. Kumaran, out of his mind a few moments ago, was now cheerfully enjoying art. Thomas didn't know whether to be hopeful or not. In any case, he would have to try one more time to get Kumaran's help. "Will you speak to the King on my behalf, Kumaran?" he said bluntly.

"Don't expect much," said Kumaran as he stood admiring the bas-relief with his back to Thomas. "Karikal is not Pari, you know. Their temperaments have as much in common as this *yakshi*"—impulsively he smashed against the floor the figurine he was still carrying—"and this ivory masterpiece."

"But I think he must know I'm innocent. Surely the Queen has told him. Maybe he just needs a way to free himself from his own command. I suspect Charishnu put him up to it. And Charishnu is his guru."

Kumaran began to limp his way back to the entry. As he wound around the last obstacle between himself and the door, he said, almost to himself, "I'll see what I can do."

"One more thing, Kumaran." Almost on a whim and with some misgiving, Thomas reached behind him for a large weighty sack. "Many of my writings and translations, even a dictionary of Greek words, Greek to Tamil, they're all in here. Also a letter addressed to a certain Valluvar of Mayilapur—he is a poet and a convert—and another introducing Mochikiranar to the church back in Jerusalem. This Mochikiranar will be my successor, the second Bishop of India, if I don't get out of here alive. I'm not sure I'll have a chance to see anyone else, so would you—could I trust you—with this? Not even the Queen has come. I have no idea what's happened to her. Do you?"

Kumaran shrugged his shoulders.

"Kumaran, the proper administration, the very life of the Christian church in India depends on you. You haven't always agreed with me, and I wonder now if you still hate me. But we are still brothers. Please don't disappoint me now. Take this to Mochikiranar, who lives in the Paradavar quarter. Anyone will be able tell you where he lives. Please do this one last thing for me. Please!"

Kumaran took the sack and with a final careless nod said, "Good-bye."

"'Good-bye'? Is that all?"

"I'm already late. Kadyalur is waiting. Guard!"

"Don't forget. Mochikiranar!"

Mahadeva unlatched the door, and Kumaran, carrying Thomas' sack over his shoulder, departed without a backward glance.

As Mahadeva turned the key in the lock and bolted the door, Thomas turned his attention to the clepsydra. He tried to detect movement in the level of the water. He could not, yet he knew the cup was filling, slowly and steadily filling, and that at a given instant it would drop to the bottom of the basin. He stared hypnotically at the cup. He wanted to see the water swallow the cup; he wanted to witness the exact moment when the cup sank.

He remembered the cross Kumaran had torn off his neck and thrown out the window. He went to the window and looked down at the ground. For a long time he looked, but he could not see it. Then he happened to look up, and there it was, dangling by its thong from a lower branch of the mango tree like a piece of airborne litter.

48. The Eunuch's Visit

The sun flooded Thomas' prison with morning light. He stood up with his wash basin and wound his way across the room to the windows. Every dewdrop still clinging to leaf and blade glistened, while birdsong enveloped the park, but he felt oppressed by all this beauty. Looking down, he saw colorfully dressed women move gracefully along the paths under the trees while monkeys played in the branches above; and he prayed to God for the strength to endure another day. Suddenly he recognized one of the women, one of Queen Adimanti's ladies-in-waiting.

"Uma! . . . UMA!"

Uma and the two women with her stopped and looked up, trying to see where the sound came from, but a branch cut off their view. Thomas waved his hand and repeated, "Uma! Here! It's Thomas!"

"No calling from the windows!" Mahadeva yelled as he unbolted the door and rushed a few steps into the room.

Thomas backed away from the window, still holding the wash basin.

"You know the rules! If you break them again, I'll have to shutter the room!"

Thomas did know the rules, and he also valued Mahadeva's friendship.

"I can't allow it, Sire. Please, not again. You'll force me to . . ." Mahadeva didn't finish the sentence but only nodded his head as if they had come to a better understanding. Then he went out and bolted the door behind him with a forceful clank.

"Where are you, Aiyer?" Thomas heard Uma cry faintly from below. "I can't see you . . . I can't see you." He returned to the window and caught a glimpse of her orange and blue dress as she hurried away toward the buildings on the far side of the park. She was gone, but his heart beat to a new hope. He had gotten through; she had said the word "Aiyer."

He threw his bath water out the window and watched it splash on the grass.

A man and a woman, both elegantly tailored and dressed, passed beneath the prison window, turned off the pebble path onto the grass, and sat in two swings hanging side by side from a tree limb. Thomas, whose eyesight was still sharp when there was ample light, could see their mouths moving, and he wondered idly if they were lovers. The woman wore a golden headdress and had reddened her lips; Thomas let himself imagine what she smelled like; she carried Adimanti's scent. At one point their conversation became animated, and he could hear their voices, even make out some of the words. Watching them finally became tiresome, and his mind drifted off to Kumaran. He remembered how he and Kumaran had sat on swings hung from a tree in another royal park six years ago—in Muziri outside King Attan's palace. He remembered their conversation, in particular how he condemned the King's maids frolicking in the park.

An elephant trumpeted outside in the park, and Thomas stepped over furniture and between busts to have a look. The elephant had apparently gotten loose and was bathing in one of the ponds. Its driver came running up, gesticulating and brandishing a goad. He pointed to the flower garden around the pond that the beast had stepped through and cursed it for its negligence. Then he waded into the water, mounted the elephant, and guided it out onto the path, shouting and grunting and hitting.

Thomas felt vaguely dejected about what he had seen. He felt sorry for the elephant, just as he felt sorry for himself. He, like the elephant, wanted to be free. He watched the mahout guide his elephant down the path out of sight beyond the trees.

It was almost noon; the sun's rays struck the floor in a thin strip just under the windows. In another minute the strip would disappear as the sun reached its zenith. Thomas stared down at the floor as the strip grew thinner and thinner, teetered on the point of extinction, then vanished.

It was mid-afternoon, and the tedium of prison life lay heavily on him. He picked up stylus and palm leaf and began to work on his dictionary as he held it against the window ledge so he could see. Working along, he was roused by Mahadeva's voice on the other side of the door. There was a snap and formality about the way he called out "Sire!" that suggested someone important.

Thomas heard an unfamiliar voice mumble something, then the latch being lifted. He rose, not knowing what to expect.

An old man clad in a gold-trimmed white tunic, wearing a cap, and carrying a cane came in. The door closed behind him, and the latch fell into place. Thomas knew the man's face, but he couldn't remember who he was. He greeted him as courteously as he could under the circumstances.

"I am Kakanthan, Guardian of the Women's Quarters," the man said.

Thomas never entertained gossip, so he didn't know what everyone else living in the palace knew: that this Kakanthan was born a prince; that his father was the king of the Chola Empire before Karikal's father defeated him in battle; that he had been castrated as a baby and nursed by some women of the elder Karikal's court, and then, quite naturally, had grown up to command the women who nursed him; and that he was vain—thus the cap, which served to disguise his bald head—a grumbler, and a spy for the King. All Thomas remembered was that he was a eunuch and that Adimanti didn't trust him.

"Sit down here if you like," said Thomas, pointing to a marble slab he used as a seat.

"I will stand," answered the old man, leaning on his cane amid all the clutter. "I come from the King. Are you being well cared for?"

Was the man being sarcastic? "I'm a prisoner," Thomas answered with a hint of irritation.

Kakanthan shifted his position, then brought his cane down on the floor with a crack. His eyes seemed now to take in the room; they shifted back and forth, settled on Thomas for an instant, then continued to rove. "I have heard that you are a raja from the west, that you are descended from a king. Is that correct?" he said without looking at Thomas.

Thomas hated any lie, and it pained him a little to make this claim. It was true that his foster father had been descended from King David, but Thomas had no idea who his true father was. On an impulse he decided to tell the eunuch the whole truth.

"So you are an impostor," said Kakanthan.

"I grew up in the family of a descendant of King David. I was treated the same as my brothers, who carried David's blood. If I am not a raja, then what am I?"

"A bastard," said Kakanthan, whose shifting, wily old eyes for once settled calmly on Thomas' face.

"Well, then I am a bastard."

"Actually you and I have much in common," said Kakanthan, trying to smile, "for I, too, am a displaced raja. My father was king of the Cholas. You have heard of my father, King Kakanthan?"

"Your father was King Kakanthan?"

"How do you think I came by my name? And even you must know that Puhar was once called Kakanthi. It too came by its name from my father. Like you, I came into this world in curious circumstances. No sooner was I born than my father was killed and I castrated. They would have killed me too, but the women of the new court begged the king to show mercy. Mercy! It would have been better if they had killed me."

"Do you mean that?"

"I suppose not," said Kakanthan, leaning on his cane.

Thomas pitied the old man. Kakanthan, his defenses beginning to melt, quickly straightened and came to the point. "The King's Guru, Charishnu, accuses you of adultery with the Queen. It would go better for you if you confessed. The King has commissioned me to take the confession. I have come directly from his apartment."

"Charishnu? Charishnu, you say?"

"Charishnu, the King's Guru."

"Charishnu. I never thought I'd hear who my accuser was. Well, you may tell the King that Charishnu is lying."

"This is not what the King wants to hear. It will not go well for you if you persist in this," said the eunuch.

"But it's the truth."

"You are asking the King to disbelieve Charishnu and believe you. Charishnu consecrated Karikal king when he was only three days out of his mother's womb. Charishnu has been the King's spiritual teacher ever since. You ask the King to believe you and disbelieve Charishnu? You are a yavana, you teach a foreign religion. Why should he believe you? If he cannot trust his Guru, who can he trust? I tell you, it will not go well for you if you persist in this! If you confess, the King might show mercy."

"You ask whom he can trust. I will tell you," said Thomas. "The Queen. Let him ask Queen Adimanti."

Kakanthan began tapping his cane loudly against the floor. "But she is your accomplice!" Immediately he coughed, as if regretting his own words.

"Beg the King to ask her. He will believe her. Adimanti never lies. He knows that better than anyone."

"'Adimanti' you call her," said the crafty eunuch. "Not 'Queen Adimanti,' but 'Adimanti.'"

"She is my shishya," said Thomas.

"Charishnu says she is your lover."

"A lie!"

"'Adimanti,' eh?" Kakanthan lowered his eyes and snickered, then looked back up at Thomas and said, "Do you know what the King told me once? 'It is easier to find a white crow, or the imprint of fishes' feet, or flowers on the sacred fig tree, than to know what a woman has in her heart.'"

"He applied that saying to the Queen? Surely not."

"Look at you! I wish you could see how your face reddens. You yavanas always give yourselves away when you lie. And you say you don't love her. Yet you call her 'Adimanti.'"

"When did I say I didn't love her? Did I say that? Did I say that, Kakanthan? All I have said is that I haven't . . . Not love her? By everything that is sacred to me I do love her! And you may tell the King that, if he doesn't already know! Tell him, Kakanthan!"

"Lower your voice. Such ardor does not become a yogi—even a yavana yogi," said Kakanthan sarcastically. Then in a pompous, threatening tone he announced, "No one loves the Queen except the King!"

"Love her? Kakanthan, you are aware of the King's concubines. I believe they are referred to as his 'junior queens.' If you dare, ask him when he visited the Queen's bed last."

"No doubt you have visited it more recently!"

Thomas almost sprang at the eunuch. Kakanthan, seeing the rage in Thomas' eyes, held his cane out for defense and, with a contempt compounded of fear, said in a low hissing growl, "Don't touch me, you son of a yavana whore."

The words exploded inside Thomas' head. He took a deep breath, calmed himself, and said, "Kakanthan, I *am* the son of a yavana whore. And as God is my witness, I am not the Queen's lover."

Kakanthan studied his face intently, and Thomas felt that the eunuch saw the truth in his eyes and believed him.

Declining to offer the courtesies of leavetaking, Kakanthan knocked his hand against the door, then turned to go. As the latch was being lifted, he turned his face back and spoke into the room without looking at Thomas: "Unless you confess, you will be burned to death sometime this week." He waited a few moments in silence, glanced back furtively one last time in Thomas' direction, and said, "All right, then *be* a fool!" He rapped the door with his cane, and Mahadeva led him out.

For a moment the words paralyzed Thomas. "Burned to death." That is what Kumaran had said, too. Yet he could hardly believe it. Once before, at Kurinchi, he had been certain he would die, but thanks to Kumaran he had escaped. Now he not only had Kumaran on his side, but Kakanthan. He was sure Kakanthan believed him.

As he stared down at the water trickling into the cup of the clepsydra, he prayed that Kakanthan would speak well of him to the King.

49. Treachery Halved

It was very late, well after midnight, when Kumaran was summoned. He followed the guard to the innermost building of the palace. Back and forth up the wide marble staircase they climbed by the light of the messenger's torch. Eight stories Kumaran counted. They came out onto a giant pavilion open on all four sides; the entire ninth storey consisted of this single room. Flickering lamps were mounted on the posts supporting the two uppermost floors, and Kumaran leaned against the balustrade and looked out and down, deep down into the cool dry night, as a shiver ran through him.

Soon a light appeared in the hatchway leading to the upper storeys, and down the ladder came several of the court mutes carrying lamps. They saw Kumaran in the dim light and indicated with gestures that he should climb the ladder. Had he been found out?

He bowed before the King and touched his feet with his forehead and folded hands. The King directed him to a rattan chair which one of the mutes, a yavana bodyguard, was pulling up.

"Alagar, prepare our guest a drink," said the King, who was clothed in simple night attire and wore no wreath in his hair.

Kumaran had no idea where he stood. All he knew was that it was very late and that the King was in no friendly mood. Had Charishnu revealed his source? It occurred to Kumaran that the drink being prepared might contain poison; he might die writhing in pain like the Pandyan King he had murdered. It would be a fit end.

"Kumaran, how did your talk with Thomas go?" the King said, getting straight to the point.

"It was not everything you hoped for, Your Majesty," said Kumaran, "but it was better than I expected."

"Better than you expected? What do you mean by that?" The King stared at Kumaran suspiciously. "Do you know him to be innocent?"

Kumaran realized he had made a mistake. There was only one way he could know Thomas was innocent, and that was by being a witness to everything Thomas did during the time he supposedly committed the crime. Kumaran was just such a witness. Had the King guessed it? Had Charishnu told him everything?

"No—I mean—he is the sort of person who might not have committed the crime," Kumaran stammered.

"Do you know that he is under sentence of death?"

"I guessed as much, Your Majesty," said Kumaran, somewhat regaining his composure.

"Have a drink, Kumaran," said the King through a scowl.

King Karikal motioned to one of the pinkfaces to give Kumaran the drink of honey mixed with water, and Kumaran called out silently to Murugan to have mercy on him as he took the cup. He stirred the mixture three times in succession with his thumb and index finger pressed together. Then, in three gulps, he swallowed the ritual drink and waited for the inner fire, about which he had studied so much, to begin to burn. He looked around the small corner room, closed on two sides and opening out nakedly into the night on the other two. Not even screens separated them from the night—it was too high for mosquitoes. Blazing torches were mounted on the walls. They lit brightly colored tapestries showing scenes from the hunt. He felt like one of those hunted animals, but the fire in his stomach did not come.

"Kumaran, I will ask you outright," said the King. "If you repeat any of this I will send you limbless down the Kaveri in a skiff. Do you understand?"

"You can trust me, Your Majesty."

"The Queen's Guru has been accused of adultery."

"Yes, Sire."

"Do you know by whom?"

"You told me the Queen, Sire."

"Not *with* whom, you idiot! *By* whom!"

"Oh! No, I don't know," Kumaran lied.

"Charishnu! My own Guru!" said the King.

Kumaran had apparently escaped again, but he knew the King might be teasing him, playing with him, as a cat plays with a mouse it has caught and is about to eat.

"Kumaran, listen to me now," said the King. "Who might have brought him this information? Who was his source?"

Now Kumaran was all but sure Charishnu had talked. The King was merely torturing him. Kumaran made up his mind to leap over the balustrade into the receptive, infinite night. His muscles tensed as he answered, "I do not know, Your Majesty."

"You know of no one who might want to destroy Thomas?"

"No, Your Majesty."

"It is rumored that you might."

"No, Your Majesty. We have both saved each other's life. In a manner of speaking we are brothers."

The King studied Kumaran with the eyes of a cobra, but the cobra did not strike. "Kumaran, I have reason to believe that Thomas is innocent," the King said. "It takes two to commit adultery, and the Queen denies any part in it. She was just here pleading his case. I cannot think of when she ever lied before."

"Perhaps, Sire, she never before had a sufficiently good reason to lie," Kumaran said with a malevolence that made him shudder.

"Exactly my thought. But the matter does not rest there. Thomas, too, denies the charge. He denies it in so striking a manner, with such passionate sincerity, that I almost find myself persuaded by him. A liar almost always gives himself away, do you not think so? You are a poet, a keen observer. A liar's voice may be unnaturally shrill, he may speak too quickly, he may blink his eyes nervously, his eyes may begin to squint, he may begin to stutter, he may cower like a dog—something usually gives him away. Indeed I have seen such signs even on men who tell the truth—as when a spy brings bad news. But Thomas showed none of these signs when Kakanthan—you know Kakanthan, as shrewd a man as there is around here—questioned him yesterday. For the moment I am persuaded that Thomas is telling the truth. Can you persuade me otherwise?"

"How might I do that, Your Majesty?"

"Well, have you ever caught him in a lie? You two have spent much time together."

Kumaran could hardly believe it. The King was playing directly into his hands!

"Yes, I *have* caught him, Your Majesty. I didn't catch him at the time. I found out later."

"He deceived you, in other words."

"That is correct."

"What did the lie concern?"

"Adultery, Sire."

"Adultery you say?"

"I once asked him if he had ever committed adultery. He denied it. I found out later he had."

"Aha! How did you find out?"

"He told me later."

"This self-styled sannyasin, holy man, guru, and what-not is an adulterer? Who was was the woman?"

"A simple convert to his religion. A widow. On the Malabar Coast. A fisherman's wife."

"A fisherman's wife!" Suddenly the King exploded with laughter and slapped his leg. "A fisherman's wife! He must have liked her smell!" He laughed from his belly, laughed hard and long, and Kumaran joined him. Gradually the laughter died down, and the King turned serious again. But not before Kumaran realized he had the King exactly where he wanted him.

"Ah, my friend," said the King, "if only the simpleton had a mistress now. You don't suppose he does, do you?"

"I can't say, Sire."

"No matter," the King said with sudden seriousness. "You can swear that this Thomas, this pretender and buffoon, is an adulterer and a liar, and that it was about a specific act of adultery that he lied, and lied so convincingly that for years he deceived you."

"Yes, Your Majesty."

"Alagar," he called to his servant, "bring some water."

The servant poured clear water from a jar into the hollow of Kumaran's hand.

"Kumaran," said the King, "say that you know Thomas to be an adulterer, a liar, and to have lied about a specific act of adultery in order to—never mind the motive. Say it."

Kumaran said so, and after each of the three accusations he sipped water from the palm of his hand and, with a conscience that was almost clear, pledged its truth.

"I still do not believe they are guilty," the King said wistfully as he walked to the balustrade with Kumaran beside him and looked out into the night. "I cannot believe that the Queen would lie—unless— unless it was to protect him—yes, it is possible, I suppose. She would never lie to protect herself, but her Guru—I suppose it is possible." He sighed heavily. "Kumaran, I am grateful to you. Charishnu is certain of his source, Thomas and the Queen appear to be just as certain that he has gotten it all wrong, that either he or his source is lying. How do I know whom to believe? You are the only one who does not bring a bias to the case. You have made my decision easier. There will be an execution in a few days. I want you to attend. There will be only a few of us. You and I together will spill his blood. If Thomas is innocent, then we will share the responsibility, we will halve the karma. Is that agreed?"

"Your Majesty," said Kumaran, feeling deeply flattered and bowing from the waist, "if I must go to the deepest hell, let it be so. It is not every pulaiyar who can share a king's karma."

As Kumaran walked home alone, he congratulated himself on outsmarting a king. Several times during the interview his life was in peril, but he had said the right thing. Once again he had gotten away with— he almost called it murder, but checked himself in time. He wondered about Charishnu, and it dawned on him that the last thing Charishnu would do is reveal his source. Why should he? Further interrogation might show Thomas to be innocent, and that was not what Charishnu wanted. In any case, not even a king had the right to challenge an allegation brought by his guru. Even to question the allegation would be an unacceptable insult. Karikal had no choice but to take Charishnu at his word, and Charishnu knew that. And what did the Queen know? Nothing. She had not even talked to Thomas since his imprisonment. And even if she had, what of it? And Thomas himself did not suspect his old "brother"! Kumaran thrilled to a sense of godlike power, as if he were Shiva orchestrating the dissolution of a world. He cackled in delight and clapped his hands.

50. The Moment of Truth

For the last two days Thomas had been telling himself Uma certainly would not fail to inform the Queen what she heard. But
the Queen had not come. Nor had anyone else. He prepared himself for another long night without so much as a lantern to brighten it.

"What is it?" Thomas said gloomily to the knock of the night guard,
who had just come on duty.

"Her Majesty the Queen."

"What?"

"My Guru, may I come in?" Adimanti said through the door.

"Is it really you?" He was delirious with joy.

The door opened, and there, holding a bright oil lamp—for it was
already twilight—stood Queen Adimanti. No goddess bedecked with
wreathes could have looked lovelier or more sacred to her most ar-
dent devotee than Adimanti looked to Thomas at that moment. She
wore a vivid vermilion dress with green vertical stripes; the dress
was cinched at the waist with a matching green ribbon. Her hair,
pulled back from her forehead and held in place by a garland of jasmines, hung down her back to her waist, and her jewelry—from the
pearl anklets that were visible just below the hem of her dress to the
pale purple amethyst nose piece that glimmered in the light of the
lantern—added grace to her already lovely form. Her "defect," her
over-long neck, had been "shortened" by means of a broad necklace
made of tigers' teeth, which, in spite of her sophistication, she believed warded off evil spirits and protected her from the evil eye. Her

extraordinary eyes ringed with thin lines of kohl shone with pleasure at the sight of him.

Thomas looked at the Queen and saw his beloved shishya, his cherished "pupil," but also his sister, his best friend, his beloved. Starved for beauty in the succession of dreary jails that had held him, he was overwhelmed by her presence. He actually stepped back when he caught the scent of her. He was surprised and intoxicated by her appearance and stepped back when the subtle scent of her perfume struck him in the face.

"Is it really you?" he said again.

But before she could answer, the face of little Puttaswamy stuck out from behind the Queen's dress, where he had been hiding.

"Puttu! Puttu!" Thomas cried out. He scooped him up in his arms. Puttaswamy clasped his "Bapu's" neck and sobbed.

Thomas became aware that another woman was waiting outside the door. It was Puttaswamy's mother. He understood that the boy would have to leave with his mother. Again and again Thomas hugged the "little brown man," as he playfully called him at times.

"I brought you something, Bapu," Puttaswamy said. "It's from all of us, especially me and Sidda."

Puttaswamy handed Thomas a beautiful wooden cross with intricate swirls covering the entire surface in typical Tamil style, not unlike the one Kumaran had made him. But at the center of the cross was a face.

"Oh, Puttu! That's beautiful!" Thomas lovingly turned the cross over and over. "Who made this?" he asked reverently.

"I had it made for you," said Adimanti, smiling all her love across at him.

He looked at her with speechless gratitude, then turned back to the boy. "And who is that face, Puttu? That's Jesus, isn't it?"

"No, Bapu, that's you."

Thomas gasped and held his breath as he tried to control the sob that rose in his throat. Sniffling, he kissed the boy over and over as he held him, then gave him back to his mother.

"You will be out soon, Bapu," said Puttaswamy. He turned an anxious face first towards Thomas, then the Queen. His little mop of hair flopped up and down as he nodded with exaggeration.

"Yes, soon!" Thomas said.

"Good-bye, Bapu."

"Good-bye, Puttu. Keep me in your prayers."

"I will. Good-bye, Bapu!"

Puttaswamy's mother had to pull him back so the guard could close the door. Thomas heard his sobs echoing outside as he climbed down the ladder. Fainter and fainter they grew until they died out altogether. Then he gave his attention to Adimanti.

"Thank you for bringing the boy," he said.

"Master, I have been frantic!" the Queen burst out as soon as the guard turned the key in the lock and withdrew a certain distance so they could talk with some privacy. "I didn't know what happened to you. You just disappeared. I thought you might have gone home on a ship. I have been looking everywhere. Then Uma told me she heard your voice coming from this building. Then I knew the King was behind it. Last night I got in to see him, and he told me what had happened. And then today I had to help consecrate a new shrine. All I could think of was you in your prison. Dearest Guru, I came as quickly as I could! Please know that your disciple came as quickly as she could!"

"Adimanti, precious Adi, how I've missed you!" Thomas said. He wanted to hold her as he had held Puttaswamy, but stopped himself. He took her lantern and made her sit on the marble bench by the windows and told her all the events of the last three weeks.

When he finished, it was dark outside. They stood side by side looking out of the window, the ledge hitting her at the navel. The air was delightfully cool and dry. Sparrows, chirping riotously only minutes before, were settling down for the night.

"Beloved friend, you are here," he said looking down at her. "Whatever happens to me, at least I have seen you."

"Dearest Thomas—may I call you Thomas?" she said.

He was startled by the question. "You've been calling me Thomas for many months now." He was saddened by the barrier between them that the question implied.

"You have lived with death," she said mysteriously. "I thought—" but she did not continue.

"More than ever now call me Thomas," he said. "Can you imagine how lonely it's been? I have only God to speak to, and He doesn't speak back."

"He doesn't?" She looked up at him appreciatively, no longer the Queen of an empire, no longer his shishya, but his friend, his confidante, the one person who understood him, who loved him, who could even tease him and joke with him.

"What's going to happen to me?" he asked. "Kumaran said something about my being burned. Did the King mention anything?"

"Burned?" said the Queen anxiously.

"The King told you what the charge is?"

"What a look of hatred he gave me!" said the Queen, whose own face mimicked her husband's. "Adultery! We who have never so much as touched each other! Do you see now why we Indians call the world *maya?* It is an absurd place. Look around and try to find God. He is always hiding."

"Did you defend yourself?"

"Yes, and I think he believed me in the end. How could he not? When have I ever lied to him? I do not have his love. But his trust? How can he deny me that? Who has better earned it?"

"I must tell you that there may be very little time. The eunuch Kakanthan was here yesterday and said I would die within the week."

"A week? Oh, that is unthinkable! Oh, Thomas, good Thomas!" She was on the verge of tears when suddenly a determined fury flashed from her eyes, and she said, "Not if I have anything to do with it!"

"But there is Charishnu. Charishnu brings the charge. Charishnu is the King's Guru. What can the King do?"

"And I am his Queen! He will have to choose between us!" Adimanti sank down on the marble bench and tapped her forehead with her fingertips, which were drawn together tightly like stems about to be put into a vase. "Poor man," she said more quietly and with sympathy. "He is in a difficult position, isn't he?"

"Perhaps you could speak with Charishnu," said Thomas, sitting down beside her, "tell him face to face you are innocent, at least find out who his source is. Perhaps you could remind him of the brahmin's sacred duty to champion the truth at all times. Would that help?"

"Oh, Thomas, my dear Thomas! Oh, if only you knew! There is *no way* to convince Charishnu. Oh, my dear man! Long ago he stopped worrying about the truth. Words, for him, are means of getting his way, that is all."

"Then the King must know this."

"No, my dear, the King cannot *allow* himself to know this."

"But—doesn't Charishnu fear retribution? Doesn't he believe he'll come back in the next life as a dog or the like, or spend some time in hell?"

"For killing a yavana? He would be more concerned if he had forgotten to purify himself after answering the call of nature! Thomas, he need only bathe in the Kaveri at the full moon to be, in his mind, purified of sin."

"Can this be true? Is he really so far gone? I saw him picking flowers only last month."

"Picking flowers!" She could not resist a laugh. "Thomas, you surprising man! I have known Charishnu for many years. Remember that he was once my Guru. He is one of those people who can't tell the truth from a lie. He is a man without a center, without an internal reference point by which to judge the truth. Not many people know this about him. All they see is his hair tuft and sacred thread and imperial emblem. He is self-deceived, utterly corrupt. Believe me, there is no way to reach Charishnu. Long ago he discovered ways to do what he pleases with impunity. Picking flowers!" She shook her head, then stood up again and looked out into the night.

Thomas stood up beside her. There were not many people now; most had reached their homes. A few sparrows chirped randomly from the mango tree.

"Is it possible I'm getting what I deserve?" Thomas said, breaking the lull. "My love for you"—he hesitated, not daring to look at her—"is not entirely pure."

"Why do you say that, you good and holy man?" said Adimanti with surprise as she looked up at him.

Thomas looked intently into the dark outside the window and said nothing.

"What is this?" Adimanti persisted. "What are you saying, Thomas? Please, dear friend, look at me."

Thomas turned his head, but not his frame, and looked at her.

"Have you ever touched me?" she said. "Have I ever touched you?"

Thomas did not answer.

"The King knows I will follow him to the funeral pyre. And you have taken a vow of celibacy." Adimanti paused for a moment as the light from the lamp reflected off her smooth bronze cheekbone. "We both live as celibates anyway," she continued. "You have chosen to, and I don't miss the King's bed—not anymore. I belong to God, as do you. Why are you afraid that we might be sinning? We are sober and discreet, we give no offense to anyone, we are friends. Our love for each other is a holy love. It brings us joy. What is wrong with that?"

"Adi," said Thomas as if his mind were elsewhere, "I told Kumaran. I told him that I loved you."

"Kumaran?"

"Yes."

Adimanti gave Thomas a questioning look. "He was here?"

"Two days ago."

"But why? Why did you tell him?"

"I'm not sure. It came out naturally in the course—now I remember. He asked me a question. He asked me outright if I 'desired' you. I told him I didn't desire you, but loved you. Anyway, he promised to talk to the King."

"But what will he *say* to the King?" said Adimanti, looking rather dismayed. "You gave Kumaran the weapon with which he can destroy you. Why did you say such a thing? 'Love.' That can be understood in so many ways."

"I suppose so. It might have been a stupid thing to do. It was a gamble. But Kumaran once saved my life. And I don't think he—I hope he—"

"Thomas, if you were to die—besides Puttaswamy, and sugar, and the unguents which make up my toilet, and of course my jewelry, what other pleasures do I have? Life without you—I might as well be a widow!" She looked for a moment out the window as if considering what she had just said, then continued in a faraway, dreamy voice: "I do not mind really, but . . . who else is there to tell my soul's secrets to? Who else understands me?" Now she looked back at Thomas, her mood again vigorous and solid. "Thomas, do you remember when?—oh, look at those moths."

Two moths flew dangerously close to the flame of the lantern. They made one pass after another at it. Sometimes they seemed to be chasing each other, playing with each other. But always they came back to the flame.

A profound, unspeakable sadness descended on Thomas as he watched the moths at play. Then he said the thing that had been trying to formulate itself for many months, but that only now escaped the confines of habit and holy discipline: "Adi, sometimes I would like to play with you like that."

As he felt the blood rush to his cheeks, he saw her eyelashes flutter. Then her face became as impassive and still as the Buddha's. Not even the stray hairs at her temple quivered. Even the sparrows, as if privy to the horrendous thing that he said, had completely quieted.

"It's true," said Thomas after a minute.

"You don't sound like a man near death," said Adimanti gravely. "You don't sound like a sannyasin. You should not say things like that, Thomas. You should not even think them. Here, let me place this cross around your neck. I brought a thong."

"They seem to think themselves," he said.

She stood before him and reached up and put the cross around his neck. Then they stood quietly side by side looking out into the dark.

He did not know how he felt about what he had said. He had never intended, or planned, or rehearsed such a confession. A year ago they teased each other about going to her village and living simple lives as husband and wife, but both understood that such an arrangement was out of the question: They had been playing; or rather they had used an artifice to convey their very real love for each other, a love which both knew could never be physically consummated. But now it was different. He had not spoken playfully. Such words he had spoken only in his unguarded daydreams—such words and much more. And it was true what Adimanti said. These were not the words of a man near death.

Confused and ashamed, he turned his mind to what he had intended to say all along if she visited him. It was almost a prepared speech, a sermon on a forbidden subject.

"Dearest friend, let me tell you what is in my heart. Please sit down."

He straddled the bench while she drew up her legs into the lotus position. They faced each other directly, the lamp a little to the side. Thomas continued: "For many weeks I have felt constrained by my office as your guru. Does a guru confess his weaknesses to the student he is trying to teach?"

"Speak your heart out," said the Queen.

"You will permit it?"

"We are friends first."

He began: "It's as if the Father is hiding Himself. All around me I see Shiva, Murugan, Krishna, and the other gods of India. Shrine after shrine, at every roadside marker, in every business establishment, in every neighborhood, they're everywhere. Even in this room, over there, on that wall, Krishna is riding on Garuda. Even if I accept your teaching, Adi, even if I agree with you that all these gods, all these Indian gods, are expressions of the Only God There Is—and I do accept this teaching—it doesn't help me get in touch with Him. Every time I try to pray to Him, the old notions storm in and threaten to take over. I thrust them aside, bury them, and set about my prayer again. Nothing. I feel no saving presence. It's as if God can come to me only through images I've cast off. In the back of my mind I've always pictured God as a stern but loving judge with the face of an Israelite. When I reject this image, I cannot find Him. It feels as though God has abandoned me.

"Feeling abandoned, I then begin to doubt. Did he make us out of nothing, as my tradition teaches, or out of Himself, as yours teaches? Is my innermost nature dark and sinful, as my tradition teaches, or is it divine, as yours teaches? Is God a Father, as my tradition teaches, or is God a Mother too, as yours teaches? Should I forbid my converts to worship God through an image, as my tradition teaches, or should I encourage them to make contact with God any way they can, as yours teaches? Is the Buddhist saint Bala Ma who rejected all teachings about God saved, as Buddhism teaches, or is she damned, as my tradition says? Is the Torah the final word of God, or is the Veda, or is there no such thing as a final word? Is the way we seem to meet God in our hearts a true revelation of Him, or is it a mere sensation, no more true than a beautiful piece of music? Is God really concerned about us? Has he numbered the hairs on our heads, as Jesus taught? Or is He remote, and does He take no notice of our littleness? Is his Fatherhood the ultimate fact of the universe? Or is it a comforting fiction?

"Questions like these roar through my mind like a great fire. And there are no final answers. Here I am only a few days away from dying, and with no answers! What a cruel fate!"

Now he began to speak with great anguish. "At least the world will be spared my hypocrisy! At least I won't be tempted to go back to my flock and tell them something is true when I'm not so sure. Oh, Adi, if you only knew what notions come to my mind! Terrible, vengeful thoughts! Arguments, imaginary arguments drum through my head! I destroy my detractors in debate and delight in their humiliation! Where is the love my Master taught me? What's happening to me?"

"Quieter, dear Thomas. The guard."

"At other times I find myself thinking about some minor problem. A few days before I was arrested, one of my converts, a woman, knocked over a flask of wine at a eucharistic supper—but instead—instead of kindly overlooking this, as I did when it happened, I took my resentment home with me and found myself despising her just because she was clumsy and thoughtless—oh, God, what rage I feel sometimes! Of course, I don't really despise her. But then there are these thoughts of you. Yes, you, dearest and fairest and purest of friends. It's shameful, this demon that rants inside me. And I've been so lonely. So lonely shut up here. You can't imagine!"

Thomas vigorously rubbed a broken statuette his hand had fallen on. "Thomas, we all have our demons," said Adimanti. "You are not evil because you think these things. Do you *will* them? Do you *act* on them? That is what God cares about. You do not! You are pure and loving!"

"No, Adi." He shook his head. "I'm no longer the sannyasin on the Vaigai. I'm not worthy to be your guru. Not worthy!"

"You—you must pray, my dear. Can you pray? Can you quiet this demon?"

"I can. And I do. But it keeps coming back. Sometimes I'm not vigilant. Can one be vigilant all the time? Can one be vigilant *all the time?*"

"You frighten me," said Adimanti. "I have always depended on you for strength. You are stronger than I. Do not waver now."

"No, Adi, I'm not stronger than you. Do you see—do you see how my hands reach out to you—and touch you?"

Shaking slightly, he gently picked Adimanti's hands off her lap and held them, one in each hand. They were warm, soft, and gave his hands a little squeeze.

"Thomas, think of your death," she said. "Now of all times you should be free of passion. For the good of your soul, come to your senses."

Through her hands he felt her whole body beginning to shiver. He released them and said, "Forgive me."

She got up, picked up the lantern, faced about, and said in a voice shaking with emotion, "Dear man, I will talk to the King. I will go to him tonight. I will find out where he is if I have to bribe my way in. Once again he will hear the truth from me. Guard!"

The night guard opened the door and escorted the Queen out. The door shut behind her, and Thomas was left alone with his featureless, all-seeing, uncommunicative God, the Only God There Is. He felt like a colorless old rag after the washerman has beaten it against a rock.

51. Devandi's Cross

In spite of the King's warning to stay away from toddy, Kumaran was out late drinking with his fellow poets on the night after his meeting with the King. When he got home, he found Devandi and the children—his daughter and new baby boy—asleep. He climbed onto the sleeping mat with them, pulled up the covers, and reached over the baby and under the cover for Devandi's ripe, swollen breast. His hand slid over and around it, caressed it, tingled to its shapely softness, passed over to the other one. He felt safe and serene in the midst of so much innocence. He forgot about Thomas and the scheduled execution.

Devandi began to stir, to groan. His hand touched her nipple, lingered there, slowly crept across—my God! What was that? His fingers felt a cross between her breasts.

He shot out of bed and went to his work room. He sat on his cushion, looked up and out into the clear moonlit night through the window over the desk, and tried to think. No, of course he hadn't intended for it to come to this! He only wanted Thomas out of Puhar, exiled. It was Charishnu who wanted him killed, Charishnu and the King. No one had consulted him about what to do with Thomas. He had only brought the charge. He had only told the truth. He had only reported what he saw. And it made sense to assume Thomas and the Queen had made love on the beach. They had not, but all he had said was that it was reasonable to *assume* they had. Or had he said more? He could not quite remember. Besides, perhaps they had anyway, at some other time, at some other place. Would Thomas tell him if they had? He lied once before! Besides, he really was a menace. A menace to the Empire. Look what he had done to Devandi. And how many other husbands of Puhar found crosses—surely he was not the only one this night to find that snake crawling between his wife's breasts! And no grand snake like the cobra, but a vile, stinking little one like the krait, whose only distinction is that it can kill you before you take seven steps.

Once before he rid an empire of a menace, and now again—so what was there to fear? On balance his karma would be good. Were not his intentions noble? Did he have anything to gain by Thomas' death? Did he wish him ill? True, he resented him for what he had done to Devandi. But did he *wish him ill?* No, he wished only that Thomas would leave them alone. "*I* didn't sentence him to death!" Kumaran said in a raspy whisper. "No pulaiyar birth for me next time! Two empires are better off because I dared to kill— No. What am I saying? *I'm* not killing Thomas!"

All that night words like these jabbed like cold lightning at Kumaran's brain. He did not sleep at all. At one point he thought he would confess all to the King. But the wheels were already turning. It was too late. At best he would only add his own death to Thomas'. Besides, he had the world before him now. He was not merely a favored poet, he was the confidant of the King. Only a fool, a fool like Thomas, would throw that away! "Think of what I'll do for my family, my distant heirs, even my dead ancestors who will look on all this with approval. I have a responsibility to stay alive!" he told himself.

Shortly before first light he was still sitting on his cushion. Swans must have already been crying out, but he didn't hear them. He heard instead the voice of his mother as it sounded shortly before her death, when he couldn't have been more than eight: "The wound that is made by fire, my little son, will heal, but the wound that is made by tongue will never heal."

He felt as if he would suffocate if he spent another moment in the room. He climbed a ladder up to the roof and let his eyes range over the sky, which was just starting to get light in the east. He noticed a large open-mouthed cistern with perpendicular sides for catching rain water. By moonlight—for the moon was still well above the horizon—he watched a dewdrop on the side of the cistern. He watched it as it trickled down. It didn't move slowly and steadily, like a snail. It didn't stop, then dart forward, like a lizard. It seemed to have no destination, but was carried downward, inch by inch, by its own wobbly momentum.

52. Adimanti's Letter

The moon was high, and it bathed Thomas in its silvery light as he lay below the window ledge and stared up. It occurred to him the moon was like God. God at that moment was bathing him in beams of divine love. An unaccustomed peace fell over him, and for a few minutes he again felt like the sannyasin living without possessions on the sandy cove of a great river. Once before, in Madurai on the banks of the Vaigai, he had felt a Love-Behind-Things at the heart of the universe beaming over the earth and bathing it in its light; and now he felt it again. Yet it was different, for it excluded nothing.

How strange this new feeling. He had joined the ranks of ordinary men, he felt a kind of oneness with them, and he felt loved by God no more than they were. He realized how immense God's love was, how wrong he had been to limit it. He forgot about the threat of execution, his flock, even Adimanti. By now the moon had passed over the edge of the roof, and it was pitch dark in the prison. But inside his soul a thin, unflickering flame glowed.

The lifting of the bolt jarred him. He looked up to see the night guard—not Mahadeva—carrying a torch and winding his way through the clutter of the prison.

"From Her Majesty, the Queen," the guard said. He handed Thomas a small packet of palm leaves wrapped in a red silk handkerchief and propped the torch on the floor.

"The Queen?" The world of *maya* swept him up again in its embrace. "Was she—the Queen—just now here?"

"Yes, she brought it herself. She put it right here!" said the man, who stared down at his hand in disbelief.

A voice inside Thomas said, Call her back! and a feeling of almost giddy delight swept over him. She was nearby. She had touched what he now touched. He wanted to linger with these feelings, to let himself feel his love for her, but the desperateness of his situation swam again into view. He took the torch to see by, dismissed the guard, and unraveled the letter.

He recognized at once the Queen's hand. Ever considerate, she had written the letter in a large, bold script for his dimming eyesight. He held the letter at arm's length next to the torch and began to read:

Thomas, it is early in the morning of the second day after my visit to you. Yesterday I went about my duties in a daze. I did not know whether I ever wanted to see you again. Last night I slept very little, and today my thoughts are as cloudy as before. But my heart beats out its message with a force that I cannot deny.

I love you, Thomas. I love you, my tall, pale, anxious, orphaned, split-down-the-middle, doubting, great-souled teacher. Do you not see that God is pleased with you, that He loves you—even as I do? I love you, and I am frightened.

Do you remember the night we lay on the beach during the last Indra's Festival and how I took off my mask under the moonlight? Do you remember what you said? "You see everything so clearly, you know exactly why you do what you do, you always see what is central and act on that. Everyone wears a mask but you!" Then you contrasted me to yourself. Do you remember what you said about yourself? "I've never done anything or believed anything for only one reason."

First I must tell you that I am not as clear-sighted and strong as you make me out. I am a weak woman who wants most of all to be loved—by God, by my husband (yes, even him), by my people, by my nephews and nieces and little Puttu, and by you. I do not always see what is central, and when I do, I do not unerringly act on it. Even now I feel something approaching dread, for I do not know what I am doing or why I am doing it. I have all day to write this letter, and may Shiva lead me! I do not know what I will end by saying. I almost feel it is beyond my control. Something larger than I, some Great Hand, propels me forward, perhaps to my destruction. I have come under its shadow; its knuckles I see as the humps of mountains. It approaches, and I shudder. But I continue writing.

Over and over I have heard your cries in your dark prison, and I must come now to your defense before the Great Hand closes around me. I see nothing wrong with you the way you are, my Thomas. Let me tell you about my father.

When I was little and he was still a very young man, I would squat for hours and watch him divert water into channels that he dug with his hoe across the terraced rice paddy. A maze of zigzagging lines was the result. There was no apparent order, and for years I accepted his hoeing as a meaningless but necessary ritual of the soil. I was surprised when I discovered one day that all the twisting and detouring around rocks and the piling up mud to make levees and dams had something to do with making the rice grow. You, Thomas, are like my clever father. Unlike my other gurus who irrigated the rich bottom land of settled truths in orderly straight channels, you farm the terraces. For you, truth zigzags. You cultivate your faith the same way my father cultivated his rice.

At that instant a bat flitted by his ear and startled him. He looked up into the dark, but couldn't find the intruder. Now the bat was still. It must have perched. "Truth zigzags." He thought about those words, then thought of the bat's jagged, zigzag flight. He was like the bat, he thought. Truth didn't zigzag. Truth was upright and straight. It was his blindness that made it zigzag, that was all. "Blind as a bat," people said. Yes, he was like the bat, all right. He brought his eyes back toward the light, again leveled his eyes at the letter.

It is not a devil inside you that makes you doubt. You are most true, most beautiful, most lovable *when you doubt*. Could I love a devil? Tell me, Teacher, could I love a devil? You cannot help doubting any more than I can help loving. You can bury the doubt, but it is always there; it will only disappear for a while. You are not weak when you doubt, but strong for facing your doubt. And does the doubt, as you say, really weaken your faith? Best of gurus, how strange that you should see it this way! In the last few months I have heard you wonder if your race was chosen, if the world's end was really approaching, and so forth.

But I have never heard you doubt your Master's gospel of love and forgiveness. You doubt a few doctrines, but you trust absolutely in God's command. And you live by the trust. What else is important?

And why do you worry yourself over your flock? Let them believe in rebirth if they must, let them worship Indra with their kinsfolk on the night of the Festival, let them think of Jesus as a black-skinned avatar like Krishna, let them worship Puhar's Guardian Deity, the Buta, alongside God the Father. Let them even worship you, Thomas! That is our way! Here we worship God *and* Guru. And why not? You are a tiny particle of God's infinite Spirit, a spark shot out from the divine Fire. God dives into matter and we are the result of that dive. How close He is to us! And you doubt his love for you. Just as soon doubt his love for Himself!

A large moth fluttered back and forth in front of the lantern and blocked out the light. Thomas swatted the moth hard, and it disappeared. Again he looked up and stared into the dark, then back down. He reread the words, "A spark shot out from the divine fire." Powerful, powerful words! he told himself. But he was a stupid, weak mortal. And God was God. He did not feel like a spark. But there were times . . . during prayer . . . when it almost seemed . . . times when he, the missionary Thomas, almost melted away . . . but he could never describe that feeling, never describe to himself what it meant. He rubbed his eyes and looked back down at the letter.

You have not failed, Teacher. Look at what you have given your flock that only you could give. "Love your enemies," you tell the man who hates. "Love the pulaiyar," you tell the twice-born. "Love the mleccha, the yavana, the outcast," you tell the pulaiyar. You needle them. You get under their skin. You prick their consciences. You make them feel that God expects great things of them, and they end by expecting great things of themselves! They are ennobled, uplifted, divinized. Sometimes you even make Christians of them. But mostly you just make them better devotees of the God they already worship.

Sometimes I try to imagine what it must have been like living in that faraway town of Nazareth that you come from. What was it like being a little child called "Judas the Bastard"? Did you accept the name as matter-of-factly as I now accept the title of "Adimanti the Queen?" Or

340

did tears gather in your shiny black eyes ten times a day? And what was it like to have a mother who was a prostitute and no father at all? Sometimes I think I see something in you, the great yavana saint from the West, that reminds me of little Judas the Bastard. Judas Thomas, you are your Master's twin! Do not forget that!

I must tell you now that I am frightened. Yesterday I saw the King, and he told me that you must be executed. "When the monsoons are over, Thomas will go into the fire," he said. But already there hasn't been any rain for a week.

I brought him into my anger chamber and shouted at him. I threatened to kill myself if he killed you. But I could not change his mind.

I have just climbed to the roof of the palace and looked at the eastern horizon. All I see is a vast plain of vivid blue stretching far over the Eastern Ocean. No hint of a cloud, of rain, of the only thing that I have any real confidence in. After twenty years I know my husband well. Seldom does he change his mind once he has set a course. I feel I must tell you this so that you can prepare. In the past I have known him to kill men he knew were innocent rather than countermand an order. You must not think him vicious or brutal. He has been taught that vacillation will bring down an empire faster than an unjustly harsh sentence. At my request he has made exceptions, though, and I will see him again shortly. But prepare to meet your God.

I am back after several hours. I ate a little lunch. I am confused and desolate and feel sick to my stomach, and my brain is boiling. I prayed in front of my Shiva lingam, but the Great Hand kept coming toward me. I should not be writing this. Forgive me, my love!

I do not know how to tell you this last thing. I do not know how to tell myself. I am following no principle that I have ever been taught. I am violating the only one I know which applies. I am appalled but tingle as I write these words: Thomas, best of men, if you wish it, I will give you all that I am—soul, mind, and body. I would like to believe that I am powerless to resist my destiny, that I am the victim of some ancient irresistible karma that never until now has been able to come to fruition. But I know better. I offer myself not as one who is pure of heart but in my sin. Perhaps I will repent the deed after it is done.

I will not deliver this letter in person. I will give it to the guard. I want you to think quietly and dispassionately. I do not want to play the temptress. I will not place myself between you and your God, especially at this momentous hour. But if, after careful thought, *you* choose, choose coolly and deliberately, to place me there, then I will come. And if I do, know that my heart will belong to you, dear Thomas, for as long as you breathe, and that we will be bound in some way for however many more lives are required of us until we go back to God. Even if you should choose rebirth in a strange yavana country, I would follow you there as your pale-faced sister or daughter.

How round the moon is as it sits on the eastern horizon at sunset! It is like this at sunset of the Indra Festival. I am thinking of the way we lay beside each other, dutiful and chaste, on the beach. Do you remember, dearest? Duty and chastity, our twin manacles: If only once the good God would let us be free! Just for a moment!

I will send my messenger to see you tomorrow morning. Tell him your wish.

You will read these leaves with the aid of a torch that I will bring you. Burn them with the same torch. Burn them to protect us both, and to protect the Empire. If you know in your heart that you will not see me, burn them as a holy sacrifice on the altar of your God. Or rather, not your God, but our God.

Be at peace, Thomas. Above all, be at peace.

Tears of joy streamed down his face as he wrapped the sheaves of the letter in their red silk handkerchief and put the letter aside. Oh, to be loved! To inspire a love so powerful that a destiny was no match against it! He sat and let the tears stream down his face. And he said, "Beloved, O my beloved. My beloved Adimanti." Over and over he said her name as he surrendered to the ecstasy of human love.

But what would he do? The thought of what lay before him thrilled but troubled him. He began to grasp the nature of the terrible choice. Human love or divine love? Or were they somehow compatible? One thing he knew with certainty: He would see Adimanti; it was unbearable to think he might not. He would not see her on her terms though, but on his. He knew he would have to be strong when she came. He would face death with doubt on his soul, not adultery. And he would lead his precious disciple out from underneath the shadow of the Great Hand. And above all he would thank her, thank her for her great, unselfish gift.

But he would not be unprepared: He would see her, but not without wearing a special armor. As he fed one leaf after another to the flame, he began to construct his inner barricade. "How silly!" he thought to himself. "How can I not resist her? I am as good as dead. A few days remaining. How absurd even to think of it. This old bag, this old body of mine, would I give it the final say?"

He told himself he was a sinner, not a madman. But he would have to be prepared. He would pretend that she was Bala Ma. In place of her youth and beauty he would see Bala Ma—her flabby wrinkled skin, her lifeless sagging jowls, her runny nose, the spit that gathered and hardened at the corners of her swollen lips as she lectured him on Buddhist doctrine back in Muziri: That is what he would see. That is all Adimanti really was anyway—just give her thirty more years. What Adimanti really was, was what Bala Ma obviously was. No more attractive. No more desirable. He would not chase a long-necked illusion. He would look at the Queen's face and see Bala Ma.

He would be like a mole digging a tunnel. The light of brilliant day might be only a flake of dirt above him, but he would not lift his snout upward. Scraping and scrabbling, he would dig his tunnel. His destination lay in soil, and his dim eyes would find nothing more to their liking than the soil they saw along the way.

"Bala Ma," he called out silently into the night. The old woman seemed to materialize in front of him like an old gunnysack. Inside the sack lay the decaying body of the Queen. He could tell it was her by the pale purple amethyst still lodged in her nose.

53. In the King's Trophy Room

Kumaran had asked for a private audience. He had never before presumed upon the King's time in such a way, and he had certainly never put himself out for a man he hated. But the demons—or were they gods?—hounded him and wouldn't let him sleep. Exhausted and almost in a panic he fled to the King.

They met in a different room of the palace, one closer to the ground and enclosed by netting. It was the legendary "trophy room" that Kumaran had heard about since he was a boy but had never seen. Stuffed heads of enemy chiefs and generals stuck out of the walls as if they were tigers or antelopes. Their wrinkled skin was the color of dead leaves.

"In the happiness of his subjects lies a king's happiness; in the welfare of his subjects, his welfare," the King said from his seat on the head of a tiger pelt laid across the floor.

For an instant Kumaran was confused. He had just been shown in, and there had not even been a proper greeting. But he recognized the King's words. They were taken from the *Arthashastra,* the manual of statecraft and warfare. Kumaran was in no hurry; he would wait for his opportunity. "No one will dispute that, Sire," he said, declining the use of the more obsequious "Your Majesty" as he took his seat at the other end of the pelt.

"The Queen must not be stained in the public mind, Kumaran," said the King. "We must find some other pretext for destroying the prisoner. The charge might leak. Adultery is unacceptable."

Kumaran tried to assess the King's mood. Was the great Chola Tiger asking for advice once again from the son of a humble pulaiyar sculptor? Or was he using the imperial "we" and merely thinking out loud?

The King, dressed in a simple cinnamon-colored cotton tunic more befitting a commoner than a king, looked hard at Kumaran, who wore blue silk. Seeing the King had no wreath, Kumaran removed his own. Then he came to the point. "Sire, would it be possible to commute the sentence? Send him into exile? He has followers up the coast in Mayilapur. Or he could be put on a boat at night and sent back to the yavana lands."

"This would show weakness," said the King. "Either he is guilty and deserves death, or he is innocent and deserves to go free. We don't know he is innocent." At this point Karikal's expression became dour. "We have been over this before, Kumaran. My policy is to be decisive and to give the clearest possible warning"— he brought his hand down like a cleaver—" to all potential malefactors. As a youth I vacillated when I was not sure. I practiced mercy. I commuted sentences or even overturned them. This was weakness, and my enemies took advantage of it."

"I understand," said Kumaran. "But no one knows about Thomas. Not even his followers have been able to find him. So you wouldn't have anything to fear from your enemies by practicing mercy."

"If I must practice mercy in this case," said the King, "then I will refrain from torturing the prisoner before executing him."

So far the King had not grown irascible, so Kumaran pressed on. "Sire, would it be possible to overlook the whole thing? To forgive him?"

"Forgive him!?" The King looked at his poet with an expression close to mirth. Then his face hardened, and he looked around the room with his right arm extended. "Kumaran, around us are gathered my enemies. I forgive them all! It is wise to forgive one's enemies, but only after they have been executed!"

This was a logic that Kumaran's artful mind had never danced to before. He was not even sure whether the King was serious or joking. In any event, his strategy hadn't worked. He looked up, and his eyes fell on the head of one of the generals. It seemed to leer at him. He was confused, and all he could think of to say was, "Will you mount Thomas' head with those?"

The King roared with laughter. "These men took lives! They're *worthy* of immortality!"

"Thomas took the Queen," Kumaran replied before he could think what he was saying.

The King fell silent and glowered at his poet. He stood up and placed his arms akimbo, as if weighing whether he should cut Kumaran's head off with a single swipe of his sword. Then just as promptly he sat down again. His face softened, and he began talking about intimate subjects. He talked of the women he had loved and asked Kumaran to do likewise. He talked about the Battle of Venni and in particular the strategy he had so brilliantly devised to turn the battle in his favor. He talked about the attempts on his life. At one point he joked, "You're not a spy, Kumaran, are you?" It was hard for Kumaran to believe what was happening. His mood had changed from momentary terror to giddy amazement. He almost slipped and called the King "Karikal," the name that inspired terror and awe in all who heard it, but now inspired in Kumaran a tender affection. Again the King came back to the topic of protecting Queen Adimanti—and the empire—at all costs.

It was Kumaran who supplied the pretext, just as he had supplied everything else. Generalizing from his own experience with Devandi, he explained how Thomas set father against son and husband against wife with his pestilential doctrines, and thus stirred up discontent in the Empire. It was a lame argument—none knew it better than the King himself, who had watched his own Queen go from one guru to another over the course of twenty years, thereby enfranchising all views.

"But all these were Tamil," Kumaran said, "whilst Thomas' religion is barbarian. He denies rebirth and the law of karma, the twin basis of all true religion." That was the best Kumaran could do, and the King could do no better. Thus it was agreed: Thomas was to be executed for sedition.

As Kumaran walked across the dark palace grounds to his apartment, he didn't feel hatred for Thomas; he even felt the urge to visit him one last time. Thomas' dream had always been to die a martyr for his faith, and that is exactly what he would be doing if he were executed for "sedition." "No, Thomas, it's not for adultery you are being executed; it's for stirring up trouble with your teachings. Just like your Jesus." That is what Kumaran could have told Thomas. It might have greatly consoled the prisoner. But Kumaran did not turn his steps toward the prison. He could not have said why at the time; all he knew was that the idea of a visit seemed suddenly very disagreeable.

As he neared his apartment, he remembered with a start that his original intention had been to save Thomas' life. Instead he succeeded only in giving the King a pretext for carrying out the execution. He even reminded Karikal that Thomas had "taken the Queen" and might deserve to be hung as a trophy. How could he have said this? Such a charge only served to condemn Thomas, and his sole purpose in seeing the King had been to save him! He was suddenly appalled by what he had said. He tried to reconstruct the conversation as it unfolded. He remembered that the King had given a reason for declining to hang Thomas' head in the trophy room and that he had responded by—and in the process he had—and the charge wasn't even—

He couldn't bear to look into it further. He told himself he was exhausted and had done his best. He had asked the King to spare Thomas' life. The King had refused, and that was that.

It didn't occur to him that he could go to the King at any time and confess he had framed Thomas. Somewhere in his mind he knew this was so, but the lie he had told Charishnu seemed almost true. Like an unnoticed insect, it crawled invisibly back and forth across the dark duff of his brain, excreting as it went, until all was sickness and death.

54. Adimanti's Second Visit

S he wore a white muslin dress studded with emeralds and lapis lazuli, and her hair, decorated on top with several small clusters of sweet-smelling jasmines, hung down loosely and unbraided to the waist. She carried a bundle of neatly folded purple silk cloth. Four servants followed, two carrying various foods, a third several bowls and a pitcher of water, and the fourth two lanterns.

Thomas and the Queen greeted each other with a silent, almost furtive glance as the servants quickly set out their articles according to her instructions. She gave her first maidservant some final advice, and the servants left. Then she told the night guard to lock the door, wait downstairs, and let no one up.

She turned to Thomas and said with reverence, "My Lord."

"My Queen," he said respectfully, almost formally, as he bowed slightly at the waist.

"You called, and I came," she said. Her expression was impossible to decipher; there was certainly nothing coquettish or seductive about it, but neither was it unfeeling.

"Did you burn the letter?" she said.

"I did."

"I have brought you refreshment." For the first time her face hinted at a smile.

But it wasn't the food he noticed; it was the flowers in her hair and the perfume he smelled even over the food. He put up his defense. "Bala Ma, Bala Ma," he whispered to himself.

"What is it, my Lord? You are—distant," she said. "I will go at once!" She took a step toward the door.

"No," said Thomas. "I'm glad you came. Sit down. Forgive me."

As the Queen sat down on the marble bench and arranged her dress, Thomas saw her left eyebrow quiver. This show of vulnerability had the effect of unnerving him, of throwing his defenses into disarray. The one thing he had not planned on was hurting her. He had been too exclusively concerned about her effect on him to think about his effect on her. Now he realized he had miscalculated. He might protect himself by treating her as Bala Ma, but what cruelty might he impose on her in the process? He grasped the situation completely and saw clearly what he would do: He would think of her as Bala Ma, but he would take great pains not to show it. He would be warm and fully present to her.

"No, Adi, I am not distant," he said with a gentle, soulful smile. "I am your friend."

She studied his face uncertainly for an instant, then smiled back. Seemingly reassured, she poured water into one of the bowls, added oils, and held the bowl out to him. As he sat down on the purple table cloth spread over the cleared space on the floor, she said, "Wash, my Lord."

As light from the oil lamps glimmered against his pale face, he bent over, washed his face and hands, then dried himself with the towel that Adimanti handed him.

"And now, my Lord," she said, "stretch out your foot."

"You need not do that," he said.

"Stretch out your foot, my Lord!" she commanded, getting down off the bench and seating herself on the cloth.

He stretched it out, and the first touch of her gently massaging fingers made him tingle and inadvertently jerk his foot away.

"What is it?" she said.

"It—tickles."

As she looked back down at his foot, which he had stretched back out, she smiled broadly. Silently he intoned, "Bala Ma, Bala Ma."

Taking care to wash between his toes with her supple fingers, she had brought him to a state of semi-intoxication by the time she washed and dried the first foot. "Now the other," she said.

He held out the other and again surrendered himself to the lovely sensation of Adimanti's touch. "Bala Ma" whirred through his mind as if part of a dream.

"Did women ever wash Jesus' feet, my Lord?" she said.

"Jesus?!"

"You jumped, my Lord!"

He fingered the new cross hanging from around his neck.

"My Lord?" she asked.

"Yes, they did. Once a woman even washed his feet with her tears—and her hair."

"Her hair?"

"They revered him."

For a moment she thought quietly, then said, looking solemnly at him, "No, my dear, they loved him." She squeezed out the rag, then added, "Did your wife wash your feet?"

"She prepared the water, but didn't actually wash. Oh, I don't know. Perhaps once. I don't remember." He paused. "Jesus once washed my feet."

"He did?" She looked up at him in surprise.

"On the day before he died he washed all our feet. Ah, that feels good."

"What a strange thing for a man to do." Looking up at Thomas with a suggestion of playfulness in her expression, she then said, "Was he as strange a man as you, my Lord?"

By now Thomas could hardly think. He had let himself surrender to the wonderful sensation of Adimanti's touch and felt almost drugged. Yet he felt safe. "Ah, what was that?" he said.

She laughed, looked up at him with a smile that would have bewitched any other man, then dried the second foot. She set the towel down and said, "Now it is time to eat, my Lord."

As she lay out the bamboo mat in front of him, Thomas remembered his approaching death. What was this game he was playing? Why didn't he put an end to it at once? Yet his conduct had been exemplary, and his resolution intact. He was aware that she might be operating under a false expectation, but she would know the truth soon enough. And in the meantime she was so happy; he would let her enjoy herself a little longer. Then he would tell her, ever so gently tell her.

In the meantime he asked about his flock. Why hadn't anyone come to see him? Hadn't she told anyone where he was? And Puttu's mother—hadn't she spread the word?

"It was the first thing I thought of, my dear, when the King told me what had happened to you. He warned me, and he was adamant. If the people found out, he would be forced to move you again, he said, and this time it would be to a dungeon, a real jail. With a threat like that he did not have to swear me to secrecy. As for Puttu and his mother, I had to swear them to the strictest secrecy. It was a risk I took. I may regret it. But I trust them."

A feeling of desolation came over him as he thought of never seeing his Christian brothers and sisters again. There would be no one to commission, no one to instruct, no one to pray with, no one to share the Lord's Supper with, no one to confess his sins to, no one to take leave of.

Not even Adimanti could entirely remove the sadness from his heart. As she set their places and served the food, he thought of the pulaiyar scrivener Mochikiranar, one of the two bishops he had ordained in Puhar, and tried to imagine him preaching up and down the coast, healing the sick, ordaining future bishops, building new churches, and doing all the things that a bishop's office demanded. A kind of panic seized him as he admitted to himself that Mochikiranar's talents fell short of his enthusiasm. Suddenly he wanted desperately to go on living. "Have you seen the King again?" he said.

Adimanti's face became somber. She did not look up or answer, except to shake her head.

"Keep trying to see the King," he said gravely. "Keep trying to see the King." He forgot about Bala Ma. All he could think about was death striding toward him with a gait swift and heavy.

He found himself seated in front of his meal, laid out on a banana leaf. There was his favorite Tamil food, *koyakattai*, made of rice and green coconut; also *paisam*, made of rice cooked in creamy milk and sugar; and slices of palmyra and mango. But he took little joy at the prospect of eating it.

"Here is your food, my Lord! May you be pleased to eat!" she said in a voice so musical and emphatic that it seemed to him to be part of an ancient brahmanic ritual. Ritual? Then he remembered the daring thing she had said many months ago. He looked at the food: there was the banana leaf, there the simple food; she had just washed his feet; she had recited the formula; she had called him "my Lord" from the moment she set foot in the prison. He realized this was no ancient brahmanic ritual; it was *their* ritual.

"A little water in the hollow of your hand, my Lord," she said. "Now a few sprinkles on the leaf."

"But a sannyasin never eats after dark," he said.

"Sannyasin? You are still a sannyasin? No more talking, my Lord."

There was now a sweetly feminine quality about Adimanti's voice. He again called up his defenses, and instead of Adimanti's lovely smile he again saw Bala Ma's sagging jowls, spittle at the corner of her lips, and oozing eyes. "Bala Ma," he repeated. Then he realized he could not, must not, wait any longer; already he had waited too long. "Tell her!" he told himself.

"Now, a little dab on the side—for your ancestors. What are their names?"

So intent was he on Bala Ma that he inadvertently said her name. "Bala M—" he said, then halted.

"Balam? You have an ancestor named Balam?" said the Queen with pleasure. "How like a Sanskrit name! Well then, my Lord, in that case, to Balam!"

By now she had spooned out with her fingers the remaining *koyakattai* onto the leaf.

"Adi, you are thinking of—"

"No talking during the meal! Now, there is your food, my Lord. May you be pleased to eat!"

"Dearest Adimanti—"

"No, my Lord, the wife of a raja does not talk to him while he eats. She does not even watch him eat." Adimanti had in fact turned her face away from him. "My greatest pleasure is to serve you, my Lord," she continued, "to wait on you. For this one night you are not a sannyasin. And I am not the King's wife."

"Adimanti, I *am* a sannyas—"

"Eat, my Lord!"

"Adi!" His voice was so emphatic and strangely tragic that she could not resist looking at him. "Adi, I *am* a sannyasin! Do you understand what I am saying?"

Holding her delicate but now sticky hands out from her body, she stared at him through stricken eyes.

"I didn't want to hurt you," he said. "You were enjoying the game so—"

"Oh, Shiva!" she cried. She buried her face in her starchy, oily hands.

Not daring to touch her, Thomas said: "Adi, I don't know how to explain it. I read your letter—so full of love, the purest love. And so honest. 'Sinner to sinner,' you said. Adi, how can I ask you to sin for me? How can I ask you to give up the bliss that you think is waiting for you after this life, this short life, for—for a petty selfish act? You say you would be willing to follow me even to a yavana country. How can I ask you to do that? I am not your God!"

"You could *become* my God!" she said with great force as she looked up at him, her beautiful face disfigured by the *koyakattai* sticking to it.

"But that isn't right!"

"It *is* right! It's our way! 'She should be beautiful and gentle, considering her husband as her God,' says Uma in the *Mahabharata!*"

"But that's—"

"It is another way to make the rice grow, Thomas!" She was fiery.

"But you would be sacrificing your eternal destiny—for *me.*"

"Not my eternal destiny! Just a few lives until we grew tired, together, of life on earth!"

"But don't you—don't you love Shiva more than me?" he stammered.

She seemed to subdue her passion at the mention of Shiva. "I love you *in* Shiva," she said quietly, looking across at him with smoldering round eyes.

Flustered, not knowing what to do, he picked up a towel, wet it, and started to wash her face.But she pulled back at the first touch of the towel and hissed, "Don't touch me!" Then she took the towel and washed first her hands, then her face. The washing seemed to sober her further, and when she looked back up she was once again master of herself.

"Forgive me, dear teacher," she said, her dignity again in place even while she dabbed at her eyes. "It has been a terrible night. First you are about to be taken from me, taken from me forever, and then—oh, it was so horrible!" Now she became almost distraught. "He received me with a woman in his bed! A woman! She was young, beautiful, haughty! How could this happen? How? I did not care about the infidelity, but to flaunt it in front of me! I had not guessed how much he hated me. Oh, how he must hate me! And after all we have been through. It is unthinkable. It sickens me. I can hardly believe it happened!" She began to sob, then got control of herself. "Do you know what I told him?"

Thomas waited for her to continue, but she looked shyly away. His eyes fell on the nipples of her breasts faintly outlined under the thin white muslin of her dress, but he made himself look quickly away, then back at her eyes. Her face underneath her eyes was smeared with kohl, and she dabbed at it with a napkin

She gathered her courage, looked up at him, and said: "He asked me outright, 'Did you sleep with Thomas?' I have been waiting for him to ask me that question for the last four days. A hundred times I imagined how I would look him in the eye and win him to the truth with my sincerity. And now what could I say? What could I say, my Lord? I had just received your message! I knew what I wanted to do! What could I say?"

"What *did* you say?"

"I told him no. I lied. I have not lied since I was a little girl!"

"But you *hadn't* . . . you hadn't . . ."

"But I had in my heart. *I had in my heart. I had received your message, dearest!*"

She reached into a pocket of her dress and pulled out a small yellow wad of balled-up string with tiny gold ornaments attached. "My *tali*," she said with an emotion so overwhelming, yet so controlled, that she seemed to shudder, like a volcano on the brink of eruption. "My marriage cord! This is the first time I have taken it off in all the years of my marriage—over twenty years. I cut it off before I came here."

Thomas understood what this meant. As he watched new tears spring up in her eyes and cascade down her cheeks, he grieved for her. Shaking his head, he could only think to say, say with a hushed awe usually reserved for God alone, say with his eyes cast down in a voice barely audible: "Adimanti, I have sinned terribly, terribly against you. Forgive me." He looked at her and said with sudden passion: "Forgive me, dearest soul, forgive me!"

"No, no! No, my love!" she replied at once with great resolution, pushing aside her tears with her fingers and again smearing kohl over her cheeks. "You misunderstand me. I am *proud* of you. Your choice is the right one. I am not accusing you, not blaming you. It is just that I—tell me—where did you find the strength? I want to understand. How did you kill your passion? If you tell me, perhaps I can kill mine!" Again she was losing control of herself. "I have been such a fool!"

"No, Adi, it was my fault. I should have told you when you came through the door and saved you this—humiliation."

"It's not the humiliation I mind!" she said. "It's the *desiring* you! You had nothing to do with that, my love! Forgive me for calling you that. I've been doing it for sometime now—in my daydreams." She momentarily buried her head in the towel, seemed to blow into it as if about to explode, then looked back up at Thomas and said, "What changed your mind? Tell me."

"My dear," he said, "I already did tell you."

"What? I forgot. Tell me again."

"You said in your letter, 'Sinner to sinner'—"

"Oh, that," she interrupted. "No, dear, tell me. Tell me the *truth.*"

"But that is the truth."

"No, Thomas!" She was almost frantic, but lowered her voice again and spoke soberly, if severely: "You are the man who told me he never did anything for only one reason. I will not let you off so easily. Look into your heart. Hide nothing from me. *Why* did you change your mind?"

He knew she was right, but he had to think a minute to discover what other reasons—selfish reasons, no doubt, for they were always the hardest to dig up—there might be.

"I'm ashamed," he said after a minute. "Of course there is something else. Oh God! Your letter, Adi, it affected me in—I don't know how to say it. It was as if—as if the *letter* was what I really wanted. As if I wanted to know you would do absolutely anything for me, go even to hell with me. I needed to *know* that, Adi. I've never been loved before like that. I swear to you I think I've never been loved in my whole desolate life—before now. And now that I know—how unfair to you—it's not that I don't want to—to love you—O Adi! It's rather that I've found—or rather you've given me the strength—to do what we both know I must do. Please don't cry! You've given me—you've given me the strength to—to *resist* you. Isn't that what you wanted all along? Wanted in your deepest heart?"

"Thomas, I wanted only—for you to die in peace," she said between sobs. "I did not know what effect the—letter would have. But I learned a long time ago— to trust the truth. The truth has taken you from me, I grieve over that. But it has given you back to your God, and for that I—rejoice. And in my deepest heart I—I think I rejoice more than I grieve!"

"How Jesus would have loved you," he said almost under his breath.

"FOOLISH MAN! FOOLISH MAN!" she exploded. Her face was contorted, her hands wringing as if she wanted to strangle him. "You know NOTHING of a woman! In my own courtyard, digging a pit! They are bringing in faggots! You are to be *burned*, Thomas, BURNED! Right in front of my eyes! Always and always in front of my eyes! And you're talking now about how Jesus would love me! You fool! You God-fearing fool!" She buried her face in both hands and wept.

Her suffering melted him. "Adi, I love you. Love you with all my soul." The words escaped from his mouth before he could think of Bala Ma.

She looked up at him and said almost frantically: "You are the lucky one! I must go on living! I must wait until my loveless master dies! Then—then I must mount his pyre to be reborn with him—in paradise. *In paradise!* Did you hear that, Thomas? With him in paradise! OH SHIVA! OH THOMAS!"

"But you don't—Adi—you don't believe—"

"What does it matter what I believe?! Oh Shiva!"

"Adi, how can I comfort you? Oh, if only I could comfort you. Adi, I—I love you dearly. Adimanti." He reached out to console her, to touch her and hold her.

"NO, NO!" she cried. "I AM STRONG! Do not touch me! This will pass, you will see! Shiva will give me strength!" She began moving away from him, weaving between the clutter. The beads in her hollow anklets jingled as she walked. "Thomas, forgive me, forgive me," she mumbled as she disappeared in the shadows away from the twin lamps.

"What are you doing?" he said, alarmed, not knowing what to expect in her present state of mind.

"I am all right. Let me sit by myself, in the dark, for a minute," she said. Something fell over, but then all was quiet. She had found a space just big enough for her to sit down in; Thomas could see only a dark lump where he knew she was.

Then came a low sibilant sound that he could barely make out over the crickets outside. "Shiva, Shiva, Shiva. . . . Om Shiva, Shiva, Om Shiva. Om Shiva, Shiva, Om Shiva. Om Shiva, Shiva, Om Shiva. . . ."

Now he knew what she was doing. She had explained it all to him, bit by bit, over the last six or seven months. In the realm of spirit they understood each other perfectly; they were like seller and buyer sitting side by side silently touching each other's hands, the pressure of the fingers alone dictating the terms of the transaction. He still did not understand her heart, but he was privy to almost every impulse of her soul. He could almost read it as she prayed. He knew she was asking Shiva to come into her heart and dance his eternal dance, his eternal dance of ecstasy. He pictured Shiva holding the sacred drum and creating the heavens and earth and all the worlds with their uncountable souls. He saw the lifted hand protecting all these souls, and the fire-bearing hand destroying all the worlds when the evil age expired. He saw the foot planted on the ground and giving rest to the weary souls caught in the web of their karmas, and the lifted foot giving eternal bliss to those who adored him. None of this had he been able to dislodge from Adimanti's devout heart in all the months he had been teaching her. She was the charnel ground where Shiva with his braided locks and ashen body walked. She was a cell in that great body of his, the universe. She was his devotee purified by fire and made empty by renunciation. She was his Uma who loved him.

As he sat in the darkness waiting for her to calm herself, to give herself back to her God, something rigid and fixed inside him jarred loose.

It was as if a great bow used by titans at a contest of strength had finally been snapped, or as if all the earthenware pots used at a huge wedding feast were simultaneously smashed against the ground. He knew that he would offer himself to Adimanti, and he rested comfortably in that knowledge. He felt no more fear at the prospect than an elephant when it delicately curls its tender trunk around one of its pointed tusks. He did not forget that he was about to die, but he felt like the acacia tree, the "Mayflower tree," which adorns the world with its vibrant orange flowers only after its leaves wither and die in the scorching summer drought. Something inside him was already dead, but something else, something radically, dangerously, foolishly new—but not foolish to him—grew where that dead thing had been.

He stood up and went to her. "Adimanti." He touched her on her shoulder as she silently meditated. "Adimanti," he repeated.

She looked up and said, "Now I am better."

"Here, let me help you." He gently helped her up and guided her through the maze of furniture and sculpture back to where they were. Then he turned to her and said, as the lantern cast its light on his inexpressibly gentle gaze, "Adi, I love you."

She stared silently back at him.

"Sit down, my dear," he said.

They sat side by side, their shoulders touching. He took her hand, still sticky, and held it between both of his as if it were a treasure. Then he placed his hand gently on her breast.

"Do not do this for me," she said, guessing what had happened.

"I love you, Adi. I want to give myself to you. That is all."

"You are pitying me," she said, still averting her glance.

"No, Adi, I am not." He took his hand off her breast. "Do you know what you've taught me?" His voice grew quiet and pristinely sincere. "Adimanti, you have taught me how to love. I've never loved like this before. I wasn't capable of loving. But now I love—love because of you. When I saw you meditating, saw how great your suffering was, how noble your character—O my Adimanti, I bent back the bars of my prison and walked straight out. I wanted to comfort you, that was all. I didn't care if it broke a thousand solemn vows. I didn't care if it sent me to hell. I just wanted to comfort you, to show you that I love you. And now everything is more lovable, everything is easier to love. Everything is the same as it was before, but I am changed. All because of you, my lovely Adimanti. I am not afraid, Adi. You've given me the gift of fearlessness. I am ready to die, my love."

While he spoke, she had kept her glance averted, but now she turned to him and searched his face only inches from her own. Then she said, "Thomas, do you know the pagoda fig tree in the courtyard of the Vishnu Temple?"

He did not know the one she meant.

She continued: "Over a century ago it was invested with the triple cord—like a brahmin. If you look carefully, you will see a margosa tree growing next to it. They are husband and wife. The same marriage ceremony performed for brahmins was performed for them after they were planted side by side. Charishnu told me this."

He looked at her face so close to his and waited for her to come to the point.

"They were just two sprouts planted side by side. Today their roots are so closely entwined that they have been incorporated into each other. You have to look closely to see which tree is which. Thomas, we are like that, you and I."

"Yes, we are like that."

"My precious husband, I want to die with you!" She reached her arms up and clasped him around his neck.

"But you must go on living."

"But I don't want to!"

"You will live a long life, the inspiration of your people," he said as he held her lightly, patting her bare arm.

"We will see," she said, drawing back from him and searching his face. Then she happened to notice the food, still untouched on the banana leaf, and said with a trace of gaiety in her voice, "You did not eat your food, my Lord."

"Leave it to the ancestors," he said.

"To Balam?"

"Balam? Oh yes, to Balam."

She reached her hands up to his head and held it between her palms. Raising herself slightly, she grazed his lips with hers. Settling back, she slowly stroked his beard. Then she stopped all movement and studied his face. For a short while they looked like statuary, like lovers on a sacred temple frieze. "Thomas, I love you!" she said with an almost ferocious passion in her voice. She wrapped her arms around him and clung to him. But only for a second. Suddenly she pushed herself back and said with great force, "It is because I love you that I leave you to your God!"

He looked at her in surprise. "But I—"

"Please! Now it is time for me to ask *your* forgiveness! Now it is all so clear. I—I wanted—I needed to see—to what lengths you would go *for me*. You have given me the very greatest gift. I have seen that you are willing to sacrifice all for me. And that is enough. Oh, my dear Thomas. That should be enough for you too. We are *willing*. Let it stop there! We have seen what we needed to see. We know how completely our hearts are bound together. To go farther, to bind our bodies, too, oh, Thomas! You made a vow! And you must honor it. And I must help you honor it!"

He felt a deep and indescribably tender love for Adimanti, his shishya, his dearest friend, his beloved. He wanted to give her what she wanted on the eve of his death, and he thought he knew what she wanted. Now he was confused. If he should take what he wanted and not what she wanted—that, he knew, would be a sin. Yet his body wanted that sin, craved it. He felt an undeniable sense of disappointment.

"But I will not," she said, "hold my body back if that is what you really want. You decide, my beloved guru, friend, my husband, my Thomas, oh, so completely my Thomas. You decide."

He was staggered. He had wanted her to make the decision for him, but she would not. He sat, waited, and breathed in the delicate lilac of her perfume while looking down at the floor. For some strange reason he had the impression that the gods of India watched him and held their breath. Then his hand instinctively rose and touched the medallion hanging around his neck, and he felt the cross. He breathed a single rapid breath and clasped the medallion as if he might crush it, then looked up at her. She stared at him, and the world was still. For a few minutes neither spoke. Then he said slowly, reverently, "You have my heart, Adi, you have mastered it. Consider it severed, cut out, my gift to you. The rest I gave, I gave long ago, to God. My mind, my strength, my soul. But my love, that belongs to you. I cut it out now and give it to you, Adi. A severed heart, yours to keep."

For a few moments she looked at him as tears gathered in her eyes. Then she said, "Thomas, for a long time I have dreamed of this." Then she leaned her head over to his breast and lightly pressed against it. "I will remember you always. And unless you are liberated at the end of this life, taken away to your God forever, I will find you again in the next."

He looked down at her precious head on its long neck, but he did not reach out and hold her. He didn't dare.

"Look for me through the second-storey window on the right," she said, pulling back her head and sitting up straight. Then she spoke with great emotion. "I will be there right beside you, my love, on the funeral pyre! There will be your Adi!"

He was speechless as he watched her stand up and begin to wend her way to the door. At that instant death became real to him. He knew they would never speak to each other again. Not in this world. He felt desolate.

He heard her say as he followed her to the door, "You are Shiva's gift to me. I will remember the severed breast, the heart you tried to give me, all the days of my life. Every day, for as long as I live, I will pray under the married trees in the courtyard of the Vishnu Temple and think of you. Through you I will find my salvation." She paused, then burst out, "But even as I say this, I cannot imagine life without you! Oh, Thomas! I am in agony!" She did not speak, but shrieked the word *agony*, her hand over her heart.

She called down to the Guard and banged on the door. As he came up, she adjusted her dress and tidied her hair.

"Good-bye, and go with God," he said stupidly. Then, in plain sight of the guard, he bent down and tried to kiss her on the lips, but she averted her face. As she pulled away, his hand fell by chance on the thick ivory bracelet around her wrist. Engraved on it were scenes from the parable of the "good mleccha."

She hurried through the door with a handkerchief held over her face.

55. The Preparations

The King had put Kumaran in charge of preparing the site of execution. None of the pulaiyars who gathered the faggots and left them outside the Queen's residence knew the purpose of their work. The stonemasons who painstakingly removed and recorded the position of the tiles where the pit was to be dug were equally in the dark. The untouchable diggers had dug pits like this one before; they assumed there would be a Sati, and they wondered out loud who had died, but of course no one could tell them. The Queen's maidservants who carried in the wood piece by piece and laid it in the pit under Kumaran's direction were especially confounded. But their Queen would tell them nothing, and in fact there were hints they would not be present when whatever was to happen happened.

Most of the work had been done the day before, and Kumaran was waiting restlessly for the pruners to finish cutting back the branches hanging low over the pit.The late morning sun beat down out of a dry blue sky. The execution was scheduled for the next day but one, at sunrise.

A welter of contradictory thoughts churned through Kumaran's brain as he watched the pruners saw down the limbs. He would go one last time to visit Thomas and tell him the sentence; no, he would not go. He had lied to Charishnu; no, he had not lied. Thomas was guilty and richly deserved his fate; no, he was innocent and had been falsely incriminated. Charishnu and the King bore the blame and the guilt; no, he, the informer, bore it. Thomas was evil through and through;

no, he was a saint, one of the holiest men in the empire. Thomas was wrong to tell him that he was uncentered and failed to understand his own motivations; no, there might be something to it, he might even be possessed.

This last thought frightened Kumaran more than the others. He hated to meditate; he hated to sit still and look into his heart and see what was there. The way of the yogi was both mysterious and repugnant to him. Even prayer did not come easy, and he found it almost impossible to pray with fervor and sincerity, as other men did. For him prayer was always one part bribe and one part absentmindedness; nothing would make his mind wander faster. He tended to feel that men who prayed for a living were society's parasites, but even as he felt an aversion to such spiritual pursuits, he suspected there was something wrong with him. The inner life of his soul seemed to lie hidden behind a shroud. He wondered if a demon had displaced his soul. Once or twice, Thomas, he thought he remembered, had hinted at this. The possibility nagged at him.

But Thomas, after all, was a fool. If Thomas thought it, the opposite was probably true. Kumaran's spirits rose as he contemplated Thomas. Why, look at him! It was understandable that a man should fail to recognize an enemy, but to confuse him with a friend, an ally, to ask assistance from that very enemy—as Thomas had done when he, Kumaran, had come to visit—only Thomas was so advanced a fool as that! But no. What was he saying? Thomas was no enemy of his. What was he saying? He wished Thomas no harm!

An especially macabre thought then occurred to Kumaran: He might be supervising his own execution! Perhaps the King knew . . . knew the charge was . . . irregular . . . and wanted to punish him in a fittingly grotesque manner. Why else, after all, would the King saddle him with such a job? Why was he, a poet, doing the job of a construction foreman? But then he remembered no one was supposed to know, and putting him in charge was a way to keep the execution out of the public eye. And why would the King tear up the Queen's courtyard if a mere pulaiyar were the victim? Nevertheless he broke out into a cold sweat as he thought about fire enveloping his body. He remembered the look of utter agony on Thomas' face when his hands came into contact with the fiery bar at Kurinchi. Merely his hands! As for the Sati's pain, that was unthinkable. As much as Kumaran feared his karma, he feared the touch of flame even more. For once he found himself praying with a heart undivided: "O, Lord Murugan, protect me from the fire!"

But the prayer was short-lived. It occurred to him that he must try to sit very still and look within himself. Why couldn't he be a yogi if he put his mind to it? As the pruners dragged branches, which made noises like a waterfall, through the public portal leading out of the courtyard, he sat on the nearest bench, closed his eyes, and tried to rivet his attention inward. He became aware of his state. He became aware that his mind felt battered and dazed and numbed by contending thoughts and that it was impossible to sort out reality from unreality. He became increasingly uncomfortable as he kept his gaze fixed on the feeling of vertigo that filled and defined his heart. He tried to go deeper, to get beneath that feeling, to discover the pure self beneath all feelings that the yogis were always talking about. He was getting nowhere, he could bear it no longer, he leapt to his feet and began to pace. Suddenly a fresh new metaphor materialized in his mind. He imagined a blacksmith's hammer pounding on a calf's soft pink tongue. The metaphor perfectly expressed his state of mind. He took a palm leaf from the pouch he always carried, inscribed the metaphor on the leaf, and felt better.

56. Letter to Simon Peter

The swans in the park called to each other, and farther away
roosters crowed. Thomas made out the first shadows of the new
day as he woke from a fitful sleep. Lying on his back against
the hard marble pallet next to the outer wall under the windows, he
saw the brightest stars fading fast from the cloudless sky. He shivered
in the thick dewy air.

Soon the dawn was filled with birdsong. As he stood up and looked out,
he smelled the scent of flowers. He felt a deep nostalgia for the beauties
of earth he was about to leave. Might this not be the last day of his life?
He thought of Adimanti, the visit of two nights ago, the strange love play,
and the way she had kept him from sin. Finally his mind turned to the
prayer he had written the day before. Closing his eyes against the brightening dawn and thoughts of Adimanti, he turned his attention to God.

But like a rutting elephant his mind refused to stay tied to its post.
He repeated the prayer up to the point where he had become distracted
and again found himself uncomfortable. He would have to fix it again;
it still did not express his precise feelings; it was unworthy of him, unworthy of the True God to whom he addressed it.

Mahadeva came in with breakfast, and Thomas greeted him with
a forced cheer.

"Sire, tomorrow," Mahadeva said as he laid out the breakfast. "It's
tomorrow, at sunrise. You asked me to tell you as soon as I heard."

Thomas was struck dumb. He thought he was prepared to receive
such news, but the word "tomorrow" was like a spear through the heart.

He stared straight ahead, seeing nothing, consumed in fear and despair. As Mahadeva turned to go, he said at last in a feeble voice, "Is it by fire?"

"Yes, Sire. At sunrise. I am sorry."

As Mahadeva bowed his way out and bolted the door behind him, Thomas turned back toward the windows. The newly risen sun threw slivers of red-orange light through the tree branches into his prison. He began to shake slightly. He realized he was watching the last sunrise of his life.

He thought of Adimanti. He wanted to feel her precious head against his breast. He sat down, sat on the same purple silk they had sat on. He indulged the memory of her loving face and touch, but he only felt the despair more keenly.

"No, I mustn't!" he said aloud. He got up and started pacing along the path he had cleared through the debris of the room. He looked around for the water clock, found it, set it next to one of the lamps that Adimanti had left behind, then placed the cup on top of the water. It began drinking up the few remaining hours of his life. He sat down to eat, concentrating on the taste of the food.

He thought of Jesus on the day of his death. Did Jesus feel then as he felt now? Those disturbing words on the cross, "My God, my God, why have you forsaken me?"—Thomas had never understood them; he hated thinking about them, and tried not to. But he had heard them. They were not a dream. And now, now at last, he thought he understood. But it was unthinkable that Jesus had died with that thought in his mind—it was an aberration. It grew out of intense suffering and loneliness. Thomas and the other disciples were sure the aberration had quickly passed. But exactly what was in Jesus' mind the moment he died, the exact moment, no one knew. They could only wonder and speculate—as they did. Now Thomas wished very much that he knew. For he wanted to die with the same thought in his mind. How, then, should he die? Now he looked at death, his own death, bravely. He did not shrink away. He did not feel despair. He decided to prepare himself. He felt invigorated. His mind focused on the momentous thing that was about to happen to him. He was almost eager to prepare himself. But how?

He knew he needed to spend the last hours in undistracted prayer. But there were letters to write. First there was the long letter to Simon Peter to complete. He found leaves of the letter in a neat bundle next to him on the floor, and his mind began to work with a strange keenness. He was troubled by what they were teaching back home; he thought he knew what Jesus would teach if he were still alive, and it was not what they were teaching. Yes, he had to finish that letter. Finish it quickly.

The sun was higher now and the warmth of the day drifted through the windows. He sat sideways on the window ledge so he could see what he had written. He picked up the wad of leaves. Suddenly he got up, emptied the water clock, and set it afloat again. Then he sat back down and, as a cuckoo in the garden outside fluted its melody, began to reread the letter to Simon Peter. He held each leaf out at arm's length so the sun's rays lit it up for his old eyes. He read until he came to the sentence, "I fear that my views have developed in a way that will startle you."

Those words triggered a series of old memories and new associations. He remembered a dream he had when he lived as an ascetic on the banks of the Vaigai in Madurai. There had been a cobra, yes, a cobra with the face of a woman, and the cobra bit him. He didn't understand the dream at the time, but now he let himself wonder if the face were Adimanti's. Then he thought of how she had suffered all her life because she couldn't bear children. But she would have suffered more if she had loved her children but then lost them. Love. He thought of his love for her. And he felt that as much as he loved her, his vow was safe. He would not even need Bala Ma if she came again. Bala Ma. He missed the old Buddhist sage. He had grown to love her in a strange kind of way. While the faces of everyone else from his past, except Jesus', grew dimmer, hers grew brighter. He wished he could tell her he understood her better. Bala Ma . . . . "Ah, stop it!" he said aloud. He brought his mind back to the letter and continued to read:

> I have looked closely at elephant flesh and seen, to my surprise, that there are bristles all over it. I have marked the way the Indian chipmunk runs with its tail straight up. I have noted the way the leopard carries its young in its mouth, while the young monkey must cling to its mother's mane. I have eaten the pulp of a hundred coconuts with spoons that I made from their husks. After years of gagging I have finally learned to tolerate cumin, which Indians like to put on everything. I have endured India's scorching heat for the better part of eight years and dealt with the sins of others while being oppressed by my own. I have discovered an Indian would rather die than submit to circumcision and have abandoned the practice. With a few of my converts I have pretended to use magic just so they could say their conversion was "forced" and could thereby save face with their families and castes. Long ago I gave up praying with phylacteries for fear of giving offense.

Listen to me, brethren. I know India.

My brothers here worship a six-faced deity named Murugan, and a little to the north they worship an elephant-headed god with a pot-belly named Ganesha. I once considered all devotees of heathen gods unfit for the Master's Kingdom. I even hated the color of their dark skin and had difficulty imagining black faces in heaven. But now I sometimes think of the face of God Himself as dark, and once or twice I have called out unthinkingly to Him as Shiva, another Indian god. Will you say that I have been in India too long? That I have been delivered over to Satan? Or that I am mad? I tell you, brothers and sisters in Christ, that I suffered from a kind of madness before I came here. For it is madness that condemns any man because of his birth. Each of you, born in India, would be a dark-skinned devotee of a strange god, at best a holy man wearing a loin cloth, ashes smeared across his chest, meditating next to a sacred river. All this scandalized me at first, and many of you, I fear, are scandalized by what I say. "Jesus Christ alone can make us holy unto God," you say. But I ask you: How can the Father be good and just if salvation comes only through Christ? Whole continents of people will be lost if you are correct, for they will never hear the name of Jesus. And of those that do, only a small number will convert to his way, and they mostly from the bottom of society. Is that because God hardens their hearts? I say to you that God hardens no man's heart. His grace is unfailing and ever-present. It is like the ocean that buoys up the swimmer. We have only to dive in and swim. If men do not know God, that is because they have chosen not to dive.

So what should we make of all those Indians who hear my word but choose not to follow Christ? Do they choose not to dive? Is that what makes them damnable? Brothers and sisters, I will tell you something hard to believe. Many of them have already dived. Many of them have already found God. In the six-faced Murugan. In the pot-bellied Ganesha. In the bloodthirsty Goddess Kali. Impossible, you say. For years I said the same thing. But I have learned something from India. I have learned that one can get to the roof of a house by a ladder or a staircase or a rope. That is wisdom. The Father, your Father and mine, the loving Father of Jesus, our Abba, is sweetest to our taste. But let us not despise our dark-skinned brothers who find dark-skinned gods sweeter to theirs.

What is finally important? The image of God that a person has, or the good he does that is inspired by the image? I say to you it is the good. Surely this is what the Master taught us: "Blessed are the poor in spirit, blessed are the merciful, blessed are the pure in heart, blessed are the peacemakers." Do you remember that day on the mount, brothers and sisters? Do you remember how his voice rang out down over the lake? What a day! What a time! Do you think I contradict one jot of the gospel he taught that day? I contradict nothing the Master said. He did not quibble over small things, and I tell you that the particular image or name of God that a man might clutch to his breast is a small thing. Men and women are good or bad for other reasons than the name they call God by, or the color of their skins, or the place of their birth, or whether they are Jew or gentile, or even whether they have heard the Master's word. Judas Iscariot ate at the Master's table and betrayed him!

I have come to see that it is not a new God that India needs, but the Master's gospel of love. When you come, join those holy men who already love the Master's gospel even though they have never heard of the Master. Take from India, then she will receive from you. Respect her gods, and in time she will honor our Father. Love her for the sanctity she already possesses—imitate her sanctity—and she will add your sanctity to hers. Do not try to take her by force, for she will resist you. She is not a guileless peasant girl. Still less is she a harlot to be bought cheaply. She will find you uncouth and uncivilized if you are too direct in your advances, as I was at first. You must court her, woo her. She will demand that you recognize her many virtues before she accepts yours. You must accept her as she is. Then she will respond.

But be prepared for something unexpected; oh, my brethren, be prepared for this! She will change you as much as you change her! If only I had understood this from the beginning, if only I had understood, how much more I might have done! What do I have to show after eight years of labor? Perhaps ten thousand converts, that is all. Of those thousands, perhaps a third have been touched by something really new. To think that I dreamed of converting all India! All these years I have measured success by the number I have baptized. I was like a man circling the base of a mountain crying out, "Come, come, start your climb *here*, not there!" I didn't see the many already climbing. All I saw was that they were not climbing from the point I wanted them to start at. And in the meantime, I was not climbing. The great achievement of my life, I tell you truly, is that I myself have started to climb.

Outside my prison windows every morning—I am writing to you from prison—the swans called to their mates, "Wake up, wake up!" Am I, too, about to wake up, to join the Master in his Kingdom of love, as the Master seemed to teach? Or must I sleep first, sleep until the Master comes back, as you say Paul now teaches? Or must I come back to the earth and live again in a new body because I am not ready for God's holy presence, as India teaches? I confess to you I do not know. But these questions are of no importance. They have nothing to do with India's needs. They have nothing to do with mine anymore. And I pray they have nothing to do with yours. Do you still call me "doubting"? Call me that if you must.

It was here his writing ended, and Thomas was agitated. Something essential was missing. What still needed to be said?

He stacked the leaves into a bundle and tied them. He looked out the window and watched golden light shimmer through holes in the fluttering leaves. For a long time he stared at the patch of clear blue sky overhead, his head craning upward like a baby bird waiting for its mother to drop in a worm. He did not see the sky even though it appeared that he saw nothing else. Instead he saw a series of memories, all of Jesus. Jesus working at the carpenter's bench, Jesus preaching, Jesus healing, Jesus jousting with the Pharisees, Jesus imploring his followers to repent, Jesus looking at him and understanding and loving him with moist dancing eyes, Jesus dying, Jesus appearing to him in his glorified but wounded body.

His mind came back to the letter. He turned back to select a leaf, placed it against a board on his knees in direct sunlight, picked up the stylus, took a deep breath, and wrote:

It is now the next day. I have been sentenced to death by fire. Tomorrow is the day. The guard just told me. I must hurry. There is a slight chance the King will change his mind, but I write to you as if from the grave.

Thomas reread what he wrote and shook his head. He felt he had written from the heart, but his simple words did not do it justice. He wanted to explain himself better but decided against it. Time was rushing by, and there were other letters to write. And he had to save the last hours for prayer. With regret he picked up the stylus and concluded the letter:

> My successor's name is Mochikiranar. He lives in the Paradavar quarter of Puhar, capital of the Chola Empire on India's southeastern coast, from where I write you now. He is a God-fearing man of simple tastes, sturdy honesty, and sound mind. He is learning Greek, and I have urged him to go to Jerusalem and meet you all someday.

> I kiss you all, and you especially, Simon Peter, whom I once sinned against through envy, and you, Bartholomew, my friend through thick and thin. Tell my daughters Tabitha and Judith and my grandchildren whom I will never see in this life that I love them. And admonish Judith not to give up on her Greek husband, and to win him over by steadfast and holy love. Above all give Mary the mother of our beloved Master, and my mother by adoption, a holy kiss from me.

> I am thinking of the Master. The night before he died he stole away from us and entered into his agony. Now I am entering into mine. Death completely mortifies us. Rejoice, my brethren!

Thomas looked behind him for the cup of powdered lampblack to smear across the Greek letters. As he smeared it over one leaf after another, he remembered the day in Vanji long ago when Kumaran first taught him this technique. Kumaran—could he be depended on to deliver the precious sack to Mochikiranar? He worried about Kumaran's unsteadiness. What if his Christian flock never found out what happened to him? What would happen to their faith if they thought he had deserted? But it was unthinkable they would never find out. The story would have to come out, surely it already had. At least it would after his death. Surely Puttu would tell his mother, and then it would spread. Even Adimanti would tell them once he was dead. Then the people would know why he disappeared. Anyway, Kumaran would deliver the sack. Surely he would.

Then he remembered with a jolt something Kumaran had said during his last visit. "I saw you next to the Queen, lying beside her, on the beach." Suddenly it occurred to him that Kumaran was the informer; Kumaran had invented the scandal or perhaps even imagined it in earnest; Kumaran had gone to Charishnu and made the charge, and Charishnu had taken the scandal to the King.

It made more sense than any other scenario he imagined. Why had he not thought of it before? But no, he was letting his imagination run amok. Kumaran and he were still brothers. They had shared each other's life in the most intimate ways. They had saved each other's lives. They had even confessed their sins to each other. Could Kumaran murder such a brother?

Thomas looked outside; the sun blazed down out of a patch of sky above his window, and the cup of the clepsydra sat silently under the water. He felt lonely.

"Mahadeva, are you there?"

"Yes, Sire."

"I have some letters. Would you take them to the Queen?"

"I can't do that. Nothing comes in or out without the King's authorization."

"But these are—can you—?"

He was about to ask Mahadeva to break the rule at risk to his life but changed his mind.

For the rest of the day he wrote short letters to his bishops and deacons, some of whom he had never met but had learned of in letters. Puhar, Mayilapur, Madurai, the various towns up and down the Malabar Coast, even Socotra—every church got at least one letter, however short and perfunctory. He would find a way to dispatch them. If necessary he would carry them to the execution with him. There would be a way. There would have to be.

It was dark. Now he would pray, pray all night long—as Jesus had done the night before he was crucified.

Mahadeva had lit Thomas' lanterns before he went off duty, and the prayer swiftly took shape in his mind—as if dictated by an angel. And the words came in Tamil, not Greek.

He played with it in his mind, made changes, added to it, reduced it, and ended with the very words that first came to him. Then he copied the prayer out in oversize letters, one line to a leaf:

Divine Father, I am your child.
Divine Mother, heal me in body, mind, and soul.
Divine Light, may your wisdom and love shine through me.
Divine Beloved, be my joy.

As he read it over, he felt no urge to change anything. He was aware that it contained none of the usual self-abasement, no cringing before the divine throne. The God of his prayer was no magistrate on high, no tyrant to be feared. There was no great, unbridgable chasm between this God and himself. They were intimates, they were one; he was a tiny expression of the infinite God Himself; God shone through him. He did not have to exert himself mightily or prove himself worthy to be heard by God. God was always there, always at the center of his soul, always home; he had merely to sink into his own depths to find God, to find joy, to be healed; God was always close.

It was a strange, exhilarating prayer. Everything about it seemed necessary, even the reference to God as Mother. He quickly memorized it, recited it three times, then set the clepsydra. He would pray until the cup hit the bottom with its dull clank, then take a break before beginning again. He took several deep breaths and closed his eyes.

Phrase by phrase, he slowly moved through the prayer: Each phrase dropped inward, dropped like a pearl falling into a clear pond. There was no discrepancy between word and feeling. When his mind wandered, he made himself start the prayer over from the beginning. He did not try to improve on the words or alter them in any way. He accepted them as they stood. When he finished the prayer, he started over.

As his concentration deepened, he grew oblivious to the tension at his joints and the itches of his skin. The chance eruptions of color and light on the canvas of his consciousness ceased to hold him. The hooting of an owl in the mango tree outside his window and the whoops of drunken courtiers returning from a party went unnoticed. He became the words that he prayed. Soon the words began to wobble and shimmer; then even the pirouettes of their dance died down, until there remained only a luminous ineffable quiet. All cravings were dumb. He knew nothing but completion, limitless, unbounded completion. And yet not he, for it was as if he no longer existed, but only the sunless Light Within. He was sunk in a vast sea of devotion.

Yet he did not fail to hear the cup hit the bottom of the basin, and again the world crowded round him and jostled for his attention. But it was changed. The sounds of the night, the buzzing and croaking, the isolated screech, the occasional human voice, the bark of a dog—there was a dreamlike quality about all these things. He had awakened, not from a dream, but into a dream.

His eyes fell on the bundle of letters beside him, and the dreamy world took on solidity. His mind began to churn and figure and worry.

How would he dispatch these letters? But then he told himself it didn't matter much if no one read them. Missionaries often died suddenly and without warning; they had no time to write letters. Perhaps it would be better if the long letter never reached Jerusalem anyway. Who would understand it? Who would understand it who had not got mixed up in India's life and swum in her bloodstream?

He realized that nothing had worked out as planned. He had failed to make a dent on Kumaran. He could count only a few thousand converts. He had been willing to commit adultery a few days before his death. He could not even mail his letters. He felt he had almost as much in common with a Buddhist holy woman in Muziri as Simon Peter in Jerusalem. It was a crazy world, a place invented by God to teach men what it is like to be where He is not, and to want to be where He is.

He went back to his prayers. But not until he briefly lay down on the purple silk cloth, put his hands behind his head, and broke out into a smile.

57. The Severed Breast

Kumaran woke in the middle of the night to a loud knock on his door and someone calling his name. Alarmed, he limped to the door.

"Follow me at once!" said the man. It was Kakanthan the eunuch.

"What is it?" said Kumaran.

"Just follow me. Hurry."

"Let me get dressed."

"Be quick! Be quick!"

A minute later Kumaran was hurrying behind Kakanthan along the brick paths that twisted between buildings and trees across the dark park. Something was terribly wrong. He wondered if someone had assassinated the King—perhaps one of Thomas' followers.

They arrived at the Queen's Residence and mounted a torchlit staircase. A woman was crying hysterically at the entrance to one of the rooms. Inside was the King, looking dazed. He was squatting, and looked up as Kumaran appeared. There was a woman on the floor at his feet. Blood drenched her garment, which was of blue silk and richly embroidered at the edges. Streams and shallow pools of blood stood on the marble floor. More blood stained the King's hands.

"Kakanthan, leave me with Kumaran for a moment. Stand by downstairs," said the King.

He motioned with a gory finger to Kumaran. Kumaran came closer and saw the woman was Queen Adimanti. A scream rose in his throat, but he controlled it. He was certain the King had slain her with his own hands. Horrified, he crouched down beside the King.

"Close the door and wait on the landing," the King called to the woman. "And don't leave the building on any account! Kakanthan, don't let her out of your sight. She is to speak to no one!"

Kumaran waited for the King to say something.

The King's voice cracked as he said in a voice barely audible, "She took her own life. What have we done? What have we done?"

Kumaran, his flesh crawling, looked at the King in disbelief.

"Just a minute," said the King.

The King picked up a piece of bloody parchment and handed it to Kumaran. It was written in ink by someone with an elegant script. It said, "To King Karikal: Many years ago you gave me a boon. Now I will use it. Burn me next to Thomas, my true husband. Adimanti."

Kumaran began to tremble uncontrollably. He tried to give the parchment back to the King but dropped it. It landed on Adimanti's lifeless hand. He buried his head in his hands and sobbed.

"That is not all," said the King, who walked over to the Queen's dressing table. "Look at this."

Blood had splattered everything in the area of the table, and on the table was a meat cleaver next to what looked to Kumaran as he approached it like a dead bloody animal, perhaps a bat, or a mouse. Then he saw what it was, and the blood in his veins curdled. It was a breast, a woman's breast, a severed woman's breast, recognizable by the nipple.

58. Fire

It was not yet dawn, but the swans and roosters were already call-ing. Thomas woke from a short sleep and listened to their sounds. He knew he would never hear them again, and a wave of nostal-gia for the simple things of earth swept over him. Then he thought of the fire, and for an instant he was overcome by dread. He sat up with a jerk and rubbed his arm, looking at it in the dark. Within the hour it would be ashes. He took a deep breath, thought of Jesus, his brother, his twin, on the cross, and tried to calm himself. He remembered the prayer of the night before and folded his hands at his chest. Slowly he swayed back and forth as he said the prayer, his heart pouring itself out into the prayer, laying itself out at the feet of God. Calm returned.

He splashed water on his face as the dark light of early dawn crept through the windows. He reached up to his face to wash it, and his hands froze. Temple, cheeks, nose, chin—he felt their familiar, precious contours as if for the first time. They had served him well, and now he was about to leave them.

As black turned to gray, time stretched out. Every pick at his teeth with the acacia twig seemed like a discrete activity: He was not mere-ly cleaning his teeth but cleaning this particular tooth with this par-ticular stroke of the twig.

Half articulate prayers darted in and out of his mind as he prepared his body for the final sacrifice. One prayer tumbled over the next. "God have mercy. Let Kumaran find Mochikiranar. Guide your church, O Lord. Receive me, Father. Jesus, Brother." Like the spidery dots that crawl continuously up and down, back and forth across the surface of the eye, his prayers came and went. He barely noticed them; they seemed to say themselves.

After washing he turned his full attention to prayer. But he could not recapture the serenity of the night before. He turned his thoughts to Jesus, tried to feel the tingle in his fingers as they slid into Jesus' wound, tried to remember what it was like.

The sound of a songbird in the park broke his concentration. He looked outside and saw it was lighter.

A key turned in the lock, and Mahadeva came in, followed by three mute guards.

"It is time," said Mahadeva.

Thomas picked up his letters, the long one to Simon Peter in Jerusalem, the shorter ones to his churches and friends. He glanced at the water clock for the last time, briefly embraced Mahadeva, and walked out of the prison ahead of the guards.

It was one of those beautiful cool days the Tamil people call winter. For no apparent reason he remembered it was the thirteenth day of Kartigai in the thirty-ninth year of the reign of Karikal. The fifth year of the Emperor Nero, he thought to himself as he remembered something he had read in one of the letters from home.

They walked under an arcade formed by small trees and flowering vines, mostly bougainvillea. Monkeys capered above them or ran ahead along the swept pathway. A few sparrows twittered around them. A crow flapped and cawed in the branch of a tall tree.

As he walked along, he tried to concentrate on the only thing that should have mattered to him anymore. "Abba, Father, Abba, Father," he prayed. When the right foot fell, he said "Abba." When the left foot fell, he said "Father."

Breaking out from underneath the arcade, he looked up at the dull-white sky. Some obscure intuition told him there was a presence there, a well-intentioned, gentle, yet powerful, unobtrusive Presence.

He tried to concentrate on the prayer of his feet, but the pungent rich smell of the trimmed boxwood hedge alongside the walkway leading into the Queen's residence brought with it images of his boyhood in Nazareth, where he had often smelled that agreeable odor. A soft, sad feeling filled his heart as he thought of his daughters and the woman he thought of as his true mother, Mary the mother of Jesus. Then the faces of women long dead flashed into his mind: his wife Huldah, a pretty leper woman who begged near the springs, a mad servant girl who carried jugs of water by the carpenter shop every morning, even his mother, the harlot. Finally the face of Bala Ma swam into view. In some strange way each was dear to him.

He made another effort to concentrate on the prayer, but instead his heart was deflected by a memory of little Puttu swabbing down his elephant. Then Puttu's innocent, trusting words in the prison, "You will be out soon, Bapu," came to him, and he choked back a sob. "Father, O Father!" he prayed. But he did not know what to pray next.

In the east a few pink splotches shone through holes in the foliage in Queen Adimanti's courtyard. Sparrows and songbirds of every kind rejoiced in the cool air. Chipmunks and monkeys scrambled along the path bordering the rectangular pond in the middle of the yard. Brilliant scarlet bougainvillea spread like flame over trellises mounted along the wall of the Queen's residence. Fig wasps buzzed around the diminutive fruits of the four giant pagoda fig trees, one at each corner of the courtyard. A temple tree stood on each of the four sides of the pond between the fig trees. Thomas stood under the outermost branches of one of these. "I am ready, Jesus," he prayed.

The light grew brighter, and he saw the pyre. His pyre. It had a white cloth on it. What was that lump under the cloth? It almost looked like a body was already there. There was even a dark patch on the cloth, suggesting blood. He stared hard at it and wondered what it could be. Then he scolded himself for wasting precious seconds on a distraction. He felt the cross around his neck, felt the words of the prayer he wrote out the night before rise in his heart.

Again he was distracted, this time by two men coming through the gate. One was Kumaran—his hitching gait identified him at once—and Thomas felt surprise. Had Kumaran's heart grown tender at last? Had his old friend come to be with him at death? The other man he could not make out until he got close. Then he saw it was the King. Together, side by side, Kumaran and the King walked into the courtyard. What was the meaning of this? There was no entourage, not a single guard attending them. Just Kumaran and the King. And the King was dressed in white, as if in mourning. Thomas wondered what it meant.

He remembered Adimanti's promise to be at the second storey window, but there was no one there. The window she indicated was closed. Had he misunderstood? He looked at other windows, but she was not in those either. He wondered why she was not there.

He looked up at the sky, now the palest of blues.

Again he looked at the shuttered second-storey window, expecting to see it open any moment. Then he remembered the letters in his hand. Thank God Kumaran had come! Except for the three guards, one of whom had mounted the roof, Kumaran and the King were the only people around. Not even Mahadeva was in sight.

"Kumaran," Thomas said as Kumaran approached the pyre.

Kumaran did not seem to hear him.

"Kumaran."

Kumaran shuffled nervously.

"Kumaran, I have these letters." Thomas held the bundle of palm leaves out. "Would you dispatch them for me? They are important."

Kumaran looked at the King. The King nodded, and Kumaran walked around the edge of the pit to where Thomas stood.

"Thank you, Brother," Thomas said in a whisper. "Did you remember—?"

Thomas wanted to ask Kumaran if he had delivered the sack with his writings and letters to Mochikiranar, but Kumaran turned rudely on his heals. He didn't even look at Thomas when he took the letters. Thomas remembered what Adimanti had said: "You have given this Kumaran the weapon with which he can destroy you!" Kumaran walked back to the King and took his spot, while the King made a gesture of approval.

The east grew brighter, and the guard, holding his spear at the ready, motioned for Thomas to climb onto the pyre.

"Kumaran, *forgive me!*" Thomas suddenly cried out. *"Forgive me!"*

Thomas' attention was now riveted to earth. He realized now that Kumaran had betrayed him, and he knew that Kumaran would take his guilt with him into the foulest depths of hell rather than give up his hatred. Unless—

"Forgive me, Brother!" he screamed again. "I was wrong, Brother! *Forgive me!"*

Sitting on top of the pyre next to whatever was underneath the white cloth, which was on his right, Thomas saw the King lean over and consult with Kumaran. Kumaran held out his hands and shrugged his shoulders as if mystified by the ranting of the prisoner.

"Forgive me, Brother!" Thomas yelled again. Even now Thomas hadn't given up.

"Silence!" ordered the King.

"I love you, Kumaran! *Forgive me!"* Thomas yelled as the guard dug the spear into his side.

"Gag him!" the King ordered. "And tie him down."

A hand slapped him in the face, and a cloth dug into the sides of his mouth, stretching his lips tightly back over his front teeth. The gag was loathsome and tasted of blood. Another guard bound him to the pyre with a rope.

Gagged and dazed, his attention shifted from Kumaran to the sky, which was brightening by the minute. Instantly, almost miraculously, his mind cleared, and what he felt emanating from the light can only be suggested. A universal love seemed to be there. It sought the good of the whole universe, yet at the same time nurtured him in the most individual and particular way. It was impersonal in its vast, impartial sweep, yet personal in the total attention it gave him. He felt it deeply understood him, understood him far better than he understood himself, and wished him well in spite of anything he had ever done or achieved. He basked in its vast good intent, its loving permissiveness, with an exuberance, a buoyancy, a desire to create and love and serve that was not like anything he had ever known before. He loved all nature, especially the cuckoo singing its flute-like melody from somewhere behind him. He loved Kumaran and wished him every joy. He loved Adimanti. He even loved the King, even Charishnu. Without effort, he forgave everyone.

The guard on the roof clacked his spear loudly against the roof, and Thomas' attention was again riveted to earth. He heard the King say to Kumaran, "That's the signal. The sun is up. Let's get this over with."

The King pointed to the jugs of sesame oil that stood alongside the pit. A guard threw oil over the faggots, front and back, high and low, even over Thomas, four jugs in all.

As oil drooled through the gag into his mouth, Thomas wondered where Adimanti was. He looked again at her window and called to her in his heart.

"Bind him tighter," said the King.

As the guard tried to bind him down against the pyre, Thomas turned his head toward the corpse lying beside him—for he knew now it was a corpse by its smell—and wondered what it might mean. He felt its stiff hand through the cloth. He remembered Jesus had died next to thieves and wondered if the corpse was that of some criminal. He felt the hand again, even the ring on one of its fingers.

He realized with a start that it was a woman's ring. He was dying next to a woman! Then a sudden impulse seized him. He hunched his right shoulder up from under the rope, somehow worked his arm and hand free, and guided his hand to the wrist of the corpse. With a shock his fingers touched a thick bracelet under the cover. Horrified, he felt more closely. His thumb glided over the surface of the bracelet. He pushed the cover back a little and saw Adimanti's ivory bracelet with scenes from the parable of the good mleccha carved on it.

He tried to jerk up his body but could only raise his head. In horror he looked first at the King, then at Kumaran, her murderers. Then he dropped his head back and with a "Maranatha" tried to put the horror out of his mind. And in its place welled up a great consolation. She would not have to mourn him! She was already gone, perhaps waiting for him at that moment—not in her second storey apartment, but—

He saw the King mumble something to Kumaran, and Kumaran came forward and took the torch from the guard.

Holding his head up, Thomas watched his old "brother" light the fire. He watched, not with hatred or desire for vengeance, but with sadness. Almost the last words Jesus ever spoke shot through his mind: "Father, forgive them, for they don't know what they're doing." Then he heard the first crackle of the fire and smelled the smoke, and a natural dread drove out every other thought and almost congealed his blood. With a supreme effort he forced himself to ignore the licking flames and fix his mind on eternity.

He looked straight up at the sky, pink at its edges. He gripped Adimanti's cool, stiff hand, closed his eyes, and imagined the face of Jesus, his beloved Master, etched into the sky. He opened his eyes and stared at the cloudless pale sky straight overhead. With his body he felt the heat of the fire rising from below. With his spirit he gave the face of Jesus his total attention.

The fire climbed fast through the pyre, and the crackling grew to a roar. Flames jabbed at his back and engulfed him on both sides, and he dug his nails into Adimanti's hand and screamed a silent sound. There was an instant, then another, of blasting pain, and his freed right arm shot backward out of the fire. Then he was free, looking down at his burning body, at Kumaran, at the King, at the whole scene, from a height that no physical fire could reach. He knew no pain, no confinement. Amazed, thrilled, he saw Jesus, the living Jesus, his beloved Master, standing in midair off to the side, his body surrounded by a glorious white aureole, his arms outstretched, his face full of welcoming love. Off to the side he saw—he could hardly believe it—Bala Ma, Bala Ma young and radiant but unmistakably herself, seated in the lotus position, encircled in a glowing aureole of bluish tint. Her eyes shone with compassion as she studied and welcomed him. And behind Bala Ma, at a great distance and in shadow—oh, how his heart went out to her when he saw her and felt her confusion and something that seemed like remorse!—stood Adimanti.

A white dove in flight swerved to avoid the plume of smoke, lifted itself over the Queen's residence, and disappeared.

59. That Old Thing

Three years had passed since that day, and nothing that Kumaran did seemed to have any purpose. If there was something he was supposed to do with his life, he had absolutely no idea what it was. He once counted himself a servant of Murugan, but now he found it impossible to offer a single sincere prayer. He once thrilled at his ability to please a king, but he had grown to hate Karikal. The gay meeting hall where the poets once sat with the King had been turned into a meditation hall, and the King, since the death of his Guru Charishnu, had ears only for the teachings of the Buddha, whom Kumaran called "the prophet of sorrow." The King had become reclusive, penitential, and, in Kumaran's opinion, dull. There were even rumors he was celibate. So was his empire: Not a single campaign of expansion had been fought since the Queen's death. His people had seen their days of glory; the sun did not shine as high over their heads. And the sea, as if bent on avenging the Queen's death, had encroached on Puhar's beaches since a disastrous cyclone struck: The city's shore district was sinking into the sea. Meanwhile foes were beginning to test the strength of the Chola Kingdom on several fronts inland. "What the Gods do not devour, men will finish up," Kumaran wrote in his diary.

He was obsessed by the Queen. His memory of that bloody scene in her bedroom was always with him even if his imagination called it forth in muted grays. So was her state funeral. He used to recall with a kind of cynical glee how the body of one of her maidservants, the same who stood by outside the bedroom on that terrible night, was substituted for the Queen's, with two hundred thousand mourners never suspecting the switch. Now there was no glee, only the memory. He and the King and the eunuch Kakanthan were the only ones who knew—they had wrapped the body themselves after the maid had taken poison at the King's suggestion. Everyone thought the "barren" Queen had died miscarrying—Kumaran thought up the egregious lie and Kakanthan spread it abroad. He told the King the best way to deflect suspicion was to manufacture a diversion. Thus everyone talked not only about the tragedy of the Queen's death but the loss of an heir.

Kumaran was especially obsessed by the Queen's motive. She had taken Thomas as her husband, no doubt in some spiritual sense, and she regarded it her duty to follow him into the fire as his Sati. But the breast? Why did she cut off her breast? Kumaran wondered often about this. Did she hate herself because of some secret, unforgivable sin she could endure no longer? Or did she hate the King, hate him so much that she mutilated herself as the best means of mutilating and destroying him? Or did her sorrow over losing Thomas simply drive her insane? All her life she had been a devotee of Shiva, but shortly before her death she was seen meditating under the trees in front of the Vishnu Temple. Did this portend madness? Or was she angry at Thomas for some reason? Did she secretly hate the very man she most loved? It was tempting for Kumaran to think this last thing, for he knew first-hand what Thomas could do to someone who loved him. But no. What evidence was there that she was anything like himself? She was the most high-principled of people. It was hard to imagine her doing anything out of hate, much less the terrible thing she did. Then out of sorrow? But that would imply she was weak and sought escape. Sorrow might explain the suicide, but not the mutilation. The Queen weak? It wasn't possible. She was the only one in the world who did not fear the King—everybody said this about her. And the way she took on the best minds in debate at the public assemblies. And the deed itself—how could she endure the pain? No, she was not weak. It did not figure.

He concluded that the act must have carried a calculated meaning, that it symbolized something as real to her, that it made as much sense to her as his metaphors did to him. Perhaps her breast symbolized her heart, and her heart's blood sealed the words of her letter to the King. Or perhaps she meant to say that her devotion to Thomas was not based on sexual passion, and thus she left behind her breast, symbol of that passion, symbol of all the dark and dangerous powers of woman. Or perhaps it had something to do with Shiva—his devotees sometimes did the bloodiest things to prove themselves worthy. Kumaran took refuge in this thought; for it was easier for him to run away from his guilt if he could be convinced she was master of herself, that she had chosen death rationally and with all her faculties intact.

He went about his business, composing with difficulty and without enthusiasm. Frequently he took up a piece of wood and whittled the time away. Once in a while the King consented to fraternize with his poets, but no recital of his virtues or the glories of his kingdom pleased him anymore. His poets pleased only themselves. Not that anything really pleased Kumaran much—except the pleasures of wine and women and dice, which helped him forget.

But he was never able to forget for long. One episode especially haunted him. As soon as the flames consumed the pyre on that dreadful day, the King gave him orders to oversee the cleanup. One of the guards was pushing Thomas' unburned right hand into the embers when Kumaran for some strange reason ordered the hand be brought to him. The hand was retrieved, and Kumaran wrapped it in a piece of dirty cloth. He brought it home with Thomas' letters and placed it in a case, which he fastened tightly. Then he put the case in the sack Thomas had given him earlier. Why? Why did he do this? Many times over the ensuing months he had come close to discarding the case, but a kind of paralysis overcame him every time, and he never carried it through. It was the only thing he had left of Thomas, and he clung to it like a relic.

Like a facial wart that grows larger by the month and at last cannot be ignored, it became clear to Kumaran finally that no one ever deserved his loyalty or love more than Thomas. He had hated Thomas because he seemed to love others, especially his converts, and for that he had had him murdered. He had hated him because he put people's salvation ahead of everything else and because he thought his way the best—in the early days the only way—to achieve it; and for that too he had had him murdered. He had hated him because he, Thomas, visited him in prison partly out of obedience to his God, and not solely out of love; and for that too he had had him murdered. He had hated him because he made light over the loss of his fortune and lied about Nallapennu and emerged from Venni a straight-figured hero and won Devandi over to his religion and been so pious and self-contained and forgiving throughout everything; and for all this he had had him murdered. "He deserved it!" a voice within him used to rage. But as the months passed, he knew better. He could not forget it was Thomas who kept him alive and cheered him up when he was rotting in that hell-hole. What did the motive matter? Thomas came. And what had he, Kumaran, done in return? Murdered him. Right down to the lighting of the fire.

Kumaran could not deny that Thomas was the best and most loyal friend he ever had. Every *"Forgive me,* Kumaran!"—those dreadful last words—were tendrils tightening and thickening around his heart. Every word cried out, "You murdered the only man you ever loved." Kumaran would try to drown these words out with prayer, but his prayers were as meaningless as monkey chatter. He looked inside himself to try to find the clue to his deed, he strained to see, but everything would get dark and dizzy and frightening. If he persisted, panic would overcome him and he would feel like screaming. It was as if the thing by which men know themselves to be who they are, was lost. It was as if he had no depths, as if a demon had stolen his soul. How could he have killed Thomas? He marveled he had done it. Sometimes he felt no continuity between the man who had done the deed and the man who he was now, just as a soldier feels no continuity between his war experiences and the rest of his life. It was a completely senseless, insane act.

He did a lot of walking, especially late at night—anything to postpone the ordeal of trying to fall asleep. But he could never walk far enough. He was like the King's parrot: Raised in a cage and accustomed to its restrictions, the parrot was unable to fly away even though the cage was lifted long ago. For years he had never budged from his large rectangular stand. His mind was his cage. So was Kumaran's.

He made a kind of truce with the night air and the starry sky. Under it the cage seemed less confining. But he could not find what he wanted even there. He vaguely remembered the ecstasies of youth when his mother was still alive as he stood under the same sky, loved it, and felt its love in return. Now it was indifferent to him. It was this indifference that attracted him now. Everything else, especially the voice in the cage of his mind, condemned him. By comparison indifference was sweet.

He also made a kind of truce with the ocean. It was so vast and mighty that his sins seemed slight beside it. And its noise muffled the accusing voice—or rather voices, for there were several, each quite distinct—inside the cage of his mind. But he could not find what he wanted there either. No matter how hard or little it rained, no matter how great or slight the current of the Kaveri which flowed into it, the sea neither grew nor diminished. In a similar way the great lump of karmic debt that silently smoldered in his soul neither grew nor diminished. He bathed in the holy Kaveri, he donated money to the building of a temple, he listened to various swamis expound the scriptures; but the lump neither grew nor diminished. He could not say the lump burned; it was beyond burning, like hunger far advanced. But it was relentless, and any attempt to find peace was like a futile effort to find some fresh metaphor to express some thought he only half understood. If for a moment, or even a day, he managed to find peace, he lost it the very next—like the *anicham* flower that withers away in the very smelling.

He had spilled the blood of his innocent brother and maimed an empire. He alone was responsible, he alone. What foolishness he had let himself believe. There was nothing "inexorable" about the events of his life. The Gods did not foreordain them. His karma was not responsible for them. He was responsible. There was nothing to do now but curse.

He could not forgive himself, and he was certain no God forgave him. He dreaded death, dreaded the hell that awaited him, yet his life now was already hell. Or at least it was hell when he was not drinking toddy or playing with the human peahens that made him spread his tail feathers and dance. He saw the world through a raging fever. It shimmered and wavered. There was no solidity anywhere.

Two more years passed, a total of five since Thomas' death. Again it was the cool season, and the breeze blowing in from the sea was dry and pleasing. The wives and children of aristocrats sat in the evening twilight on the high terraces of their cliff-like mansions and warmed themselves around braziers burning sandalwood. Devandi and the children, two little boys and the oldest girl, sat on their terrace and aped the aristocracy. Kumaran stuck his head out of the window from time to time and looked at his family lit up by the light of the fire. He wanted to participate in their contented chatter and play, to tell his wife about the events of the day as other husbands did, but he felt like an outsider. Where there was happiness and innocence, he always felt like an outsider.

He heard someone knock on the door and ask to speak to "Thomas' companion." As the servant assured the man there was some mistake, Kumaran hurried up to the stranger as fast as his crooked leg would take him. The man said his name was Valluvar, a pulaiyar, a weaver from Mayilapur, north of Arikamedu, the Roman trading city up the coast. "Valluvar." Where had Kumaran heard that name before? He had heard of a tribe called the Valluvars, but a man? He studied the man's face. He had a long white beard, thin at the middle and almost forked, and a bald head as shiny as an avocado. He looked to be about sixty. Kumaran was sure he had seen this face before.

The man had come to find out what happened to Thomas. For years he had assumed that Thomas had simply disappeared, perhaps gone back to the West. But recently he had heard a rumor Thomas was murdered by brahmins jealous of his success. Might Kumaran know what really happened? And would it be possible to recover the bones so they could be carried back to Mayilapur? For Thomas had followers in Mayilapur.

"But how did you know to come here?" Kumaran asked.

"I was told you were his friend."

Then Kumaran remembered where he had seen him. He was the man in the back row who condemned the Jain and fell on his knees at Thomas' feet after the debate.

"Stay here," said Kumaran in a state of bewilderment. He stood up, scratched his forehead, then left the room. Minutes later he came back holding a bulging dusty sack. "This belonged to Thomas. He gave it to me before he died."

"What?!" There was a look of indescribable excitement on Valluvar's face.

The letter appointing Mochikiranar his successor was on top, and Kumaran pulled it out.

"Can you read?" said Kumaran.

"Yes. Like you, I write poetry," said the man with a voice that quivered. "His very handwriting!"

Kumaran watched tears gather in Valluvar's eyes as he read the letter appointing Mochikiranar "second Bishop of India."

"He gave this to you?" said Valluvar, holding out the letter.

"Yes. And—and—in this case—is his hand. The hand that touched Jesus' wound."

Valluvar's eyes almost bulged out of their sockets, and his mouth hung open in astonishment. He picked up the case and looked at Kumaran. "May I open it?" he said.

Kumaran brought a fist to his mouth and nodded with a jerk.

Valluvar had difficulty prying open the case, but finally the hood slipped off. There, leathery but well preserved, lay Thomas' hand. Valluvar touched it reverently and softly ran a finger down its length. It held together. He replaced the hood and said, "May I have this? I would like to bring it back to Mayilapur with me. We will build a shrine for it."

Weeping, Kumaran nodded.

"And all this has been lying here for five years?" Valluvar placed the case back in the sack. "Why?—why?—"

Kumaran smarted under Valluvar's gentle accusation. Why indeed? He owed Valluvar an explanation, but where should he start? Through his tears he studied Valluvar's face and saw a kindness and a wisdom in his clear eyes. Perhaps he would understand, perhaps he could be trusted. And he was a fellow pulaiyar. And he said he wrote poetry. Kumaran decided to trust Valluvar with the whole story, he would start from the beginning, leave nothing out. All the way back to their meeting on the ship he went. And once he got started there was no stopping him. For the first time in all those five years Kumaran undammed his heart. He confessed all his crimes, all his lies. He took credit for Thomas' death. He explained the circumstances of Queen Adimanti's suicide and described Thomas' death in detail. He told how he had thrown Thomas' sack with all its treasures, including the hand, in a storeroom and left it there until this very hour. Valluvar looked at him first with shock and anger, then with pity as he shook his head, then anger again, then pity. Kumaran noted Valluvar's changes of mood, but nothing could stop him from pouring out the molten lead that had been boiling in his heart for so long. When it was all over, it was evident Valluvar forgave him everything. Together they wept, wept at the memory of Thomas, whom they loved.

"Take it to Mochikiranar in the Paradavar quarter." Thomas' instruction had clung to Kumaran like the mole behind his ear. Every month or so he would hear these words drumming in his head, but he had never acted. He had only to wait a day, and the drumming would go away. But now he would take it. Valluvar had offered to take it, but Kumaran would not let him; he insisted on taking it himself.

He thought of the words of Valluvar the night before as they talked into the early morning. Valluvar was no real Christian, Kumaran told himself, for he believed in rebirth and karma. Karma he called "that old thing." "Those who struggle on will see the backside of that old thing," he had said. Kumaran decided Valluvar was certainly no Christian; he was a Tamil; he understood Kumaran better than Thomas ever had. He did not dismiss karma as Thomas had; karma was real to him. But for him it was not what a person did in his past that mattered, but the present habits that ruled him. "Change your habits through prayer, Kumaran," Valluvar had said, "and you too will see the backside of that old thing. You too! Don't orchids grow out of the most ordinary trees?"

Kumaran reached the back edge of the broad beach. A pleasant wind rustled through the pandanus bushes and toyed with loose thatch on the roofs of houses. Along the shore dozens of fishermen tugged at ropes connected to boats out beyond the foamy surf, while others laid long fishing nets on the beach in the form of great snakes. A curly-haired boy with the help of a loop into which he placed his feet scaled a lone coconut tree to tap toddy from the stems of its leaves. Children made wreathes of tightly packed jasmines while their mother peddled them from behind a stall. Unmarried daughters, their little breasts just beginning to stick out, carried water pots back and forth between the wells and their homes; each carried three pots, one under each arm and one balanced on the head. On top of the smooth golden sand, dyers spread out their cloth in the shape of giant mazes and prepared their red dyes. A sadhu wearing a dirty saffron cloth held up a hand and stared out at the ocean as he muttered something, while next to him a traveling vendor hawked stones for making trinkets and the various powders used during festival time and for cosmetics.

Unnoticed by anyone, Kumaran limped along this busy beach with the lumpy sack hung over his shoulder. To a passerby it might have appeared that he staggered under its weight as he went. But he did not think of his limp. His step was almost light, lighter than it had been in years. If only for a day, the horrid beetle that crawls out of the seed of the soft, delicate mango fruit had crawled out of Kumaran's soul, and a new, almost palpable sense of freedom came over him as he rounded the corner leading past a stand of screw pines into the heart of the Paradavar quarter. He felt strangely vulnerable and yet safe—as if he were about to receive a spear in the chest but for some reason had no fear of it. Some small children with bright eyes ran by him, and he remembered the line from one of Valluvar's poems: "The flute is sweet, the lute is sweet, say those who do not hear the pretty prattle of their children."

"Can you tell me where Mochikiranar lives?" Kumaran asked an old fisherman mending a net.

"Straight ahead," said the man, pointing, then spitting a red quid of betel on the beach. "Over there, next to the boat."

"Mochikiranar, Mochikiranar, Mochikiranar," Kumaran told himself, as if fearing he might change his mind at any moment. He looked through an opening between two houses toward the sea, adorned with pearly beads of surf, and saw a man working on a boat. Kumaran called to him; and the man, a cross hanging from a thong across his bronzed hairy chest, stood up and faced the stranger.

"So you are Mochikiranar!" Kumaran cried out.

The man stared back and nodded once.

Kumaran, lugging the sack, hobbled straight up to him.

THE END

GLOSSARY OF SELECTED
NON-ENGLISH WORDS

Tamil Solar Months of the Year and Their Approximate English Equivalents

1. **Chitrai**	April 12 - May 12
2. **Vaikhasi**	May 13 - June 12
3. **Auni**	June 13 - July 14
4. **Audi**	July 15 - August 14
5. **Auvani**	August 15 - September 14
6. **Purattasi**	September 15 - October 15
7. **Aippasi**	October 16 - November 14
8. **Kartigai**	November 15 - December 13
9. **Margali**	December 14 - January 11
10. **Tai**	January 12 - February 11
11. **Masi**	February 12 - March 11
12. **Panguni**	March 12 - April 11

Aiyer term of address signifying special respect, "Lord"

apsaras beautiful celestial maiden whose specialty is dance

bhangi member of the latrine-cleaning caste, the lowest of all castes

brahmin member of the highest caste, priest

dharma a. the doctrine of a religious group b. a person's specific duty or calling

Garuda great eagle upon which the God Vishnu rides

ghat broad flight of steps leading down to a river, especially for bathing

ghee clarified butter used for frying food

guru esteemed religious teacher

karma moral merit or demerit that marks one's soul and determines, according to the law of karma, the soul's destiny; a person's destiny in general

karma (law of) moral law of cause and effect decreeing that a person will be rewarded or punished according to the goodness or badness of his moral choices, either in this life or subsequent ones

Kashi traditional name for the North Indian city of Varanasi or Benares

kshatriya member of the ruling or warrior caste, second to the brahmin

linga(m) phallus, worshipped as a symbol of Shiva by his devotees

Maranatha Aramaic prayer meaning "Lord, come"; a prayer used by Jesus and his disciples

maya a. God's creative power b. illusion-producing power

mleccha member of a despised caste of mixed blood

naga divinely empowered serpents of the underworld

Naraka the lowest, most painful hell where the wicked are punished

nastika an atheist, unbeliever

neem the margosa tree, prized for its purifying power

pulaiyar low caste person of humble origin

prakriti the stuff out of which the physical universe is made; Nature

raja member of the ruling or warrior caste; another name for the kshatriya

Rasa-lila ecstatic dance with sexual overtones danced in honor of the God Krishna

sadhu ascetic holy man

sannyasin spiritually advanced Hindu who has renounced all pleasures and possessions in an attempt to achieve eternal release and salvation; religious ascetic

Sarveshvara "Lord of the Universe"; God over all

Sati a. Hindu woman who chooses to cremate herself on her husband's funeral pyre to join him in the afterlife b. religious event during which one or more Satis cremate themselves

shishya pupil or disciple

stupa Buddhist burial mound marking the place of a sacred event and housing a holy relic of the Buddha

tali a thread tied around the neck of the bride in a South Indian marriage ceremony

Tamil a. language spoken all over ancient South India (Tamilakam) and in Tamil Nadu today b. a speaker of Tamil

Tamilakam the land we call today South India

vaishya a member of the respected merchant or agricultural caste group

vanaprastha "forest dweller"; Hindu who cuts his ties with society and devotes himself to meditation and study, often on the outskirts of a city in ancient India

Vanigar member of a wealthy merchant caste in ancient Puhar

Veda or **Vedas** name applied to the Hindu scriptures as a whole

Vedic pertaining to the Vedas

Velir member of an agricultural tribe or caste in ancient Tamilakam

wadi Arabic word for a usually dry gulch or wash in a west Asian desert region

yakshi heavenly-human woman of voluptuous appearance; akin to an apsaras

yavana any foreigner to ancient South India, but especially one with white skin—used pejoratively

yoga meditative discipline designed to unite the soul with God

yogi one who practices yoga

Paperbacks also available from
White Crow Books

Elsa Barker—*Letters from a Living Dead Man*
ISBN 978-1-907355-83-7

Elsa Barker—*War Letters from
the Living Dead Man*
ISBN 978-1-907355-85-1

Elsa Barker—*Last Letters from
the Living Dead Man*
ISBN 978-1-907355-87-5

Richard Maurice Bucke—
Cosmic Consciousness
ISBN 978-1-907355-10-3

Stafford Betty—
The Imprisoned Splendor
ISBN 978-1-907661-98-3

Stafford Betty—
*Heaven and Hell Unveiled: Updates
from the World of Spirit.*
ISBN 978-1-910121-30-6

Ineke Koedam—
*In the Light of Death: Experiences on
the threshold between life and death*
ISBN 978-1-910121-48-1

Arthur Conan Doyle with Simon Parke—
Conversations with Arthur Conan Doyle
ISBN 978-1-907355-80-6

Meister Eckhart with Simon Parke—
Conversations with Meister Eckhart
ISBN 978-1-907355-18-9

D. D. Home—*Incidents in my Life Part 1*
ISBN 978-1-907355-15-8

Mme. Dunglas Home; edited, with an
Introduction, by Sir Arthur Conan
Doyle—*D. D. Home: His Life and Mission*
ISBN 978-1-907355-16-5

Edward C. Randall—
Frontiers of the Afterlife
ISBN 978-1-907355-30-1

Rebecca Ruter Springer—
Intra Muros: My Dream of Heaven
ISBN 978-1-907355-11-0

Leo Tolstoy, edited by Simon
Parke—*Forbidden Words*
ISBN 978-1-907355-00-4

Erlendur Haraldsson and
Loftur Gissurarson—
*Indridi Indridason: The Icelandic
Physical Medium*
ISBN 978-1-910121-50-4

Goerge E. Moss—
*Earth's Cosmic Ascendancy: Spirit
and Extraterrestrials Guide us
through Times of Change*
ISBN 978-1-910121-28-3

Steven T. Parsons and Callum E. Cooper—
Paracoustics: Sound & the Paranormal
ISBN 978-1-910121-32-0

L. C. Danby—
*The Certainty of Eternity: The Story
of Australia's Greatest Medium*
ISBN 978-1-910121-34-4

Madelaine Lawrence —
*The Death View Revolution: A
Guide to Transpersonal Experiences
Surrounding Death*
ISBN 978-1-910121-37-5

Zofia Weaver—
*Other Realities?: The enigma of
Franek Kluski's mediumship*
ISBN 978-1-910121-39-9

Roy L. Hill—
*Psychology and the Near-Death
Experience: Searching for God*
ISBN 978-1-910121-42-9

Tricia. J. Robertson —
*"Things You Can do When You're Dead!: True
Accounts of After Death Communication"*
ISBN 978-1-908733-60-3

Tricia. J. Robertson —
*More Things you Can do When You're
Dead: What Can You Truly Believe?*
ISBN 978-1-910121-44-3

Jody Long—
*God's Fingerprints: Impressions
of Near-Death Experiences*
ISBN 978-1-910121-05-4

Leo Tolstoy with Simon Parke—
Conversations with Tolstoy
ISBN 978-1-907355-25-7

Howard Williams with an Introduction by Leo Tolstoy—*The Ethics of Diet: An Anthology of Vegetarian Thought*
ISBN 978-1-907355-21-9

Vincent Van Gogh with Simon Parke—*Conversations with Van Gogh*
ISBN 978-1-907355-95-0

Wolfgang Amadeus Mozart with Simon Parke—*Conversations with Mozart*
ISBN 978-1-907661-38-9

Jesus of Nazareth with Simon Parke—*Conversations with Jesus of Nazareth*
ISBN 978-1-907661-41-9

Thomas à Kempis with Simon Parke—*The Imitation of Christ*
ISBN 978-1-907661-58-7

Julian of Norwich with Simon Parke—*Revelations of Divine Love*
ISBN 978-1-907661-88-4

Allan Kardec—*The Spirits Book*
ISBN 978-1-907355-98-1

Allan Kardec—*The Book on Mediums*
ISBN 978-1-907661-75-4

Emanuel Swedenborg—*Heaven and Hell*
ISBN 978-1-907661-55-6

P.D. Ouspensky—*Tertium Organum: The Third Canon of Thought*
ISBN 978-1-907661-47-1

Dwight Goddard—*A Buddhist Bible*
ISBN 978-1-907661-44-0

Michael Tymn—*The Afterlife Revealed*
ISBN 978-1-970661-90-7

Michael Tymn—*Transcending the Titanic: Beyond Death's Door*
ISBN 978-1-908733-02-3

Guy L. Playfair—*If This Be Magic*
ISBN 978-1-907661-84-6

Guy L. Playfair—*The Flying Cow*
ISBN 978-1-907661-94-5

Guy L. Playfair —*This House is Haunted: The True Story of the Enfield Poltergeist*
ISBN 978-1-907661-78-5

Carl Wickland, M.D.—*Thirty Years Among the Dead*
ISBN 978-1-907661-72-3

John E. Mack—*Passport to the Cosmos*
ISBN 978-1-907661-81-5

Peter & Elizabeth Fenwick—*The Truth in the Light*
ISBN 978-1-908733-08-5

Erlendur Haraldsson— *Modern Miracles*
ISBN 978-1-908733-25-2

Erlendur Haraldsson— *At the Hour of Death*
ISBN 978-1-908733-27-6

Erlendur Haraldsson—*The Departed Among the Living*
ISBN 978-1-908733-29-0

Brian Inglis—*Science and Parascience*
ISBN 978-1-908733-18-4

Brian Inglis—*Natural and Supernatural: A History of the Paranormal*
ISBN 978-1-908733-20-7

Ernest Holmes—*The Science of Mind*
ISBN 978-1-908733-10-8

Victor & Wendy Zammit —*A Lawyer Presents the Evidence For the Afterlife*
ISBN 978-1-908733-22-1

Casper S. Yost—*Patience Worth: A Psychic Mystery*
ISBN 978-1-908733-06-1

William Usborne Moore—*Glimpses of the Next State*
ISBN 978-1-907661-01-3

William Usborne Moore—*The Voices*
ISBN 978-1-908733-04-7

John W. White—*The Highest State of Consciousness*
ISBN 978-1-908733-31-3

Lord Dowding—*Many Mansions*
ISBN 978-1-910121-07-8

Paul Pearsall, Ph.D. —*Super Joy*
ISBN 978-1-908733-16-0

All titles available as eBooks, and selected titles available in Hardback and Audiobook formats from www.whitecrowbooks.com

CPSIA information can be obtained
at www.ICGtesting.com
Printed in the USA
FSOW01n1538190216
17110FS